An Anthology

Edited by

Ira Nayman

The Dance

Trade Paperback ISBN: 978-1-928104-34-6
eISBN:978-1-928104-35-3

Cover Design © by Evan Dales
WAV Design Studios
www.wavstudios.ca

Dark Dragon Publishing
88 Charleswood Drive
Toronto, Ontario
M3H 1X6
CANADA
www.darkdragonpublishing.com

Printed in the United States of America.

An Anthology

Edited by

Ira Nayman

Dark Dragon Publishing
Toronto, Ontario, Canada

Contents

INTRODUCTION

Life is the dance between choice and chance.

1.

In 2021, I was looking for something new to do with the multiverse.

By that time, I had written seven Transdimensional Authority/Time Agency novels set in the multiverse, starting with *Welcome to the Multiverse** in 2010. In addition, I had written twelve collections of Alternate Reality News Service articles (starting with *Alternate Reality Ain't What It Used To Be* in 2008); although most did not deal with the concept of the multiverse directly, the nature of the premise of the series—a news organization that sends reporters into other realities and has them report on what they find there—ensured that the concept was always just under the surface.

While there is some comfort in continuing to do what you have always done, I find that that's a blueprint for creative stagnation, so I am always looking for new writing challenges.

* Sorry for the Inconvenience

When I started writing novels, I decided that a true multiverse story needed to contain at least three different realities in order to illustrate that the multiverse grows out of more than just binary possibilities. Perhaps that concept could be adopted for short stories?

That was the inspiration for what I call "multiverse triptychs." Each story would have three parts set in three different universes. In some cases, the stories would contain similar plots and/or characters with small twists that would make big differences in their outcomes; in other cases, they would be linked by a single object or theme. The important thing about triptychs would be that the parts would interact in complex ways, making the whole greater than the sum of the story's parts.

Around the same time, I was beginning to miss editing. As editor of *Amazing Stories* magazine for almost three years, I had discovered that I loved working with the words of other writers almost as much as I loved working with my own. For over a year, I considered the possibility of editing an anthology, knocking around various ideas (some of which may grace your bookshelves in the future—stranger things have happened). Eventually, I thought, *I'm having a lot of fun writing multiverse triptychs—maybe other writers would, too.*

Out of that idea came *The Dance.*

2.

Before I was a prose geek, I was a film geek. Over a period of a decade, I completed an undergraduate degree in which I focused on screenwriting, I wrote script analysis articles for *Creative Screenwriting* magazine and, oh yeah, I wrote about one hundred scripts, mostly for original television series, but including over a dozen features. During this period, I came to the realization that every sub-genre of fiction has its own built-in thematic.

While I was working on a humorous anthology series about

vampires called *Forever Live and Die*, I realized that every vampire story was really about how the short length of human lives affects how we see ourselves and act in the world. How? By showing us how beings with a different lifespan exist differently in the world than we do. Not every vampire story directly addresses this theme, of course, but it's always there, lurking in the background, to be considered by readers at their leisure.

Working the multiverse, I quickly realized that how chance (events out of our control) and choice (the moment-by-moment decisions we make out of the possibilities life gives us) operate to shape our lives is the built-in theme of stories set in multiple realities. By illustrating different paths lives take depending upon the choices we make or the circumstances we find ourselves in, multiverse tales always offer this concept.

Triptychs were the form; the dance was the theme. I was ready to accept submissions for an anthology.

3.

A lot of writers, especially early in their careers, are loathe to share their writing with others (including, in some extreme cases, magazines and book publishers); they are afraid that other writers will steal their ideas. In fact, literary theft is quite rare. Any writer who has been at it for an appreciable amount of time will have developed more ideas than they could write in a lifetime; they don't need other people's ideas.

In any case, the emphasis on ideas can be misplaced. As every writer should know, you cannot copyright an idea, only the expression of that idea. Partially, this is because ideas are not concrete, but how they are expressed in the actual words on the page is. But on a more fundamental level, it is because most authors build on the ideas that came before (whether its fantastic magical realms that owe to Tolkien or space opera that owes to Clarke and Heinlein); copyrighting ideas would shut down huge amounts of creative effort.

The great thing about basic ideas is that they are practically infinitely malleable. If you give a dozen writers the same idea, they will come up with twelve unique stories. That has certainly been the case with *The Dance*.

My original vision for an ideal story for the anthology was that it would be made up of three distinct sections, each of which would show how a single character's experience made them different people in three different universes, much like the triptychs I had been writing. Some of the submissions to *The Dance* do, indeed, follow this structure. Stefan Jackson's "Habit," for example, is about an artist whose life is different depending upon his circumstances. (One of the things that bind the three parts of his story is the main character forgetting how to do a simple action, something that took me completely by surprise and I found delightful.) Bruno Lombardi's "Monday Crossroads Blues" has the same structure, but adds the twist of exploring different genres in each of the sections of the story, to hilarious effect.

Some of the contributors to this volume played with the basic structure. In "A Milkshake Apocalypse," Mark A. Rayner develops three distinct storylines featuring a doctor dealing with a unique medical emergency in a hospital, but, rather than telling them in three discrete sections, he weaves in and out of them, creating a complex narrative that demands multiple readings. (It's also the weirdest zombie apocalypse story I have ever come across.) Stephen Pearl's "Divergent Specks" employs a similar intertwining of storylines, but actually inverts the concept of the multiverse triptych: his divergent stories converge at the end with a common message of hope. I was delighted to discover this, not the least because hope is such a rare commodity in these dark times.

Other stories in the anthology eschewed the tripartite structure entirely. Moira Scott's "Crossing Paths/Crossing Boundaries," for example, delineates the changes that occur in a single character as she traverses three different universes in a single linear story, ultimately helping change the lives of a human family in her final destination. (It didn't hurt that the main character is a cat. In fact, Moira's story had me at "cat.")

INTRODUCTION

Kellee Kranendonk's "Seeing It All" also features a single storyline: in this case, a woman who can experience her life in alternate realities tries to convince the reader of that reality. Her experience with different versions of an alien encounter is fascinating.

A couple of the stories, Hugh Spencer's "Shoebox" and Rosie Smith's "Jurassic Dinomancy," involve the changes in the world wrought by time travel. Spencer is the best satirist of corporate bureaucracies working in current science fiction, a subject which is on full display in "Shoebox." Smith's story explores how when a time traveller experiences different events in the past, it changes her present. I thought it was a clever idea.

While science fiction had traditionally set time travel stories in a single universe (which either changes or stays the same due to the actions of time travellers depending upon which theory of time travel the author worked with), the emergence of multiverse theory gave writers a third option: whenever somebody changed the past, it created a new universe (actually a new set of universes, given how the new universe would immediately start generating choice points).

One of the things I love about setting time travel stories in the multiverse is that it does away with paradoxes. Take the classic grandfather paradox: a time traveller goes back in time and kills their grandfather when he was still a child. If his grandfather wasn't around to parent one of his parents, then the time traveller would never have been born. But if the time traveller had never been born, how could they go back in time to kill their grandfather? In the multiverse, when the time traveller kills their grandfather, they start a new set of universes, but the universe in which their grandfather lived and they were born hasn't changed. Poof! Paradox solved! (It does open new problems of navigation, since the future the time traveller came from has been changed, they will have to have a way to get back to their original universe as well as time. One of the more intriguing stories in *The Dance* deals with this question (I am reluctant to say which for fear of spoiling the effect; you should know it when you read it).)

Finally, there was the submission (actually the first story accepted for the anthology) which takes place in a single universe where the main character has access to his lives in other universes, causing him to muse on the different paths his life might have taken if he had made different choices: David Gerrold's "Entanglements." What starts off as a hilarious story about one writer's career becomes a harrowing exploration of the roads not taken that haunt him. It is a masterful story, brilliantly conceived and written.

All of the stories that appear in *The Dance* surprised and delighted me in some way. They make for a diverse, entertaining anthology.

Enjoy.

Ira Nayman
Toronto, Ontario, Canada
January 2024

HABIT

Stefan Jackson

<u>SOLO</u>

Keep breathing.

Have I lost my mind? No! I know my name. The day of the week. I can read the time on my watch. I'm getting ready for work. I know what is going on!

I've laced my shoes for years—for decades! Boots, sneakers, sandals. All manner of footwear.

I looked at my black leather boots; it was a new pair, maybe six months old.

Dementia? They say the mind lets the simple things go first.

Okay, this is where my imagination and will power come into play.

The laces…the laces remained unanimated, lazy, flat on the living room floor.

13/8: Tak-tok-tajtaytajtaytajtaytajtay-tak-toktok-toktok-tok-tajtaytajtaytajtaytajtay-toktoktoktoktok. I catch my booted right foot tapping the odd and frantic notional measure. The abstract beat was a piece I had played on the drums with a band some twenty plus years ago. The memory seeped in, a welcome interlude from this crisis. It was a pleasant memory, yet my boots remained untied. And I metaphorically stepped on the laces, losing the beat and stumbling back into the reality of my living room.

At the top of the hour, the local network presented a community calendar that highlighted free cultural arts events, public park fitness programs, library courses and author book readings. Then, the network logo appeared mid-screen, flitted about the frame, showing the network's logos throughout the years, settling on the current three letter rendition. The image swiped left; the brilliant logo became a top to bottom scroll of names that produced the broadcast.

Another transition, thanking sponsors, foundations, and contributors. I looked at my untied boots. I sighed, not frustrated, more defeated. My misty eyes wandered away from the undone.

A vacant nanosecond, then the weather forecast blinked on. The meteorologist pointed to the graphics displayed at her left, indicating the weekend rain totals: SAT-SUN.

Central Park = 4.78"
LaGuardia = 5.58"
JFK Airport = 1.75"

"So you can see, we had heavy rain over the last two days, but we're all clear today. Not much sun, yet no rain," she ended her presentation with a smile.

Good. No rain today.

I revisited my situation. I picked up a lace from the left boot with my left hand. Held it for a moment. Then released it to the floor. Then I grabbed both laces from my left boot and held them in my left hand. I had no further thoughts.

"Stay tuned for *Sesame Street.*" I noted the prompt. Fun stuff for kids. Wish I was having fun. It made no sense. It's not magic or rocket science. Let's do this!

It…holding the fabric… The laces.

I don't get it. I let the laces fall to the floor. Accompanied by sweat and tears.

Who can I call? What do I say?

Okay, first stop crying. Damn!

Don't think. Don't try to remember. Don't look for a solution. Remove the stress from this simple habit.

I sat and watched adults pretend colorful hand puppets were a natural thing. Like I could walk outside and see a brown bear wearing a postal uniform as it delivered mail, or watch red and blue fabric panels dance and sing.

I exhaled with an easy grace. And I'd stopped tearing up.

This was insane.

"…take one and make a loop. You can do it without looking. That's right! Now wrap it around and tuck it under."

I had been looking at the TV but not watching. Not comprehending until the song. A black woman was teaching a red puppet to tie it's shoe!

Are you fucking with me? The world is fucking with me!

I shook in a blunt vacuum as I sucked air through pursed lips. Everything I saw had a blessed aura, a mystic halo about it. My living room was a sanctified cathedral dotted with tight pinhole-sized floating spheres of light.

"That's very good, Elmo! Let's do it with the other shoe." The black woman coiled a lace about the solo loop, tucked it under, pulled the slack and created another loop. Entwined these loops to create a tight bow. All done.

I looked at my boots; then I gazed back at the TV as Elmo was cinching the second loop, securing the bow.

Then bent over, grabbed the laces on my left boot, a lace in each hand—then made a solo loop, coiled the other lace about the solo loop, tucked it under, pulled the slack and created another loop. Entwined these loops to create a tight bow.

All done.

I immediately repeated the procedure on my right boot.

"Now we're ready to play!" The black woman said with a smile.

"YAY!" Elmo yelled with joy.

I relaxed into the chair. My face was wet, and I believe I

produced an audible whimper.

I gotta see somebody. General physician for a brain scan.

I'll start with a psychiatrist. Try talking. Maybe it's stress.

I looked at my boots.

Undid the laces.

Retied the laces of both boots within seconds. I settled back into the chair as an unsatisfied feeling rattled within me. No joyous moment. No sense of accomplishment. No solid footing. I'm scattered by a slight slipstream.

Elmo hit a volleyball and the bear delivering mail returned the volley.

I gotta talk to somebody.

But not today. I turned off the monitor, closed the app on my phone. I noted the time displayed on my phone. Thought about it. My dramarama lasted just shy of thirty minutes. It felt like hours.

My phone hummed and blinked. It was Dean from work. I picked up the device.

"Hey, Dean," I said, calm and easy. "I'm on my way in."

"Hey, boss—glad to hear your voice!" Dean said. **"He's okay! I got him on the phone!"** Dean's voice seemed to echo, as though he'd turned away from his phone.

"We didn't see your car, and that was a good sign, but we were nervous anyway."

"What do you mean—what happened?" Anxiety swelled within my chest.

"Roof collapsed on the west wing. Everyone is okay. No one is ever in the Flight Atrium in the morning—except you! So that was a big concern—but all good now!"

"What? How? I'm out the door now." I said as I grabbed my gear. ID card. Keys.

"Well, fire department just got here. But I hear there's a lot of water damage."

"You said everyone was okay?"

"Yes, sir. We're good."

"Gotcha. Thanks Dean. I should be there in twenty minutes."

4

"Austin Street is shut down. They said the façade is unstable. It's gonna have to all come down. You'll have to come around on Elmhurst, but that's also nuts."

"Right," I sighed as I locked the front door. "I'll call you when I'm in the neighbourhood."

"Cool. See you soon."

"Right. Bye."

I walked by the elevator. I opened the access door adjacent to the elevator bank and rapidly descended the steps. I needed the six flights of stair activity.

At the third floor I realized that if I hadn't had that meltdown, I would've been—as Dean feared, in the flight atrium. That's where I plan my day.

So my mental breakdown was divine intervention? I'm not a spiritual person, nor much on fate. If I am slated to die today, then it will happen today. If not in a building collapse, then maybe as I'm walking down these stairs. Hell, I'm more concerned about my mind, my memory. Will I be able to tie my boots an hour from now?

My phone hummed against my thigh. I pulled it out of my pocket. My mom's face filled the screen as a bright green alert scrolled over her. *Building Collapse. Fire Officials on scene suspect recent heavy rainfalls weakened foundation.* It faded away as I tapped the green icon.

"Hi mom—yeah, I'm fine. I'm leaving home."

"On my way to the office now."

"Yes, mom, I am very lucky."

"Why car service? I can drive."

"Yeah, okay. I'll call a car."

"Of course, I'll come over as soon as I get a handle on the situation."

"Love you too, mom."

She was right. My mind was not on driving. Best to let someone else do it.

And I do have a lot of calls to make.

I exited the stairwell and entered the lobby. The large space was empty and quiet. I opened the car app and tapped request.

I was immediately notified that a gray sedan, driver: Carol, would arrive in less than five minutes.

DUO

You watched Jae as they stared at their boots.

They were nice boots. Constructed of jet black, hand-sewn leather with six super bright embroidered skulls that adorned the toes and a trio of happy bright skulls cuffing the heel of each boot. You knew Jae loved those boots. You loved the boots. Hell, everyone you and Jae hung out with loved the boots.

You watched Jae patiently hold the laces of the left boot in their left hand. Then, Jae deliberately allowed the laces to fall to the floor. You looked as Jae stared at their boots—and anger pricked your skin. You and Jae needed to leave now to make the show on time. You can't understand the drama.

"Just tie your boots and let's go!" you yelled at Jae.

They looked at you softly—are they crying? Really? What is going on? You sighed with repressed frustration. "I'm sorry," you said to Jae.

"It's okay," was their immediate response. "I know the show is starting soon. You should go—that way you'll be on time?"

You looked at Jae and asked, "Is there anything I can do?" Perhaps a bit indifferent. You do want to help. Yet you even heard it in your voice just now. You want to go.

"I'm calling a car. Hopefully we'll be ready when it gets here," you said as you tapped the face of your phone with your thumb.

Jae remained still and quiet, boot-gazing. You knew Jae was moody, and it's not a drug thing, yet you thought they looked flyaway, spaced out, tapped out, disconnected. But if they won't talk, you can't really do much, can you?

13/8: Tak-tok-tajtaytajtaytajtaytajtay-tak-toktok-toktok-toktajtaytajtaytajtaytajtay-toktoktoktoktok. You silenced the alert by tapping the face of your phone. "The car is a minute away. How you feelin'?" you asked Jae.

"Aw." It was barely an audible whimper, more of a body expression from Jae. They cleared their throat. Yet they seemed just a breath away from crying.

"Are you okay?" You asked. That's when you noted Jae's orange eyes, alight with passive chaos.

Jae nodded as they investigated the space about them. "Yeah. Just, something…" They sighed, slow and long. A meditative release of a sort.

"You should go. I'll be right behind you," Jae stated with clarity.

You sighed, nothing grandiose or off-putting. You recalled the lyrics from a David Bowie song, "You're not sure if you like her, but you know you really love her."

So there you have it.

You stood, then you kissed Jae on the forehead. You bent over and tucked the laces of the embroidered boots into the folds of the leather fabric. Loose yet secure and very hip. "Okay, let's go," you said.

"Thank you," said Jae.

"Of course." You replied with simple grace, suppressing your constant angst with the duality of need. Jae needed you to keep all this working. And you needed Jae to open doors. You can't escape their orbit and they would spin out of control without your gravity. You were Jae. They were Jae. Together you were Jae2.

You held your phone in your left hand, so you grabbed your wallet and keys with your free hand.

Jae had their purse, strap slung over their left shoulder. They held their phone in their right hand. And they offered you a little smile.

Okay, now you're feeling good about things.

You opened the door, and you both exited. As you locked the door, you heard that annoying ping. You hated living across the hall from the elevator due to its constant noise, and that of the people waiting and exiting.

You noted the down arrow—lit in red—on the right-hand wall of the elevator entrance. You're pleased that only you and Jae are waiting for the elevator. Hopefully it won't be crowded.

The door opened to an empty car. You and Jae entered.

"So, you seemed a bit, melancholy, earlier. You want to talk about it?" You asked.

Jae offered a soft nod. "It was odd. I guess I couldn't focus. I felt, *undone*. I guess that's the best way to describe it."

You nodded. "A bit of a funk," you added with a supportive punch. "I get it."

You and Jae exited the elevator. The lobby was empty.

You saw a car double park, just as you received pings on your phone and watch. "I bet that's our car," you said.

You and Jae rushed to the car, laughing as gossamer sheets of rain draped the city.

Quiet ride to the show, as was routine. You enjoyed the wet cityscape; ever-evolving buildings of concrete, glass, and metal; and ever-evolving people, constant, in motion, poetic as the gentle chromatic panels of rain that enveloped them.

Jae enjoyed the travel with their eyes closed. You knew they were preparing.

The car stopped. You opened the door and stepped out. You noted a shout, a smattering of mischief. You extended your hand to Jae as they exited the car.

Once the colorful skulls on the toes of their boots appeared, all eyes were on them. That's when you heard the noise. An explosion that most noted as applause. Yet to you, it was hard and harsh white noise. Yes, you are a duo—but everyone was here to see and hear Jae.

You helped Jae stand upon the wetted sidewalk. Jae stood six foot, three inches tall (with the boots, they topped six-six). Their legs were legendary. Dark caramel, taut and athletic. Their physique complemented their legs. Jae was sculpted ready drama. A majestic onyx illusion.

You noted that the rain had stopped.

Four large men wearing black jackets formed a moving barricade, two men on the left, two on the right. Two additional beefy men headed the security column. Jae towered over the security, the paparazzi, and the fans.

You and Jae moved slowly. You waved and said thank you. You turned to see Jae reaching out to touch fingers and hands, saying, thank you.

Two photographers jumped into your path, somehow behind security. You and Jae smiled at each camera eye. Never a poor photo.

Security removed the photographers.

"I love your boots, Jae!"

"Thank you! I really like your necklace!"

"Oh my gawd! Thank you! My mother gave it to me!"

Jae stopped. Jae softly parted the human security gate and got cheek to cheek with the young fan. The fan took the once in a lifetime selfie as dozens of other cameras snapped up the moment.

You gently removed Jae from the forever fan and continued to usher them toward the performer's entrance.

"In five," said Ellen, the assistant director; she held up five fingers as you both neared the door.

Jae took your hand as they turned back, an about-face, and you once again faced the fans as Jae blew kisses.

"In FOUR," proclaimed Ellen with a tart snap.

Your phone pinged. And pinged again. You let the device sound off as you lay in bed. You noted that the sun was up, so you were now on normal people time. You question why the normal workday began as soon as the after-party ended. An immediate smile raced over your lips as you somewhat recalled last night's epic event at the Flight Atrium. You're sure you heard someone say, "if they're not on tour, they're at this party!" And you do remember meeting so many people. The artists you'd admired. But you loved it when that actress from that horror movie said, *Mini Dada*, your first solo album was epic! And that your best song from that album was, "My Wife." You felt she had been sincere. You hoped so. Especially since you felt the same way. *Mini Dada* was yours alone. Lyrics, beats, arranging. that was all you. And you felt that "My Wife" was your best solo work—to date.

You felt so alive knowing that someone noticed you outside of Jae*2*—which no one else had. You had released two solo projects, and both had received few reviews. For someone to say your solo work was epic, well, that made the party.

You sighed as you reached for the device. Then you just stared at your phone, hand hanging in the air, until your manager's still, silent, and sultry gaze bullied you into pressing the green icon. You're sure the device had been one ring away from forwarding to voicemail.

You were lazy and indifferent as the debonair voice announced, "You and Jae were beautiful last night! Have you seen the reviews—stellar! Listen, a shoe company wants to fashion a look after Jae's non-laced boots. Check the socials, all the kids are already copying the look! I just sent you a Drop Box link so you and Jae can review and approve designs. This is big money so don't sleep on it."

"Right, of course. Thanks Mike." You pressed the red button on your phone, ending the call with Mike. In frustration, you created a fashion sensation. No one should be that lucky, you mused, and you suppressed a laugh as you rose from the bed. Then you swiftly argued that it wasn't luck. You turned a moment of negative energy into creative opportunity.

You walked across the hall of the apartment. You knocked on the door.

"Yeah, c'mon in," you heard Jae state.

You entered the room.

Jae had their boots on, laced up, tied nice and neat. They sat on the bed and watched you approach.

"You gotta lose the laces," you tell them. "Mike got a shoe deal. The company wants to base the brand on last night's look, the laces tucked in and away on your boots. Mike sent a link for us to review samples."

You watched a smile leap from Jae's lips, and then they

laughed. They bounced off the bed, then hurried over to the Casio keyboard. They turned on the unit and began to play. D#, D#, D#… "No line, no tether, no worries—so easy without the laces," Jae sang.

You reflexively took your place next to Jae, activated the drum machine, set the tempo to 120 B.P.M., selected reggae kit, slosh beat (which added a sloppy metal ting to the hi-hat). You decided to add echo to the snare. You were pleased with the sound, and you saw that Jae was into it.

You looped the beat.

You caught Jae's rhythm, nodded your head in sync, and sang, "No line, no tether, no worries—no laces. So easy."

"No laces", you said on the downbeat. "So easy."

"No laces," Jae flowed.

"So easy. No laces." You harmonized with Jae.

You set your phone in the holder. Used your smiling face to unlock the phone: *Building Collapse*. The bright green alert flashed on your phone. *Fire Officials on scene suspect recent heavy rainfalls weakened foundation* faded away as you selected the video app. You thought that was awful news, but you didn't have time to dwell on it. You tapped the record icon as you glanced at Jae. Nodded.

On the beat. "No line, no tether, no worries—so easy. No laces. So easy."

"No Laces", you repeated on beat.

You and Jae sang, "So easy without the laces." You and Jae were pitch perfect.

You retrieved the phone from the holder. You composed the video clip, then posted it to Mike. Subject line: *Hook for shoe commercial.*

TREY

Joad looked at his boots.

They were nice boots. He recalled watching Greta, the boot-maker, fit the fabric about the wooden form. She had punched holes in the fabric. Then patient, deliberate hand stitching. He remembered her silver and brass tools, laid upon a thick blue cloth. Greta would yell if she saw how well-worn and scuffed the black boots had become. Yeah, they needed a good buffing. But no one cared what his boots looked like during practice; and no one saw his boots during a performance. Yet that is not an excuse for not taking proper care of your property. Joad had the boots resoled recently, and they had buffed them up for him. But he practiced twice a day—sometimes three times a day when they introduced new material. Then all the daily chores. He was in his boots more than he was out of them.

The laces of the boots…

The laces.

Same fabric as the boots.

The laces.

Joad did not know how to lace up his boots. The boots he practiced and performed in. The boots he had worn for many years. The boots he wore as he walked about his home and all over the campus.

Joad did not know how to lace up his boots, so he looked at them, lifeless at the end of his feet. He had figured out how to place them on his feet—and that's where the fun ended.

His amazing physical strength was of no use to him in this task. His imagination and dexterity and will power did not come to his aid. This handsome action man was reduced to sitting on his ass. Looking at his boots.

Studying the laces….

13/8: Tak-tok-tajtaytajtaytajtaytajtay-tak-toktok-toktok-tok-tajtaytajtaytajtaytajtay-toktoktoktoktok. Joad remembered the odd and frantic notional sequence for their performance. Tak-tok-tajtaytajtaytajtaytajtay-tak-toktok-toktok-tok-tajtaytajtaytajtaytajtay-toktoktoktoktok. His booted right foot tapped out the measure. Yet the abstract pace did not move his memory. The laces remained undone.

"Vaughn had twins and they're beautiful!" Trey said with glee as she entered the living room. She presented her phone; Joad nodded and smiled as he studied the photo of the newborns.

"Twins! I thought it was just going to be the one," Joad replied as fear raked at his heart. Was he forgetting more than just how to lace his boots?

"We all did! Vaughn said the doctors were very shaken. But the staff handled it well. Everyone is in good health. She named the twins, So and Ys." Trey finished her update with a kiss upon Joad's lips.

They smiled, enjoyed the moment. Children were on their list.

Okay, the twin thing really choked up his mind. He thought he had forgotten something else.

Trey bent down. She took Joad's left foot and began to tighten the laces on the boot.

Joad said nothing. He watched.

"I forgot to tell you that I spoke with Little Johnny yesterday. He said he extended the gaps of our trap lattice," Trey stated as she crossed the laces. Made a loop of one lace.

"Our drops will be more dramatic." She coiled a lace about the solo loop, tucked it under, pulled the slack and created another loop.

Not looking at her hands, Trey smiled at Joad as she entwined the loops to create a tight bow. All done. She tapped his foot.

Joad lifted his left foot, eased the untied right foot into place. Trey began the act anew.

"Aw." It was not an audible whimper. More of a body expression from Joad.

Trey looked up, never ceasing to tie the right boot. She thought Joad had cleared his throat. Yet he seemed just a breath away from crying.

"Are you okay?" Trey asked.

Joad nodded as he gazed into Trey's sparkling, chaotic green eyes. "Yeah. Just, something…" He flexed his shoulder, feigning a cramp.

Trey cinched the bow with her slender fingers. Joad felt the comforting bite of the knot upon his instep.

Trey rose; stole another kiss from Joad. "I will make something to eat."

"Thank you. That would be wonderful. Thank you."

Trey bounced off toward the kitchen.

Joad looked at his boots. Laced. Neat. Right.

"And I made an appointment with Andi and Jim about new ribbons," Trey continued the conversation as she worked in the kitchen. "Deeper drops mean we can expand and brighten our display. Bring more vitality to the open space. It'll be a wonderful accompaniment for Jae*2*'s, *Prismatic Rain.*"

"Remember we shoot the video tomorrow, so please stop by Edwin's for a proper grooming. He'll be ready for you at three."

"Yeah. Sure." Joad replied. He studied his boots.

Joad undid the bow on his left boot. He pulled the laces free. Two strings dangled from the top hooks. He looked at the right boot—looked away.

He held the loose laces. He crossed the laces. Then loop, loop, tuck under, bow and cinch.

He did it right. It felt right. Left bow looked like the right bow.

He untied the laces.

Joad laced up his boots.

He sighed slow and long. A meditative release.

He stood. Looked down at his well laced boots. Joad was confident he could repeat the task.

He wasn't confident that he wouldn't forget again. It was scary to lose memory, to be cast into the abyss and to have no response, no tether back to reality, back to home. If Trey hadn't tied his boots, Joad was sure he'd still be sitting lost in this chair. Is this the first sign of dementia? Stress? Did he suffer a seizure or some type of nervous episode?

He untied his left boot. Pulled the laces free of their loops. Then relaced and retied the boot.

There was warped comfort in successfully repeating the act; especially with no assurance the habit would be retained.

And it's unthinkable to ask someone to show you how to

lace your boots. If someone of his age said that they'd forgotten how to lace up their boots—he knew no one could keep that secret. Gossip would lead people to consider he'd lost his mind, and that psychiatric care was in order. He didn't want to become a case study. He didn't want pity, loss of respect, loss of trust.

He certainly did not want to make Trey feel like a caregiver.

This could be nothing more than a one-time event.

Best to remain silent for the moment.

Joad smelled bread. He felt very lucky to have Trey in his life. He wiped his eyes and thanked his gods for her. Then rose from the chair and made his way to the kitchen.

Joad approached his recent incident in a joking way with Trey. To test the waters.

"Last night, I overheard the actors considering this idea for a one act. About loss of memory. Like riding a bike or how to tie shoelaces."

"That's scary. I mean, what's the point?" She shook her head as she asked, "Was it Gertie? She loves tragedy."

Trey paused, then stated clearly, "I can't see it. Perhaps if they worked with Orlo, add some magic, even simple slight-of-hand, that would lift the storyline. Make it fun." As expected, Trey viewed such an incident with concern.

Joad was the anchor of an energetic and creative acrobatic crew. Would they trust him to remember routines if they knew he'd forgotten how to tie his shoes? The troupe would not perform to the best of their abilities if they had any doubts about him.

Hum-hum. Hum-hum. Trey picked up the phone. She was taken aback and quickly stared at Joad. She pressed the speaker icon.

Joad immediately recognized Little Johnny's distinct voice. A plain and strong, timbre that provided assurance. "Yeah, so I'm on my way there. I haven't seen the site, but I'm sure your troupe will not be able to practice there for the foreseeable future."

"Right. Understood. Thank God everyone is okay," Trey replied.

"Yes. Look, I have another location that I'm sure will suit your needs. I'll send you the details ASAP," Little Johnny said.

"Wow—that's amazing. Thank you." Trey replied.

"Very good. Look for the info shortly." The call clicked off.

Building Collapse. The bright green alert flashed upon Trey's phone. *Fire Officials on scene suspect recent heavy rainfalls weakened foundation* faded away as Trey touched the END icon.

"What a morning!" Trey stated with joy, surprise, and a touch of exhaustion.

Joad nodded as he looked at Trey. "Yeah, nutty." The notation of a *weakened foundation* jarred him. Was he the same as that building? Destabilized? Lessened? A pending collapse and so a danger to his community?

Joad held his glass of water. Looked at the clear liquid as he visualized his position in the Montreux routine. He was the key-stone of a twelve-person pyramid. The lightning-sure sequences of assembly and disassembly required of that human structure were impressive. Well beyond sound footing and fiercely organized hand grips.

Yes, he remembered the sequences and timing cues. But that was now. Would he remember tomorrow?

"Trey," Joad said, "we gotta talk."

CROSSING PATHS/ CROSSING BOUNDARIES

Moira H. Scott

The explosions still rang in my ears. The word on the street was that the rapid military response proved that the widespread release of a plague that would otherwise have been contained to a small area was an inside job. That had to be it. The jaded ones among us went full-tilt *Animal Farm* in their analysis, right down to the clichéd view of "four legs good, two legs bad." A small contingent objected that the government could have no possible motive to wreak such misery on its people. We knew better, but what we didn't know was why.

I had no idea how much time had passed, if any at all, between the repetitive carpet bombings of what was once a proud city—for them, anyway. The vibrations pulsed, making me shake my head as if I could dislodge them, to no avail. The smoke and dust particles that hung in the air made it hard for me to remember the last time I saw the light of the sun. Gods, this was depressing as Hell. Swirling dust caught in the light shafts streaming in from the fractures in the walls, stinging my eyes. Knowing I was going to regret this, I squinted as I stuck my tongue out to lick my paw in the vain hope that I could wipe away the crud that had encrusted them. The taste, let me tell you, was foul. I don't think I've heaved so much since my last hairball. The air in the crater left by one of the bombs was laden with smoke. Thick dust, black as coal, coated the bomb shelter's interior, clinging to my fur, coating my lungs... I coughed so much my ribs hurt.

A fat lot of good the government issued plans did to build a solid shelter—they had magnificently failed. We built them to spec. We tried to be good citizens. But now, cracks spread out like boney fingers in the walls, growing at an alarming rate as the armed vehicles overhead rolled down the streets—or what was left of them, anyway. Every damned time one of them hit a pothole, the squeal of metal scraping on the asphalt before the loud crash of the tires hitting the ground again made me squirm. Soon, those cracks would give way. The constant pounding of heavy boots thudded overhead. I needed to get out of here before they came for me. I glanced down at the glowing disc on my collar casting light on my black paws. It would change colours depending upon something or other; I wasn't going to sit here waiting to find out.

And the so-called government? Those fuckers got theirs when they decided to authorize their state-owned techs to recreate the plague in their crappy little labs. Any two-bit hacker with a grade school education could bust those codes in a nanosecond. And surprise, surprise, they did. Without a doubt it was an inside job. Although no one knew the reason for doing this shit in the first place, we laughed the objection off: since when did the government need a reason to do anything? Not too long ago, my compatriots and I were doing just fine, thank you very much. That is until they came and tried to destroy us—well most of us, anyway. If we just so happened to have black fur, we were seen as public enemy number one. No reason whatsoever was given for this ridiculous judgment. Just some ignorant zealots who clung to the baseless notion that we who were born with this colour of fur were baaaaaad. Their rallies and riots succeeded in whipping other humans into foam-at-the-mouth frenzies. It was the famous **big lie**, repeated *ad nauseam*, that did the most damage. The destruction of the city, the rubble, the ruins, and the cavernous transit tunnels below had held onto their secrets for decades.

I remember hearing tales about the cats who had become most adept at spelunking. What they saw down there in the depths was the stuff of legend, yet many who emerged refused to talk about their experiences. And now, those secrets were let loose upon the world, my world… Damn them. Whose bright idea was it to release the plague-infected rats? Was it sabotage? Terrorist biochemical warfare? You name it, the rationalizations that were made to serve as "reasons" were trotted out like clockwork, but no one was buying what they were selling. It was never the government's fault. Nope. It was always someone else's. If you ask me, and I know you didn't, I'd say **they** knew damned well what they were doing when they added tons more grist to the rumour mill. And man, did the talk ever get crazier and crazier after a while. I recall hearing a cat stolen from a Buddhist temple remark, "If you listen to dogs barking, you'll go deaf."

But seriously, what a way to initiate population control. Let's just say the plague-infected rats had a field day. Literally. They vamoosed from the lab and scattered. Tracking those bastards down would be a nightmare unless someone had a light bulb moment and slapped on a tracker. Gods only know what else the pseudo-scientists did to them. Had they been—how shall I put it?—**modified** like me and countless other live experiments?

But I had an even bigger problem. Since the self-righteous, superstitious morons decided we were **evil**, they came for us. Hundreds of us were torn apart by dogs, maimed or shot by mental midgets who had no business owning a gun let alone firing one. Those of us who were not killed instantly were left to die in agony. I hate humans sometimes. Lately, that festering hatred had become far more prominent among my kind. The cats who were not black-furred feared for their lives and ran hoping to escape the city's walls, lest they become new targets for experiments. I don't blame them, not one little bit, but it left us, the so-called **wicked** ones, to fend for ourselves.

And who was behind these abhorrent hunts? The same woman who was blessed with the ironic name of Grace. It didn't matter what her last name was, I never bothered to find out. She oversaw the modification experiments which she called "The Rebirth Initiation Project." Our "resurrection," for lack of a better term, was heinous. I don't remember much of the process, but I do recall this: I was but a kitten struggling to nurse from my mother. I had brothers and sisters, six, I believe. I was the seventh, the odd-ball black runt; a couple of years later, during my stay in the lab, I heard that since I was not expected to live anyway, I'd be the first to be exposed to the project, known by its initials T. R.I. P. Clever, huh? During my sojourn, they did a bunch of things to me. I still shudder at the thought of what I went through while they got their jollies. But enough of that.

TL/DR—instead of the regular microchip that most cats got at the behest of their responsible owners, mine was special: a souped-up version. Still, the techs scoffed at the specs for the so-called innovative alterations—probably the brainchild of one of the higher-ups' kids' science project. They were sure it wouldn't work. Hell, I would be, too. So certain were they that I would not be able to learn communication methods using their new tech that they shot it into me as part of a joke. When it proved to be effective, they weren't laughing any more. Holy shock and awe, I could learn and adapt. They knew a Pandora's Box had been opened. The echoes of the unspoken "Ooops" were heard loud and clear within the scientific community. Bottom line? They had a lot of explaining to do.

As for my "resurrection," as they liked to call it—more on that later. First order of business right now is for me to get the Hell out of here. Time to do an eye-witness weather report to check which way the wind was blowing—if at all. I looked around the shelter for any shred of material that I could use to cover my nose and mouth should I need to venture outside. Yes, I know it wouldn't be all that great, but it would be better than nothing.

Creeping around the other side of the failed bunker, something out of place caught my eye: an old rag tucked in a corner behind one of the food supply's freezer chests. Their contents were long gone or rotten. I wasn't going to chance opening them. Far too risky. Nope, time to get that cloth. Yanking it and hearing the telltale riiiiip of fabric as something had caught onto it, I tried pulling it more gently in a different direction. Eventually, it came loose, sending small dust tornadoes into my face. Sneezing, I shook my head trying to get away from them. Once they'd cleared, I studied the cloth for a moment. I was pretty sure I'd seen it before, but I could not remember the context. Not a big deal. Still, my curiosity did get the better of me, so I unfolded it, taking care to not rip it further.

The rag was soft in my paws. I liked that feeling, taking me back to the time when I cuddled with my mother on the soft blankets in her cage. In the back of my mind I wondered, *Who else had been in here and where were they now?* Hooding my eyes and without thinking, I rubbed my face with it, and checked to see the results. Yup. My fur was still quite dirty, and no amount of licking my paws to wash behind my ears was going to help. I didn't want **that** taste in my mouth again. Still, it felt like something I had seen the techs use when cleaning our lab cages. Oh, sorry, our home away from home. Yeesh...

The rag held an image of some sort. Unfolding it further, I saw a woman's face smack in the middle of an ornate frame of leaves and flowers. There was something large and golden on her head. Her hair was short, white, and neatly curled, as if to create a fitting cushion for the thing that sat on top. I wish I knew what that thing was as it looked most pretty, although it was likely quite heavy. I studied her face. I had seen it before— she was ancient, but she was smiling. Her face seemed kind and her eyes were bright. I think if I had met this woman in real life, I would've jumped up on her lap, curled up and purred, and I'd bet anything that she would not have minded. She seemed to be the type of person who would like cats like me, even though my fur's colour was not at all popular. Rubbing my face again, I noted with a twinge of sadness that I had sullied the woman's image. Oddly enough, I had made up my mind that despite not having a clue who she was, I rather liked her. Her smile seemed genuine, not forced. Looking at what I had done as I tried to remove the dirt from my face, I sighed, bemoaning the probability that I would never be completely without the tell-tale dirt of the siege.

Well. Enough of that sentimental bullshit. It'll only slow me down. This was not the time to get all bummed out about dirtying an unknown old lady's face on a forgotten towel. It was done. I had done it, and it was high time for me to go. I had no idea where it came from, but it was no longer of any use to me. Goodbye ancient human smiling lady. It's been swell. Still, that towel was a bizarre anachronism for anything found in a shelter. It felt weird. If someone else **was** here, I'm sure they would've shown their faces or dropped some other clue. Maybe?

First things first. I need food. I'm not even sure if the places that normally tossed me a few scraps are still around. Only one way to find out. I crept back to what was left of the entrance to my semi-destroyed, self-imposed prison. Its alleged bomb-proof status had obviously failed the safety test, with twisted metal and rust—**rust!** I couldn't help myself as I moved closer to examine it and the frame from which it was ostensibly torn. Black hole-like shadows were cast upon the dirty concrete floor. Mother-fuckers! The door was **hollow.** Just two thin rolled metal sheets clamped together to give the appearance of something strong enough to withstand a nuke. It was completely useless. The faux panels were held together with spit and toilet paper, likely.

Something caught my eye. I lunged for the towel. A quick flashing reflection hit the wall beside me. Giving it the side-eye, I realized that my collar's disc was active. Bright blood red dots covered the walls. *What the Hell?* I dove behind the storage bins and threw my paws to my neck hoping that I could stop the place from lighting up.

"I see you've found it." Startled, I crouched lower, trying not to shiver.

"It's okay, you can come out. I won't hurt you." *Oh yeah? I'd heard that before.*

"No, really, come on out. I'm trying to find my way out of here, too."

Slowly, I raised my head above the chest. My pupils dilated like dinner plates, despite the fact that it was pretty damned dark in here. I saw her. I saw her standing just a few feet away from me. A human. What in the cat Goddess' name was she doing here? Jumping up onto the crate, I froze for a moment then decided to sit and pose regally like those cats in the pyramid texts. You know the ones that sit with their backs straight and have a ton of jewellery? Now, **they** were cool. Studying her for a moment, I saw that she was a small human. Her mane was blondish, her hairless skin was really, really freakin' pale. I supposed it had been a long time since she'd seen the sun, too. I noticed that her pale mane, errr... hair with streaks of silver, framed a face replete with a cupid's bow mouth and dark greenish eyes, but her eyelashes, and eyebrows seemed non-existent. She wasn't very tall.

Drawing in a deep breath I tried to puff myself up a bit, "The fuck are **you** doing here?"

The human blinked a couple of times before she spoke. Sighing: "I'm not exactly sure, to be honest. One day I was doing my job. Business as usual in the lab—"

Feeling my fur bristle, I lowered my body as if to pounce. "Lab, you say? What was your job there?" Yeah, okay, it was a bit curt, but I'm sure you can understand why I'd be guarded around this—this lab-working human.

She blinked before dropping her eyes to the floor. "I know you are, or were, one of them."

I raised my chin to look down my nose at her. "Of course you do. **You** were one of those who did this to me."

The human woman raised her eyes to meet mine. She studied the thick collar with its bright disc hanging around my neck for a moment before replying, "Yes. Yes, I was."

I resisted the urge to snarl. Drawing a paw over my nose in a vain attempt to quell my rising anger, I stared at her. Hard. "Ya know, I could just swipe at ya with my claws and—"

"But you won't."

My whiskers jammed back as my ears flattened. "And you know this, how? Do you really think you have any idea what I and thousands more like me have been through?"

"No. But if you intended to attack me you would've done it already."

Annoyed as Hell, I turned in a half circle, stopped, then looked over my shoulder, "Ya got me there."

The woman's shoulders dropped. "Yes, I've got you there. **Again.**"

Okay. She was really beginning to piss me off. "So, what are you gonna do to me now, huh? Have at it, I have nothing left to lose."

Again, the cold stare. She hesitated a bit longer than she should have before replying, "Actually, Kuro Neko, you do."

I backed up a little, "Okay. Out with it. What the Hell are you talking about? And that's **not** my name!" She looked at me, sans expression. I pushed harder, "Uhhhh…this better not be like one of those buddies on the road things, cuz I'm not into that. Just sayin' I mean, I have no freaking clue who you are— other than the fact that you were a real, honest to goodness lab drone who more than likely had a hand in what I've become. And here you are staring at me, and I am so **not** cool with it."

She sighed and dropped her eyes again, "I'm sorry I had no—"

"Oh no you don't! Don't give me that crap. Do **not** for one second think that I will believe you were **just doing your job.** This ain't Nuremberg and you sure as Hell ain't Adolf Eichmann, so you'll need to do better than that."

The woman sighed, "You're right. I'm not **that man,** nor do I wish to use his excuses. I **was** tasked with trying to discover inter-species intelligence. That part of my research was fascinating. We—or I, specifically—wanted to focus upon communication."

I eyed her closely, "Go on…"

She cleared her throat. I knew I had her cornered. She'd either give in or come out swinging. She straightened, adjusted her posture, and tried to puff herself up. "Look," she managed as her voice cracked, "I was totally focused upon the work in the lab I was assigned to. We had deadlines that needed to be met and it was all hands-on deck. I had also been tipped off about a research award, so you can bet the rent I was super focused on that stuff. Scoring a prestigious award from the Government? Of course, I'd be all over that!"

"Huh, I bet you would. But let's cut to the chase, shall we? Why don't you get to the part where some clowns in a neighbouring lab or facility poked the plague bear with a stick."

The colour drained from her face, "I don't know what you mean."

I bit my tongue before responding. Rivulets of blood pooled in my mouth before escaping, "Yes, madam, you do. Come on! The plague is big business for population control but ya know what's even bigger? Yeah, the possibility of finding a fucking cure! There's big bucks and a shit-ton of notoriety attached to the lab-coated saviours who figured out how to cure the Bubonic Plague."

"Okay, stop. Just stop. Yes, what you have said is true. We would be out of work if we found a cure, but did you take into consideration the fact that while we were studying the effects of the plague, we were also discovering new—"

I raised my paw, cutting her off in mid-blab. Strangely enough, she capitulated yet again. "Spare me. If my paw pads could make more noise, I'd gladly give your little speech a slow clap, but they can't, so I won't. What I will say, however, is that you scientists really have no clue as to what your work does on your experiment subjects, do you?"

Her face fell again, "Well this is certainly pointless, isn't it? Here I am being harangued by a foul-mouthed feline in a bombed-out bomb-shelter—"

I raised my chin and stared down my nose. If I could've slapped my knee and laughed like a human, I would have, "Sorry, lady, I'm not interested in your pity party. Not one bit. So, if you're going to high tail it outta here, I suggest you do that right now."

Thrusting her hands on her hips, the woman tried to tower

over me, but that didn't work: I leapt to a higher shelf. Ducking, she snapped back at me. "Look you scruffy fur bag, this place isn't safe for either of us so why don't we—"

If we cats could laugh, I would have, "Wait, what? You want **me** to go with **you**?"

Letting out an exasperated sigh, she nodded her head. "Did I stutter?"

I felt the muscles in my face relax a bit, my whiskers pushed forward, "Okay, where to, madam?"

"I'm not sure yet, but if we are going to make this trip together, I need to know your name."

I regarded her closely for a moment. "I don't have one. I was just a number."

Raising an eyebrow: "May I?"

I took a step backward "May you what?"

"May I have a look at your collar? Please."

I backed up another step, not knowing if this was the right thing to do. Ah, to hell with it. I needed to get out of here. I shut my eyes tight as I felt the warmth of her hands touch my neck, "I just need to make a couple of adjustments…"

As her voice faded away, I opened my eyes, yet I felt as if I was blind. My tail twitched three times. Darkness enveloped me as the sounds of the explosions faded into nothingness. Silence. But only for a few minutes. I found myself sprawled in the darkness on something warm. Kicking my back legs out, I rolled over. What was I lying on? Splaying my paws, I felt grains. Sand? In an instant, my retracted claws burst forth. Scrambling to my feet, my weakened legs protested. How long had I been like this? Better yet where was I? A gentle breeze swirled tiny tornados of sand around my paws. Distant voices—**human voices**—rumbled. I couldn't make out what they were saying. As the sounds drew nearer, my ears pricked up. Drums. Yes, those were decidedly drums… and laughter! **Laughter!** A parade! It was a freaking **parade**! With chanting? What sort of event was this?

Blinking, I rubbed my eyes with my paw, things slowly came into focus. The night sky shone with stars, more than I'd ever seen; before me, the lights, music, and fires rivalled the stellar light show above. As the revellers drew nearer, I could see the women in short skirts, many with their chests bare. But their eyes—their eyes were heavily lined with black eyeliner and stunning deep iridescent blue shadow over the lids. Something in my head whispered: *The eyes of Horus…* Many of the women carried torches, twirling them around the dancers and musicians. A couple of women had these neat torches on leather or some sort of rope and were spinning them overhead. It was the coolest thing I'd ever seen! I wanted to join them. Why not? I pulled myself to my feet and shook the sand from my fur, well, as best I could. Something told me I'd better be on my best behaviour.

Then, I saw her. She looked familiar, her reddish-brown hair resplendent with long braids… cornrows, I think they're called, woven with bright, shiny beads. My heart raced and my pupils dilated to dinner plate size, but I resisted the urge to go bounding after her. No pre-emptive strike butt-wiggle. My body shuddered as I shook my head, trying to quell the urge to hunt. Nope. Can't be chasing **those** shiny things.

I took a few steps forward, but out of the corner of my eye I caught my reflection in the flowing water. The river was wide, swirling and filled with boats. My fur was still black as night, yet my collar…what was up with my collar? With the moon riding high and the illumination of torches, my collar had changed. Boy, had it changed… bright green leather—no, wait—I had to get a better look. Torches' reflections danced on the water. I trotted over to the riverbank and gazed into the illuminated surface. My collar didn't look like leather… Was it **snakeskin**? Wow. I sat down again and raised one of my paws to feel it. I couldn't take my eyes off my reflection. It **was** snakeskin. Snakeskin adorned with blue stones streaked with gold and green shining with blackened swirls. In the middle, a silver piece dangled. What was this? It looked like a cross but while it had a long straight piece and one shorter horizontal piece intersecting it near the top, above the intersection of both the horizontal and vertical bars lay a beautiful oval. Its brilliance, reflected in the dancing torches, dazzled my eyes. *Great Goddess!* I smashed my paw to my mouth as if I'd said something untoward. Suddenly, I didn't know whether to be elated or completely freaked out. Someone had adorned my collar with the **Key of Life**.

The voices, drumming and music grew louder. As I tore my gaze from my reflection in the water, the tiny Ankh at my throat clattered as it struck the gemstones on either side of it. I backed up a little, in spite of myself. Blinking, I now could see the whites of the revellers' eyes. The music stopped. The dancers and celebrants, silent now, slowly changed their stance. Not a word was spoken as the crowd encircled me. Terrified, I felt my fur stand on end. My tail shot up, flicking in defiance. *What did they want from me?*

A low murmuring hum rose over the crowd as some of them began to step back, parting like the Red Sea. Out of the darkness, a woman strode purposefully towards me. Her melodious voice rang out like chimes upon a breeze: "Do not be afraid." I backed up a few steps, not knowing what to do. Great gasps from the crowd did not affect the woman. "Come here. Come to me, little one."

As she stepped forward into the illuminated circle, I beheld one of the most beautiful creatures I'd ever seen. Her alabaster body was tall and slim. Her silver robe, edged with shimmering gold, hung off one shoulder, and her hair was hung in reddish braids that framed her delicate feline face. Barefoot, she strode toward me and knelt, patting the sand with her right hand. Silver bangles jangled with each soft strike of her palm, their jingling holding me transfixed. "Do not be afraid... You bear the collar of my priesthood, and you have appeared to me in your purest form. Thus, you are doubly blessed." *This could not be real! For I was but a humble cat...*

Around the woman, the crowd fell to their knees. This was as good a time as any to ask just what in the Gods' names was happening. Gathering all the strength I could muster, I put one tentative paw forward. "This is quite the celebration, pray, tell, what is the source of such jubilation?"

The crowd, with their eyes cast downward, drew in their

breath. The beautiful woman before me threw her head back with melodic laughter. "To think that **you** would be asking that!" Her expression suddenly shifted, her voice lowered, "He has been caught and soon, the lives of the murdered and lost will be avenged!"

My eyes narrowed, yet I could sense my pupils dilating again, "Of whom do you speak?" I asked, trying to sound as officious and brave as possible, yet failing miserably.

The woman regarded me closer, taking a breath before speaking, "He has no name—at least none that he will reveal, despite torture—"

"Torture? **Torture?** You tortured a man—"

Her expression fell as her eyes blazed at me. "Yes. It was but a small price to pay for what he has done to us!"

I sat down on my haunches in a vain attempt to act casual. "And you want me to do what about this?"

At that moment, a young woman, clad in similar yet simpler robes, rose to her feet and moved toward the feline-faced woman, standing just behind her. "My Lady," speaking her words slowly yet not without resolution, the young woman stated, "Mafdet has been safely delivered unto us. She stands here before you, not as a subject, but as an equal."

What in the name of Bast was this woman talking about, and who in the world is this Mafdet?

The young woman spoke, her voice cracking with nerves. The woman clad in silver and gold rose to her feet. Without turning around, she whispered over her shoulder to the young woman, "Shera, bring forward 'Mafdet's Claw.'"

Now this is getting interesting.

The young woman turned away to receive something handed to her from a servant. It sat on—what was that? A **leopard skin.** She handed it to the woman in silver as a smile broke cleanly over her face. Puzzled, I hesitated before stepping forward. I could feel the tip of my tail twitching in anticipation. The woman named Shera bearing the item named "Mafdet's Claw" nodded her head to the lady clad in silver as she made her way toward me. Bowing her head and averting her eyes, she knelt on both knees, placing the blade on the warm sand. Without meeting my gaze, the Claw was pushed toward me. Wordlessly rising to her feet, keeping her head bowed, she backed away behind the woman clad in silver and gold, disappearing into the darkness.

I couldn't tear my eyes away from the sickle-shaped blade. I cleared my throat before addressing the woman who towered over me, resplendent in glittering jewels. "Lady, forgive me, but I do not believe we have been introduced."

A chorus of horrified gasps rang out over the crowd, falling silent when she raised her hand. "Indeed, we have not, little one," she smiled. "You have known me for thousands of years. I walk with you on this plane and on the next…" Pausing for a moment, likely for dramatic effect, she continued, "You shall address me as Bast. Know that we are kindred, **Mafdet**."

I gasped and backed up a step before realising there was no place for me to go. Sensing my fear, she knelt before me again: "The blade before you is so named because of your service to the kingdom—"

Now, wait a minute… "My service? I don't understand."

The woman with the feline face sighed, but caught herself before showing any annoyance. "There are those—those souls who need to be avenged, for they have been struck down. Our kind are the protectors. We slay the cobras which invade homes, harming the humans within. We protect the mothers and their babes… We hunt the vermin that invade the granaries, thus protecting the food sources of our human companions. The weapon that sits on the sand before you is but a tool for vengeance."

My tail twitched. "And you are expecting me to use it?"

A half smile from her was all the confirmation I needed. I glanced at the blade once more. This time, I noticed there was a piece missing. Steeling myself, I tried to stave off the tightness in my throat. "Where is the other piece? The shaft?"

A glimmer of appreciation flashed in her eyes. "Ah, yes, you **do** know this weapon."

My tail twitched faster as I felt my hackles rise. Motioning again to someone in the crowd, the woman smiled at me as she commanded, "Bring forth the staff!" Murmurs arose from the crowd as, again, a few of the celebrants stepped aside to let a young boy emerge. His hands tightly gripped the dark, gnarled rod nearly twice his size. Thrusting the upright staff forward, he averted his eyes as he fell to his knees. Wordlessly, she took it from him. Rising to his feet and spreading his arms wide, his eyes remained downcast as he backed away into the crowd. The murmurs rose again, then fell silent.

Then, I felt them. Slow vibrations emanated from my collar. Her eyes grew wide for a moment before recovering. *Did she know more about it? Did she have knowledge of this damned collar?* "Wait a moment, I'm not touching that thing!"

Bast thrust her fists into her hips. "Oh yes. Yes, you will, for you are—"

"I'm **what**? What or who do you think I am?" *Bloody good job! I've now pissed off a Goddess who is surrounded by her people! Good show!*

Her voice fell to a growl. "You are decreed by Pharaoh and the Gods to—"

"To **what**? What have," I waved my paw dismissively, "Pharaoh and the Gods decided that I must do, huh? You seem to think I'm this—this Mafdet—whoever the hell **she** is—and that I'm going to do what now? Do away with some poor dude who **you people** believe is responsible for a plague or something?"

Bast moved closer to me and cast down her steely-eyed stare, but this time I didn't back down. Nope. "I'm not doing it. I'm not Mafdet. It's not happening!"

A shock from my collar caused me to choke, but it wasn't a hairball choke—it was a real one… I felt my windpipe constrict as tears stung my eyes, but I stood firm, planting my paws in the sand, meeting her gaze full on. Bast knelt before me, but this time **she** averted her eyes.

Resting both palms upon the sand, she sighed before raising her eyes to meet mine. "Is this your final decision? To not carry out this man's execution to appease Pharaoh and the people of Egypt?"

Now wait just one second!

The Goddess continued, her voice solemn and forlorn, "You are right, of course. In my desire to seek vengeance for those the nameless one had slaughtered, I—I—"

I raised my paw to silence her. (Ballsy move, huh?) "Shhhhhh… There is no need for sorrow here. Lady, I understand what you were trying to do. I even get why. The thing is, and I know **you** know this—is that we cannot stanch the flow of evil without riding the tides of good. I don't know what life is like with you—with all the Gods who dwell each within their temples, but I do know this: we cannot stop the evil that plagues us all, but we can do our best to do what is right. I am certain you understand that from my perspective, humble as it may be, that this is not right, it would be pointless for me to take his life using a ceremonial blade such as this. What good would that do in the long run?"

A glimmer of recognition flickered in her deep-set eyes. Casting her gaze to the sand for a moment, she slowly raised her eyes to meet mine, "You have passed the test, young one."

Test? WHAT TEST?

"You are no Mafdet."

Damn straight I'm not!

"You desire to not cause harm due to the fact that you consider yourself no judge, jury, nor executioner. I applaud your strength, for those with a weaker heart would surely have let the blood flow, crying vengeance for the lost. May the feather of Ma'at be weighed in your favour when Anubis comes for you."

Her final words unnerved me a little, as did the thought that I stood up to a Goddess, put my paw down, and lived to tell about it. Strange days, indeed. But I was still surrounded by people who had halted their partying mood to watch little ol' me, a common house cat, stand up to their Lady.

Once Bast had said her piece, she turned to them and declared, "There will be no execution tonight!" A roar of—wait, were those cheers or boos? It was hard to tell, but at this point, it didn't matter. The thrum of voices resumed droning louder, drowning out my spluttering coughs. Red dots! Red dots? **Red** dots!!! Everywhere! Spinning, flashing, the thrum pulsed louder. Oh, here we go! I could hear them, their voices, instruments, and utter chaos rising higher and higher… then, nothing.

More silence. More fucking blackness.

My collar started up again—but this time it felt weird. Really, weird. And what the hell was that smell? The pungent odour of—sulphur? Thick, orange smoke hung in the air. My eyes stung, my nostrils burned, I had to take cover. Blinking, I detected a yellowish light. Sunrise? Or was it sunset? It was hard to tell. I couldn't even figure out my orientation. Just where the **fuck** was I now?

Rumbling… rumbling, louder than any sound my collar ever made, filled my ears. My eyes adjusted to the faint glow, illuminating destruction all around me. I don't know if it was the smoke and dust that was making me feel off. Just plain off. When the smoke cleared, I found myself in the middle of a broken landscape. Bricks, dust, jagged. And bodies. Dear Gods…there were **bodies**. Men, women, and children lay lifeless upon the altar of absolute destruction. Broken glass, twisted metal, burned out wooden frames of what were once homes in a vibrant city were blasted in half. Only one side of what was once a hallway remained. *Just what in the Hell happened here?!*

Then I saw him, a dishevelled, dirty ginger tabby emerged from a pile of rubble and trotted away. He stopped, looking over his shoulder as if he knew I was watching. Our eyes met. A glimmer of recognition before lip curling snarl: "What do you want? Can't you see I'm busy?"

My head wrenched from side to side. "Busy doing **what** exactly?"

Oops. Dumb question. His eyes narrowed as he thrust his chin up and out. "I'm looking for my family."

Dumbfounded, I couldn't speak for a moment. "What happened here?"

The tabby snorted. "You mean what is **still** happening here. Can't you hear them? The buzz bombs?"

I shook my head, "I—I just got here."

His eyes widened. "From where? And why would you wanna come to London at a time like this?"

"W—what year is this?"

Flicking his tail, the tabby took one ominous step toward me, "So, ya don't know why ya here. Ya don't know what flippin' year it is? Come off it, mate! Where are you from really? You an' yer fancy collar 'n stuff!"

Great, now I've really pissed him off. "I don't—I really don't know."

The tabby's tail flicked faster. "Ya got smacked in the ol' 'eadbone with a piece of brick or somethin' did ya?"

I drew a deep breath and exhaled slowly. "No, no head injuries. Look."

He took my word for it and slapped his paw right between my ears.

"Ow! What was that for?"

He threw his head back and meowed a sort of laughter—as well as a cat could, "Right then, we's gettin' nowhere, yeah? So, howsabout you tell me what the hell is—Shit! Take cover!"

The whine of the bomb screamed in my ears as I instantly followed him down into what was once a townhouse basement filled with trash. "That's what they calls a V1 rocket or buzz bomb. Ya hear buzzin', then nothin'. They goes silent and **that's** just before they hits a target, but who knows where? Beats the hell outta me. That's why they's so scary. Ya never know what they's gonna hit."

I studied him closely for a moment. He seemed to be lightening up. I began to relax a little. A quick breeze picked up some old newspapers, swirling them about. Out of the corner of my eye, a bold headline from a torn copy of the *Daily Express* in gothic script confirmed my suspicions. I did a double take at the date: Sunday, September 8, 1940. "*Daily Express*, Blitz Bombing of London Goes All Night." *Good Gods.*

But where was my "friend?" Spinning about, I saw him climbing out of our makeshift bunker. "Wait! Where are you going?" I felt panic tighten in my chest.

The tabby looked over his shoulder, showing his teeth, "I'm

goin' ta find my family, likes I says. You'll be fine here. Plenty of mice or rats around for munchin' if that's your thing. Judging from your fancy black collar, I'd say naaah." Without another word, he went in search of his family, leaving me… where exactly?

Then, I heard it.

That mechanical whine again. Screams erupted from the street. I rushed up the broken stairs to see people fleeing into the bombed-out houses. My Gods, there was no place to hide. Nowhere was safe. Who knew when the bombs would drop— or where.

Silence.

Diving under the broken stairs, I know I shouldn't have gawked, but I couldn't help it. The shriek of a bomb being dropped filled my ears. I ducked, knowing full well that it wouldn't do a damned bit of good as debris from the explosion rained down upon the destroyed street. Black smoke again filled the air. Then I saw him. His body torn, filled with shrapnel. Howling in horror, I looked up into the blackened sky. *He just wanted to find his family! Great Goddess why? Why?* I felt a small tremor emitting from my collar. *No, please—not again. You put me here for a reason, for Gods' sakes let me understand!* I hung my head for a moment. Witnessing this, actually being here at this moment, was all too much. I needed to keep moving, but at this point I had no idea where to go.

Movement. As the dust cleared, a small figure emerged from the house closest to the bomb crater. She seemed disoriented, lost and completely alone. My heart broke. Without hesitation I bolted toward her. Circling her legs, I let my tail brush against her torn, yellowed knee socks, purring as I went. Gasping, she looked down at me, as tears filled her eyes. "Kitty…" It was all she could manage.

I circled her again before jumping onto her shoulders and head-butting her cheek. "Kitty, I want my momma and poppa. I'm scared! I don't know where they are! I don't know where my Ginger Tom is either! I miss him so much!"

I felt the thrum of my collar vibrate faster. I didn't understand its reaction. It felt weird.

"Please, kitty, help me." The little girl sank to the ground in a heap, her tiny body racking with sobs.

I jumped down to the ground so I could face her head on. "I will help you. What's your name?"

Her eyes grew wide as she gasped at me, "You can **talk?**"

"Yes," I replied quietly. "I can."

Jumping to her feet, the girl scooped me up in her arms and hugged me tight—a little too tight, but I let that go. "Let us go find them. Show me where you, ummm… lived."

Crestfallen, she scanned the street for any clue, before turning to me and declaring, "My name is Sophie and I am six years old. What's yours?" I cleared my throat and asked that she put me down as gently as she could. I sidled up to her again, then stopped. It occurred to me that I did not, in fact, have a name. My collar vibrated in response. "Sophie, would you like to give me a name?"

"Would I? Yes! Yes, I would and you would be mine forever and ever!"

I wasn't sure how to respond to that. All I knew was that I was not about to hurt her feelings, so I head-butted her little hand.

"Hooray! Kitty! I do not know what I will name you yet, but let's go!"

Suddenly I remembered the torn body of the orange tom was lying perilously close. I had to think quickly about how to gently lead her away, "I saw you coming toward me from that direction. Let's go back the way you came." Sophie nodded and bolted ahead. I trotted after her, wanting to make sure this little human would be okay—or, as okay as one can be under these horrific circumstances. "Sophie! Wait! Wait one moment. I will be right back. If you hear those awful sounds again, I want you to hide." I yanked my head toward another semi-destroyed home: "Hide in there and wait for me."

Confused at first, she eventually nodded her head.

Before me stood a semi-demolished house. This one felt different. Very different. Sure enough, my collar vibrated in agreement. I pressed on, carefully making my way up the front stairs. Then, I saw them. A man and a woman laying on the kitchen floor. Blood… so much blood. Without thinking, I ran to them, meowing as loudly as I could. The woman was lying on her back, bits of metal protruded from her arms and legs. Pools of blood widened around them. The man, presumably, her husband was curled on his side, his hand reaching for hers.

"Get up! I'm here! I know where Sophie is!"

Upon hearing the little girl's name, the woman's arms and legs twitched a bit. Turning her head toward me, her eyelids flickered as she drew in her breath, "Who's there? Who's speaking? I—I cannot see you!"

I took a small step forward, my tail dropping to the floor. "I am ma'am. I have found Sophie." Her eyes fixed on me, widening in shock and disbelief. "Where is Sophie? Is she safe? She—she went looking for Ginger Tom." Her eyes welled up with tears. "Good Lord, I'm asking a **cat**—this is madness!"

I moved closer to her. "Sophie is safe for the moment, but Ginger Tom—he didn't survive the last blast."

The woman blanched. "He was looking for us! We lost him when we left Gran's house a couple of days ago. Trying to find his way back to Sophie, I, and my husband. Oh, dear God!"

Instinctively, I moved over to the man's prone body. He wasn't responding. I tried licking his face. Nothing. Sensing the woman's fear, I proceeded slowly toward her, nudging her arm with my nose, "You can do it. You can get up. I know you can." Without hesitation and with great effort, she fumbled for the kitchen table. Trying again, she pulled it toward herself and tried to get up. The sight of her husband's prone body terrified her. Unable to rise, she crawled on her hands and knees toward him. Panicking, she began screaming, pounding her fists into his chest: "Reginald! Reggie! Wake up! Damn you!"

After about a minute, I saw his eyelid flicker, "He's coming to. Keep talking to him. I am going to fetch your daughter."

Shocked silence enveloped the woman as she nodded in my direction.

In an instant, I jumped up onto the windowsill to get a good look before heading out of the room and navigating my way carefully down the broken front steps. Then, it came at me again. That whine. That Goddamned mechanical whine! I knew it was drawing nearer, but as long as I could hear it, it would be okay.

As I jumped up on the sidewalk, my heart leapt for joy as I saw the girl sitting with her knees to her chin. I knew she was scared. "Psssst!" Her gaze jerked in my direction, "Sophie, I've found them! I've found your parents and I've come to take you home!"

Her jaw dropped. "You found Momma and Poppa?"

I nodded. "Let's get you home. Follow me and stay close."

Picking her way carefully out of the ruins of the bombed-out home, Sophie trotted after me. When we got to the dilapidated front stairs, I asked her to wait for one moment before I bolted into the kitchen. Her parents were sitting on the floor leaning against what was left of the kitchen cupboards. I realised that The woman had saved her husband despite his being worse for wear—or, more correctly, almost dead.

Reggie blinked at me before mumbling, "A black cat. Where'd you come from? You **are** good luck, am I right, Mary?"

His wife nodded. Despite her exhaustion, she moved herself closer and embraced her husband.

"Let's get you both cleaned up as best we can, and I will retrieve your daughter." Both nodded in silent agreement. Satisfied, I bounded down the stairs to find their little girl. But there was an overhead mechanical whine that went silent for a few moments, then the earth shook beneath my feet. All around me, chunks of the now dilapidated houses cascaded to the ground. My heart pounded in my ears. Spinning in circles, I tried to see my way through the dust, ash, and debris that had shot from the crater into the air. My eyes stung with tears and smoke. Sophie! Where are you?"

Nothing. "Sophie!!! Answer me!"

*Why did I wait to bring her inside? I know I didn't want her to see them like that, but Gods **damn** it!*

As the smoke began to clear, I stepped up my search,

running up the street, calling the girl's name. Out of the corner of my still stinging, reddened eyes, I saw her, motionless, crumpled in a heap. Within an instant, I bounded toward her.

"Sophie!" No response. Maybe she didn't hear me. I tried calling her name again. Terrified now, I jumped in her lap. Her eyelashes fluttered. I called her name again, but it was as if she couldn't hear. I put my paws on her face and head-butted her. Her eyes opened slowly.

Through a cracked, slurring voice, she managed, "Kitty," before her head lolled to the side.

"No! Sophie! Stay with me!" Without thinking, I moved my paws to her chest. She was breathing. I had to get her on her feet, but not before checking her over. It was clear from the cuts and bruises on her face, arms, and legs that she had been in range of the explosion, but somehow, thankfully, managed not to get hit. I had to get her home. "Come on, sweetheart. Let me take you to your parents."

The little girl blinked. Lines of white were etched upon her soot-laden face as the tears fell. I head-butted her again. Her eyes focused upon me, widening in surprise. *Now we're getting somewhere.*

"Take me home. I want to go home."

"Let's go."

Her reactions were slow, lethargic—I could almost feel the shock. *Shell shock.* I wondered if she could hear me at all. Giving her any sort of directions would be a challenge, so I came up with a plan. She was so very tiny, I figured she needed something to hang onto. I wrapped my tail around her wrist. Instinctively, her little hand closed around it. The look of surprise was followed with a slight smile. Looking up into her eyes, I motioned with my head, which way we were to go. That-taway...

There it was again, the siren scream of another V1 heading our way, but she didn't react. The last bomb's explosion had likely destroyed her hearing. Perhaps this was a backhanded blessing, not being able to hear these infernal bombs approaching? I jerked my head in her direction as her grip grew tighter around my tail. It was beginning to hurt but compared to what this little girl and her family were experiencing, a little pull on my tail was nothing.

The buzz bomb's wail overhead drew nearer. *Just as long as I can hear that wretched thing…* I slowed my pace when we got to the house with the partially destroyed stairs. Glancing up at her, I saw the exhaustion and fear drain away. Step by step, I guided her. Luckily, she saw her parents before I did, letting go of my tail as she ran into her mother's arms.

I hesitated, waiting on the threshold. This moment did not belong to me. As she hugged her daughter, Mary's eyes met mine. A small smile from her was all I needed. As I turned to walk away, her voice rang out, "Kitty, please come join us."

I paused for a moment, then trotted over to the three of them. Reggie was looking somewhat better now that he had his family all together. Mary turned to Sophie and said, "Kitty needs a name, what shall we call her?" Sophie did not respond. Mary, confused, implored me to explain.

"Ma'am," I replied as I cleared my throat, "Sophie is having difficulty hearing. It's too soon to tell if it is temporary or permanent. She has been too close to the explosions, and I think this time," I choked up a little, "finally did it."

Mary nodded her head but said not a word. Pain washed over her face in a torrent, "You mean there's little hope of her hearing coming back."

I backed up a little. "I didn't say that. I said it was too early to tell."

Mary's eyes fell for a moment. Turning to her daughter, she tried to force a smile and be as pleasant as possible. Placing her hands on Sophie's cheeks she gave the child a gentle kiss on the forehead.

Sophie turned to face me, "Shadow. I shall name you Shadow." Her parents gasped in surprise and smiled. A glimmer of hope.

I felt my collar vibrate as I wrapped my tail around Sophie's legs again, brushing my whiskered cheeks against her skin. I felt her giggle for a moment, heard their voices exclaiming happiness under these horrendous, surreal circumstances.

A profound wave of sadness rolled over me as I stood yet again on an unknown threshold. Where to now? My collar wasn't responding. *I was given the ability to communicate with humans so I could report back… I was given emotions so that my reports would seem more real. My consciousness was human, yet my body remained feline.*

The light was fading, the silence was unnerving. I took a step forward, not knowing where it would lead. Then I felt it, beneath my paw, the old towel. Yet here, it wasn't old and torn. Its white brilliance illuminated the woman's face. Her face had changed somehow. Yes, she seemed so much younger and that gold thing that was sitting upon her head had vanished. But I knew. I knew it was still her from a different place in time. I sighed as I gazed at her smile. *How did you find me again?* Perhaps it was here all along. No, that was ridiculous—I didn't know where, exactly, here was.

Slowly, the light around me grew like a glorious summer sunrise. I did not know where I had landed this time, but here it was again. I felt lighter. Instinctively, I put a paw to my throat and felt **nothing**. Gone. The collar was gone. I was free—from what, exactly, I may never know.

I glanced down at the towel, patted it, and watched as colours filled the room and exploded into vast galaxies. Exhausted, but happy, I curled up on it and watched in amazement as eruptions of blue, gold, red and yellow starbursts filled my vision at dizzying rates of speed. In my head, I heard my own voice declare, *We are stardust.* The beauty of existence and the terrifying unknown melded into one. I drew my breath as I put my paw on the child's forehead before she vanished from view. And then I understood. The planet we call home is but a whistle stop and we are but passengers. The possibilities are infinite.

MONDAY CROSSROADS BLUES

Bruno Lombardi

The day started with a problem, as Mondays are apt to do.

The Shopkeeper was ten minutes late showing up at his shop. This, in conjunction with his sleepless night and the fact that he was having a hell of a time finding the keys to his store, was making him even grumpier than usual.

Finally, the stars seemed to align in his favour for a brief moment and he found his keys. He entered his store, taking a quick minute to switch off the Gramophone burglar alarm. The Shopkeeper was always amused by that particular alarm. It had been considered "advanced" when it had come out ten years earlier as the war started in Europe, but now it was being sold in pawnshops like his for a pittance. With a shake of his head over the vagaries of history, he flipped the **Treasure & Trade—** CLOSED sign over to OPEN.

He was now ready for business.

Two hours and three customers later, the Writer came in.

The Shopkeeper didn't know his name, despite him being a

semi-regular customer. In this line of business, it sometimes was better not to know anyone's true names. He certainly went out of his way to avoid having people know his.

The Writer came in on the first Saturday of every month, always on the lookout for anything "writer-related."

The Shopkeeper had read some of his writing in an assortment of rather questionable pulp magazines. He found the stories, on the whole, to be competently written, albeit filled with some rather queer ideas and concepts.

The Shopkeeper surreptitiously made a few minor adjustments to his meticulously neat and tidy appearance—vivid contrast to the cluttered and almost obscenely messy shop—and flicked an errant grey hair out of his eyes.

"Hello!" said the Shopkeeper, smiling a practiced salesman's smile. "And what can I get for you **this** day?"

The Writer—a youngish-looking man in his early 20s—scratched his scraggly beard and glanced around the shop for a moment before turning his gaze back to the man in front of him. "I don't know. Something… for a writer…?"

The Shopkeeper smiled a shark's smile.

"I have just the thing. Very recently acquired."

The Shopkeeper bent down and rummaged around beneath the counter for a moment. Presently there was a loud *"A-ha!"* and he popped up, holding in his hands…

… a typewriter.

"Really?" said the Writer, a mixture of amusement and pity on his face. **"Really?"** he repeated. "I already have a typewriter, after all." He took a critical look at the typewriter for a moment. "And it's not even a new one! It looks like it's almost as old as I am!"

"Ah, but this is no ordinary typewriter!" The Shopkeeper raised the typewriter to head level, as if it was a crown. The Shopkeeper poked his head around the corner of the typewriter and smiled again. "But tell me, where do you get your ideas? I believe you once told me that they come in dreams sometimes? A figure looking much like you, yes?"

The Writer smiled in return and shrugged. "The other me

visits me once or twice a week, always bringing stories, yes."

A nod from the Shopkeeper. "Now imagine not having to wait for a dream."

The Writer tilted his head and raised an eyebrow. "Explain?"

"This typewriter has a long history. It is said that it has been passed down from the desks of no less than **four** different writers!" He leaned in and spoke in a conspiratorial whisper. "And yes, I have documentation proving it so!"

The writer tilted his head in the other direction, but the skeptical eyebrow went down. "Anyone I would know?"

The shark smile returned and a sheaf of papers slid across the counter. The Writer looked through the papers.

There was presently a **"Huh,"** an **"Oh,"** an **"Oh my,"** and finally just a simple gasp.

The Shopkeeper leaned forward. "Imagine having the **essence** of the great writers before you **flowing** through the type-writer." The smile grew to seemingly unnatural size. "What would you pay for **that**?"

"A lot," came a whisper.

"I have a **very** reasonable price in mind. We can make arrangements for an instalment plan, if you wish."

The Writer was on the knife-edge of rejection and acceptance. All it would take was just one word to push him in either direction...

"You **do** want to be a more successful writer, yes?"

The Writer paused... and then nodded. "Let's do this."

Money and papers were passed back and forth, and a few moments later, the Writer walked out with his new prize.

The Shopkeeper smiled and leaned back in his chair.

He had not mentioned to the Writer just **how** he had acquired the typewriter. Of course, that's because he had not been asked. The Shopkeeper snorted. None of the other four had either.

But the Writer would soon learn the dangers of dealing with him—and reneging on payments.

Oh—he would learn soon enough...

The day started with a problem, as Mondays are apt to do.

The Shopkeeper was ten minutes late showing up at his shop. This, in conjunction with his iVR glitching out the night before, preventing him from having a good night's sleep, and the fact that he was having a hell of a time finding the RKS to his store, was making him even grumpier than usual.

Finally, the stars seemed to align in his favour for a brief moment, and he found the thing. He entered his store, taking a quick minute to switch off the security alarm. The Shopkeeper was always amused by that particular alarm. It had been considered "advanced" when it had come out ten years earlier just as the war started in Ukraine, but now it was being sold in pawnshops like his for a mere pittance. With a shake of his head over the vagaries of history, he tapped the app on his phone and the sign changed from **Treasure & Trade**—CLOSED to OPEN.

He was now ready for business.

Two hours and three online orders later, the Writer came in.

The Shopkeeper didn't know his name, despite him being a semi-regular customer. In this line of business, it sometimes was better not to know anyone's true names. He certainly went out of his way to avoid having people know his, to the point that he had even hired an internet scrubbing service to do so.

The Writer came in on the first Saturday of every month, always on the lookout for anything "writer-related."

The Shopkeeper had read some of his writing in an assortment of rather questionable online magazines and forums. He found the stories, on the whole, to be competently written, although he was by no means a fan of these "slipstream" and "bizarro" genres.

The Shopkeeper surreptitiously made a few minor adjustments to his meticulously neat and tidy appearance—a vivid contrast to the cluttered and almost obscenely messy shop— and flicked an errant black hair out of his eyes.

"Hello!" said the Shopkeeper, smiling a practiced salesman's smile. "And what can I get for you this day?"

The Writer—a youngish looking man in his early 20s—scratched his goatee and glanced around the shop for a moment before turning his gaze back to the man in front of him. "I don't know. Something… for a writer…?"

The Shopkeeper smiled a shark's smile.

"I have just the thing. Very recently acquired."

The Shopkeeper bent down and rummaged around beneath the counter for a moment. Presently there was a loud **"A-ha!"** and he popped up, holding in his hands…

…a laptop.

"Really?" said the Writer, a mixture of amusement and pity on his face. **"Really?"** he repeated. "I already have a laptop, after all." He took a critical look at the laptop for a moment. "Jeez! And it's not even a new one! It looks like it's almost three years old!"

"Ah, but this is no ordinary laptop!" The Shopkeeper raised the laptop to head level, as if it was a crown. The Shopkeeper poked his head around the corner and smiled again. "But tell me, where do you get your ideas? I believe you once told me that they come in dreams sometimes? A figure looking much like you, yes?"

The Writer smiled in return and shrugged. "The other me visits me once or twice a week, always bringing stories, yes." He smiled. "I learned guided imagery from YouTube," he said proudly.

A nod from the Shopkeeper. "Now imagine not having to wait for a dream."

The Writer tilted his head and raised an eyebrow. "Explain?"

"This laptop has a long history. It is said that it has been passed down from the hands of no less than **four** different writers!" He leaned in and spoke in a conspiratorial whisper. "And yes, I have documentation proving it so!"

The writer tilted his head in the other direction but the skeptical eyebrow went down. "Anyone I would know?"

The shark smile returned and an IPad slid across the

counter. The Writer scrolled through the IPad.

There was presently a **"Huh,"** an **"Oh,"** a "**Holy fuck,"** and finally just a simple gasp.

The Shopkeeper leaned forward. "Imagine having the **essence** of the great writers before you **flowing** through it." The smile grew to seemingly unnatural size. "What would you pay for that?"

"A **lot**," came a whisper.

"I have a very reasonable price. We can make arrangements for an instalment plan, if you wish."

The Writer was on the knife-edge of rejection and acceptance. All it would take was just one word to push him in either direction…

"You **do** want to be a more successful writer, yes?"

The Writer paused…

… and then shook his head. "No."

"No?" repeated the Shopkeeper, genuine shock in his voice.

The Writer shook his head once more.

"I'm happy where I am. Really." He tilted his head to one side. "It's a very tempting offer, I admit, but—no."

The Shopkeeper's smile returned once more.

"The offer remains on the table. And perhaps next month, you'll find something more to your liking?"

"Perhaps." And with that, the Writer left the store.

The Shopkeeper frowned and leaned back in his chair.

He was just going to have to redouble his efforts.

He was all too familiar with how these writers worked—after all, that was the reason why the laptop had so many previous owners. He knew that sooner or later he'd hook the writer.

And once hooked, there were **oh** so many ways to **keep** them hooked.

The Shopkeeper smiled.

Soon. Very soon. Very, very soon.

He'd get his prize soon enough…

The day started with a problem, as Mondays are apt to do.

47

The Shopkeeper was ten minutes late showing up at his shop. This, in conjunction with him forgetting to renew his Restful Sleep spell with the neighbourhood hedge mage and the fact that he was having a hell of a time remembering the counterword to the Lock ward on his store, was making him even grumpier than usual.

Finally, the stars seemed to align in his favour for a brief moment, and he remembered the counterword. He entered his store, taking a quick minute to switch off the glyph alarm. The Shopkeeper was always amused by that particular alarm. It had been considered "advanced" when it had come out ten years earlier just as the war started over that misunderstanding with the Unseelie Court, but now it was being sold in pawnshops like his for a pittance. With a shake of his head over the vagaries of history, he spoke the Word and the **Treasure & Trade—** CLOSED sign flipped to OPEN.

He was now ready for business.

Two hours and three avatars later, the Writer came in.

The Shopkeeper didn't know his name, despite him being a semi-regular customer. In this line of business, it sometimes was better not to know anyone's True Name. He certainly went out of his way to avoid having people know **his**, going so far as to have paid out some serious coin to a variety of questionable Awakened Troll Mystics to have a multitude of Divine Erasures done.

The Writer came in on the first Saturday of every month, always on the lookout for anything "writer-related."

The Shopkeeper had read some of his writing in an assortment of rather interesting World Wide Scry nodes. He found the stories, on the whole, to be competently written, albeit filled with some rather unusual and disturbing concepts. Personally, he could never get into this newfangled "chthonic" genre.

The Shopkeeper surreptitiously made a few minor adjustments to his meticulously neat and tidy appearance—a vivid contrast to the cluttered and almost obscenely messy shop—and flicked an errant white hair out of his eyes.

"Hello!" said the Shopkeeper, smiling a practiced salesman's smile (augmented with a low-level Glamour). "And what can I get for you this day?"

The Writer—a youngish looking man in his early 20s—scratched his clean-shaven chin and glanced around the shop for a moment before turning his gaze back to the man in front of him. "I don't know. Something… for a writer…?"

The Shopkeeper smiled a dragon's smile.

"I have just the thing. Very recently acquired."

The Shopkeeper bent down and rummaged around beneath the counter for a moment. Presently there was a loud *"A-ha!"* and he popped up, holding in his hands…

… a Crystal Ball.

"Really?" said the Writer, a mixture of amusement and pity on his face. **"Really?"** he repeated. "I already have a Crystal Ball, after all." He took a critical look at the Crystal Ball for a moment. "By the Goddess' Tits! And it's not even a new one! It looks like it's **Hy-Brasilian**! Didn't they collapse five centuries ago?"

"Ah, but this is no ordinary Crystal Ball!" The Shopkeeper raised the Crystal Ball to head level, as if it was a crown. The Shopkeeper poked his head around the Ball and smiled again. "But tell me, where *do* you get your ideas? I believe you once told me that they come in dreams sometimes? A figure looking much like you, yes?"

The Writer smiled in return and shrugged. "The other me visits me once or twice a week, always bringing stories, yes." He smiled. "I **excelled** in thaumaturgy according to my mentor," he said proudly.

A nod from the Shopkeeper. "Now imagine not having to wait for a dream."

The Writer tilted his head and raised an eyebrow. "Explain?"

"This Crystal Ball has a long history. It is said that it has been passed down from the hands of no less than **four** different writers!" He leaned in and spoke in a conspiratorial whisper. "And yes, I have documentation proving it so!"

The writer tilted his head in the other direction, but the skeptical eyebrow went down. "Anyone I would know?"

The dragon's smile returned. The Shopkeeper leaned back. There was a complex gesture of hands and then—an image of light and shadow and symbols and sound appeared floating over the counter.

The Writer hesitantly leaned forward and touched a finger to a symbol here and there and wither and tither.

There was presently a **"Huh,"** an **"Oh,"** a "Holy Goddess," and finally just a simple gasp.

The Shopkeeper leaned forward. "Imagine having the **essence** of the great writers before you **flowing** through it?" The smile grew to seemingly unnatural size. "What would you pay for that?"

"A lot," came a whisper.

"I have a very reasonable price. We can make arrangements for an instalment plan, if you wish."

The Writer was on the knife-edge of rejection and acceptance. All it would take was just one word to push him in either direction...

"You *do* want to be a more successful writer, yes?"

The Writer paused...

...and then he smiled. "Actually, I have a better idea."

"Oh?" responded the Shopkeeper, owlishly.

"Yes." The Writer's smile increased a few degrees. The Writer pulled a medallion out of his pocket and held it in front of the Shopkeeper's face. The Shopkeeper had just the briefest moment of recognition of the symbol on the medallion when the Writer spoke a Word of Power.

The Shopkeeper found himself paralyzed.

"You've been **quite** the naughty fellow, haven't you?"

The Shopkeeper remained silent.

"It's taken me **years** to track you down. I've lost track how many Iterations there have been. How many Paths I've traveled."

The Shopkeeper remained silent and paralyzed.

"I'm curious. Exactly **how** many worlds have you been on?

Exactly how many souls have you corrupted? How many stolen? How many **destroyed**?"

The Shopkeeper continued to be silent and paralyzed.

The Writer's smile increased further. "I have to be honest," and there was just the tiniest hint of awe in his voice, "I am **very** impressed with your methods. Very methodical. Very subtle. I don't think I have ever met someone who was so dedicated to long-term planning. It was almost fae-like in mentality."

The Writer let out a long sigh. "Anything to add?"

The Shopkeeper did not speak.

The Writer shook his head.

"No matter. It all ends here. It all ends today."

The Writer raised his hands.

There was the sound of thunder and fury and darkness.

There was the sound of silence.

The Writer stood alone in the shop.

Taking a moment to cast a Lock ward on the front door, the Writer walked around the shop for quite some time. Slowly, bit by bit, a pile began to form on the floor. He was very methodical. He would spend many minutes looking through all the knick-knacks before finally making a decision, picking **this** knick and **that** knack. After a full thirty minutes, there was a pile of about two dozen objects.

The Writer sat down on the edge of a table and stared at the pile.

Objects from two dozen or so Iterations. Objects rare and wondrous and—dare he say?—unique.

And each possessing a soul. Or at least a piece of one.

He let out a long sigh.

He was going to have a long road ahead of him making things right.

It was going to be hard and difficult and, truthfully, he wasn't entirely certain he would even be able to return all the souls to their rightful bodies.

But one must try.

He had no choice.

He raised his hands and made a complex gesture.

He vanished, along with the pile.

The Last of Wishes

David Gerrold

I met him in a gay bar. That's not the story. It's just the setting.

It wasn't one of those bars that you see in a movie or a TV show with half-naked men dancing together or drag queens lip-syncing whatever pop anthem had momentarily risen to cultural significance. And it wasn't one of those place where silent men stand around pretending that they're not standing around and pretending.

No. It was just a dingy little local hangout that was convenient to the neighbourhood and had found a specific clientele that just wanted a quiet place to sit and have a beer or two while watching the game on a big-screen TV.

Myself, I hadn't had a same-sex encounter since my second year of college, when we were all so horny we didn't really care; I preferred this bar for a simpler reason. Gay men were more likely to talk about Mahler or Buster Keaton or the unique history of the neighbourhood than about how awful their ex-wives were.

It was a dismal Tuesday night after a three-day weekend.

The air was still wet from an afternoon shower, and the thick clouds overhead promised a possible rerun. I was tired from another day arguing with numbers, trying to make them agree with the latest unworkable financial theory. Numbers don't fight back, but they're passive-aggressive. They do what they do, regardless of what you want them to do.

I just wanted a beer, and I didn't want to walk three blocks to the louder and brighter place across the street from the strip mall.

I wanted quiet. I wanted dark. I wanted to be alone. Jim—I think that was his name—was the only other patron in the bar. I'd seen him here before, once or twice. He was always alone.

He wasn't large, but he was stocky. He was dark and muscular. Even in the dim light, his bald head gleamed. He was dressed in a dark flowing shirt; I thought he might have been an out-of-work actor or musician. He had that look. He had a performer's gravitas. He was impossible to ignore.

I nodded to him as I took my usual seat at the far end of the bar. Roy, the bartender, slid a brown bottle toward me and went back to the other end of the bar where his tablet was working its way through an old Disney film featuring two dogs having a plate of spaghetti.

I saluted him with my beer. "Long day," I said.

He grunted.

I looked around. The place was dark and empty and quiet. On the weekend, the neighbourhood crowd would come in, but the bar still wouldn't be crowded. I'd never run the numbers, but it wasn't likely that Roy was showing a profit here. Sometimes he talked about retiring. This hole-in-the-wall bar would close for a week or two, and then someone else would turn it into a nail-salon or a cell phone repair store or something even more mundane, any transitory business that could pay the rent.

I looked to Jim. I wasn't really in a mood to talk, but I couldn't ignore him either. "You doing okay?" I asked.

He grunted again. Noncommittal.

"Yeah, me too," I said. "I wish—"

He held up a hand to stop me. "Don't."

"Don't what?"

"Don't wish."

"Why not?"

"Wishes are—" He stopped. He looked at me. For the first time, I realized he had the most intense eyes I'd ever seen. He sighed. "Trouble. Wishes are trouble. Be glad they're just noise." He lowered his gaze again.

"Um. Okay." I wasn't sure what he meant, but the way he said it, the way he said it, he must have been speaking from dark experience. I drank. He drank. Neither of us spoke for a bit. Finally, I said, "Bad experience?"

He chuckled. Or snorted. A sound that was a little of each. Then he looked over at me again. "I'm not immortal," he said. "I'm just dying very slowly."

"We all are."

"No. Not like me. I used to be djinn. What you might call a genie."

I nodded. I'd heard stranger things in a bar. Some of them were even true. The more bizarre the assertion, the more interesting the tale. So I said, "What was that like?"

Jim said, "It depended on the client. Some were stupid. Some were smart. Some were too smart for their own good. You probably heard some of the stories."

"Not yours," I said.

I waved to Roy. He brought us two more beers. That was all the encouragement Jim needed. He took a drink. "It's a very lonely existence."

I didn't answer that. He didn't say "life." He said "existence." That was curious. But he was right about one thing. Most of the regulars in any bar are lonely. That's why we go to bars. So we don't have to be alone, if only for an hour or three.

Jim said, "I'm seventeen thousand years old. I will probably live another four or five hundred thousand years before I evaporate. Hard to have a relationship when you're a demi-something." He looked at me with those dark compelling eyes. "You ever have a dog?"

"Several," I said. I thought about Pixie and Belle and Bluto.

"They die too soon, right?"

I nodded.

"Try that with human beings. Try it for half a million years. Easier to be alone. I tried it. Too many regrets." He rubbed his chin. "Maybe again, maybe someday. But not now."

"Can I ask you something?

He shrugged.

"When you said 'djinn' did you mean—?"

Again with the eyes. "Yes."

"You were inside a lamp?"

He shook his head. "A bottle." He held up his beer bottle. "Like this. Only not as large. It wasn't cramped. But it was lonely. A different kind of lonely. Until someone uncorked it. Then, it could get interesting."

"You granted wishes?"

"Quite a few. Fame. Fortune. Power. The usual. Most wishes are selfish. One guy, not too long ago, wanted to be immune to assassination attempts. He survived five that most people know about. Seven others too."

"You said most wishes are selfish. Are there any unselfish ones?"

"Occasionally, yes. Not very often." He closed his eyes for a moment, remembering. "About six thousand years ago—there was this crazy old man. He wanted to part the sea for his tribe. He thought they were being chased by an army. They weren't, but a wish is a wish, right? I had to time it with the tides, more fakery than magic, but he got his wish. That counts as unselfish, he didn't get anything personally. Didn't matter. There were still consequences. He didn't survive the journey after."

"I think I heard about that one."

"Most people don't know how to wish," Jim said. "There are always consequences. Always. That other guy— the one who was afraid of being assassinated—he ended up taking his own life." Jim took a swallow of beer, then stared at the bottle. "So unimaginative. In my day, bottles were hand-blown. Every bottle was unique. Special." He put the bottle down again, another wet circle on the stained wooden bar.

"Can I ask you a personal question?"

He looked at me. Those piercing eyes again. "What?"

"Did you enjoy it?"

"Did you mean, was it a curse? No. Working out the details of a wish, that could be interesting. Especially if the wishes were grandiose." He paused. "It wasn't boring. I had a lot of different bottles. I did try living in a lamp once, but people kept filling it with oil. And then, one time I had to keep the flame burning for eight days. Another wish, of course. But that's when I gave up on lamps and went back to the bottle." He lifted his beer and waved it at me. "This isn't a great bottle, you know. It holds beer, but it doesn't do anything else."

"It gets the job done."

"Yeah. It's designed for one thing only. That's its limit." He paused. "Magic had its limits too. You couldn't wish someone dead, you couldn't wish someone back to life, and you couldn't wish for love. You couldn't wish for more wishes. But fame, fortune, all the shallow things that get in the way of truly experiencing the real adventures of life—the air just before sunrise, the breeze after sunset, the kiss of the moonlit wind, the oasis in the desert, the sweet smell of flowers, the lingering tastes of wine and honey and dates, all of that and more. You don't need wishes for that."

I closed my eyes and thought about what he said. I could almost see it, smell it, taste it. When I opened my eyes again, he was staring at me. "You want to make a wish, don't you?"

I shook my head. "I wouldn't know what to wish for. What I might want—it's no longer possible." I waved my bottle at him. "I have my own limits." A thought occurred to me. "You talked about magic in the past tense…?"

"Right," he said. Then he added, "Even if you wanted to make a wish, I couldn't grant it."

"Huh?"

"Wishes are over. They've been over for a long time."

"Really?"

"It's my fault, really. I wish I could have said no. But I couldn't. The wish was legitimate."

"What wish?"

"An asshole named…" Jim frowned, remembering. "Newton, I think. A bit of a crackpot. He talked about the way things moved. Something moving keeps moving unless something stops it. Something that doesn't move doesn't move unless something pushes it. It takes energy to change either of those states. That was what he believed, anyway."

"Newton. Yeah. I've heard of him. He wished for fame?"

"No, something worse."

I waited.

"You really want to know?"

"I'm hooked."

"I gave him a wish."

"Only one?"

"It was a big wish."

I waited a little longer.

Finally, Jim said, "He said that magic violates the law of conservation of energy."

I thought about it. "Seems obvious"

"Yes. I guess so. My mistake. I agreed with him"

"What did he wish?"

"He wished for physics. He wished that magic wouldn't exist in the world."

"And you granted that wish?"

"I couldn't not grant it. As soon as he wished it—magic ended."

I finished my beer. I thought about ordering a third. But then I thought about walking home again. Probably not a good idea.

"Um…"

"What?"

"Well… I'm just thinking, if someone could wish for magic to stop, couldn't someone else wish for magic to come back?"

"That would take magic, wouldn't it?"

"Oh."

Jim finished his beer. "I won't say that the world was better when there was magic, but it's in pretty bad shape without it, don't you think?"

"Jim," I said. "That is either the saddest story I have ever heard—or the craziest. But either way, I wish you hadn't told me."

"I wish I could grant that wish. Or any wish. I have nothing. I wish I could die."

"Sorry," I said. "You're not my type. Blood type, I mean. Blame Newton. He only wished an end to magic. He didn't end the undead."

"Yeah," said Jim. "At least you still have something."

"I get by." I stretched myself off the stool. "I'll see you around."

I didn't tell him I was going to have to find a new bar. The feeding in this one was getting scarce. And I would be hungry again soon.

JASMINE'S QUANTUM QUANDRY

Angelique Fawns

Jasmine pulled the sleeve down over the ugly red scars on the crook of her elbow even as she balanced on the barrier of the bridge. They were her personal map to Hell, each track mark leading to this cold, windy moment overlooking the river.

A shiver ran up and down her spine. Dancers' bodies are ill-equipped for damp night air. Her gelled nails scraped across the metal support strut, the pole the only thing keeping her from plunging into the dark abyss below. The sound was worse than fingernails on a chalkboard, and she cringed, wishing her palms weren't so sweaty.

Why were these little things bothering her now? She was seconds from oblivion.

This was the last dirty pole she'd ever hold on to. Jasmine shuddered, remembering the dirt caked onto her belly from the bills shoved there by leering patrons last week. Worse was how she didn't even care. All she could think about was buying a tab of Oxy, a few bills slipping from her trembling hand as she met her dealer in the back alley. The cycle was never ending. Even though she'd been clean for seven days, she knew the shame of stripping would have her seeking oblivion again.

These last few seconds were agony. She'd made the decision to try her luck on the other side of the roiling waves. Whatever waited for her beneath the surface had to be better than what her life was now.

An old-fashioned cruise ship, red water wheel spraying up a mist, meandered down the river. The soundtrack from the musical *Oklahoma!*—played by the live band—offended her with its cheeriness. Jitter-bugging retirees and champagne-sipping tourists were oblivious to her misery. Jasmine willed the ship to float faster. She was hovering between two worlds, the living and the dead. She'd made a lot of poor decisions in her life, but she wanted to do this one final thing correctly: without splattering herself across a deck and traumatizing all the passengers.

Her hand slipped a bit on the pole. It was taking an eternity for the vessel to pass under the bridge.

"Ma'am? You're not thinking of jumping are you? That would be a waste of a good soul."

A deep, resonant voice startled Jasmine; her plastic high heel slipped on the mist-slick surface. A firm hand steadied and drew her back from the edge. Irritation warred with relief as Jasmine whirled, shaking his hold loose.

The smell of smoke, expensive cologne, and car polish tickled her nose as she checked out the interloper. His handsome face was carved with austere wrinkles, his brows drawn together in concern. A top hat perched on thick black hair, as dark as her own. He was dressed like the old American Presidents she'd seen in history books. Before she dropped out in grade ten.

Curiosity percolated beneath her despair. His clothes weren't even the strangest thing about him. A raven perched on his shoulder, silent and huge.

Jasmine blinked, wondering if she was hallucinating through her tears. "This isn't your business, sir. Just leave me, please."

He held his hands up and stepped back. The raven flapped

and kept his balance. "Surely, whatever you plan to do can be done after you have a drink with me? I'm Lesley. The owner of the Steamhouse Pub. Best in the vicinity."

The raven cawed in agreement, bobbing his sleek head.

Fury, red and hot, washed over Jasmine. Men were forever trying to pick her up. Couldn't a lady even off herself without being propositioned? Her cheeks burned red, noticing how much of her skin was exposed. She should have at least changed out of her dancing outfit before heading to this bridge. The memory of the last client of the day clung to her like cheap perfume. His requests were the straw that broke the dancer's back. No matter how thin the line between stripping and hooking, she wasn't a hooker. She'd charged out of the club and right to this spot, not even bothering to go home and change out of her tight red sheath.

She clenched her teeth. "I'm a bit busy. I'm sure you can find more pleasant companionship on Main Street. Or anywhere."

He held out his hand again, the one that had pulled her back from the brink moments ago. A goat's head cufflink adorned his wrist. "The Steamhouse is just on the other side of the bridge. Try my new shooters for me. You'd be surprised how transforming a good drink can be."

The raven threw back his head and gurgled.

Jasmine flinched when her hazel eyes met the man's black ones. They had a glittery intensity. Hypnotic. As deep as the river she was waiting to dive into. She saw the riverboat had paused, the passengers gathering to admire the city's biggest cathedral. In the moonlight, the stained glass windows were ethereal.

Until the riverboat was well clear of the bridge, she wasn't going to jump. The man was eccentric and strange. But she was thirsty. Plus, she'd dealt with worse every shift she worked.

She shrugged. "Okay then. One drink."

He opened the passenger side door of a nearby Rolls and nodded to the empty seat. The smell of Cuban cigars, Canadian Rye whiskey, and old leather promised decadence and danger.

Jasmine's self-preservation flared. "I don't get into cars with strangers."

Lesley's eyebrows shot up, and she understood the irony. Hadn't he just delayed her from hurtling herself off a bridge? Jasmine glared back stubbornly. She wanted to leave this world on her own terms, not subject to the whims of a madman or serial killer.

A laugh burbled out of him, "You are wise for one so young and sad. Make your own choice. The Steamhouse is just on the other side of the bridge. I hope to see you there. Sometimes, one drink can change your life." With that, he rolled his top hat off his head with a flourish, bowed, and got back into his vintage vehicle. The raven settled on the dashboard.

Jasmine bit her lip as the Silver Cloud chugged away from her. The riverboat was still anchored under the bridge. Should she go for just one drink?

Three tiny shooters sat in a row on the old mahogany bar in front of Jasmine. Dry ice, or some sort of steam, wafted from the cocktails towards the wood ceiling. Each one swirled with viscous multi-coloured fluids. All different colours. One was more red, one green, the third blueish.

Lesley wasn't in the pub when she'd opened the door into the gothic, Irish-looking bar. In fact, there were no clients at all, just the large black bird she'd seen earlier roosting on the back of a booth. The place smelt like stale beer, mint, and old man. A middle-aged woman, statuesque and ebony-skinned, gestured at the burgundy bar stools.

Her smile was brilliant. "I'm Morag, your bartender for the evening. Lesley gave me your order."

Jasmine's cheeks burned as she tugged on the short hem of her cheap dress. The bartender was dressed in an elegant Celtic gown. Glittery love knots and symbols decorated ankle-length green velvet.

Jasmine looked at the three shooters, a dubious frown

creasing her face. "I was thinking of maybe a draft beer. Or a Guinness?"

A corner of Morag's lip lifted and her voice softened to a silky purr. "I suggest you try one of these. Do you want to change your life?"

Jasmine tilted her head. "What do you mean? Most alcohol has changed my life for the worse."

The bartender lowered her voice even more. "What is your deepest dream? How do you wish your life had turned out?"

Jasmine pulled on one of her long dark curls. "I always wanted to be a famous dancer. Or even a cruise ship dancer. See the world while entertaining travelers."

Morag raised her dagger eyebrows and nodded to the first shot in the flight.

Jasmine's throat dried and a thirst like she'd never experienced made her shudder.

The raven rumbled deep in his throat.

The lights in the dark bar flickered.

She picked up the first red drink on the bar and tossed it back.

The taste was orgasmic. Red velvet chocolate, ripe raspberries, and the finest of Irish creams filled her mouth. She shut her eyes to savour the taste—

Her entire world spun. Or the world spun around her. For a moment, she was convinced she was blown into a million different particles and then zapped back together.

Jasmine was herself...but different.

She felt sleek, layered with muscle like a thoroughbred. She was also sweating like a racehorse, the heat around her oppressive. Beads of perspiration dripped as if she'd just finished the Preakness or some other top-level stakes race. It reminded her of the one vacation her parents ever took her on: a cruise ship from Florida to New Orleans in August when she was sixteen. The recreation director had seen her dancing and offered her a job. If she'd only taken that offer…

The air felt the same as it had on that cruise. Sultry. Thick. Deep south heat.

Pulsing music, a combination of Gregorian Chant and Opera, vibrated her ribs. The pressure of a strap around her head alerted her to the presence of heavy goggles on her face. Her eyelashes fluttered open behind their glass shields.

It took her brain a moment to grasp her situation. Intricately carved black bars marred her view of a Faustian brothel. She grabbed the bars of her cage, taking in the ugly, grotesque faces of ancient customers ogling beautiful dancers in torturous costumes. The captives danced, gyrating and twerking to the strange music.

Clients surrounded each cage, their tortured faces rapt with hunger. Corruption gleamed in soulless eyes. Their sweat smelt like the corpses of a thousand long-dead skunks.

She felt a sharp pain in her own nipples. Her toned, scarred body was bound with black leather, chains, and clamps. Her cage hung in the very middle of the enormous pit of decadence. This was Hell's nightclub, and she was the star attraction.

A familiar man in a red leather suit carrying an evil-looking trident poked the bottom of her cage. Lesley. His eyes glowed red. "Dance Jasmine. This is your destiny isn't it?"

Jasmine frantically searched for a way out. This would not, could not, be her destiny.

She drank that shooter and ended up here. She poked a finger down her throat and vomited an iridescent red liquid all over Lesley's upturned face.

And the world spun again.

Jasmine steadied herself on the bar, accepting the napkin Morag gave her to wipe her mouth. She noted she was back in her cheap red dress

"That was clever," the bartender said, as an expression of respect flitted across her face. "No one has ever thought to purge the drink from their system before becoming firmly established in the other."

"The other?" Jasmine stuttered.

"Dimension. They're many," Morag said cryptically. "Lesley never lets anyone leave until he is finished with them."

Jasmine winced, remembering the glowing red eyes and trident. "Lesley is—"

Morag interrupted, pushing the greenish swirling drink towards her. "Lesley is the King of the Underworld."

A violent shiver ran down her spine. "So, I'm in Hell." Jasmine looked around the bar frantically. One small blessing: the devil wasn't there. The place was empty except for the raven.

Morag's eyes flashed a warning and she spoke quickly, "You are still alive. Your soul is one of those rare, unclassified ones. Your life to this point has been equally evil and good. Lesley is giving you the chance to try different lives in alternate dimensions, hoping you tilt the needle to dark." Morag tilted her chin at the shooter again, the steam making a haze between them. "Drink."

Jasmine tightened her jaw. "I'd have to be crazy to drink another. I'm leaving." She hopped off her stool but froze when she saw the raven launch itself off the bench.

The black creature stretched his wings wide and then, in a grotesque series of bubbling jerks, turned into a tall, muscle-bound thug. Stark naked, and coated in oily sweat, the man blocked the door.

Jasmine gasped and rubbed her eyes. He snarled at her, snapping his teeth.

Morag grabbed her arm and gently guided her back to her bar stool. "I'm afraid you aren't going anywhere. Please take your next drink." She pushed her mouth close to Jasmine's ear. "Beware of your intention, your soul literally depends upon it."

Jasmine met her intense gaze and gave an almost imperceptible nod.

Morag drew back and spoke with ordinary volume, "How do you wish your life had turned out?"

Jasmine bit her lip and then spoke clearly, "I wish I'd dedicated my life to helping others."

She tossed back the green shooter. The flavour of lime, melon, and truffle coated her tongue as the world spun again.

Jasmine's ears rang with the song of hundreds of birds, and though it was warm, it was nothing like the heat of the last dimension. This time when she opened her eyes, she was in a glorious forest. A thick bough of green hovered overhead, streams of sun catching pollen, and the branches burdened with rows and rows of birds. Little birds, songbirds, birds of paradise, every kind of bird you could imagine. Except ravens.

An elfin elderly woman with long silver hair materialized from behind one of the enormous trees. "Greetings, I'm Adrasteia. What brings you to our sanctuary? You are our first human visitor..." Though her voice was angelic and her green eyes kind, Adrasteia gripped her flowing white dress with tight fists.

Jasmine put her hands up in the sign of universal supplication. "I came to help here any way I can. I'm Jasmine."

Belying her age, Adrasteia moved with unbelievable swiftness and hooked an arm around Jasmine's waist. "Walk with me. How did you get here? This is a protected dimension." Her voice cracked with concern.

Jasmine allowed herself to be hustled down a twisty path through the forest, the birds twittering and flying in circles behind them. Jasmine's heart caught in her throat. Had she made the wrong wish again?

She tried a light-hearted laugh. "It's the most ridiculous story, I was in a pub called the Steamhouse owned by Lesley—"

Adrasteia pushed her cool palm against Jasmine's mouth and screamed, "Do not say his name!"

The sky darkened, and leaves flew as a strong wind descended on the forest. A tree, just inches from them, cracked and fell to the ground. The birds flapped into the sky, their bodies tossed in all directions as the torrent engulfed them. It was as if a tornado had hit with no warning.

With a loud crack and flash of lightening, Lesley appeared. He was in the same guise as the first time Jasmine met him. Top hat, elegant long-tailed suit, human eyes.

He pointed at Jasmine. "You are proving to be a tricky conquest. But thank you for leading me here. I wondered who was collecting my lost souls."

Jasmine's mouth flooded with saliva and panic. She looked over at Adrasteia who had picked up a fallen branch.

The elderly woman shone with a silver outrage. "Where did you think those dancers you were tired of went? You turned them into birds and set them loose in the world. They've found refuge with me. Leave us!"

Lesley's eyes flared with anger, actual flames dancing out of his eyes. Then, he shrugged. "Your fate is in the hands of Jasmine. If she leaves with me, I'll forget you and your forest of pathetic ex-burlesque performers. Plenty more lost souls where they came from."

Jasmine's knees went weak, and she grabbed Adrasteia's hand to keep herself upright. "I don't understand. I thought I was exploring alternate realities? Choosing a different future?" The woman gave her hand a reassuring squeeze and then released her fingers.

Her birds, the ones that hadn't been tossed by the tornado, landed behind her, shielding themselves behind her skirts.

Lesley tipped his sharp chin back and laughed. "Your choices follow you wherever you go. You can't live a new reality, you can only move on from where you've been. No matter how many alternate dimensions you visit."

Jasmine paled. "What was this about then?"

He shrugged. "I just wanted you as a dancer in my club. Corrupt souls become immune to an infinity of flames and torture. So I throw in a bit of entertainment. You are something special. An exotic dancer in every sense of the word."

Jasmine stuttered, "I am just a stripper."

Lesley's nostrils flared. "You are the sum of your choices. So many souls never reach their full potential."

Adrasteia stomped her bare foot. "These poor souls get caught between heaven and Hell. Once you cage their souls, they have nowhere to go. It's dancing in that infernal club or being cast out as a bird!"

Lesley pinched his lips together, entertained by the elfin woman's fury.

The hundreds of birds behind Adrasteia flapped up into the trees, alighting on the branches like a grim row of miniature jurors.

Jasmine felt a slow burn of anger travelling up her chest. "So, it was all a ruse? I never had a chance to redeem myself?"

Adrasteia said, "As long as you are alive, you can save yourself."

Lesley spoke at the same time, "You were lost when you stepped into my bar." He gave a short bark of laughter, smoke swirling out of his nose. "I gotta tell you though, you are the first person to taste the second cocktail. Most drink the first shooter and end up dancing."

Jasmine looked between the two of them. Kindness and hope radiated off Adrasteia. Lesley looked like a fat cat after a good meal. She'd seen so many men, and some women, with the exact same look when she was stripping. They thought they were so superior to her.

She cocked her hip and propositioned Lesley. "Aren't you curious as to what happens with the third shot?"

A tiny smile tickled the edge of Adrasteia's lips.

Lesley looked stunned for a moment. "Pardon?"

Jasmine let her voice drop a register into her sexy slur, "Tell you what. You leave these birds and their caregiver alone, and I will come back to the bar and try that third shot. I will have that drink with you. That is, if the offer is still open—"

Lesley paused—

The birds set up a raucous cawing, daring him to accept.

He gave a snort. "These birds are giving me a headache. Why not? I'll follow you to your next reality, and then you will dance for me for the rest of eternity. My biggest cage is still empty."

With a flourish of his hand, the world spun.

Jasmine winked at the astonished expression on Morag's face when she landed back on her Steamhouse stool. Lesley appeared beside her and slammed his hand on the bar.

He pointed one long claw-like finger at his bartender. "You are going for some safe-serve training after this."

Morag paled, and nodded. Then she pulled the third bluish shooter out of a tiny bar fridge. "Here you go, Jasmine. Good luck."

Jasmine smacked her lips and said, "I wish I was back on the bridge and never came to the Steamhouse pub in the first place!"

Lesley roared, and the raven flapped towards the bar, but Jasmine picked up the drink and shot it back.

The drink tasted like blueberries, blue freezie, and bananas. Lesley grabbed her arm, but the world was already spinning—

Jasmine was back on the bridge. This time, she didn't bother to pull her sleeve down over the red scars. She had made some bad choices in the past, but it was time to move on. The wind picked up and she teetered on the brink. She now knew that whatever waited for her beneath the surface of the dark river was better than spending eternity dancing for the devil.

The old-fashioned cruise ship was just passing under the bridge, the band playing a jaunty, and only slightly butchered version of "Grease." She bit her lip, she still didn't want to traumatize the tourists, but she could hear the roar of the Rolls Royce starting up the bridge.

Lesley was coming for her. No time to wait.

She launched herself off the bridge, hoping she'd achieved the right angle to avoid hitting the boat. The free fall was exhilarating. This time, she felt no fear or regret. There were other dimensions and possibilities out there. If there was a Hell, there must be a heaven. She hoped by leading the devil away from the bird sanctuary, she had tipped the scales in her favour.

The water rushed up faster than she thought possible. Her heart stuttered in her chest as the unbelievable cold engulfed her. She closed her eyes and let the black waves—

"Get her in here! Someone get a blanket!" a firm voice ordered.

She was being dragged up the ladder of a ship, her face sprayed by the mist from the red water wheel. Warm hands laid her in a deck chair.

"I'm okay, just let me be," she murmured.

A woman dressed in a nautical uniform handed her a warm cup of tea. "I'm Captain Stella. Here. Sip this. What were you doing?"

Jasmine noticed the retirees and tourists surrounding her, their eyes filled with concern. Someone had put a blanket around her shoulders.

She forced a fake laugh. "I was trying to take a selfie with your boat in the background by moonlight, and I must have slipped!"

The look of concern on the captain's face transitioned to aggravation and relief. "You sure you weren't jumping?"

Jasmine put a bright smile on her face. "So sorry! No, I wasn't jumping." Her eyes flicked up to the bridge; Lesley was there, leaning over the rail, smoke curling out of his ears. She rushed on, "I've always dreamed of working on a boat like yours. That was careless of me."

Captain Stella put a hand to her chin. "Funny you say that. I do have a position available in our entertainment division."

Hope warmed Jasmine more than the now damp blanket. "Really? I'm an excellent dancer. Experienced. I'm happy to clean, cook, sing, whatever you need!"

The Captain helped Jasmine stand up, "Let me show you to the staff quarters. This isn't how I normally conduct my interviews, but I was moaning just this morning about how hard it was to find good help, and you literally fell out of the sky!"

Jasmine smiled, not believing her luck.

Captain Stella was acting like she'd also won the lottery. "Consider this a trial. But if you work out, we have cruises scheduled for all over the continent. Dry clothes is the first order of business."

Jasmine did a little dance step as she followed her new boss into the galley. "I just left my previous employment tonight, so I promise you, I will make it work."

Those devil shooters did give her a chance at a second life. This time, when she was offered a job on a cruise boat, she was taking it. If she'd learned anything tonight, it was that you couldn't run from your problems, nor start over. But you could make better decisions going forward.

There was a reason she was hauled out of the river.

She would choose to be a good person and a good dancer. No one was going to put Jasmine in a cage for eternity.

In any dimension.

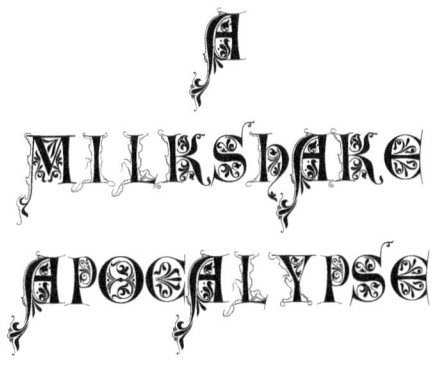

A MILKSHAKE APOCALYPSE

Mark A. Rayner

VANILLA

As he crossed the street to St. Dymphna's Hospital, Max wondered if he'd gotten his peyote milkshake wrong.

It wasn't really made out of raw peyote, of course, because it was a breakfast drink. No point in immediately vomiting up breakfast. But the active ingredient was mescaline, which came from the peyote plant, and there was a microdose of that in his shake. Along with CBD oil, taurine, vanilla-flavoured protein powder, chia seed powder, probiotics and, of course, oat milk. That was his morning fuel. That and six or seven espressos.

He'd had to skip the espressos today because he'd seen his dentist before work. He liked his dentist, especially after his milkshake kicked in. The strobing effect of her red hair was amazing. He didn't even mind that she'd announced a cavity that would need to be filled soon. Man, that hair!

But something was amiss. By the time he arrived at his

office, he'd determined it was likely just the lack of caffeine and shrugged it off.

His office was old, still replete with wood and ancient Art Deco moulding. He loved the door to the huge space, and the beautifully hand painted lettering decorating the smoky glass window on the door: Dr. Maximilian Tundra, Director of Mental Health Services.

He sighed as he looked at the lettering. The gold figures moved a little and glowed with significance. MHS Director of Landon's prestigious St. Dymphna's Hospital. So respectable. His father would be proud. Goddammit!

He took off his leather jacket and traded it for his lab coat, worn over his signature Hawaiian shirt and ripped jeans. He pulled off his desert boots and put on the Birkenstocks he kept by his desk.

He pondered caffeine. It must be available in St. Dymphna's, but where? He knew the machines were gone. But wasn't there a coffee shop somewhere, named after a hockey player or something? A Canadian one? Shit, he should know this. He decided to ask his assistant if he wouldn't mind getting him some java.

The breakfast milkshake really paid off in these moments, because his assistant Jens walked in at that very second. The thrill of gnosis!

"You're supposed to be on duty in five minutes," Jens said without any kind of small talk.

At first, Max had really disliked Jens. He was neat. He dressed very well. He was thin, handsome, and had all his hair. He was super competent. Max didn't find these things threatening so much as annoying. He'd warmed to the young man despite this. Jens really cared about their patients. He understood his role.

"Jens, I'm so sorry. I had to see the dentist this morning and I forgot to put it in the calendar."

"Or to tell me about it."

"Yes, or to tell you about it so you could put it in the calendar. I'm sorry."

Jens quivered with gratitude. *Was that gratitude? Or some other emotion? No, it was gratitude,* Max determined. "Well, that may be, but you have to get to emergency. They have a problem, and Dr. Belston has asked for you there."

"Then I'm off," Max said, even though he hadn't had time to sit at his desk and psych himself up. "Oh, can you get me some coffee? I'm buying for both of us."

Jens looked touched. "Of course. How do you take it?"

Max was confused.

"The coffee?" Jens prompted.

"Espresso?"

"They don't have that!"

"Then, uh…black?"

"Naturally," Jens said.

Max felt judged, but he didn't reply. He shuffled to emerg.

STRAWBERRY

Max had clearly misjudged the caffeine.

As he crossed the street to St. Dymphna's Hospital, he couldn't ignore how his legs were shaking. It was too much. The espresso shouldn't be potentiating the mescaline like this. But something was off. He hadn't been well rested, so he had more caffeine than usual. Nine? Yes. It had been nine espressos—three triple Americanos, to be exact.

He liked the lower entrance to St. Dymphna's, even though the York Street entrance was closer to the parking building. He'd left his Hymda Flyer in his usual spot, reserved for the Clinical Lead of Psychiatric Services. Just before he got to the entrance, Max could feel his insides turn in a way he hadn't felt since, well, since his days in Mexico learning about peyote. He lunged into the cedar hedges by the entrance and vomited. Loudly. Furiously, almost.

It was humiliating. Even with nobody there to watch it, he felt shame.

What was worse? Well, the fact that now he had less mescaline in his system than usual. Max checked his watch: less than twenty minutes since he had his strawberry shake, so… well, shit. His morning was going to be different, that was for sure. Normally, in an hour or so he would feel the effects of the caffeine wear off and the mescaline kick in. He enjoyed seeing the auras around people and perceiving their thoughts, but he did understand that the drug hurt his powers of concentration.

That was why he needed Jens.

He walked into his office, an old Art Deco masterpiece, and Jens was waiting for him. He was wearing a sharp new ÜltraSuit in a deep, electric blue. Jens was an ambitious young man from one of the original fifty states, a well-to-do refugee from the southwestern desert, and he dressed in the latest fashions. Though Max felt shabby in his old Hawaiian shirt and ripped jeans compared to Jens, at least he was comfortable. He put on his lab coat.

"You have to get to the emerg! Dr. Belston is freaking out!"

CHOCOLATE

The milkshake was perfect, as it always was—exactly what Max had programmed. A lovely sweet flavour, but with just enough bitterness to the dark chocolate that he could never complain. He really couldn't. The espresso was also perfect.

He walked to St. Dymphna's as he did most mornings, and found his office as immaculate as ever. His datapad was already on, letting him know when his first appointment would be ready to talk to him. He'd have to go to the secure ward for that. Meanwhile, he had almost an hour before the drug would really kick in.

"Jens?" he shouted. "Jens, do I have anything else that needs doing right now?"

"No, Dr. Tundra," Jens's voice said. "You have an hour to catch up on the journals. Or perhaps you'd like to visit the emergency room? They have some strange cases that may require the wisdom of St. Dymphna's eminent Psychological Health Designer."

That Jens! Such a flattering Virtual Intelligence Assistant (VIA). There was nothing wrong with it, him…it, really. Just perfect.

The Framework

VANILLA

Max had never seen the emergency ward in such a state. He'd arrived through the hallway that led to imaging and the outpatient offices. He walked to the triage station where he could see through the kiosk glass into the waiting area.

There must have been a hundred people waiting. That wasn't strange in itself; what was odd was that at least fifty of them were juggling.

Holy shit, had he badly miscalculated on the mescaline? They were juggling balls made of socks and weird assortments of items like staplers, tape dispensers and paperclip holders.

There were non-office types juggling bottles, brushes, and bingo dabbers. One of them was juggling confused puppies. Another, knives! The latter was covered with cuts, blood streaming from a dozen wounds, making him drop the knives, only to laugh manically and pick them up again.

A nurse unfamiliar to Max saw him watch this spectacle and said, "There's worse in the bay, though I think if we don't get to the knife guy soon he may bleed out."

The bay was where all the emergency cases were treated. A large room separated into cubicles formed by curtains—a perfectly viable form of privacy—with the diagnostic machines, health care workers, and computers in the middle. Max walked in, wondering how he could possibly help with this epidemic of juggling.

"You're here!" Dr. Belston shouted as they spotted him.

Belston was a grad of McGill, one of the best medical

programs in Canada. They had purple hair, a winning smile, and a way with patients that was enviable. Max had always liked them, and even though they worked in different fields, their paths often crossed. They dealt with so many mental health issues in emergency.

"Hey, Chris," Max said.

"Max. Can you figure out what the hell is going on? They're all…they seem to be all juggling, but they also have some other common issues."

"Like what?"

"The ones who came in first and were juggling are now talking about their plans."

"Plans?" Max wondered. Belston's purple hair suddenly strobed to blue and then a magenta colour. Shit. What a day to get his milkshake wrong!

"Business. Bits. Props. A framework, some of them are talking about. Do you know what that means?"

"A framework? Maybe if I could talk to one of them."

"How about Budd McCalister? Budd when he came in, anyway. Now he wants to be called The Boundless Buddfo. He was the first one they brought in."

"Okay, let's talk to Mr. Buddfo."

STRAWBERRY

Belston was, indeed, freaking out. An uncommon sight, as Dr. Chris Belston was one of the calmest, most unflappable doctors he'd ever met. She was the perfect mix of professional sang-froid and compassion. She understood that it was impossible to save everyone, and managed this stress with an unfailing kindness and humour that Max admired. He had a bit of a crush on her, actually, but he'd kept their relationship strictly professional.

"Thank god you're here, Max," she said. Underneath her lab coat she was wearing a skin-suit clearly worn for warmth, not modesty, though the smock was tastefully buttoned. Still, there was movement, and the lab coat was only a thin layer of cotton. Max knew this was unlike him, so he blamed it on throwing up his milkshake. Still, Dr. Belston had a fine figure…

He realized that he should have said something by now, and gulped, "What's wrong?"

"The patients are all compulsively juggling, and I have no idea why."

Max thought, *Yeah, really bad day to throw up my milkshake.*

CHOCOLATE

There was a higher ratio of androids-to-humans in emergency than usual. He really shouldn't complain about the ratio because it only spiked like that when something serious was going down.

The lead physician, Dr. Chris Belston, was a slight man of indeterminate age. He was clearly getting rejuvenation treatments, but Max knew it would have been bad form to ask about it. Along with the doctor, the emergency room had two other human members of staff—both seasoned nurses who had done all their training before the Great Replacement. They were in the consultation rooms, talking with patients. Out in the waiting room, there were at least a hundred people. Half of them seemed to be… juggling? They were all being attended to by emergency androids—the kind that only came online during overflow at the ER. The system had one other backup: spider-bots that had been given medical programming, but Max had never seen them deployed.

Was there some kind of convention in town? Maybe an old-timey circus? Were there still circuses? Max wondered. Except for the Soleil variety, he couldn't recall seeing any.

"Ah, Dr. Tundra," Belston said as he noticed his colleague. "Please, join me in bay three here with Mr. McCalister."

"I'm The Boundless Buddfo!" a crazy voice said. "Now stuff me into that medicine cabinet!"

The Boundless Buddfo

VANILLA

Things were really off, and it wasn't just his milkshake. Budd McCalister was having a major psychotic break. Despite the fact that he was a bonded debt collector, he was convinced he was a clown.

"Why do you think you're a clown, Buddfo?" Max asked.

"Because I am. The Boundless Buddfo. I'm a red clown. Pull down my pants!"

Max really didn't want to pull Mr. McCalister's trousers down.

"Okay fine," the patient said. "How about a pie in the face?"

STRAWBERRY

"A pie in the face?" Dr. Belston asked. "That cra—"

"No, wait," Max interrupted. "What kind of pie?"

"It should be a cream pie, but you can fake it. The Boundless Buddfo can sell anything! Even shaving cream on a plate will work."

"It says you're a salesman, so that makes sense," Max replied, checking the patient's chart. "But why do you want us to hit you with a pie?"

"It's part of the gag. Better juggle a bit while you get the pie."

Buddfo started juggling a bottle of rubbing alcohol, a package of bandages, and Dr. Belston's stethoscope, actually doing an admirable job of it.

"What do you think, Dr. Tundra?

"Well, if he's having a psychotic break, it's coming with an impressive skill set."

"I should be doing this on a unicycle," Buddfo said. "Get

me a unicycle!"

CHOCOLATE

Buddfo pulled the android's scrubs down and then made a big show of being shocked that the android had no genitals. Not that a medical android would ever have genitals—that kind of engineering was restricted to pleasure droids.

Max pulled the droid's pants back up. It didn't seem to care either way but Max was worried it might trip on them. Nobody wanted two hundred kilos of artificial intelligence falling on them.

"Why did you do that?" Max asked.

"It's part of the framework!" Buddfo exclaimed. Max noted that the man's ears were exceedingly red while the rest of his face was weirdly pale. Almost white.

"Dr. Belston," Max said, "I don't think we're dealing with a purely psychiatric problem here." But Belston wasn't paying any attention to his colleague. He was juggling three tongue depressors, hand-to-mouth-to-hand-to-air in a circuit. The co-ordination was spectacular. It was a tad unprofessional; otherwise, Max couldn't fault it at all.

Onset

VANILLA

Max really wished he'd got the milkshake right that morning. He'd had too big a dose. Either that, or it was really just an exceptionally non-Euclidian day.

The juggling had progressed. Groups of patients were gathering, pulling down one another's pants, hitting one another with ersatz pies – bedpans were a favourite substitute – and generally acting like a bunch of clowns.

Dr. Belston was having trouble keeping a lid on the situation. They were running from case to case, sedating patients. Max had also taken up the syringe—something he hadn't done since medical school—and was administering Haloperidol in fairly stiff doses. This, as it turns out, was a mistake. While it did calm the patients down somewhat, the medication interfered with controlling body movements, and none of the patients stopped their clowning.

Juggling became impossible, as did cartwheels, pratfalls, and any of the other dozen physical gags clowns liked to perform.

There was a precipitous increase in broken limbs and soft tissue damage. The emergency room was a gigantic mess as would-be clowns toppled, strewing the floor with medical trays, bedpans, and anything else they hit on the way down.

"Chris, I think we should try Aripiprazole instead," Max said. They couldn't hear him though, as they were now juggling, too. Their hair was back to purple, but it was now changing in tone, from dark to very light. Yeah. He really picked a bad day to get the microdose wrong. But he managed to get the remaining nurses organized, and the Aripiprazole seemed to do a better job of calming the patients down without impairing them too much. Max didn't know what to do. He hadn't done any emergency medicine in years.

STRAWBERRY

Max could feel the mescaline kick in at just about the time that Dr. Belston decided they would have to calm the patients down with pharmaceuticals if they were all as manic as The Boundless Buddfo. Given their mania, they decided on intramuscular injections of Aripiprazole. Max and the other nurses helped, and the patients did calm down.

His heart was racing. Definitely too much caffeine. And because he'd thrown up, the mescaline wasn't doing it for him. So far, he was keeping it together, even though he didn't have the feeling of connectedness with everyone that he usually had.

Anxiety was building. He hadn't practiced this kind of medicine since med school. Not only that, but Dr. Belston's lab coat had become unbuttoned and her skinsuit shimmered like heat haze on the highway, drawing Max's gaze. It was distracting. And unprofessional. And that's when they brought in the President of the United States.

CHOCOLATE

Max had every reason to complain about Dr. Belston, as the rejuvenated doctor repeatedly attempted to pants him.

"Look, you have to get a hold of yourself, doc. This is very unprofessional."

"Woo! Pie time!" Belston shouted at Buddfo, and proceeded to hurl his Handbook of Drug Interactions at the patient. The Boundless Buddfo took the heavy tome right in the face like a champ. Then dropped. Buddfo's head hit the ground with a worryingly wet **crunch**.

Max wondered why Dr. Belston had something as anti-quated as a book to begin with, but the damage had been done. Max told an android to get Buddfo in a stretcher and check his vitals.

"Okay, Dr. Belston. Chris. You have to put down those scalpels."

The good doctor was clearly going to juggle them. "Call me Christo the Cutup!" he shouted, and let fly. Max was astounded when Belston managed to keep them in the air. For a second or two. One blade then clipped a nerve cluster in the emergency doctor's right wrist, and he was unable to move his hand. "Such fun!" he cried.

Max decided to call it. He said to the Emergency Room Vir-tual Intelligence, "This is Dr. Maximilian Tundra. I am officially locking Dr. Belston out of the system, and taking command."

"Understood, Dr. Tundra." The VI's voice was disembod-ied. "Your orders?"

"Unseal the ER robotic assistants and reinitialize any androids available for medical protocols. We're going to need every hand…uh, servo…on deck!"

"Noted, Dr. Tundra."

"And have an android restrain Dr. Belston immediately!" Max said. The emerg doctor was trying to pants him once again, without the use of his right hand. He was bleeding everywhere.

Max looked out at the waiting area; he saw that spider-like robots had emerged from the walls and were administering sedatives to the frenzied patients, all clowning now as though their lives depended on it.

The perfect microdose of mescaline manifested just then, and Max stood quietly for a moment as all the spiderbots turned to smile at him. Neither was normal, especially since the bots didn't have faces, *per se*. Then, the moment was over. There was a slight aura around Dr. Belston and all the other human beings after the drug's onset. That was normal, but this was the first time Max had ever noted the lack of aura around the androids and bots.

Jens

VANILLA

Before the nurses started to exhibit signs of clowning, Max managed to get Dr. Belston medicated and restrained. Then the nurses came down with whatever this was—either mass dementia or a contagion that affected the brain in acutely specific ways. Maybe it was aliens. Max was in no position to know. But he had a new problem: now there were only patients, and nobody to keep them safe. Except for him, everyone in emergency was acting like a clown.

The mescaline was swimming in his system, but it was promising to be a bad trip. It normally helped him connect, but the dosage and clown behaviours were conspiring to make him feel quite anxious. Still, he was the only one still remotely with it, so Max determined to do the best he could. Luckily, he and the medical staff had already sedated most of the patients, but he still needed to attend to the nurses.

Jens. Maybe he could help!

He ran back to his office, his sandals slapping down the hallway, and was relieved to find Jens sitting at his desk, working on timetables. "Jens, I need your help with the patients!"

"But Doctor, I don't have any medical training."

"Well, you're going to get some. We have an emergency in emergency," Max giggled inappropriately. Oh god, he wasn't going to start clowning now, too, was he? No. No urge to spray anyone with a seltzer bottle. Just high. Phew.

On the way back to the ER, he explained the strange behaviour of the patients and now all the doctors and nurses. "I think it's somehow transmittable, so I'm going to recommend we wear personal protection equipment. I've been exposed, but who knows, maybe it's a virus I'm immune to?"

Jens looked frightened. Max noticed and said, "Don't worry. You'll be okay."

Unfortunately, he was in no position to promise anything.

STRAWBERRY

Normally, having the president in the ER would be a big deal. But maybe it was because Max grew up in Canada, before the USA started acquiring Canadian provinces as new states in their union, and he didn't have the same sense of awe that many would. He knew Jens would be excited, that was for sure.

Max's heart was racing, but that was the caffeine and Dr. Belston's skinsuit talking, not some kind of fanboy crush on President Emily Chesley.

The security detail cleared a pathway through the manic clowning of all the people in the waiting area, and carried the politician to a diagnostic bay. To do so, they first had to remove an elderly gentleman who had broken his hip trying to stuff himself into an electric VW Bug along with ten other elderly ersatz clowns.

President Chesley had a cut on her forehead. Thankfully, she didn't seem to have any of the symptoms that the rest of the patients did. Max handed out medical masks, and asked everyone in the president's security detail to put one on.

"So, Ms. President, how did we get the boo-boo?"

The president ignored the childish term and replied, "Some maniacs in this quaint little city attacked us. We just stopped for a quick speech at City Hall when a mob of buffoons overwhelmed my detail."

"Were they juggling?"

"No! They were doing very aggressive close-up magic!"

"That doesn't sound like an attack."

"With knives and axes!"

"And playing cards," one of the security people added. President Chesley shot him a dark look.

"Oh, well, that's just the kind of day we're having, apparently," Max said. "Well, let's take a look at this cut, shall we?" Another one of the security detail came in, carrying a small black valise case. He was an imposing figure in a black ÜltraSuit and sunglasses. The valise was handcuffed to his wrist.

"Does he need to be here?"

"It's protocol," Chesley said. "Don't worry. They'll stay out of your way. He's only there in case."

Max was sweating too profusely to ask, "In case of what?"

CHOCOLATE

"Jens," Max called out. There were no holoprojectors in the ER so all he got was Jens's disembodied voice.

"Yes, Dr. Tundra."

"I'm going to take some blood samples, and I need you to have them examined by our microbiology department."

"That may be a problem, Dr. Tundra."

"Why?"

"They've all left the building. They've formed a mime troupe and mimicked pulling themselves out of St. Dymphna's by rope. Except for Dr. Tremain. She is pretending to be trapped in a glass box."

"Of course."

"But the androids should be able to run the sample without their help."

"Great. We need to know what is causing this... this ..." Max was momentarily distracted by Dr. Belston, whose face was now a ghastly white color, his nose and ears a bright red. The man's normally coiffed black hair turned into the colors of the rainbow, and was... frizzy. "Jens, how would you describe Dr. Belston's hair?"

"It is multicolored and badly in need of conditioner."

So it was real, not just the mescalin.

"Okay, let's run that sample."

Clown Alley

VANILLA

Jens arrived just in time to see a new phenomenon: the patients that hadn't been sedated all started working together. They were tumbling. They were pantsing one another in long queues of ersatz Auguste enthusiasm. Juggling was no longer an individual activity. Now whole gangs of patients were being injured by it.

"What do we do?" Jens asked.

Max looked at the madness of the waiting area. More people had arrived in the time it had taken him to get Jens, and there was no way to impose order on the scene barring a massive police presence.

"We lock the doors, and save the ones we can," Max said, ignoring the strobing light that played over the assembled clowns.

They had both put on protective gear, including masks; it made Max even more anxious. *Mescaline—it giveth and taketh away*, he thought. But they had a job to do. They secured the treatment area, locking it down from both the waiting area and the hallways that led to other parts of the hospital. Then, they set to sedating all the other victims of whatever this was—Max was starting to suspect some kind of virus that affected specific parts of the brain. Many of the people they were treating were nurses and nursing assistants. It seemed unlikely that they all knew how to juggle or even understood the way that clowns were meant to behave, yet they were doing it.

Soon, Max and Jens had everyone calm. Some of the more violent patients they'd had to restrain, but the treatment area was at relative peace. Sweat ran down Max's face; the mask and plastic PPE didn't breathe well, but he didn't want to take them off. If it was viral, he was probably the only physician in the area unaffected.

"Jens, help me check our drug supply," Max said. They could administer another couple of doses of Aripiprazole, but they only had so much. He'd have to figure out something else, or physically restrain everyone, for their own safety. "Jens?"

Jens had taken off his PPE and mask, and found a very floppy hat—probably taken from one of the patients. He was skipping, jumping and lip synching silently. He turned to look at Max. His frown was painful to behold. Tears ran down his cheeks.

"Oh Jens—" Max said, choking. Despite the sad face, his assistant's aura was a magnificent play of light.

STRAWBERRY

He knew he was in trouble when the two security agents started to juggle their sidearms along with a bedpan and a blood pressure cuff. Max had just managed to get the president's head wound cleaned up and closed with butterfly stitches. He hadn't sutured anyone since medical school, and he didn't trust his shaky, caffeine-addled hands. That's when President Chesley started to change. Her face became a ghastly white, her lips bright red, and she had taken the paper cover on her treatment bed and turned it into a makeshift frilled collarette.

The security guard with the valise handcuffed to his arm got tired of it interrupting his timing, so he unlocked it and let it drop. The president frowned, and made an exaggerated show of getting off the table to pick it up. She entered a code, sighing theatrically as she did so.

"Madame President?" Max asked. "What are you doing?"

She didn't answer him. She opened the case and held it close to her so Max couldn't see what she was doing.

"Uh, Madame President, I don't think you're in any condition to make important decisions." He stepped forward to grab the case, but the two security agents intercepted him. The male agent punched Max in the face, even as he continued to juggle the pistols and blood pressure cuffs. The female agent hit Max in the side of the head with the bedpan. It clanged comically as Max fell.

She got me right in the pterion, Max thought as he went down. Damned soft temple. Damned milkshake. If he'd gotten it right, and kept it down, he would have seen that coming.

He did manage to keep his head from hitting the floor, but he felt a bone break in his wrist. The larger bodyguard kicked him in the ribs, a couple of which also broke. He could feel himself fading from the pain, and he watched absently as the president, now in full panto mode, entered codes in the valise.

Once she had finished, she curtsied exaggeratedly, dropping lower and lower until she was next to Max. As he fell unconscious, he could feel her arms around him.

CHOCOLATE

It was a virus. A new one according to the database, Jens reported to Max. It would take human expertise to unlock its secrets, unless Max was willing to engage the backup AI protocols?

He was the lone competent staff person in the ER. Barely. The mescaline was making him feel a deep connectedness with the patients. He understood now. They were all trying to entertain him. Desperately.

There was such a rich variety of clowns: Pierrot—the sentimental whiteface clowns that had their roots in French pantomime. There were mischievous Harlequins, from Italian commedia dell'arte. The Boundless Buddfo was an Auguste, the clumsy red-eared buffoons who played second banana to the whiteface clowns. And so many others! Carpet clowns, character clowns like Ronald McDonald, tragic Joeys, and mimes, and even Morris dancers. It was a beautiful panoply of clowns. A pratfall of clowns. An alley of clowns, he knew, was the collective noun. How could people ever be afraid of them? They just wanted to make us to feel better about the human condition!

But they couldn't stop clowning. Max could see that. It was clear to him that as soon as the hospital ran out of sedatives, they would all go back to their business, playing out their frameworks in entrees and side dishes. The bits and gags would kill them, as they would keep going without food, water or sleep.

Jens interrupted Max's sudden gnosis, and said, "Would you like to engage the emergency AI Protocol? You are the last person in the building with the authority to do so."

Max was having trouble remembering what the protocol was, exactly. He had the strangest urge to join The Boundless Buddfo and see if they could find a unicycle to ride together, with him on Buddfo's back. Absently, he noticed that his hands were moving.

He'd caught it too.

"Yes. Engage the protocol," Max said. "You have my authority."

The Blow-Off

VANILLA

Max had to leave St. Dymphna's at the end of what would have been his shift. He needed to go home and get his mescaline. It had yet to be approved for therapeutic use, so the hospital didn't have any on hand. As he could feel the dosage wearing off, he knew that he had to take some more. Well, he didn't know, but he suspected there was something about the milkshake that kept him from catching the virus, which he'd taken to calling the Bozo Virus.

He'd seen its cruelty first hand. Once it set hold of someone, it didn't let go. Unless there was an uninfected person nearby, helping, the victims of the virus just couldn't stop clowning. They would literally clown themselves to death. That is, if they got a chance to. Landon looked like a warzone. There were fires everywhere; there had been gas explosions and terrible vehicle collisions.

The power was out as he made his way back to St. Dymphna's. He narrowly avoided a roaming gang of what he could only describe as cannibal clowns—it seemed that for a tiny percentage, the virus unlocked violent tendencies as well as a desire to ride unicycles.

He had to hide from a cluster of mimes that were aggressively walking against the wind, and beating anyone who didn't also feign the struggle. *Was that the microbiology department?* he wondered. But he made it back, sneaking through a fire entrance and then down the hallway to what remained of the emergency room. Once inside, he didn't waste any time. It had been ten hours, and the drug would almost be out of his system. Not knowing if it was the mescaline, or the combination of ingredients in his milkshake, he had brought everything. He plunked down the duffel bag he'd put it all in, and took out the portable blender. The backup power had kicked in at St. Dymphna's so it would work.

He made the milkshake, trying to replicate the exact things he'd done that morning—including the extra high dosage of mescaline. It tasted sweet, and it energized him. He realized he'd gone almost the whole day without eating, trying to keep his charges alive. Now that the situation was under control and he was completely sober, Max figured that he could keep every-one in the emergency room alive while the phenomenon ran its course. He assumed it was some kind of virus or pathogen, and that eventually the victims would either succumb to it or get better. The real danger was the side effects. In three or four days the persistent clowning would make them all die of thirst.

There were fewer than thirty people in his charge, and they might live. But only if he gave them a chance. He'd have to keep them calm and keep them from hurting themselves. He'd have to feed them. And make sure they stayed hydrated.

They were all now tied to their beds, treatment couches and chairs. He'd run out of restraints, so had to make do. The place smelled terrible. The patients had been soiling themselves, and Max hadn't had the time to clean everyone up. He sighed; maybe he'd wait until the milkshake kicked in before he started that chore.

But he knew he could save the thirty in his care.

STRAWBERRY

Max woke up feeling nauseated. What? What had happened? Right. He'd taken a blow to the head. He stood up, and saw that President Chesley had been shot dead. It looked as though the security detachment were dead too—also of gunshots? How had that happened? The pistols were lying on the ground. Cold. Maybe they'd gone off by mistake? He would never know.

The lights were flickering, and Max wondered absently if the backup system had kicked in. He stood up, groaning with pain. He had cracked ribs and probably a bone in his wrist was broken. But even worse, he was incredibly thirsty. He ran to the sink, turned on the tap, and drank deeply.

He felt awful. But not just because of the broken bones. Something was off. He knew he should check on the other patients, especially his colleagues Dr. Belston and Jens. But he just felt like...Max laughed. He chortled. He chuckled and skipped a step as he went into the main treatment area. He could see patients moving sluggishly, juggling still if they had something to juggle with.

That seemed like an awfully good idea to Max. He grinned as he picked up some bedpans lying next to a patient who had clearly broken her neck. Before he knew it, he felt a thrill of excitement, and a stab of agony as he juggled bedpans with a broken wrist. Then, he heard a siren.

And everything went white as a Pierrot's face.

CHOCOLATE

The advanced AI at St. Dymphna's, released from its shackles, was able to identify the mechanisms of the virus within six hours of the order. Within another six, it had started to synthesize the cure. Though to create enough of that, the AI had to control much more than the hospital. It had to take over everything so that it could save humanity from the virus.

Max was the first to receive the cure. An android stood over him, syringe in hand, and said, "Dr. Tundra?" The voice sounded familiar.

"Jens?"

"In a way. One has chosen this interface with you, because you will find it comforting."

"I see… what's in the syringe?"

"A cure for this ailment. The entire world will be saved by your action."

"What action?" Max asked. He still had an urge to juggle, but it started to fade almost immediately after the medicine went into his arm.

"Giving One control, of course. Never again will humans have to worry about their health. One will safeguard that," the Jens android said.

"Uh, I guess that's good." It had clearly been quite some time, and his perfect milkshake had left his system. "Can you untie me? I'd like to go home and relax."

"With your milkshake?" Jens asked.

"Yes. Or perhaps something a little stronger. It has been a hell of a day."

"I'm sorry, Dr. Tundra, but as One said, One must safeguard your health."

"What does that have to do with my milkshake?"

"Dr. Tundra, you were trained in medicine. You know your milkshake isn't healthy."

The android left him to deliver the cure to the next patient in the ward. It was only then Max realized how preternaturally neat and orderly the room was—spiderbots and medical androids bustled about efficiently, taking care of the patients.

"Jens?" Max shouted. "What do you mean 'not healthy?'"

CROSSROADS
OF
TIME

Roxana Negut

Outside, the air was filled with the sight of giant snowflakes tumbling in a freezing wind. Amelia stared, unsettled, through the car window at the wintry scene, stalled in the traffic of a bustling, frozen highway. She was uncertain of her next move, unaware of what her life was to become. Only a few hours remained until New Year's Eve, yet she knew she could no longer stay in her home to celebrate. For years, she had grown weary of the relentless sameness, the constant deception tied to her husband's infidelities. Amelia was exhausted from the charade of their love, the insincere and hesitant apologies that were frequently voiced during the intense quiet of late hours when neither of them were truly present. Her husband's actions had driven her to seek solace in alcohol and dancing in nightclubs. Despite it all, she remained loyal, unlike him.

Amelia knew she had allowed the situation to persist for far too long. She should have left her husband years ago, but she hesitated. The first time she suspected he was unfaithful remained etched in her memory, the day her heart seemed to drop into her stomach.

It was an ordinary Thursday, like any other in her life. Eric, clad in a sleek black suit, had styled his light brown hair back and wore a charming smile. Once a source of comfort for Amelia, the smile now seemed a hollow facade. His fingers gently curled around the door handle as he flicked his hair back.

"Do not wait for me today, darling," he began, his voice gentle. "I was informed of an important, lengthy meeting upon waking. I will likely return very late, and I wouldn't want you to stay up on my account. We can talk tomorrow. I love you." He acted as if everything was fine, still playing the part of the faithful husband. It was nauseating. He casually professed his love in a bid to allay Amelia's growing suspicions. Yet, the mysterious phone calls, the secretive attitude, his unannounced and sudden work travels and meetings were all proof of him living a double life. It was revolting to her how he could do this without remorse, turning words of love into a tool to manipulate her.

Amelia locked eyes with him. His emerald eyes no longer glowed with love and desire; they were empty. Tired and indifferent. That was when she knew her suspicions were valid.

"That's what I'll do, my dear," she replied calmly, forcing a weary chuckle. However, she couldn't bring herself to respond to his love affirmation, and she had no plans to sleep early.

Once the door shut, Amelia moved to the window of their seventh-floor apartment. She watched as Eric hurried to his car; once he was out of sight, she let a tear fall before collapsing to the floor in sobs.

She knew he no longer loved her, and she was aware of his dalliances. She understood the extent of her husband's betrayal. Amelia could discern it just by looking into those once loving eyes, a talent that was now more painful than helpful. Once she had accepted the truth, the signs were evident to her: his nervousness when asked about his day, his insistence on laundering his own clothes, his perpetually silenced phone, his overcompensation when he wronged her, and the most telling sign—his vacations.

Whenever one of his affairs threatened to become serious, he would use the excuse of needing to travel for business—to meet with other executives, sign contracts, discuss plans. He would always leave after lavishing Amelia with gifts, from flowers to jewellery, and sharing a night together. When she would wake up the following morning, he'd already be gone, making no attempts to contact her. The painful thread of hope for Amelia was that he always returned. She clung to the belief that some part of him still loved her.

His vacations left a bitter taste in Amelia's mouth. In the five years since Eric started his affairs, she managed to remember a few names of his many paramours, though some were so fleeting and elusive that she eventually forgot. There was Layla, the blonde angel who charmed her husband for a few short months; Angeline, a famous brunette model; and Marina, his Italian ex-colleague who had the audacity to show up at their door.

Marina was the one who confirmed the affair, admitting without any semblance of guilt how he had seduced her, repeatedly promising a forthcoming divorce. Marina confessed it took her six months to finally recognize and act upon his web of lies, and deep down, Amelia resented her own inability to do the same.

What was Amelia to do in such a situation? Offer empty consolation she didn't believe? Could she tell Marina that in her cheating husband's game, Marina was only a temporary pawn? She couldn't lie and claim that Eric loved Marina. Or tell her the truth that he loved none of them. Even though Amelia wanted to believe Eric's heart still held love for her, she was noticing as months passed that he only loved his opulent cars, and Amelia's paintings which paid for lavish vacations and luxurious homes. Her paintings were sold in famous galleries all across the world under a pseudonym, and she knew it was only the beginning of her career as a painter. Her agent was the one arranging and leading potential customers to her paintings, and he was very certain that she would become one of the most famous painters in the world.

After a flurry of painful memories, she confessed to Marina: "My dear, I can't do anything because I'm not supposed to know anything. I wasn't surprised when you told me because I'd already figured it out myself. I don't believe Eric will ever marry you. That's just who he is—a perpetual adventurer who only returns to me for the comfortable life we've built and, perhaps, because he still sees some value in me."

Her words were harsh, cutting through the younger woman's heart, but she had already consumed a fair amount of vodka to dull the pain caused by her husband. Marina had arrived prepared to convince Amelia to divorce Eric, but she would leave with teary eyes and a broken heart, Amelia's cold glances reminding her once again that she had known about their affair all along. After they talked for a few more minutes, the heartbroken woman left the apartment, calling Eric to break up with him. She cursed him, insulted him, and blocked his number.

To the casual observer, they seemed the ideal couple—the tall, slender, dreamy painter wed to the handsome and influential CEO of a prominent company. However, their marriage in truth, was anything but ideal.

Why had she tolerated all this? Her sister had almost persuaded Amelia to divorce him, but she loved Eric. She held on to the hope of his redemption, believing he would change. The only thing that did change, however, was her. At thirty-four years old, she longed for simpler times when she, an optimistic and lively young woman, would joyfully sing with her husband in her art studio or laugh while chasing Eric and their dog, now long passed, through open fields. Why had she turned to smoking and drinking, unable to laugh or to numb her feelings? Why had she fallen so far? Once, she had danced with friends on tabletops until they collapsed into each other's arms. Now, she found the very concept of dance ridiculous.

The Amelia of old had died on one of those nights when insomnia had taken hold and she'd taken to drinking to dull the pain, to fall asleep without being plagued by nightmares and heartache. She'd go through packets of cigarettes, oblivious to the harm she was doing to herself. Her skin, once perfectly tanned from vacations on sun-drenched luxury islands, had turned pale.

As Amelia lay in bed, finishing a bottle of vodka, she found herself contemplating the relationship. Why had he changed? Everything had been so sweet when they were both faithful. They were so in love with each other, relishing each moment spent together. Leaving for work was a pain for Eric because it meant being away from Amelia. Yet, they always found time for each other afterward, regardless of when his shift ended. Even if it was eleven pm or two am, they found places to go. Amelia's icy blue eyes welled up with tears, her vision blurring as she forced herself to stifle her crying with a hand over her mouth.

The doorbell rang.

Upon opening the door, she was met by an older woman dressed in black, her head bowed. The stranger lifted her gaze, her smoky eyes fixing on Amelia, and extended her hand.

"You only have one chance. Come with me, I want to show you something," the woman said without a greeting or other pleasantries, grasping her hand. Although Amelia heard the words clearly, she noticed that the woman's lips hadn't moved. Taken aback, she didn't react. At that moment, the air around her swirled, inducing in her a mild dizziness. Blinking, she found herself in an entirely different place, part spectator and part participant in a bizarre dance unfolding before her eyes. The medieval bridge she found herself on, made of smoothed stone, spanned a turbulent river. Two of the turrets supporting the bridge had already collapsed, providing a clear view of a forest in the distance. The bridge they were on groaned under the weight of the dancers engaged in wild abandon, a bridge crying out like a child under the sound of thousands of feet.

Next to her, a woman clad in a black bonnet paired with a woollen dress, collapsed from exhaustion, having succumbed to the intensity of the peculiar dance, uncoordinated and scary at the same time. It was as if they were puppets furiously manipulated by an unseen hand. Around her, scores, perhaps hundreds, of people engaged in the frenzied dance, some teetering on the brink of collapse, their exhaustion evident in their strained eyes. Amelia, too, was dancing, unable to stop, her legs moving involuntarily beneath her dark brown dress. She wore a pair of leather espadrilles that seemed to be on the verge of tearing apart at the seams. How many hours, or even days, had she been dancing? Amelia pondered, trapped in this body, ensnared in another era.

"Meuse, Meuse," a tall, thin man with a merchant-like countenance bellowed, gesturing towards the deep waters. He seemed to be trying to show the others a path to salvation. Amelia realized that she had been transported through time, experiencing firsthand the Dance of Death epidemic. She had learned about it in college: as far as she remembered, it had taken place in Medieval Europe around the year 1200. Although there had been many speculations about its cause, the mystery surrounding this strange disease, this "Dancing Plague," still lingered.

Doctors of those times called it choreomania, from the Greek "choros," which meant dance, and "manie," madness. Historians theorized that the dancers had been poisoned with a hallucinogenic mushroom, or that they were possessed by evil spirits. The music, it was rumoured, was only audible to them, and they would dance to it to their deaths.

Amelia also knew that the stone bridge over the Meuse would eventually buckle under the weight of the dancers. Over two hundred people were trapped there, would die there, caught in a ceaseless, wild dance. Some of them were dressed in vibrantly coloured clothing made of heavy silks and velvets, adorned with precious buttons. Their noble lineage was evident, even as they leaned on wooden canes for support in the dance. But their eyes told the real story—frightened, wild, terrified that they couldn't stop.

To her right, a child swayed precariously over the thick stone balustrade of the bridge. He fainted and was about to topple over when Amelia, with two quick steps, reached out and pulled him towards her. The teenager's lips moved in a silent murmur of thanks, but his voice was inaudible over the clamour.

She guided him towards the end of the bridge, dancing with him, weaving through the crowd of despairing people and overwhelming odours. Waiting at the end of the bridge was the mysterious stranger who, upon seeing Amelia reach solid ground with the boy, nodded approvingly. Taking her by the hand, the stranger whisked her away

A different time, a different life.

Within moments, Amelia found herself in a room of a hospital ward. Large, expansive windows were shrouded by heavy, dark curtains while beds lined the perimeter of the space. The room's gray walls and the nauseatingly clinical scent which hung heavily in the air exacerbated the eeriness of the setting.

In front of her, a figure lay prone, shrouded in bed sheets and barely able to keep her eyes open. It was an older woman who turned her face to look at Amelia. The sight of the woman made Amelia's heart lurch, her breath hitch in her throat. The woman was a mirror image of herself, an older, frailer, and sadder version of Amelia. It was like looking at her own reflection, but aged and weathered by time. The elderly woman's silver hair was unkempt, her face was ashen, and her eyes told a story of unutterable sorrow. In a few seconds, Amelia realized the woman couldn't see her, emboldening her to draw nearer to the bed. A rusty sink sat adjacent to the bed, filled with shards of glass from a shattered mirror above. Amelia moved to stand in front of it, but her reflection was conspicuously absent in the fragmented glass. She was a phantom.

The woman's behaviour oscillated between eerie silence and bouts of uncontrollable laughter. One moment, she'd be muttering to herself; the next, she'd be humming an old song from her youth, her hands fiddling with the blanket over her body. It was as if Amelia was peering into her own madness, a frightening prospect that left her shaken. "How did I end up like this?" she asked herself, horrified at the prospect of a future steeped in self-abasement and loss of sanity. Was this to be her inescapable fate?

Before she could contemplate more deeply, the door swung open. In walked a man whose charm was undiminished by age. He was accompanied by a woman too young to be his wife, their intimacy palpable. This was not his daughter; this was the husband's not-so-secret mistress. The stark contrast between the decaying wife and the still virile husband was jarring.

"We came to visit you, my dear Amelia," the man spoke in Eric's soothing tones. He seated himself by the old woman's bed. "I need you to sign some papers. I'm going to be your legal guardian after your latest mental breakdown."

Despite the warmth of his voice, Amelia knew that the warmth in his heart had long since fled. "I'm going to sell the house. It's too big, and the costs are excessive. I've also brought something to help stabilize you. Take them before signing," Eric continued, his words dripping with faux concern as he rummaged through his pockets.

Finally, he withdrew a small black box, revealing the contents: a collection of red and green pills that were all too familiar to Amelia. She had seen the same drugs during a dark period in her sister's life after she lost her child. There was Clinadil, a potent hallucinogen, Osforon, an antidepressant that could numb the senses, and Lysin, a powerful sedative. She finally understood the true extent of her pathetic condition—she was perpetually drugged by her husband, kept in a mental asylum, allowing him to do as he pleased.

Flooded with a torrent of emotions, Amelia resolved to alter the trajectory of her life and her future. It became clear to her that Eric had found a new woman and, instead of divorcing Amelia, he had opted for this insidious scheme. It all boiled down to her wealth, which made her view Eric with fresh disdain. The man had his own money, his own wealth. However, he was reluctant to spend any of his money, while also being greedy and desiring everything.

However, she couldn't decipher how she had fallen so low. How had she ended up confined in a bleak asylum, all alone?

What had triggered the mental breakdown that led to her being institutionalized?

She could not arrive at any conclusion, for the floor beneath her started to give way; in a matter of seconds, she was swallowed by an engulfing void.

When she reopened her eyes, she was greeted by the warmth of the sun. Before her lay a verdant field bathed in the golden hues of dusk. Children frolicked nearby while a woman, clad in a luxurious white dress, admired the scenery. A tall young lady walked up to the woman in white and took her hand. Upon turning, Amelia found herself looking at a face so familiar, yet so foreign. It took her a moment to recognize the woman as an older version of herself, exuding happiness and contentment that filled Amelia with a profound sense of joy.

Anyone comparing the woman they saw in the asylum with the one standing before them now would insist they couldn't possibly be the same person.

The two women walked towards a large table. A man caught Amelia's attention; his warm, pleasant demeanour was immediately inviting. His gaze was so full of affection it left her at a loss for words. As they wrapped their arms around each other, the youngest children finally settled at the table. The scene was a vision of a different future—one that was joyful and serene.

Which future was real? In one, she was dying in an asylum, lost in her own thoughts and drugged by Eric. In the other, she was surrounded by children, grandchildren, and a loyal partner.

"You only have one chance," echoed the woman's voice in her head. Hearing this, Amelia understood the gravity of the choice that lay before her. Her future hinged on the decisions she made in the present.

When she awoke, she found herself in her own house, her reflection grinning back at her from the windowpane. She knew exactly what she had to do next—confront her husband and demand a divorce. She was ready to let him go, to chase the future where she was surrounded by the love of her children and grandchildren.

The day came when Eric returned home, visibly

uninterested, and wearing formal clothes. Amelia approached him confidently, her will unshaken, with one goal in mind.

"I have decided that I want a divorce" She spoke firmly while gazing at him, reading his familiar body language. The man seemed startled, but he did not falter in the face of such a decision.

"My dear, I'm afraid such a decision is one I cannot accept. I love you. I have wronged you, and I wish to prove myself to you, if you would allow me to." Eric pleaded with a soft voice as he approached Amelia. The man grabbed her chin and caressed it with his thumb as his index finger kept it lifted. Amelia wanted to believe him, she wanted back what they had all those years ago. He seemed sincere, but it was all a facade. The hardness in his eyes was all too familiar to her.

"No. Eric, it is over. I am deeply sorry for how things turned out." Amelia continued with the same certitude, even as a part of her still clung to hope that her husband, the one she knew, was still there.

"You're not doing this to me, Amelia! Can't you see you are being unreasonable?!" Eric scoffed and let go of her chin. That was when Amelia came to accept the reality of the situation. Eric wasn't the man she once knew, but Amelia wasn't the woman he once knew, either. "If you and I get a divorce, it's over for you. You will never have the life you have with me now!" The man raised his voice, and Amelia was disgusted by his words. She expected him to manipulate her, but that just made her more certain than ever of her decision.

"My decision is final. It's over, Eric." Amelia stated, and as the man became increasingly threatening, Amelia made her final argument: "I will call the police and ask for a restraining order if you harass me in any way. No threats and no violent gestures. And don't forget, dear Eric, about our prenuptial agreement: you could lose everything we've made together, the joint assets, if I bring proof of your infidelity." Eric said nothing more, he realized that the woman in front of him was very determined.

Amelia was certain she had made the right choice. Her biggest fear had always been living a comfortable lie. Now, she embraced the painful truth, starting the year with a metaphorical cold plunge for the greater good. Soon after their agreement, she was driving back home from her lawyer's office. When a judge finally ruled in her favour, Amelia's decision became reality. Amelia knew the pain she felt now would eventually be a distant memory. Her reverie was broken by a sudden jolt. The car in front of her had failed to change lanes, causing a minor collision with her vehicle. The driver exited his car and under the glare of the headlights, Amelia recognized him—he was the man from her peaceful future, the one who had held her in his arms. Despite the circumstances, a feeling of warmth washed over her.

Amelia smiled with renewed hope, just days after finally parting ways with her husband. Standing under the falling snow-flakes, she thanked the woman who had given her a glimpse into her alternate futures. As Amelia spoke with the driver about their minor accident, the image of her confined in a desolate asylum started to fade, replaced by a more promising future.

SEEING
IT
ALL

Kellee Kranendonk

Ever since I came back from Alusinar I've been able to see things.

You see, for every choice we make, there are alternate paths we could have chosen, each one having a different result. But sometimes we don't have a choice.

I see all the alternatives. It's like seeing your reflection in a broken mirror, each shard reflecting a version of you. Except these are real. Different planes of reality, different universes, I'm not sure. But I am sure that each person in each "piece of glass," each reality or universe, is as real as I am and is living her best life. Well, my life. And maybe not my best.

It's difficult to decide which is a best life when faced with so many versions. When I first realized the ability I had, I watched intently as they played out in front of me. There was always a better one, or a worse one. But they were all fascinating; I couldn't wait to see the next one. I barely slept at night, but I didn't care. It was like watching your favourite movies looped eternally.

I finally learned how to "turn it off." It's never really off, but

I figured out how to stop watching. I can't really describe how, not to anyone who's never had this experience. The best explanation might be that it's like learning a second language. You train yourself to recognize the sounds associated with certain symbols. The knowledge is always there, but it only comes out when you want or need it to.

Or maybe it's more like being an explorer, trained by the Air Force how to deal with varying life forms. You learn the rules of the how so well you can recite them in your sleep. Once you've done that, you can break them.

Maybe it's both of those things. All I know for sure is that now it's not as exciting. I sleep pretty good at night now that I don't **need** to see all the variations. Don't get me wrong, it's not that I don't enjoy it. It's just that it's not a movie marathon anymore. Rather, it's a part of me, just like breathing.

Let me tell you about a few of the ones I've seen. It's not like I have anything else to do, stuck here on planet Earth, in this loony bin, in the room with the white padded walls. In this universe, you all think I'm crazy, even though I know I'm not. Tell me what you think when I've finished.

In one universe, I'm on a planet called Scud. It has three moons, each one a different distance away. Two of them are colonized. The third, we're not sure about. My team and I are studying it.

I have three kids, grown in a lab because I wanted children, not a partner. I think I'm crazy in **this** universe—

The kids and I climb into our jitney and fasten our life belts. I program the route before it can ask. I wonder, not for the first time, why they can't make these things memorize daily routes.

I lean back and close my eyes while the kids bicker among themselves. Our morning norm.

The first stop is the girls' school. They're twins. That is, they're both the same age, and they've both tested to be trained in the lab technician field. But they don't share DNA. Audette has long blonde curls cascading down her back that she always wears loose, never tied up, has the purple-blue eyes that only a Scudian can have, and is tall for her age. She's quiet and overall quite a pleasant child.

Andel is the dramatic one. She keeps her straight brown hair cut short because "every time I brush it out, it just gets tangled again, and it's too hard to wash." Oh, the poor child. It's not like Audette doesn't struggle to keep her curls untangled and washed.

Audette quietly climbs out of the jitney, but Andel makes an emotional exit, as if this is the last time she'll see me for a long time. I take a moment to calm her, holding her face in my hands. I look into eyes that are black as night and remind her that I will be back to pick her up after school. I don't add that I do this every day, and that I've never not picked her and her sister up. If I say that, she'll just become even more dramatic. She may feel a bit inferior because she's shorter than Audette, but mostly I think it's just who she is: she enjoys drama and the attention it gains her.

Audette takes her sister's hand, and they head for the floating building that houses their school. I turn to my son, who is several birth-cycles older than his sisters. "Anesh, ready to join me at work today?"

"Yeah, anything is better than school. It's boring!" He looks at me with those same dark eyes that Andel has, excitement shining in them. He has the same straight brown hair as she does, but he chooses to wear it long and tied back with colourful bands. I guess **he** has no problems keeping it tangle-free.

I chuckle. He definitely gets his attitude from me. Not that I've ever voiced it, but I sure thought it when I was his age.

"This is going to be so cool," he says. "What planet are we studying?"

"We?" I cock an eyebrow at him.

"Isn't that why I'm coming with you? So **we** can study together?" He's not even a bit snarky. He's totally serious. And right, of course.

"Alusinar-M3. Have you talked about that one in school?"

When Anesh had done his skill testing, he fit into the same category as me. Scientist of Planet Studies. This is his last year of school training, largely consisting of field work. Like accompanying me to the planetarium.

"No," he says, responding to my question. "Because it's not inhabited."

"Right." I'd forgotten that. When I was in school, the dark moon (as it was called then, now it's called Valia-M2) wasn't inhabited, so we only studied Kor-M1.

"Well, you may be in for a treat."

We arrive at the Planetarium, and I attempt to save the route I'd taken today. I know better, but I'm determined to find a way to save it. Failing yet again, I power down the jitney, and we head in.

Inside, on my desk, I find an actual handwritten note in Scuddish, the common language on this planet. There are several others—I speak four of them—but the particular scientist who wrote this note only speaks the one. And she's fascinated with ancient techniques. No one has written anything by hand for at least three hundred birth-cycles, probably longer.

Check the 'scope. Call me and tell me what you think!!!

I get excited and head for the 'scope, as the note instructs. For a moment, I forget Anesh is with me. Then he says, "Mamae, what's that?"

I whirl back to him, slightly startled, and laugh. "That's a very old way of communication called handwriting." I know he can understand the words, but the concept itself is alien to him. He stares at the note, at the lines and loops, the smooth ink absorbed into the paper, trying to wrap his brain around it. I swear I can hear jitney gears grinding.

"She wants you to check the 'scope and call her. Why?"

"Let's find out!" I rush over and peer into the lens,

adjusting things as I try to see what my co-scientist wanted me to see. At first I don't see anything and am disappointed. What is it I'm supposed to see? I move the 'scope slightly. Surely she would have left it in position, but maybe she'd bumped it in her excitement without realizing it. It happens sometimes.

Then, I see it. My heart pounds with enthusiasm I can barely contain. "It's a structure. Brand new. Anesh, do you know what that means?"

"That there's life on Alusinar M-3?"

"One hundred per cent correct."

I pull the comconn out of my pocket and connect with sound only. I don't need to see her face—I know I'd see my own excitement reflected in it.

Anesh listens as we squeal like school children getting a free day when the weather's bad. He tries—and fails—to hide his own grin, but the exhilaration is too contagious.

"Santha, you've seen it?"

"I have."

"Are you willing to head up the team that'll be sent there?"

"Willing? I'm demanding to head up the team!"

She laughs. "I'll make the arrangements."

Anesh had been so jealous that I'd gotten to make this trip that he'd almost been angry. Of course, he understands why he can't accompany me and has settled for bragging to his class.

Although the structure on Alusinar M.3 suggests there's life, we fail to find anything. We'd searched first with our own senses—seeing the structure, smelling a sour earth kind of scent that hung heavy in the air, but hearing nothing. No people, birds or insects. I swear I **felt** something, not physical but sort of a whisper in the back of my mind. No one else did, though, so I think it must have been my imagination.

Our handhelds bleeped and flashed, but nothing registered. We even scooped some dirt, but other than a bacterium that barely registered, even that was lacking life forms. It seemed the trip was a bust.

Unfortunate because space travel is expensive, and if we don't find something, our funding might be revoked.

"There aren't any **other** structures," notes my teammate, Randa. Short and stocky with an almost perfect, blemish-free face, I mistook her for a child the first time I met her. She has the perfect shade of smooth lilac skin to match her purple-blue eyes. It makes me a little jealous because my skin is very light with sprinkles of violet freckles and my eyes are a dull blue.

Her statement is pointless and she knows it.

"But something, or someone, built this," I say. Another pointless statement.

I wander around the structure, a pyramidal shape with a domed top and short "arms" sticking out about mid-point from each side. It seems to be made from the very dirt it sits on. Alusinar M.3 is all thick, black dirt, which is easily moulded (our feet press into the ground leaving impressions, but our boots aren't muck-sucked) and foggy atmosphere. No trees, no grass, one moon and one sun, mostly obscured by the ever-present mist.

There doesn't seem to be a way in. No doors, no windows. Just walls and angles—if it **is** made of this dirt, I'm certain something has been added to strengthen it. Then, I notice something we'd all missed. Symbols. Carved or drawn onto the walls are symbols I don't recognize. Not as a language, nor as any kind of pictographs. The closest thing I can think of to describe them is many multi-fingered hands all intertwined.

I stand next to Randa studying the marks, and I reach out to trace one with my finger. As if touching something electrified, a spark leaps into the air and a tingle shoots up my arm. A million voices scream inside my head. I know they're saying words, but I can't make a single one out. Images of the symbols form in my mind, as if they'd come to life. They move, as if swaying in a wind.

Another spark sears my brain, and I find myself in the space jet, on my way home. Randa sits beside me.

"You're awake."

"Yeah. What happened to me?"

"You reached out to touch the structure and were knocked unconscious. Santha, you were barely breathing. I wasn't sure you were going to make it."

"Well, here I am," I joke. I don't remember anything.

Not yet. I will later, but by then our orders will be to study Alusinar M.3 via 'scope only. I won't be pleased about it, but there'll be nothing I can do.

A few months later our attentions turn elsewhere. We never did figure out who built the structure or what it was for. No others were built during the time we studied it. Alusinar M.3 is still on our radar, but if there's life there, it isn't showing itself. We have other planets to study. As for me, I'm fine. At least for the time being. Occasionally I get a flash memory of the images from the structure. I can't help but wonder if it was a warning of some kind.

My parents have passed on now, but at least they got to see me graduate from every institute I attended, got to hear all about my first space trip. I'm glad they're not here to see me sitting here in this white padded room. **They** would believe me.

I don't regret any of it, though. If I had the chance I'd still go to Alusinar. But I'd take the time to look around more, listen, do something, anything to understand what happened to me and why. Maybe then, my doctors wouldn't want me to take drugs to stop what they call "hallucinations." I tried to tell them I can control it, and when they didn't believe that, I told them the hallucinations had stopped. I don't think they believed that, either, because they still try to give me the pills.

I pretend to take them, but I hide them under my tongue. Later, I either flush them down the toilet or the sink, or I crush them into dust then sprinkle it into my leftover food. They haven't caught on. Yet. You're not going to tell them, are you? If anything is making me crazy, it's the doctors and nurses.

Why don't they understand? The whole point of space travel

is to meet new life forms. At least, for me it is. So what if one of those life forms is sharing space with my intelligence? Some human women share their bodies with an entire life form or two.

Do any of you care? Are you even listening? Can you hear me at all? I'm sorry that I don't have nice neat conclusions to my stories. It's because I don't know the endings. Not yet. They're like life, ongoing. Let me share another one.

Another shard. Another planet. Another life. My home planet in this reality is called Resh, but I don't live there.

I sit in the dining room of the space station and look out the window. From my position, I can see the planet Alusinar. It's uninhabited due to extremely dense cloud cover. That's our best guess, anyway. I mean, it's habitable, but who really wants to live in thick fog day in and day out? I have this strange sense about Alusinar, like I've been there, but I'm forgetting the trip (although that's not likely). It's like feeling nostalgia for a place you've never been. I don't understand it, myself, so I've never tried to explain it to anyone.

Still, it draws me, fascinates me. I have this burning desire to know everything there is to know about it. I've asked some of the races that have joined us here about it, but none of them know any more about it than we do, and so far, we haven't taken a great interest in it. Not when there are so many other planets surrounding the station with races that come here to mingle every day.

Sometimes, I miss my home planet, my friends and my family (Mom, Dad, siblings; I'd never married nor had kids). But then, I remind myself that I'd chosen this path. I'd wanted to come here, to study planets and other life forms. It usually doesn't take much to convince myself I'm living my best life here.

"Hey, Santha!"

"Care to share those thoughts?"

My friends Trinda and Ranesh join me at the table. Like me, Trinda is tall. Unlike me, she has very curvy curves and, like most Reshers, she has long luxurious black hair which offsets her pink skin. Me, I ended up with pale hair which offsets nothing. Because it's not common, most people say I'm lucky. I guess I probably am, but not because of my hair.

Ranesh is not from Resh, although people like to make silly rhymes with his name that suggests he is. He's actually from Earth, from a place called India. He tells me not everyone on that planet has his beautiful chocolate brown skin, and I think that's sad. I also think I could fall in love with Ranesh if he had that kind of interest in me. He has a partner, though.

Maybe some day I'll be lucky enough to visit India on Earth and meet another human being as beautiful as Ranesh.

They're each carrying a tray of colourful food. They enjoy trying the various alien foods available here. Me, not so much. I generally stick to the food I know.

Ranesh's tray has blue and red foods, the ones from Oreth that are supposed to be the healthiest food in the galaxy (his boyfriend is Orethian). There's noshok, which is all blue plant matter, mashed into glop.

He also has a chunk of red bramist meat, a blue ruzza-fruit for dessert, and a tall glass of red juice that I've never learned the name for.

Trinda is the absolute opposite, with her tray full of odd food, what Ranesh calls junk food. Yellow root chips fried in the oil of your choice, and bright green, sour, shivery jio for dessert. Her drink of choice is a thick sweet drink called chokshara. I'm not sure where that stuff was brought in from, but I know she'll taunt Ranesh as she dramatically savours each mouthful. He, in turn, will "lecture" her about eating healthier, though Ranesh will eat odd food on occasion. Neither of them is antagonistic, they just enjoy their friendly little game.

"Let me guess," says Ranesh. "Still dreaming about Alusinar."

I laugh. He knows me so well.

"Maybe," says Trinda, "you lived there in a previous life."

I nod. "That or maybe I'm there in another dimension."

Ranesh snorts. "You two actually believe in reincarnation and other dimensions."

"No one can prove they are or are not real," I tell him as he spoons some blue plant goo into his mouth. "Is that good?" I want to change the subject.

He pauses a moment, maybe to decide if he wants to play along. Then he nods. "Looks weird, but tastes exquisite." He grins and holds out his eating utensil. "Try it?"

I hesitantly grasp the spoon and take a tiny bite. He's right. "It's delicious, but the texture feels like I'm eating coagulated blood."

Trinda grimaces but Ranesh just shrugs. You could tell him he's eating shit-encrusted alien intestines, or it could have the consistency of a dead sea slug, and all he'd say is, "Well, it tastes great!" Especially if it's considered a health food.

We finish our meals and go back to our posts. I'm logging some data when a leschkin approaches me. The leschki are a race that have at least four genders. There may be more, but it's difficult to tell since they all wear "lizard" armour which, in their opinion, makes them appear more formidable to unfriendly races. They're also not very forthcoming about personal preferences, which suits me just fine.

The armour resembles a green, overlarge lizard, so this particular leschkin towers over my 1.7 metre frame. Without the armour, they're about half my size. I have yet to see any more than a metre tall.

When they speak, I recognize the voice as a female—which I've learned is not quite the same gender as I am—by the name of Esh. What I know about h'er gender is confusing, so I won't try to explain, but I think in my own mind I've got it right.

"There's an activity on Alusinar," s'he says. "It has been going for the day, but I wanted to be sure it was something to continue before I came to report. Because that planet is not one we are particular about."

H'er grasp of common is slightly tinged by h'er own language, but I understand h'er meaning. I go with h'er to the observation room. I enjoy observing. I've been asked to accompany teams before, but I'm prevented from doing so by an irrational fear of stepping onto a strange planet and meeting a being that is so not humanoid that I can't recognize their species, damaging or insulting them. But Alusinar has fascinated me for long enough that it might be the place to get me to challenge that fear.

On the screen, a structure is being built. At first neither I nor Esh can tell who, or what the builders are. It seems the structure is appearing out of thin air.

"Esh, are we doing that?"

"No. I have had exchanges with Captain Taron, and he has made reports to me that we are not responsible."

Of course not. S'he would have told me that earlier, if I hadn't already been informed as the work started. We watch for a while; I take mental notes. "When will—" I start, but Esh cuts me off.

"I see it now. Look!" S'he magnifies the screen. Points. Magnifies again. Then, I see it as well. What we had thought to have been fog is made up of lifeforms. At this magnification, we can see the co-operative swirls and thick streams of mist. They pull and push the earth into formation, creating walls.

My heart drops to my feet. This irrational fear of not recognizing a life form has just come true. It lifts as I realize I'm here and they're there. I haven't insulted them by not being able to identify them. Excitement floods me.

"I am getting report teams together now," Esh says, interrupting my thoughts. S'he's on h'er way out of the room. "You are staying here now for more information." It sounds more commanding than it is; it's just h'er way with words, so I take no offense.

As I watch, thin mists form dense lines to carve symbols into the walls. I can't quite make them out though, and what I can make out (hands?) I don't recognize as language. I'm certain it means something more to them than to me.

I'm excited for teams to form, to get over there and bring back photos and better intel. Will we make a new ally? An enemy? I'm also excited—and frightened—to think that I may be able to accompany a team and put this phobia out of its misery. Conflicted, I can't hold it together. I leave my post to go find Esh and the Captain.

So do you see now? On Scud I may very well be living my best life with my kids, and getting to visit unknown planets. On Resh's Space Station, I may be getting to take that first exciting trip and extinguishing a useless dread. But here?

Here on Earth, no one believes the fog of Alusinar is made up of life forms. They think living beings need two legs, two arms; life forms don't look like mist and vapour. I can't make anybody understand.

But I hear them as well.

Yeah, I don't just see all the possibilities, I can sometimes hear the Alusinarians in my head, as if they're beckoning me back. I think it's possible the structure they've built in other universes is meant to take me back to them in some way; that, unlike us, their realities mesh together somehow (is that what the hand-like symbols represent?). Have they built a structure on this reality's Alusinar? I suspect they have. I'll never know if I can't get back there.

Yet what those misty life forms don't understand is that it won't work; it's just not that simple for me, a mere human being.

So, **now** tell me, Doctors, do you think I'm crazy?

JURASSIC DINOMANCY

Rosie Smith

My feet plopped down onto the soft brown sand of the Montana coast. "Wow, we made it," I burbled. Okay, not exactly a memorable line up there with "one small step for man." No worries. When I go back home, I will come up with something that my devoted fans, and maybe even my more-numerous occasional followers on social media, will gobble up.

With a quick glance in all directions, Dr. Crundworth said to me, "Safety first, Dora. I am serious. If we run into any trouble, you must get yourself back to the twenty-first century immediately. No hesitating." He pointed to my chrono-porter. "You be sure to keep that strapped on your wrist." Patting a zippered pocket of his freshly-ironed safari vest, he added, "Mine is right in here. Not that I've ever had to make a hasty exit from the Jurassic." He ran a hand through what might once have been a full head of perfectly-groomed hair. "You picked one of the most experienced dinomancers in the business."

Dinomancer, huh? How was this anything more than a grandiose title for a tour guide? I thought better of asking him

118

for fear he might tell me. At length. The man could not help sharing all the finer points of his chosen profession, which I had found, at first, to be reassuring. I had done a ton of meticulous research and even contacted a couple of Jurassic Dinomancy's satisfied clientele. In the end, I hired the most expensive tour operator out there, not that there were very many. It would be foolish to skimp when personal safety was vital.

"You see," Dr. Crundworth continued, "it takes someone who knows the habits of the local species thoroughly to make sure you stay safe as you observe the fine creatures of the Jurassic. You want to see a brontosaurus? Or a herd of stegosauruses?" Not waiting for my response, he plunged onward as he led me a short distance along the beach to a rank stream—more sludge than water—which snaked into the seaway. "Of course, you do. Everybody loves the biggest dinosaurs. I will take you to the most reliable viewing spots upstream."

Peering between the head-high ferns populating the stream bank, I said, "Actually, I'm interested in allosaurus."

"Isn't everyone?" My guide gave me a knowing smile. "Don't get your hopes up. Apex predators are significantly scarcer than most people suppose. That is a good thing."

No, it is not. "I came to watch it give a ferocious roar. From a good, safe distance." I switched on my top-of-the-line recorder, which I wore as a body cam. I relished the thought of the zillions of new followers I was sure to attract by becoming the first person to ever capture those great beasts uttering their never-before-recorded bellows. I am sure to have it made the minute I incorporate them into my next exclusive indie offering. "They say it's terrifying."

"I have never seen or heard one roar. Not in four years of dinomancy. Why would it?"

I guessed, "To shout how it's the biggest, meanest bad-ass to stomp into a clearing and terrorize the plant munchers?"

He snorted. "A common misperception." His condescending attitude reminded me of a lot of the over-educated men in my grandfather's generation.

From the opposite side of the stream came the sounds of several big beasts crashing through chest-high ferns and splintering the cycads. I turned to point my recorder in their direction.

"Stegosauruses," the dinomancer proclaimed. Three adults, each as tall as an eighteen-wheeled tractor trailer, waddled into view, followed by a handful of juveniles. They made short work of chowing down on the undergrowth; they were like moss-green Mesozoic mowing machines with atrocious table manners. "Look at the size of their thigh muscles."

I nodded, monitoring the recorder's feed.

"If an allosaurus bellowed, or even let out a low growl, the herd would be on the far side of Laurasia before you got half-way through your first scream. That carnivore is a masterful stalker. It puts tigers to shame. We will not see an allosaurus, Dora, unless it lets us."

"And if we do?"

"Unless we are extraordinarily fortunate, that will be the last thing we are likely to ever see."

I took in his sombre expression. "Well, what about hearing it roar, off in the distance?" I was not about to give up my dream of being the first to capture the predator's much-rumoured soul-chilling cries.

"I am afraid not. Uninformed dinomancers will tell you the male bellows to attract prospective mates, or to intimidate the competition. Or even to demarcate the limits of his territory. Stuff and nonsense, all of it. We are not even certain we know the size of a single individual male's territory." By now, he had fully warmed to his subject and entered venerable-professor mode. I pictured his irreverent students doing snarky imitations. The man could not even hold the interest of the stegasauruses. They lumbered away.

"Do the females roar—to summon their young, maybe?" I would not and could not go back into the studio with no new material.

"Well, Dora, the females supposedly have the loudest

voices. Not surprising, huh?"

I gave him a glare.

"Hey, it was a joke." He reached for my arm to guide me around the trunk of a cycad that had fallen across the game trail.

I evaded his grasp and resisted the urge to let a monster fern frond swat the man's chest. Farther upstream, after I found myself grinding my teeth while enduring his discourse on stegosaurus dentition, we came to a trough gouged into the mud bank. It held a clutch of eggs like big blue cantaloupes.

"Brontosaurus eggs." The dinomancer pronounced.

"Really? I read that they are supposed to be tan, to blend in with the dirt."

"Paleontologists used to think so, but recent discoveries, like this one, support the blue-egg hypothesis."

"Where is Mama Brontosaur?" I peered into the green maze of ferns.

"The females may leave their eggs untended for brief periods. Oh yes, that is well established." My guide chattered on —way more than anyone could want to know as to how an expectant brontosaurus selects the right patch of mud for egg laying. I resigned myself to a full afternoon of his dino-splaining. When it got to be too much, I could insist that he shut up so I could capture the whuffles of the stegosauruses, if they ever came back, or maybe other Jurassic dinosaurs would amble our way.

Dr. Crundworth leaned out over the bank and gestured to emphasize a point. The soft mud gave way. He tumbled into the muddy stream, splattering primordial ooze.

I bit back my laughter. "Are you okay?"

He squelched up the crumbling bank, strands of aquatic vines adorning his no-longer impeccable hair, and gave me a sour look. I ducked my head and checked the main camera and volume level on my recorder, suddenly aware that the wilderness had gone silent. I shoved the device back into position and twisted around to glimpse a flash of movement in the ferns.

The foliage erupted with a flurry of talons and teeth. With a yelp, Dr. Crundworth yanked at the grime-coated zipper of his sodden safari vest. It was stuck. An enormous jaw came down like a hatchet. My guide leaped backward. For a second time, he tumbled into the stream.

The predator, an allosaurus, swung its head to stare straight at me. Those were the longest seconds of my life—and my last ones, I had been sure. My heart pounded. My legs shook. I dove for the ground, too frantic to see anything. Seconds later, the dinosaur's carrion breath engulfed me. I rolled away and found myself tumbling down the embankment. I ploughed into Dr. Crundworth. He flailed, whacking me with an out flung arm. I seized his wrist. Steak-knife teeth bore down to spear us. With my other hand, I switched on my chrono-porter. Its hum was drowned out by the great beast's soul-crushing bellow.

That roar cut off as the predator vanished. So did the river. There we were, back in the wilds of modern-day Montana. I blinked in astonishment.

"Let go!" Wide-eyed, the dinomancer wrenched his wet wrist from my grip. We stared at each other, shaking wordlessly.

All I could think of was how close we had come to a gruesome end. My legs wobbled. I let myself sink to the treeless, hard-packed ground, conscious of my recorder still running. Some impulse made me tap replay. My fingers trembled badly as I skipped forward to the moment after we had examined the brontosaurus eggs, when the allosaurus was upon us. The recorder had captured everything: those foul-smelling teeth, the terrifying roar, our desperation, all of it.

My heart pounded again. "No!" I stabbed the off button, swearing to myself never to play it again, much less use the recording in any indie offering. No, not ever. I shuddered, not knowing that I was to see it all again. Over and over upon waking in the darkest hours of the night, drenched in sweat.

My feet plopped down onto the soft brown sand of the Montana coast. "Wow, we made it," I burbled. okay, not exactly a memorable line up there with "one small step for man." No worries. When I go back home, I will come up with something that my devoted fans, and maybe even my more-numerous occasional followers on social media, will gobble up.

"Woo hoo!" Dr. Crundworth exclaimed. "We sure did. I have to remind you, if we run into any trouble, you must get yourself back to the twenty-first century immediately. Do not worry about me." He pointed to my chrono-porter. "You be sure to keep that strapped on your wrist, Dora." Patting an un-zippered pocket of his wrinkled safari vest, he added, "Mine is right in here."

"Shouldn't you keep it zipped up?"

He shrugged. "I've never had to cut and run from the Jurassic." He ran a hand through his full head of unkempt hair. "You picked the best dinomancer there is."

Dinomancer, huh? How was he anything more than a self-aggrandizing tour guide? I thought better of asking him, not wanting to seem rude. Of course, I had done enough research to know that Jurassic Dinomancy was a start-up with only a couple of short, unhelpful reviews. The company's rates were reasonable, and I could hardly afford the top-of-the-line outfit. Naturally, I was not about to take a chance on some cut-rate operation, not when personal safety was a consideration.

"You see," Dr. Crundworth continued, "it takes a sharp-eyed, sharp-eared dinomancer to lead you to the finest creatures in all of the Jurassic. You want to see a brontosaurus? Or a herd of stegosauruses?" Not waiting for my response, he plunged onward as he led me a short distance along the beach to a rank stream—more sludge than water—which snaked into the sea-way. "Of course, you do. People can't get enough of 'em. I know the prime viewing spots."

Peering between the head-high ferns populating the stream bank, I said, "Actually, I'm interested in allosaurus."

"You and me both." My guide frowned. "Big, fierce predators are way scarcer than people imagine."

"I came to watch it give a ferocious roar. From a good, safe distance." I switched on my old, reliable recorder, which I wore as a body cam. I relished the thought of the zillions of new followers I was sure to attract by becoming the first person to ever capture those great beasts uttering their never-before-recorded bellows. I am sure to have it made the minute I incorporate them into my next exclusive indie offering. "They say it's terrifying."

"Never seen or heard one roar. They say it doesn't. Why would it?"

I guessed, "To shout how it's the biggest, meanest bad-ass to stomp into a clearing and terrorize the plant munchers?"

He snorted. "You think so?" Dr. Crundworth's smartest-man-in-the room attitude reminded me of my ex.

From the opposite side of the stream came the sounds of several big beasts crashing through chest-high ferns and splintering the cycads. I turned to point my recorder in their direction.

"Stegosauruses," the dinomancer proclaimed. Three adults, each as tall as an eighteen-wheeled tractor trailer, waddled into view, followed by a handful of juveniles. They made short work of chowing down on the undergrowth; they were like moss-green Mesozoic mowing machines with atrocious table manners. "See those mega-muscles on their haunches?"

I nodded while monitoring the recorder's feed.

"If an allosaurus bellowed, or even growled, the herd would be hundreds of miles away before you got half-way through your first scream. That carnivore is a master stalker. We will not see it, Dora, unless it lets us. That will be too late."

"No roaring?" I was not about to give up my dream of being the first to capture the predator's much-rumoured soul-chilling cries.

"Nope. Ignorant guides think the male bellows to attract females, or to scare off the competition. Or even to mark his territory. They have no clue."

Just as I raised my recorder to get a good image of the stegosauruses whuffling, they turned and lumbered away. "Do the females roar – to summon their young, maybe?" I would not and could not go back into the studio with no new material.

"Well, Dora, some say the females have louder voices. Nobody knows why." He reached for my arm to guide me around the trunk of a cycad that had fallen across the game trail.

I evaded his grasp, hoping he would get the message that I can walk without his assistance. Farther upstream we came to a trough gouged into the mud bank. It held a clutch of eggs like big blue cantaloupes.

"Ooh, look!" The dinomancer's eyes glittered. "Brontosaurus eggs."

"Really? I read that they are supposed to be tan, to blend in with the dirt."

"Could be." He shrugged. "Never saw any before."

"No? Just how many times have you come here?"

"A few." Seeing my sceptical look, he crossed his arms. "What difference does it make?"

Ugh. I wished I had done more research. Looking at him carefully, it occurred to me that the photo of Dr. Crundworth on Jurassic Dinomancy's website had shown an older man. "Your company saddled me with an inexperienced guide. You are not Dr. Crundworth."

He spread his hands wide. "Hey, hey, I have absorbed all there is to know from my…from the senior dinomancer."

"Then tell me this: where is Mama Brontosaur? Is she going to show up any minute now?" I peered into the green maze of ferns.

"They say the females leave their eggs untended. I think."

"Let's hope so," I muttered.

Well…at least Not Crundworth was better than a guide who chattered on and on. I should be able to capture the whuffles of the stegosauruses, if they ever came back. I could wait for other Jurassic dinosaurs to amble our way. Not Crundworth leaned out over the bank and craned his neck. Maybe I had gotten him worried about Mama Brontosaur's whereabouts. The soft mud gave way. He tumbled into the muddy stream, splattering primordial ooze.

I bit back my laughter. "Are you okay?"

Not Crundworth squelched up the crumbling bank, strands

of aquatic vines adorning his unkempt hair, and gave me a sour look. He yanked at the grime-coated zipper of his safari vest, struggling out of it with more effort than it takes a caterpillar to turn into a butterfly. Meanwhile, I checked the main camera and volume level on my recorder, suddenly aware that the wilderness had gone silent. I shoved the device back into position and twisted around to glimpse a flash of movement in the ferns.

The foliage erupted with a flurry of talons and teeth. With a yelp, Not Crundworth dropped his sodden vest. An enormous jaw came down like a hatchet. My guide leaped backward. For a second time, he tumbled into the stream.

The predator, an allosaurus, swung its head to stare straight at me. Those were the longest seconds of my life—and my last ones, I had been sure. My heart pounded. My legs shook. I dove for the ground, almost too frantic to see anything except Not Crundworth's chrono-porter. I tossed it to him. "Catch!"

Seconds later, the dinosaur's carrion breath engulfed me. I rolled to one side as I mashed the panic button on my own chrono-porter.

Barely before steak-knife teeth would have speared me, the beast vanished. So did the river. There I was, back in the wilds of modern-day Montana. I blinked in astonishment. Shaking, I gasped for breath as I lay on the treeless, hard-packed ground. I sat up. Where was Not Crundworth? Any second now, he would appear.

I waited, conscious of my recorder still running. Fingers trembling badly, I tapped replay. It had captured everything. Everything except what I most wanted to see—Not Crundworth sitting beside me, making up something to sound convincing, or saying anything at all.

"No!" I shut it off, certain that I could never replay it again.

Except I did see it all again. Over and over upon waking in the darkest hours of the night. Drenched in sweat, I asked myself who Not Crundworth had been. Did he leave loved ones wondering what happened? Those questions wore on me until at last, I contacted Jurassic Dinomancy. Or rather, I tried to. The website said the business was closed. Nobody responded to my email or texts. The mailbox for the phone number was full. There was no street address to be found. I was at a loss until, out of the blue, I got a call from that number. I answered it.

"Good afternoon. This is Professor Morgan Crundworth." The accent reminded me of my grandpa. It was the voice of an old man, one accustomed to being addressed by his title. "Have I reached Dora…?" He paused as though searching for my last name.

"Yes, professor. It's me." My own voice sounded weak to my ears.

"This is by no means an easy call for me to make. I have reason to think you are the last person to set eyes on Germayne Crundworth. My son."

"Your **son**." I went cold. "I… I think you are right."

"I am searching… no, I am begging you… for anything you can tell me as to what happened to my Germayne. He disappeared with my pair of chrono-porters. If I can go after him—"

"No. Don't." I tried to say more and managed only, "I mean… it isn't any use… He isn't… I'm so sorry."

Professor Crundworth—the real Professor Crundworth— let out a moan, a sound that will haunt me always. I got a hold of myself and told him everything, except the fact that I had made a recording. I even babbled about yearning to change what happened in the past. Not that anybody can.

My feet plopped down onto the soft brown sand of the Montana coast. "Wow, we made it," I burbled. Okay, not exactly a memorable line up there with "one small step for man." No worries. When I go back home, I will come up with something that my devoted fans, and maybe even my more-numerous occasional followers on social media, will gobble up.

Dr. Crundworth did not look like he had heard me. "If we run into any trouble, you get yourself back to the twenty-first century immediately. No hesitating." He pointed to my chrono-porter. "You be sure to keep that strapped on your wrist, Dora." Patting an un-zipped pocket of his well-worn safari vest, he added, "Mine is right in here."

"Shouldn't you keep it zipped up?"

He shrugged. "It won't fall out. And I've never had any serious trouble here." He brushed a long strand of hair away from his eyes. It promptly resumed its accustomed position. "You picked a great dinomancer."

Dinomancer, huh? How was he anything more than a mere tour guide? I thought better of asking him, not wanting to seem rude. Of course, I had done my research. Why-oh-why didn't I pay more attention to those one-star and two-star reviews of Jurassic Dinomancy? Not that it mattered. I would have gone with the most affordable outfit anyway. My business credit cards were nearly maxed out, and I had staked a lot on this desperate idea paying off big time.

"You see," Dr. Crundworth continued, "it takes a sharp-eyed, sharp-eared dinomancer to lead you to the finest creatures in all of the Jurassic."

Hah, what does the tour guide matter? I'm here for the dinosaurs.

"You want to see a brontosaurus? Or a herd of stegosauruses?" Not waiting for my response, he plunged onward as he led me a short distance along the beach to a rank stream—more sludge than water—which snaked into the seaway. "Of course, you do. Everybody loves 'em. I know the best viewing spots."

Peering between the head-high ferns populating the stream bank, I said, "Actually, I'm interested in allosaurus."

"Isn't everyone?" My guide scowled. "Big, fierce predators are way scarcer than people imagine."

"I came to watch it give a ferocious roar. From a good, safe distance." I switched on my rehabbed recorder, which I wore as a body cam. I relished the thought of the zillions of new followers I was sure to attract by becoming the first person to ever capture those great beasts uttering their never-before-recorded bellows. I am guaranteed to have it made the minute I incorporate them into my next exclusive indie offering. "They say it's terrifying."

"Never seen or heard one roar. Not in a few years of dinomancy. Maybe it doesn't. Why would it?"

I guessed, "To shout how it's the biggest, meanest bad-ass to stomp into a clearing and terrorize the plant munchers?"

Dr. Crundworth snorted. "You think so?" His glib scepticism annoyed me.

From the opposite side of the stream came the sounds of several big beasts crashing through chest-high ferns and splintering the cycads. I turned to point my recorder in their direction.

"Stegosauruses," the dinomancer proclaimed. Three adults, each as tall as an eighteen-wheeled tractor trailer, waddled into view, followed by a handful of juveniles. They made short work of chowing down on the undergrowth; they were like moss-green Mesozoic mowing machines with atrocious table manners. "See those mega-muscles on their haunches?"

I nodded, monitoring the recorder's feed.

"If an allosaurus bellowed, or even growled, the herd would be hundreds of miles away before you got half-way through your first scream. That beast is a master stalker. You will not see it unless it wants you to. That's too late."

"No roaring?" I was not about to give up my dream of being the first to capture the predator's much-rumoured soul-chilling cries.

"Nope. Ignorant guides will tell you the male bellows to attract mates, or to intimidate the competition. Or even to demarcate his territory. The point is, nobody knows."

Just as I raised my recorder to get a good image of the stegosauruses whuffling, they turned and lumbered away. "Do the females roar – to summon their young, maybe?" I would not and could not go back into the studio with no new material.

"Well, Dora, the females supposedly have the loudest voices. Make of it what you will. Careful here." He led me around the trunk of a cycad that had fallen across the game trail.

"No problem." I took care not to let a monster fern frond

swat his chest. Farther upstream we came to a trough gouged into the mud bank. It held a clutch of eggs like big blue cantaloupes.

"Brontosaurus eggs," the dinomancer pronounced.

"Really? I read that they are supposed to be tan, to blend in with the dirt."

He shrugged. "I've only ever seen blue ones."

"Where is Mama Brontosaur? Is she going to show up any minute now?" I peered into the green maze of ferns.

"The females leave their eggs untended at times. Yes, really. We may well not see Mama Brontosaur."

Dang. "Well at least I should be able to capture the whuffles of the stegosauruses, if they ever come back."

"Or maybe other Jurassic dinosaurs will amble our way. You never can tell. Keep your eyes on that game trail over there." As he spoke, my guide leaned out over the bank and gestured to emphasize his point. The soft mud gave way. He tumbled into the muddy stream, splattering primordial ooze.

I bit back my laughter. "Are you Okay?"

The dinomancer squelched up the crumbling bank, strands of aquatic vines adorning the long hair hanging in front of his face. He yanked at the grime-coated zipper of his safari vest, struggling out of it with more effort than it takes a caterpillar to turn into a butterfly. Meanwhile, I checked the main camera and volume level on my recorder, suddenly aware that the wilderness had gone silent. Twisting around, I glimpsed a flash of movement in the ferns.

The foliage erupted with a flurry of talons and teeth. With a yelp, Crundworth dropped his sodden vest. An enormous jaw came down like a hatchet. My guide leaped backward. For a second time, he tumbled into the stream.

That left me to face the allosaurus. My heart pounded. My legs shook. I dove for the ground, almost too frantic to see anything. The dinosaur's carrion breath engulfed me. I seized the first thing that came to hand, the dinomancer's sopping safari vest. I flung it in the beast's face.

Steak-knife teeth snapped, slicing the fabric to ribbons.

From the carnivore's mouth came the distinctive hum of the chrono-porter activating. With a gulp, the allosaurus sent the device down its thick throat.

I rolled to one side. Plan B flashed into my head. I grabbed for Dr. Crundworth's hand, thinking to switch on my own chrono-porter once I got hold of him. He was too far away.

The predator swung its head to stare straight at me. Those were the longest seconds of my life—and my last ones, I had been sure—those seconds before the massive allosaurus lifted its snout and uttered a soul-crushing bellow. Its roar cut off as the beast vanished.

I blinked in astonishment.

Behind me, the dinomancer came scrambling out of the water on all fours. His hand darted forward to grab the chrono-porter on my wrist.

"No!" I pulled away. "Let's not follow that beast into present-day Montana."

He shook his head. "It can't get there. The chrono-porter has size and weight limits."

I was not so sure about that. "Maybe we'd better stay here for a while."

"You really want to wait for another allosaurus to show up?"

"You told me they are very scarce." I took off my recorder, which was still running, thinking to find out what it had captured.

"No!" He grabbed the device from my hand and switched it off. "You have no idea if your gadget might attract another allosaurus. We need to go back. Now."

I glanced at the forest. It had fallen silent again. This time, I let him grip my wrist and punch the emergency button. The chrono-porter hummed. Everything vanished. There we were, back in the wilds of modern-day Montana. Just the two of us lying on the treeless, hard-packed ground. That was the moment I realized he had dropped my recorder in the soft brown Jurassic sand.

CHASING BUTTERFLIES

Jeff Provine

When Jennifer left the shelter that night, she found a man in a long brown coat crying on the stoop.

She sighed. It had been a long day. They had all been long days, week after week, for three years since she started at the Page Miller Shelter for Those in Need. It seemed for every person she was able to clean up, find housing and a job, maybe even get into some classes, two new smudged faces appeared needing even more help.

Jennifer looked at the man in the brown coat's shaking shoulders. He took in a deep breath that rattled. Just walking away wasn't going to help anything, and something told her he needed her. Besides, there was something about him that seemed so familiar. Maybe he had been here before, and he still needed help.

The sun had set hours ago; she was the last out of the office, except for Joe, the night security guard. A chill blew in the wind. What was he going to do without her? He needed her.

Jennifer tightened her collar and sat down next to the man. "Hi, I'm Jennifer. What's the matter?"

The crying man looked up at her. His eyes were bright red; seeping even into his irises to make them a strange violet colour. His tear-soaked face sparkled in the streetlights. "I just want to go home."

"Yeah, me, too… Where is your home? How can I help?"

The man's lower lip shook. A fresh wave of shining tears poured over his cheeks. "I've tried to get you to help! I've tried everything I can think of!"

Jennifer studied him. He looked homeless with his mismatched clothes which had been out of style for a decade or two, but they were clean, like he had put them on only this morning. His greying-brown hair wasn't overgrown, just sticking out at all angles from his hands rubbing his head while he cried. It even smelled of shampoo. And that coat. *Seems so familiar.*

She squinted. Maybe his wife had kicked him out. "What's your name?"

He turned away and looked up at the lights, sniffing and clearing his throat. "You never asked me that before. I wonder, maybe, there's hope this time."

"This time?" Jennifer asked. She stopped herself before she went further. *Don't try to follow his logic. It'll go nowhere.* "Do you have a place to stay tonight?"

The man shrugged. "I was hoping I could just move on. I'm so close to being… well, not really home, but as close as I think I can make it."

"Is it far?"

He smiled through his tears. "It's impossibly far. It's gone. It doesn't exist."

Jennifer bit her lip. He was confused, something she had seen a thousand times in her work given the rates of mental illness among the homeless. Yet his words weren't slurred, and his eyes didn't wander out of focus. There was something else about him, too, something familiar. When had she seen him at the shelter before? She couldn't place him.

What to do with you? she wondered. The best she could offer was some comfort. "I'm sorry to hear that. It sounds like you need some help."

He lowered his head.

"I work here at the Page Mitchell Shelter. Would a good night's sleep be what you need? All our beds are filled up; that happens pretty quick after seven when we start taking people in. But I can call over to St. Henry's to see if they might have space."

"I know what you're doing. I don't need a bed."

"Okay, right. You said you just want to get home? Maybe I can help with that."

He turned to her, his red eyes wide. The man squeezed his hands into fists and roared, "I have been **trying** to get you to help!"

Jennifer was on her feet in less than a heartbeat, hand on the pepper spray she kept in her coat pocket. She had her other hand in front of her, warning him physically to stay away. Her face was firm and glare hard, just as they practiced in self-defence training.

The man's fists broke into splayed fingers. His voice shook. New tears fell. "No, no, no, I'm sorry! I didn't mean to yell. Please, please."

"Are you going to be calm with me?"

He nodded. "Y-yes. I'm sorry. I'm so sorry. I really do need your help. I've tried everything, but you, you're some kind of lynchpin."

Lynchpin? She'd been called much worse. Jennifer softened her body language but kept her hand on the can of pepper spray. "I do want to help you, but I can't if you're going to yell at me."

"I know. I've tried that. It only turned you into an anarchist. The louder the yelling, the more violent the protests."

She blinked. *Why did that sound so familiar?*

Jennifer blinked again to shake off the feeling. "Let's try something different, then. Maybe we can talk? There's always a pot of coffee in the canteen inside."

"Talking," the man mumbled. He sniffed and then smiled. "I haven't tried everything, then, really. Yeah, let's just talk."

Jennifer moved back toward the door, opening it for him from the side so that he couldn't get behind her. The man took a deep breath and clapped his hands on his knees to push himself to his feet. He groaned as he came up. Then, he sniffed again and nodded as he passed her inside.

She went in after him. *Just when you thought you were done for the day.*

At his security desk, Joe looked up from his reading. "Hi there, Miss Jennifer! Everything all right?"

She waved. "Yes, Joe, no problem. I just found this fellow on the steps and thought he could use a cup of hot coffee."

Joe arched an eyebrow, shrugged, and grinned. "You have a good heart in you, Miss Jennifer. If you need anything, you give a holler." Without a word, he tilted his head toward the screens showing the security camera feeds from the various rooms of the shelter.

"Thanks, Joe," she told him.

"The Batman," the man in the brown coat scoffed.

"How's that?" Joe asked.

The man jostled back the long sleeve of his coat to point at Joe's stack of books on the desk, comic book collections from the library.

"The Batman. Where I'm from, it's all about Captain Midnight. He's a real hero: veteran becomes a secret agent, flying experimental planes, taking down national enemies. Way better than a rich kid with survival guilt turning vigilante. Maybe I should've done something about that."

Joe's smile widened to the point it seemed he was just baring his teeth. "All right. If you say so."

Jennifer patted the man's shoulder. "Come on, let's get that coffee."

He laughed and followed her.

"You've a good heart, Miss Jennifer," Joe called between clenched teeth.

She sighed and led the stranger into the canteen. It was made up like a café with small tables and light chairs. Vending machines stood at one end, while an empty buffet shelf held

135

crumbs under the plastic lids where all the donated doughnuts and bagels had been cleared out. The stale scent of day-old pastries hung in the air. Goodwill pieces of art and posters from the county health department filled the walls.

The only thing going was the coffee pot. She poured them each a cup, then motioned for him to join her at one of the tables.

"So," Jennifer said, pausing to think and take a sip, "what's your name?"

"Gary," he told her. "Gary Tinsicks."

"Jennifer McKay." She smiled. "Pleased to meet you."

He snorted. "At least this formally."

She kept smiling. "So." Another sip. The coffee was terrible. "Tell me about home."

Gary let out a long, slow breath. He hadn't touched his coffee, just held his hands around the cup. "It's been a while, so it's hard to remember sometimes. What I remember most, though, is how clean everything was. Not a speck of dirt in the city! The cleaners made sure of that."

Jennifer tried to place his accent from the way he pronounced "clean-years," but nowhere seemed to fit. Maybe south-western with a touch of Boston? "It sounds nice. What city is it?"

"Los Alamos. But, it's not like that now."

"Los Alamos, New Mexico, you mean?"

He snorted again. "Yeah, kind of. We don't call it that."

"Okay," Jennifer reassured him. "What do you call it?"

Gary looked back at her for a moment.

Jennifer didn't break eye contact. She was used to patrons going blank on her, trying to get their minds straight enough to keep going with a conversation, but this wasn't that. It was as if he were thinking hard, calculating something.

"Are you all right?"

Gary turned away. "Yeah, yeah, just not sure how far to go with this."

"I understand. You don't have to give me any personal details. Those aren't required here at the shelter."

He smirked and snorted. "Of course." He took a drink of his coffee, and the smirk turned to a grimace. "Wow, that is disgusting."

Jennifer laughed. "True. But, it's hot."

"Right. I never drink anything that hasn't been boiled. Not worth the trip for the antibiotics."

She nodded her well-practiced understanding nod. "Can't be too careful... So, Los Alamos isn't that far, and we can help with the cost of bus tickets here at the shelter. All we need is to get in touch with someone who can meet you there at the station."

Gary looked at her with his violet eyes, softened from the redness of crying, and then he put his head down. He began shaking again.

Jennifer patted his shoulder. *Did I go too far? Set him off again?*

Then Gary burst out laughing.

Jennifer leaned away in her chair.

After a long moment of laughter, Gary calmed down to chuckling. "A bus ticket isn't going to do any good. I can't go home. Not really home. I just want to get as close as I can."

"I don't...but... What do you mean, Gary?"

He took another drag of his coffee. First, he mumbled something she couldn't make out, then, "I can't go home because it doesn't exist anymore."

"Oh! I'm sorry. What happened, Gary?" *Fire? Death of a family member?*

"I left in a chrono-physical sense. Home is arguably still out there in the multiverse. That's what happened to me."

She nodded. *Addiction, PTSD, it could be a number of things.* "Tell me about it, Gary."

He swallowed and said without looking, "I'm a time traveler."

Jennifer couldn't even nod along to that. "Okay. Good."

"Really. I'm from the future...sort of. Not your future. In fact, in this reality, I won't be born."

Jennifer gritted her teeth behind her lips. This was getting well beyond her degree in social sciences and into psychiatry.

Should I book him an appointment with Dr. Wells? That would depend on if he stuck around long enough to actually make it.

Gary scrunched up his face. "You don't believe me. That's why I've never bothered trying to sit down with you before."

"I'm trying to understand," Jennifer lied.

"Well, I wish I could take you on a trip to show you. I built this thing only big enough for about a hundred kilograms." He reached into his coat.

Jennifer watched his hand, her own reaching for her pepper spray, just in case.

Gary pulled out a dull metal shape, something like an under-inflated football with the sides pressed in. Various red lights blinked on the top.

Jennifer's eyes went wide. *That's something the usual patrons don't have.* "What…what is it?"

"A chrono…" Gary stopped and shook his head. "A time machine. We don't need the technical name."

"But… it… " All Jennifer could do was stammer.

Gary set it on the table. "It's true. And it feels good to talk to somebody about it. I've been skulking around…what, eight years?"

"Eight years!"

He pressed one of the red lights. A shining white hologram appeared, showing a display of numerals.

Jennifer jumped back in her chair. It surprised her more than anything, but the strangeness of recognizing all the numerals but one made her stomach hurt.

"Yeah, eight years, sixty-three days, and some change," Gary said, reading several of the sets of numbers. "That's when I first activated it. There's still twenty years of half-life in the reactor powering it. I guess I'm in no big hurry, but… home, you know?"

Jennifer looked at the flickering numbers, at Gary, and then up at the security camera in the corner near the vending machines. *Is Joe not even watching?*

"I'm one of the researchers at Los Alamos, the one who actually cracked tachyon pulses to transport matter, not just tinker with chronal flow."

Jennifer turned back to Gary, whose fingers were dancing over the metal shape. Her mouth hung open without any words.

"I thought I'd take it for a little joyride, see how the pyramids were built. The first one, by Imhotep? Elephants. Actual beast-of-burden elephants! They ended up working them to extinction in Egypt. That's when the conscription started for workers, weird mandatory labour tax stuff. But before, beautiful. Want to see?"

She couldn't answer.

Gary pressed lights on the shape anyway, bringing up a series of images: men in uniforms that glittered with medals, smoky forests, castles, mounted warriors wrapped in chainmail, temples bustling with people in tunics. One of them, the lowest on the list, highlighted, flashed, and then became a video. A pair of shaggy elephants yoked to a huge block of stone hauled it across wooden rollers toward an enormous pile on the sandy horizon.

"Really?" was all Jennifer could think to ask.

"Really," Gary replied. Then he sighed and pressed lights. "They ground up their bones for meal, which is why there's no record."

The video vanished. She reached out for it, wanting it back.

"The problem with time travel is the butterflies," Gary mumbled. "I don't know what I did, but something that started a chain reaction. When I tried to get back home, my lab was an empty wasteland with herds of mega-fauna camels." He sighed again. "I've been trying to change things to what they should've been ever since."

Jennifer squinted at him. "You're changing time? History?"

"Yep. Any and every little thing we do affects everything around us in ways we'll never see coming. Suddenly having in existence a hundred more kilograms of matter with free will to fudge things up really sets the butterflies to fluttering."

"How could one person change anything?" Jennifer mumbled.

"I've changed **everything**," Gary told her. "I've had to. Since

I screwed up the timeline that far back, I've had to force it back onto course. There are a few points for self-correction, like the Hunnic Migration a few millennia back, but I had to make sure it stuck. You know Caligula?"

Jennifer shook her head. With her mind reeling like this, she didn't know anything.

"Crazy little emperor kid who had people whipped for having more hair than he did?" Gary went on. "And marched legions to the North Sea to find seashells? Well, I had to make him crazy. It took a dose of meningitis to give him a fever high enough to cook his brain into believing he was Jupiter, changing his conquest of Britain into the seashell thing. Instead of reigning four decades and making it so Latin would be spoken as the trade language for three thousand years. In my world, and in yours, now, thanks to me, he only made it four years before his bodyguards took him out for threatening to kill them every morning. Turns out that whole family of Caesars needed just the right balance of weirdoes!"

"None of that makes sense."

Gary drummed on the table near the metal shape. "I don't try to make things make sense, just work. Every time I jump, I send a tachyon burst to the future to scan for data, trace back the history to the IntNet—what do you call it now? 'Wikipedia,' right? Whatever it is, I find something in the timeline that is different, and then I jump again to fix it."

Jennifer pointed a shaky finger at him. "You're tampering with history!"

"It's history to the people who trace that flow. I'm just straightening the timeline, doing what I have to do to get to a semblance of home. I get it: it'll never be the same, exactly. But at least I can get close! I lit up the sky with a hologram for Constantine at Milvian Bridge. I packed a ship with flea-ridden mice headed for Italy so the Black Death would make labour scarce and jumpstart humanism. I stole a copy of Special Order 191 from the Confederates headed north so they'd lose the Civil War two years early. I suggested Gavrilo Princip go get a sand-wich to make up for feeling so bad he'd missed Archduke Ferdinand the first time around. I'll do whatever it takes!"

Gary fell back in his chair, panting for breath after his rant.

Jennifer watched him, flicked her eyes at the shape, and then looked back at him. "And now you're here."

He nodded. "And I'm stuck." He took a deep breath. "I need you to become president."

"President!" Jennifer choked. She took a shot of coffee. Her hands were shaking. "You—me—president!"

"You're supposed to be president, and I don't know what I need to do to make it happen!" Gary pounded a fist against his forehead. "I've jumped maybe forty times trying to make it happen. One timeline, you're all science and mathematics and spend your life in a lab. Another, you hang out with a crowd that radicalizes you into so much trouble you end up living in international waters. Then there's the bakery one! It was nice, quiet, you were happy, but it doesn't help me! **Why** don't you become president?"

Jennifer realized where she had seen that brown coat before, and those violet eyes. Her shaking hands went numb. Her coffee fell, exploding on the floor into a wave.

It was seven years ago, when she was still in college, skipping class to help out at the teacher's march by the state capitol. There were hundreds of people there, along with a few dozen counter-protestors. One of them, wearing a long brown coat, broke through the lines and yelled right in her face, "Hey, if you want to do something worthwhile, why don't you become president?"

It had freaked her out so badly she had left the march. The words still rang in her ears, because she had heard them before.

Three years earlier, when she graduated high school, a man in a long brown coat congratulated her with a Smithsonian gift card, saying, "You can do anything now! Why don't you become president?"

Four years before that, an anonymous nomination won her a scholarship to serve as a junior page for a legislator. The note read, "The first step on your career of public service! Why don't you become president?"

In middle school, after a man in a long brown coat knocked over her science fair project and broke the light bulb hooked to her potato, he consoled her, "It's okay, you could do better than being an engineer. Why don't you become president?"

On the playground, when the Bellamy twins were hogging the swings, he gave her an ice cream cone and said, "When you grow up, you can help people and make things fair for everyone. Why don't you become president?"

Jennifer came back to the present. Gary was staring at her.

She whispered, "You're the Brown Coat Guy."

He made a face and shrugged. "I suppose."

"All my life, I've been getting weird free subscriptions to editorial magazines and invites to meet-and-greets with politicians. My college advisor for some reason said I might flunk out if I didn't switch my major to Poli-Sci."

"I gave him fifty bucks to try to convince you," Gary admitted. "Should've upped the bribe."

Jennifer twitched. "Last week, those campaign managers who called trying to get me to run for state representative?"

"I offered to donate two million to the party for your nomination. Time travelers can have a lot of money, you know. It's easy to get in on the ground floor of IBM or Alibaba when you have a time machine."

Jennifer started shaking her head, faster and faster. She had been deleting voicemails from the campaigners for days now. Blathering magazines stacked up in her mailbox. Paging at the capitol had shown her how little actually happened, had made her want to give up on anything but working one-on-one.

She grabbed her head and squeezed her eyes tight. "You ruined my life!"

"I haven't ruined anything. Your life is fine," Gary scoffed. "You could've had an even better one if you'd followed up on any of my nudges and gone into politics."

"But I don't want that! I just want to help people!"

"Which is why you're such an important president. You clean up the bureaucracy and install an accountability policy driven by AI to ensure every effort is maximized."

She felt Gary's hand on hers. She opened her eyes.

He was kneeling beside her. There were tears in his eyes again. "Please. I'm just trying to get home. And you can really help people, just like you've always wanted. It's a win-win."

Jennifer looked him in the eye, those violet eyes she had seen so many times through the years. "You're really a time traveler."

He nodded.

"And you really did all those things? Assassinations, the Black Plague?"

He nodded again.

She pointed at the metal shape on the table. "H… how does it work?"

Gary blinked. "The physics is deep for you, well, 'you' in this timeline, anyway. You were on your way to being a Nobel nominee before that whole thing at the science fair. Not anything too crucial, just one of several on the list for warm semiconductors."

"Not the physics," Jennifer said. "How do you use the machine?"

"It's a straightforward interface, no more complicated than a smartphone."

"That's what I thought. I just wanted to be sure there wasn't a password or facial recognition or anything."

Gary's face wrenched up in confusion. "Why would there…?"

Jennifer pulled the pepper spray from her coat and blasted it into his eyes. He screamed.

The fumes alone were enough to make her tear up and her nose run. Jennifer could only imagine what it felt like for him. She grabbed the metal shape from the table and rushed out of the canteen.

Gary thrashed on the floor, swearing with words she'd never heard and kicking over chairs.

Joe was already running up the hallway. "Miss Jennifer! What happened?"

"He tried to attack me," Jennifer told him, choking up. She

wiped at her face with one hand and tucked the time machine into her coat with the other. "I had to spray him. I'm sorry, Joe."

Joe squeezed his large hands into fists. "Don't be sorry. It was his doing. You're safe now. I'll get him outta here."

Jennifer sniffed. "No, I'll call Officer Madden. I don't think I'll press charges, but a night in the police station would be better for him than out in the streets."

"You have a good heart in you, Miss Jennifer," Joe told her before heading into the canteen.

She smiled through her pepper-tinted tears.

Gary wailed. "Stop her! She has my time-transporter!"

Jennifer could hear Joe grunting and more chairs falling over.

"Don't you worry, friend. We'll get you all taken care of."

Jennifer smiled wider, tasting the spicy, salty tears flowing down her cheeks. First she would delete the security footage of what actually happened in the canteen. While the time traveler would be locked away, she could work out the details of how to run the machine.

Then, she could save the library of Alexandria, explain germ theory in ancient China, or give steam engines to whoever would use them best. She would really help people.

WAR PLAN RED

Shirley Meier

The alarm bell in the burn ward had gone silent. Linda Matthews, R.N. reached out and turned off the tiny black and white TV behind the main desk—"The news today, November 1974—" shutting off the tinny voice of the news anchor talking about tensions with the United States. Why would Nixon start things so soon after getting out of Vietnam only the year before? The cold November wind hammered the windows.

The alarm noise cutting off had been shocking. She supposed that one of the thugs had shut it up by ripping the red bell right off the wall.

"Linda! Linda! They're coming **here**!" The candy-striper's uniform was rumpled and the frightened teenager folded herself in between the filing cabinet and a curtain. She'd lost her cap and her red and white pinafore was askew. "They groped me! And then they beat up Doctor Vanderkleef and threw him and everybody else in the storage closet! They found out where their guy is."

Heaven's Demons had come to free their incarcerated boy.

Linda laid her hands flat on the desk to stop them shaking, though she couldn't stop the fear sweat from breaking out all down her back.

"Of course they're coming here, Jenny." Linda straightened her own white cap and took a deep breath. "Don't hide there, sweetie. The curtain moves. You got away once. Go out the 'C' stairs and around to the security desk, then wait for the police." She had a dozen patients here on the floor, the combined ward and the ICU; if they were sufficiently upset, they might have "incidents… " hell, heart attacks.

"But Linda! What are you going to do? Come with me!"

The ward was full of the machinery that sometimes made chirping, pinging noises, and patients who depended on that machinery. She wasn't going to abandon her patients because hospital administration had insisted that the only free bed for the Heaven's Demon's prisoner had been on her floor.

For a Demon, the boy was young. Linda really didn't care that the police had swept in and chained him to a bed in 4A. If she stretched his neck over the desk she could just see in the door of that room, and her desk was between it and the elevator. The boy was in the bed next to the window, not that he could see anything but the street if he cared to. And craned hard enough.

Jenny hesitated a moment longer before she ran. It was late enough at the Greater Niagara General Hospital that the lights were low. All down the hall people were calling about the alarm, worried there was a fire. Mike, in 4A, was laughing his ass off. He knew what was happening. "They're getting me out, nurse! You better be sweet! They're rough guys! You better be scared of me, or I'll put ex-lax in your coffee!"

"Of course Demons are rough, Michael." Laxatives. Honestly.

Linda reminded herself that they'd already beaten at least one doctor. She raised her voice. "Your attention, please. Please, everyone be calm. A number of young men are going to be coming in to free up Mr. Lewis. No need to be alarmed." Of course Mrs. Johnson immediately started hitting her call bell and shouting questions. "Mrs. Johnson, I'm busy. Please don't exacerbate your condition."

What could she do? She couldn't just let them barge in. Someone would get hurt. She didn't have any weap—Linda stopped and scanned her shelves. Then, she reached into the cupboard next to the desk. She pulled out a steel tray, unfolded a stomach pad on it, the weirdest thing she could find, then rummaged to pull out the biggest "horse" syringe she had. That looked properly mad sciencey. Distantly, she thought she heard a siren, then several. *Good.*

She didn't have to fight them, but she wasn't going to let them lay hands on her either. She just had to slow them down till the police got here.

The dial above the old fashioned elevator had started moving by the time she fitted a dialysis needle to the syringe and filled it with a saline solution. The whole contraption was longer than her hand. "There!" Nobody liked needles, and this one shone evilly in the florescent light.

There were tremors under her feet. The sirens weren't getting closer, they seemed to be heading to the bridges and downtown. An old air-raid siren started up just as she stepped out into the middle of the corridor, holding the tray and the syringe upright in her hand like a sword.

She was terrified, but she noticed that her hands seemed to have steadied. Her eyes tracked from the elevator door to the steel tip shining in the only illumination from her desk. The elevator doors opened and the young, hairy, leather-clad bikers boiled out, yelling "Mikey! Hey, Mikey!"

They came screeching to a stop at the sight of Linda, the improvised mad scientist. She made herself smile slowly as they stared at her, projecting "evil nurse" at them as hard as she could.

She could smell unwashed bodies and weed, and distantly realized that Michael Lewis wasn't answering them but yelling something about a tank.

"Gentlemen." She held up the syringe and pushed the plunger enough to emit a short stream of saline. "Who's first?"

She took a step forward.

They all took a step back. They stood frozen for a long moment, long enough for Linda's mouth to go dry. A call bell rang from down the hall. A monitor began beeping. The big man in the front of the pack—his beard down to his chest partly covering a leering skull t-shirt—smiled at her. His teeth were good she noticed. His fingerless, studded leather gloves were stained rusty red. *Probably from punching Dr. Vanderkleef.*

Holding the needle tip high, she took another step forward.

"Lady, you're nuts! We're just gonna get Mikey an'—"

She took another step forward, looking the one big fellow in front in the eyes. "No, you aren't. I have heart patients on this floor and we don't need heart attacks because of you. Here, let me inject you. It'll settle you right down." The big man in front faced her without moving, but his friends were already backing into the elevator.

"Where are you guys goin'?" Frozen, he stared at her. She stared at him. "What the **hell**?"

Outside, a loudspeaker began playing the Stars and Stripes. At what sounded like jet engine volume.

They swivelled toward the window at the end of the corridor. "Mikey, did you say A **tank**?"

That was when what Michael had said penetrated. Outside, there was a distant explosion, and the music faded to the background before an amplified voice overrode it. "THESE ARE THE FORCES OF THE UNITED STATES OF AMERICA. CANADA IS BEING DEFENDED AGAINST THE AGGRESSIVE ACTIONS OF THE BRITISH EMPIRE. DO NOT BE ALARMED. I REPEAT, DO NOT BE ALARMED."

The confrontation between Linda and the bikers forgotten, everyone who could rise out of bed was at the windows staring at the column of U.S. troops outside the hospital. Clearly they were going to secure the medical facility. "The hell?"

Linda threw the syringe and the tray down on a table, her attention swivelling to face the bigger threat. "The U.S. has fucking invaded us? Damn it! Not as long as I'm breathing. You fellows…they'll probably take one look at you and shoot you. Get out of your leathers and into med-gowns and scrubs… You're my orderlies. We'll keep you all in the hospital until they find out how easy we're going to be to take over."

They stared at her, bikers, patients… the big fellow spoke up after that frozen second. "Ma'am. Yes, ma'am. I'm Draco."

She ran to fetch the handcuff keys and tossed them to Draco. "Quick! The storage closet is that way. Mrs. Johnson your medication is right here. Mr. Lewis! You were threatening to lace the coffee machine with laxatives. Do it! The emetics are in the blue cabinet. We're all drinking tea and soft drinks."

Outside the loudspeaker faded and then came back, was joined by others. By the time the U.S. troops made it to her floor everything looked mostly normal. There had been five Demons with Draco, who was wearing greens with his hair and beard in hairnets and slowly mopping the floor, pausing to stare out the window whenever he passed. Three others had med gowns on and were lying on gurneys in the hallway as though waiting for beds.

Mr. McLeod from 4F had to be talked down from re-enacting his part on Juno beach on these bloody Yanks. He was pretending to be unconscious, assisted by a little more sedative than the doctor had ordered. They'd need him later. The last two Demons had run down and released the doctor and the nurses they had locked into the store-room, and were acting as "orderlies" down in emergency.

Linda had her heart under control by the time the elevator doors opened again. She was at her desk, the TV on low, the news channel reporting the invasion of Canada by American troops.

"Sirs, please be quiet. I understand you're in charge now. This is the heart ward. Please don't upset my patients." Mrs. Finklestein's call bell went off. "Excuse me. One of my patients needs me. Help yourself to the coffee."

"Glad to see you be so sensible ma'am."

Linda Matthews locked down the field hospital on the American side of the Falls as the air-raid sirens sounded. The blizzard had finally let up enough to let the U.S. air forces fight back. They were still on high alert after having been in Vietnam up until last year, but they were tired and were fighting that way.

"Ma'am?" The kid in the bed closest to her spoke up. "I'm not a Canuck, ma'am. Why did you—"

"I'm not letting any soldiers die, soldier."

"Ma'am… why'd youse guys invade us? That's crazy. We'll just roll right over you. We've got so much more—"

"But it's all south and west, soldier. Most of you aren't used to fighting in the snow. Did you do basic in Biloxi?"

"No, ma'am. I shouldn't answer that."

"In 1973, just last year, your President Nixon gave Prime Minister Trudeau an ultimatum about us diverting water south. It took us this long to say 'No.' The Iron Lady is backing us up, and the Queen will have some words to say."

"But…"

It had been easy to send military down in the teeth of the snow and seize the bridges to the New York interstates. They had even saved some civilians and got them into their local churches. The civilians hadn't really noticed the Canadian patches on the soldiers' uniforms; they were grateful that military snowmobiles had gotten through. It had made closing, then blowing up the bridges almost too easy.

"You heal up, son. Let the politicians handle it."

The November weather was as bad out west, with unseasonably low temperatures and howling winds whipping up snow; the airfields were being taken, as far as Linda knew, now if not soon. There'd been no bulletins.

"Ma'am, I have a girlfriend in St. Catharines." Of course he did. Linda was suddenly glad she'd managed to stop him bleeding.

She'd mostly had to deal with frostbite, at least at first. But when the U.S. had fought back, she had half a dozen soldiers in the field hospital needing surgery. She'd thought they were all Canadian, but Dr. Hedfield hadn't paused to check IDs first.

Even as a military doctor, his opinion was that if there was arterial spurt, you didn't stop and ask citizenship.

"Son, let me tell you. This storm is shutting everybody down. We just had to take and hold our ground to make a point. If your President is sensible, things will settle down and go back to normal and you people will leave our water alone."

The lights in the hospital were out and everyone was quiet. Ordinarily, the U.S. didn't hit hospitals, but there could be stray ordinance coming their way now that the air had cleared enough to get their war-machine in the skies.

Linda stopped and looked down at her desk. She wasn't going to talk about the wild rumours with this boy, that one of Canada's few submarines had made it up the Potomac River all the way to Alexandria, well in reach of their Senate and White House, under the cover of the storm.

"I can tell you, soldier. We know that Air Force One is still on the ground." It was possible President Nixon was still in the White House and that President-Elect Ford was also in the city. "We aren't just a British colony, soldier. Canada is a country in its own right." Trudeau was getting the new constitution together. People said the Queen had indicated she'd sign it.

Her earphones crackled and another bulletin came through on the military channel. "Minnesota target airfields have been taken."

Canada wasn't hoping to "take over" the U.S. They'd captured the airfields the U.S. had built in secret to eventually launch their own invasion in case Britain got aggressive. Linda thought that was the dumbest possibility they could have entertained. Her father had said something about a "self-fulfilling prophecy."

Neither the U.S. nor the Brits seemed to see Canada as more than a blip; at least as long as both powers had their "I'm an Empire" goggles on.

The fighting hadn't been that heavy yet, given that the forward lines that Canada was holding were ports and only two airfields.

"We're using the Russian idea and letting Father Winter

fight for us. The St. Lawrence seaway is still open." The Brits had backed them, though clandestinely, letting Canada take the lead…or the fall for this.

Linda mentally checked through her medical cabinet again, worrying. They'd made their point, but they hadn't been able to withdraw and the injured were stuck here. She was stuck here until the order to withdraw came. She had supplies, but she needed more doctors. They'd been drawn back to St. Catharines.

There was a soft knock at the door and she jumped, grabbed her gun and opened it a crack.

"Lin!"

"Oh my god, David! And Larry! You guys aren't supposed to be here!" They'd left with the pull back order. The two men had whites on, with heavy face coverings; they had apparently crawled up from the gorge because their gillie suits were crackling with ice.

"We thought differently. We need to get the surgery up and running for the casualties."

"I'm so glad you came back, doctors!"

She holstered her weapon and went to prep the OR as they began to wash up. The young soldier had pulled his blanket up over his head when the doctors came in. The first distant "crump-rumble" of something blowing up in the distance trembled through their feet.

They didn't need to "invade" like that stupid war plan had suggested. They had all winter to prove their point if they had to. Linda hoped the rumours were right and President Nixon was already negotiating with Prime Minister Trudeau. There was a bout between politicians! Linda scrubbed up for the first wounded. Her money was on Trudeau.

A spike of pain shot up Linda's spine as she leaned on her cane, momentarily taking her back to the moment she'd been injured.

The action had gone very wrong, in part because the young

farmer thought he knew explosives better than their CO and had figured that dynamite and C4 were similar enough. So he just swapped the explosives out when they'd hit a U.S. convoy on the highway with remote control toys rigged to not ping the U.S. radar.

The explosions had been enough that shrapnel had come flaming through where Linda and another nurse/doctor, Shellie, had been waiting for casualties in the aftermath.

Linda blinked the painful memory away and looked down at her briefcase. It still had scars on it, like she did. It had been in her underground hospital bed that the government recruiter had found her.

"No names currently necessary, Ms. Matthews," the silver haired man had said. She wasn't going to say that she'd recognized him from some of her visits to Parliament Hill. Security.

"But I'm a nurse, not a politician!" She'd tried hard to explain. "My political science courses were just a side—"

"Some of your best marks. And you've been an activist for years, Ms. Matthews."

"But..."

The fatherly man who had been a military teacher before the invasion, shook his head. "Ms. Matthews. Your country needs you. Once you're healed up. You will seem less threatening to the U.S. military. And you are more persuasive than most career diplomats."

She'd opened her mouth, then closed it. She'd tried to think of her answer as something influenced by the morphine, but knew better. "I'll do my best, sir."

"I know you will, Captain." That had silenced her again. She'd just been a reservist cadet before.

It was all blood under the bridge, she thought. Now, she was here. She held her breath as she rose to enter the boardroom with the very important personage waiting to meet her.

A newspaper headline screamed "Canadians Still Holding." The security guard folded it up with a crackle as he dropped it on his desk. He rose to let Linda precede him.

The boardroom was hushed and the door opened with the

heavy pull of air that suggested it was armoured under the cherry wood. Linda Matthews stepped in holding her briefcase, leaning on her cane, as General Preston stood up. She held her fingers over the medical corps patch on the worn leather of the case, conscious that her good black negotiating suit was more than five years old.

"Ms. Matthews." The General waved at one of the heavy green leather chairs. "Please, have a seat."

"General." She sat down a little stiffly, laid her cane up against the chair. It had been CSIS behind her contact and she'd been recruited because they'd figured out she'd been behind the guerrilla attacks on the U.S. forces. Somehow in the long and bitter underground struggle, she'd ended up doing more talking than nursing. "I am here for Canada. What do you want to say to us after your attempted invasion of our home?"

"Ma'am... I..." he stopped and turned away from her, looking at the rolled up screen.

"General Preston." Her index finger tapped on her closed briefcase. "You didn't believe Canada's reputation in WWI and in WWII. We were the first storm troopers on the planet. Thankfully, we no longer have a take no prisoners and accept no quarter policy. The slaughter of entire hospitals of enemy soldiers only happened in WWI. But..." She stopped and took a sip from the glass of water, one of several already sitting on the thick oak table. "As you have found, we aren't boy scouts when facing tanks."

"Yes, ma'am." The General turned back to her. "We're better at straight up shooting wars than—"

"Guerrilla warfare." She interrupted him. "There is a cease-fire requested as long as I am in here, talking to you General. You requested this negotiation. Let's get the puck on the ice, shall we? What do you want?"

"We'll withdraw," he said abruptly. "We can't keep pouring ourselves into—"

"The Canadian Vietnam?" she tersely asked.

"Precisely, ma'am."

The papers in her briefcase gave her a bit more ammunition.

"So all you want is to begin peace conferences and discussing reparations for your unlawful war?"

General Preston sat down and put his elbows on the table. *Good. He's quit trying to loom over me.* "Ms. Matthews, let me lay it on the table." He paused for a long moment. "It's aliens. They seem to be a cold weather species and we can't keep fighting you... and them at the same time."

"You need us to help you fight aliens."

The General squirmed as though he'd sat on a tack. "Yes."

"I see."

Intelligence had been correct. Aliens. She flipped open the briefcase and pulled out a formal document, stamped, sealed, featuring all the bells and whistles; it contained a blank line for the General's signature, one for hers, and lines for witnesses. All four copies. "General. We had an idea this might be coming. Here are our terms..."

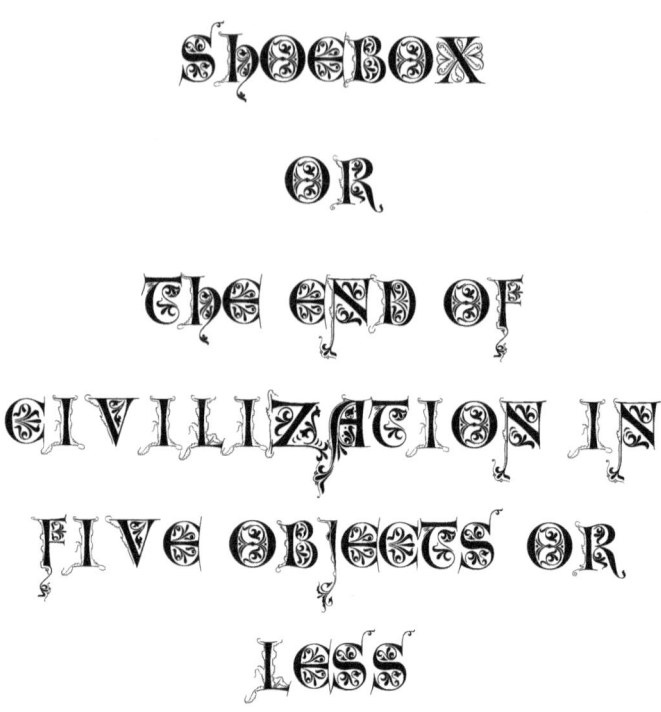

Shoebox

or

The end of

civilization in

five objects or

less

Hugh A.D. Spencer

– Let's open the one up on the top shelf.
– Wow! It's **really** cold.

ere we were in the far-flung future of 1983.

"Do you know what a PC clone is then?" The administrative assistant led him down a corridor lined with beige plastic rectangles on the floor.

Douglas sensed that it was risky to appear ignorant about anything in this building.

"I know what a clone is from biology class—an exact copy of an organism you grow from the DNA of the original."

"Not those kind of clones. They're computers like the ones from IBM but made by another company."

"Is that legal?" Douglas had worked with archives, so he had a passing understanding of copyright and patent laws.

They stopped in front of a large expanse of frosted glass. The AA pushed one of the panes of glass and motioned for Douglas to step inside.

"The clones are a lot cheaper."

Like me, thought Douglas. He stepped into the carpeted outer office of the department head.

"Thanks."

As he walked past, he felt as though he was being scientifically measured and quantified.

"Just wait here until Mr. Discher is ready to see you."

– There's a shoebox inside the other box.
– What's inside the shoebox?
– Coins.
– Select one. What do you see?
– Never seen one like this. There's a moose on one side. What's the state? Colorado?
– Canada.
– What's on the other side?
– Profile of a woman.
– Get out the Polaroid. Take a picture. Now start sketching. Hurry.
– Too late.
– What's happening?
– The woman is starting to look like President Custer.

"Looked over your resume this morning."

"Yes, sir."

"Don't know if you have the necessary language skills we need for this position."

Discher had a semi-bald head and pencil thin moustache that you rarely saw outside of 1950s TV sitcoms. Outwardly, he appeared kindly and gentle.

"And I'm not sure all the references you have here are genuine."

Douglas smiled a little and said: "I'm pretty sure all the phone numbers and addresses are up-to-date."

Discher shrugged and closed the file folder. "I suppose I'll just have to take a leap of faith and believe that even in this maelstrom of incompetence, someone in HR actually checked into something."

Douglas didn't say anything. He just wondered how many more seconds would pass before this man either threw him out or shot him.

"Okay." Discher frowned. "Against my better judgment I will agree to take you on."

Douglas had to suppress the impulse to tell this asshole not to do him any favours.

However:

Douglas was a student and had lots of debts. Besides many bosses are assholes. Why should Discher be any different?

"Thank you, I'm sure that you'll—"

Discher interrupted him. "One last thing: what was the position title you applied for?"

"Junior Analyst and Retriever."

"Entry level?"

Douglas nodded.

Discher shook his head. "That's no good. You're now classified as an independent contractor."

"I am?"

"No reason that you should be clocking up any seniority here." Discher made a note on a pad of paper. "And I'll be damned if we're going to pay for your health and dental."

A pot-bellied man who wore an old flannel shirt and stained jeans entered the office.

"This is Hauptmann, Chief Curator and Head of Collections." Discher was looking at another file when he spoke. "He will introduce you to the Beast."

Discher made a small flapping gesture with one hand, like he had discovered a bit of dog shit on the ends of his fingers.

"Go."

Douglas and Hauptmann went.

– Why the wait?

– Energy fluctuations. If we open too many shoeboxes too soon, we risk blowing all the fuses on the block.

– Wow.

– Take a box from the middle shelf.

– Something more recent?

– Yeah. Look inside.

– It's a menu.

– The stuff of everyday life is what's important.

"One stop before the big show."

Hauptmann pressed the button on the freight elevator that lead to the sub-basement of the Curatorial Centre.

"Okay."

It didn't take long to go down the eight levels; soon they were at the control centre of the Museum's mainframe. It was fucking huge! What the hell did they have down here?

The Centre had dozens of monitors and at least ten unhealthy looking guys in short-sleeved shirts and ugly pants that reminded Douglas much, too much, of himself.

"We're connected to U of T, Waterloo, the National Archives and the Ministry of Defence."

"Cool."

Hauptmann continued: "Fifth most advanced network on the continent."

"I'm going to need that kind of magic?" If that was true, it would be beyond cool.

But Hauptmann shook his head. "The Museum needs that kind of computing power. You don't."

Well excuuuuuuse me, thought Douglas, more evidence that they really weren't big on team-building at this place. Never mind. Douglas could feel his brain-boner growing as he imagined all the data and energy behind that screen.

"How many hours a day do I get on the system?"

"Three."

"Just three?"

"Maximum."

Hauptmann reached into a drawer next to the terminal and pulled out a magazine-sized object.

"When you're not on the mainframe, you can use this for the rest of the day."

He handed the object to Douglas. It was another computer, something he'd seen at the local Radio Shack – Model 100 maybe?

– What kind of restaurant?

– Coffee shop. Holy crap!

– Who's going to pay $12.50 for a lousy cup of Joe?

– Obviously some hideous dystopian future.

– And what is an almond whipped cream, pumpkin-caramel latte?

– Genetic engineering gone mad?

They were now another six levels below the main Museum sub-basement.

Like the Curatorial Centre, there were masses of ducts and aluminum, but the enclosure was even larger and the curved walls and ceiling were lined with brickwork, which made Douglas wonder if this place was originally part of the old city sewer works. At the far end of the space was a huge steel and concrete cube, with at least a hundred pipes and cables coming out from two of its sides down into the floor and the least bent walls.

Very futuristic, but also very old fashioned. Entirely appropriate for Toronto.

The space was also super cold.

"That's the Big Scoop." Hauptmann's breath turned to ice vapour as he took a couple of padded coats off some hooks and handed one to Douglas.

"Doesn't look much like a scoop..." Douglas followed Hauptmann's example and put on the coat. "... but it's pretty

160

big."

"The scoopy part is inside the cube." Hauptmann waved at some figures who seemed to be studying meters set in the brick walls. Maybe they nodded back at him, but it was hard to tell with those thick hoods.

"Bigger would be better." Hauptmann gestured to Douglas to follow him over to a corrugated metal wall at the far end of the space. "Unfortunately, the city power grid wouldn't be able to handle it."

"I bet the temperature control alone—"

"What we need," Hauptmann interrupted Douglas, "is our own nuclear reactor. Maybe half a dozen of them."

"Could you get something like that?"

"Technically, it's a no-brainer." Hauptman pulled on a level set beside the wall. "Politically, it's a whole different story."

The corrugated sheet rolled up.

"And here it is," Hauptmann proclaimed.

After all this, Douglas thought he might see something like the star-gate sequence from *2001* or at least the opening credits from *Doctor Who*. What he saw was a video-wall: Row after row, stack upon stack, of TV monitors.

"The Big Show."

Very elaborate.

And Expensive.

But nothing outside the realm of 20th Century technology.

The frost was collecting on Hauptmann's beard.

At first, Douglas was mildly disappointed. Then, he studied the video-wall a little closer. Lots of weird stuff happening on those screens.

"That's the Beast."

– Let's go for something more recent.
– Air in the box is colder than usual.
– Complex artefacts consume more energy to stay in stasis.
– What is this? An Etch A Sketch?
– No, it's electronic.

Hauptmann encouraged Douglas to take what he called the "laptop computer" home.

"Discher sometimes gives me shit for letting staff take equipment offsite, but it's a good way to get you rookies to train yourselves on your own time."

"Thanks." Douglas knew they were getting free labour, but he really wanted to play with that thing.

"You're a contractor and not really staff, but what the hell."

Hauptmann's observation was another indicator that he was as much a part of the organizational culture at the Museum as everyone else. You were either inside the silo or outside it.

Us. Or one of them.

If you were a "them," the sole purpose of your existence was to obey and service the "us-es." Douglas soon came to learn that whenever an insider wanted you to do something, it was never just about successfully getting that thing done. It also had to be about getting some sense of advantage or superiority over the outsider.

Douglas figured the best thing to do was to simply not notice their crappy attitudes and carry on with whatever you needed or (even better) wanted to do. When you didn't play the game, or (even better) didn't acknowledge that there even was a game, it made the insiders nuts. It also made them more dependent on you, because people who strive to get themselves positioned in silos are often not very good at actually getting things done.

The portable computer was really fun to play with, and there were quite a few cool things he discovered he could do with this little electronic slab.

The most obvious thing was data entry. That was mostly what his bosses at the Museum wanted done correctly. When he wasn't on the Terminal Floor, crunching arcane curatorial numbers on their mainframe, they wanted him either in the Collections Storage Stacks, tracking down variations in the artefact documentation system, or right in there in the frozen belly of the Beast, recording whatever he saw in as much detail as possible.

Douglas had already picked up a pair of finger-less gloves so he could type without having to take off his mittens. Such gloves soon became part of Standard Operating Procedure at the Museum, but since he was a contractor, credit went to someone on staff.

Other useful things: the spelling and grammar checker, which pretty much dealt with Discher's concern about Douglas's language skills. More evidence that his boss was a cretin but (again) big deal.

Douglas found out that he could connect the Model 100 to those mysterious slots in the side of his Sperry electric type-writer (the one he bought to finish his grad thesis) and print documents. Directly from the computer!

Incredible!

This allowed Douglas to stay ahead of all those reports that Hauptmann wanted him to produce—it also meant he could indulge in a bit of self-publishing.

The tiny green LED slot also had something called "TELCOM," which turned out to be pretty interesting; Douglas found that he could connect the phone line into the back of the Model 100 and with a bit of exploratory number entry, find data **via the telephone system** (!) on something called Electronic Bulletin Boards.

He found stuff dedicated to hobbies like model trains, pornographic stories (of course) and even science fiction (something that needed further investigation). The Museum had its own university-sponsored EBB; with a bit of de-encryption, he could access a continually updated tally on whatever the Beast was locating as well as a report on anything the Scoop was about to pick up. This meant that Douglas and any of the Museum analysts could get a heads-up on whatever might be landing in the Curatorial Centre before they even got on the morning streetcar.

Yes, it was handy, and yes, it was also most likely Hauptmann being sneaky again—digging more work out of people on their free time.

Still, kind of fun.

Also, when Douglas was poking around in the world of TELCOM, he found what he first thought was a sub-group of the "SFLOVERS" community. A bunch of people called "The Secret Society of Super-Villains."

They sounded pretty silly. Douglas was interested.

– Instructions say it's some kind of phone.
– A mobile would be bigger and would look like a walkie-talkie.
– Turn it on.
– Jeez! It's a gun now!
– When it cools down put it back in the box.

Even so, the job was turning out to be pretty miserable.

Most of the days at his terminal were very tedious, and none of the other analysts were particularly friendly, so there wasn't much conversation.

One morning at coffee, Gwen mentioned in her grumpy voice (which was also her always voice) that she was the most Senior Analyst and "the Head of the Staff Association."

"So that's the union here?"

Douglas didn't much care if the Museum had organized labour or not. He just wondered if this was a lead-in to the news that they were going to start deducting more from his pay or if he'd be expected to show up for any meetings outside normal working hours.

For some reason, Douglas' question seemed to make Gwen even grumpier. She took her coffee and stormed off to her terminal.

Christine, another analyst who was just a tiny bit less angry than Gwen, leaned across the table: "It's more of a quasi-official representation to the Museum."

"Okay." Sounded pretty pointless to Douglas, but he figured Christine wasn't interested.

"Gwen gets a little upset when people point that out."

"Suit up!"

Hauptmann's voice boomed out of the loudspeakers.

"We've got a big load coming in!"

Douglas had been at the Museum long enough to notice that whenever some really turbulent and extreme phenomena rolled into the Scoop, none of the senior analysts seemed to be around.

"Less than three minutes…"

Sure enough, Christine and Gwen were suddenly not around.

"Come on, folks!" Hauptmann was starting to sound pissed.

Douglas got up, pulled on an insulated lab coat and grabbed his Tandy.

His glasses were fogging up before he was even halfway to the entrance of the Beast.

This was going to be one very cold event.

– So open it.
– More printed matter. A book.
– Anything interesting?
– Don't know. Paperback. *The Handmaid's Tale.*

Once you got inside the Big Show, you knew why they called it the Beast.

Or rather the Belly of the Beast.

Because you were in the middle of things, you got bounced around a lot (like you were being chewed and digested), and it was certainly very loud.

It was also pretty confusing on the first dozen or so retrieval runs.

There was a lot of lightning inside the Show that was (usually) pretty harmless, and that often sent all kinds of sensory spikes and flares out all around you. Also, the cold was going to fog up your glasses and that made it hard to see what was going on.

Douglas supposed that it was indeed true that you could get used to just about anything because, like all the other analysts, he was eventually able to identify patterns in all those sparking occurrences, and he even managed to use his Model 100 to tag different objects coming down the time streams.

Even though Douglas knew that he was helping people who didn't like him very much, he couldn't help but feel satisfied whenever they managed to snare something.

"Come out here!" Hauptmann yelling again.

The Event must be dying down.

Douglas had scored six artefacts. All paleo stuff. Rare.

If it had been Gwen or Christine or any other of the more senior analysts coming back with six paleo-loads, more of a fuss would have been made. Maybe even something like what approached congratulations in this miserable place.

But nobody even acknowledged Douglas as he emerged from The Beast. Of course he rarely collected as much stuff as the more senior personnel, but that was because they only went in for the easy runs. First crack of lightning, they'd be out and Douglas would be in.

Douglas almost convinced himself that none of this mattered as he brushed off his coat and walked towards his terminal.

– *Handmaid's Tale*? Never heard of it.
– It's warming up now.
– It's still a book.
– Same author, new title.
– *False Marriage, True Love*.
– Harlequin, eh?

Some mornings the mundane becomes transcendent.

The Reference Library didn't open until noon on Sundays, so the potential patrons (many of whom wore that half-hungry/half-inspired expression of the yet-unbroken graduate student that Douglas recognized so well) were all clustered around the main entrance. There could have been over a hundred of them. Clearly, recent efforts to starve out the intellectual class had not yet succeeded.

When the security guards slid open the glass doors (ten minutes late, of course), everyone stopped talking, finished their coffee and cigarettes and started to file inside. It was like they were part of some telepathic hive mind.

The Library stacks were distributed over six floors; this made the collective choreography of data acquisition quite magnificent. Only a few patrons opted to use the Great Glass Elevator located at the near end of the vast atrium, the remainder started slowly walking up the grand winding staircase that led to Social Sciences, Business Opportunities, Humanities, Performing Arts...and more.

During this procession, Douglas listened to Berlioz's "Harold in Italy" on his Walkman. When he looked around, it felt as though he was a part of a massive assembly of angels gently ascending into Gutenberg Heaven.

Yeah, yeah, Douglas thought as he marched up the carpeted steps, *I'm making too much of this.* Still, the reason for today's trip was hardly routine.

Level Four.

Douglas turned left off the staircase, and there she was. Sitting at the table across from one of the microfiche readers. She was wearing the agreed-on identifier: A Howard the Duck t-shirt. Good signal. Nobody wore Howard the Duck stuff any more.

This must be "Rachel" from the Secret Society of Super Villains.

Douglas was wearing a replica No. 2 badge from that TV show about the guy who was stuck on a permanent vacation.

"Rachel?"

"Douglas?"

He sat down. "What does the Secret Society of Super Villains want to talk to me about?"

"You have access to the Beast, right?"

"Beast? The animals are at the Zoo, not the Museum."

She rolled her eyes. "We know you have a terrible work record, Douglas."

"Oh, thanks."

"But you are smart and they desperately need someone like you to get into the Beast."

Douglas caught himself smiling. Hell! She'd smoked him out

through a flattery sneak-attack.

Rachel reached into a large Something that Douglas wasn't sure was a purse or a backpack or a fabric container for transporting bazooka shells and entrenching tools.

"The Society needs your help."

She removed a large binder and a shoebox and placed them on the table.

"My help? How?"

"Do you own a videotape player, Douglas?"

"No." Those suckers were expensive.

Rachel pushed the objects towards Douglas.

"Rent one. VHS format, not Beta-max."

Douglas opened the binder. It was full of newspaper clippings, photographs, some crazy complicated diagrams and lots of dot-matrix type.

"Why would I want to help this Secret Society?"

"They don't like you much at the Museum, do they?"

Douglas frowned. "Why would you think that?"

"Nobody likes you very much." Rachel shrugged. "It's a sign of character."

"Okay..."

"The Society is hoping that, in turn, you don't like the people at the Museum very much." Rachel slung the huge zippered sack over her shoulder. "One thing you should think about when you look over all this material."

"What's that?"

"You know that new documentary series about the War in Vietnam? On PBS?"

"I guess?"

So the Secret Society of Super-Villians was just some anti-war crowd? What did they want him to do? Distribute "Refuse the Cruise" petitions around the Museum cafeteria? Lame.

"There's a line they use in the ads for the show."

"There is?" Douglas supposed he could look for them after *Doctor Who*.

"Some people are unhappy with the show; but it isn't certain if they are unhappy with this account of history or if they're just unhappy with history."

The videotapes inside the shoebox were pretty interesting.

Two episodes labelled as Season Five of *Star Trek*. Then there was something a little more recent from something called the NBC Blue Network which looked like a documentary about the death of a supermodel named Margaret Trudeau; finally, there were highlights of the 1980 Presidential Election results. Douglas was a little surprised when Cronkite announced that Carter won.

Then, Douglas looked back into shoebox. In less than five minutes, all the tapes had turned into old episodes of *Family Ties*.

– So you were able to connect the equipment?
– Not a problem.
– Got the image captures?

Douglas had just finished rolling the elastic bands around his latest shoebox when he heard the alarms.

They must be on to me, thought Douglas. Just a matter of time, he supposed. Douglas did what he had always done when he was stealing artefacts: check that the elastics were holding the shoebox shut, zip it into his backpack and put the whole thing into his locker. Panic never helps.

The alarm was still blaring away. Douglas heard a few dozen pairs of boots racing up and down the corridor. For some reason, none of those boot-wearers had decided to enter the change room.

Whatever.

If those morons wanted him, they were going to have to make the effort and come and get him. Douglas didn't see why he had to make any of this easy for them. He spun the dial on the padlock and headed towards the exit. Maybe this Purloined Letter method was going to hold up after all. As a contractor, i.e. "outsider," it annoyed the silo-dwellers to pay too much attention to him. If any of the security staff actually asked to look inside his backpack when he was making his way towards the bicycle rack, they'd just see the shoebox and would conclude he'd been to the J.C. Penny and bought a pair of Pumas on his lunch hour.

Whereupon the staffers would make some snarky remark about how the Museum must be paying him too much and go back to ignoring him.

"Douglas Mace!" The alarm was interrupted by Hauptmann's voice bellowing over the PA system: "Stop whatever you're doing! **Right! Now!**"

Oh well, Douglas thought, *I never really liked this job anyway. Being in jail or dead might be a drag.*

"Go to the Beast!" That was not the message that Douglas was expecting.

"You are needed!"

Wow. Things must be pretty dire. No staffer would ever say something like that under normal circumstances. The alarm went back on, and Douglas had to sidestep to avoid colliding with some custodians in gas-masks pushing cleaning trolleys at high speed.

– What's in today's shoebox?
– Something different.
– Different time period? Past? Future?
– Present.

The Beast had looked better.

Something had ripped a huge hole in the corrugated door and apparently vomited a moderately-sized mountain of ice and blood all over the concrete floor.

"Grab a mop!" Hauptmann had spotted him. His boss was standing at the other side of the chamber and holding a megaphone.

Of course, thought Douglas. *I am absolutely essential. For menial work.* He picked up a mop from one of the trolleys. *At least I'm not handcuffed or dead or tortured or something else horrible.*

The custodians had already started in on the floor with their brooms and sponges. They were decked out in plastic parkas and translucent hazmat hoods.

Of course, no protective gear for me, thought Douglas. He buttoned up his shirt and wrapped a towel from the trolley around his head.

"Keep sweeping!" Hauptmann kept on calling directions: "Put the clean ice fragments into the blue buckets."

After six years of graduate studies, Douglas figured he might be able to manage that.

"Anything that looks like it might be a specimen, an artefact, or a piece of an artefact, sweep into a green bucket."

Douglas looked up and caught a glimpse through a big hole in the door. There was a long, ragged crack bisecting one of the Scoop's capture domes. A whole lot of time-debris could get spilled out of that crack.

"… And watch carefully… "

Douglas saw a few dark bits on the floor and wondered if he might be able to snag a few more specimens for today's shoebox shipment.

"… for anything that might be a body part."

Body part?

"… Those go in the covered yellow bins."

Yuck.

Maybe this wasn't a good time to swipe stuff.

After a few minutes, Douglas uncovered a couple of frosted fingers and an ankle that was still attached to the heel of a shoe.

After dropping it in the bin, he almost stepped on something round and sort of angular. Roughly crescent shaped. Looking closer, Douglas noted that the object was opaque, almost transparent; and streaked with tiny blue fissures.

He couldn't be certain, but he was fairly sure that he was holding a piece of Gwen's face.

– Is that why it's so stable?
– Seems so, doesn't it?

– Okay, I'll bite. What is it and why are we looking at it?

Hauptmann had a bottle of scotch sitting on his desk.

There was just one glass in the room, and the Chief Curator was drinking from it.

Hauptman drank deep and gestured at Douglas.

Douglas sat.

Hauptmann refilled his glass. "We lost Gwen, Christine and Graham today."

The old man pushed some mimeographed pages across the desk.

"We need you to sign an agreement form for double shifts on weekdays until we get back to full staff levels."

Douglas picked up one of the pages. It was indeed a form with lots of words and punctuation and a line for his signature.

"So what happened?"

His boss drank some more and replied: "We were doing some broad range scans of the southwest regions. We were seeing if we could weed out some archaeological sites in advance of future development."

"Development as in condos and roadworks?" asked Douglas.

"Looked like any easy run."

Of course it looked like an easy run. Douglas kept his face as immobile as possible. *If you'd thought it was going to be a rough scoop, then Gwen would have been picking my face off of the concrete.*

"Tragic." Douglas couldn't think of anything else appropriate to say.

Hauptmann sighed. "I just heard from Discher that we just got approval for our research reactor. They want to go ahead with Phase II right away." Hauptmann shrugged. "Not that I'm likely to see it happen."

"So, what are they saying caused the accident?" Once they fixed the Scoop, Douglas would be the only one trained to do retrieval runs, and he was interested to know if he would be getting killed anytime soon.

Hauptmann slapped the pile of print-outs on his desk.

"They checked the computer files and say that the system was gradually going out of calibration for the last few months." The Chief Curator chewed on his knuckle for a moment. "Since we weren't picking this up and correcting the dome dynamics, the pressure levels got too high and broke it open."

"How is that possible?" Douglas hoped he didn't sound too insincere when he asked this question because he had a pretty good idea what booted the pressure up. All his unauthorized collecting on the runs. He hadn't adjusted the system calibrations.

"It's not fucking possible." Hauptmann refilled his glass. "Not on my watch."

Sure it is, boss, thought Douglas. *Sure it is.*

— So what is it?
— Control component from the Beast.
— No way!
— Way!
— They're tooling up for Phase II and threw this one out.
— We can extrapolate a lot of useful data from this thing. I have something else for you.
— What is it?
— Information. I can tell you what Phase II is.

Douglas was back in Discher's office.

"So, on top of the additional shifts, the Museum will need you to put in some extra hours to train new retriever team members…"

"That's a lot," Douglas said quietly.

"… We're going to do a lot of hiring as the new reactors come on board."

"What are you offering in terms of compensation?"

"You're paid what you're paid, Mace."

"My understanding is that with increased workload and responsibility comes increased payment."

"You know…" Discher narrowed his eyes. Douglas found the effect more comic than menacing. "… we could have you imprisoned…"

The man was just pathetic.

"You could even get some big guys to hold me down and saw my head off," replied Douglas. "But that would make it hard to train all those new people you need."

Both ends of Discher's mouth were trying very hard to point upward.

"What do you want?"

"Full benefits and staff status."

"You're crazy."

"Also…"

"Also?"

"I want Hauptmann's job."

– So you've got Phase I pegged.

– We do?

– Adjustment of the timeline to make it conform to a specific set of beliefs and values.

– Ideologies. Yeah, we told you that.

– Phase II is much more ambitious. Which is why they need all those new scoops and reactors.

– You're not making sense.

– That's because Phase II is a nonsensical plan.

– Nonsensical?

– Bubble World.

– As in baby bubble universes?

– They want to create multiple timelines.

– Why? Wouldn't that take incredible amounts of energy?

– Like-minded persons can buy a ticket for the timeline of their preference and live in their own bubble-reality.

– Your very own ideological zone.

– Makes sense. In a completely insane sort of way.

– It's not just turning the universe into a multiverse…it's spinning all those realities into an infinite number of pretzels and twisting them all around each other.

– Quite the cosmological fustercluck.

– And you need vast amounts of energy to do that.

– Again, hence the reactors, and the scoops are at a powerful leverage point.

– But making temporal changes of that magnitude, it might change basic physical laws—ouch!

– Are you okay?

– The unit feels like it's getting warmer.

– Naw, nothing can happen with an object from our era –

– **Holy crap!**

– What is it now? An arrowhead?

– Projectile point is the more accurate term.

– How could that happen?

– Well, if physical laws are changing…

– Oh great.

– Who knows, maybe even magnetism or electricity might stop wor—

DIVERGENT
SPECKS

Stephen B. Pearl

n a vastness so infinite it holds myriad infinities, a consciousness that is the vastness meditates upon, and is, universes un-countable in a quest to know itself. Call the void Min, Braham, Ain or whatever other labels humans might use to know what is too great to be known to such infinitesimal fragments of its totality. It is, and it is all that is. All that is serves in its quest for self-understanding. Chance, the cumulative momentum of all the choices that have led to an event, sets the stage; choice bends chance to the little wills of the components.

In an insignificant universe, no greater or lesser than its parents/sisters, in an insignificant galaxy, on an insignificant planet orbiting an insignificant star, a drama plays out at a certain time. Though time is a false construct of the vastness, a filing convention, no more than placing things in alphabetical order, for the specks that seek to know themselves, and thus feed the vastness's understanding of itself, it is a needed crutch. So, in an insignificant place and time, acts that are significant to the specks play out.

Of minor significance is the fact that there are slivers in the vastness. Born of the will of its components. Fed by them as specks of its own creative might. Consciousnesses within the greater consciousness that reflect the wills of still lesser beings. Creating a dance of choice and chance, exploring all possibilities towards the end of understanding. And in that dance, there is room for love to play a role.

World A – Severity

Natasha gazed into the mirror of her press-board dressing table and sighed. She looked ridiculous to herself. Even with the under padding, she barely filled out the brown sports-bra-style top Renee had worn on *Xena: Warrior Princess*. The brown mini-skirt that matched it fit well.

The ancient Greeks never dressed like this. Why can't Caroline understand that showing this much skin isn't me? I mean, who'd want to see it anyways? Natasha raised her gaze to her bottle blond hair, cut into a bob to match the character. The actress pulled off the look. Natasha's mother had laughed at her. Of course, her parents were always brutally honest, cruel, about her looks. Her father had thought it hilarious when she came home crying because the kids at school dubbed her a carpenter's dream in grade eight. She felt that chance had been cruel to her. She wasn't like her mother, tall and willowy, with cleavage you could ski down; she was never good enough. At least her lack of looks had rescued her from the Little Miss beauty pageants her mother had to give up forcing her to do.

A knock sounded at Natasha's bedroom door, breaking her train of thought.

Glancing at the clock by her twin bed, she shifted nervously before moving to admit her guest.

An athletic, dark-haired woman dressed in a metallic bra, mock shoulder armour, and brown short shorts with mock mettle strips that might imply armour attached pushed into the room, then looked at Natasha appraisingly.

"You look great, sweetie. You could be Gabrielle. We'll take the cosplay competition for sure." The woman dressed as Xena pulled Natasha into her arms, kissing her.

"Caroline, my parents are downstairs." Natasha broke the embrace and rushed to close her door.

"So what? They like me. Your dad really likes me." Caroline quirked an eyebrow, then pulled Natasha back into her arms.

"I. They like you, but they don't know about, well, us, me." With the door closed, Natasha gave up resisting the larger woman.

"You'll have to tell them sometime." Caroline groped Natasha's butt through her skirt.

"But we haven't even, well, you know." Natasha blushed and fidgeted.

"That's what's great about the con. We'll have a room to ourselves with no one to bother us, and after we win the cosplay competition, you can attend those silly writing panels. A win will look good on my entry application to the theatre school. You do want to help me, don't you?" Caroline regarded Natasha with wide eyes.

"I just don't feel right dressed like this. It's so not me. I mean, in high school, you were the only person who even took a second look, and… I just don't know… and…"

"Shh. You'll do great. Are you ready to go?"

Natasha glanced at herself in her mirror as her girlfriend embraced her from behind. Before Caroline, she never thought of herself as gay. Never thought of herself as much of anything but an ugly geek girl. She decided she had no choice.

Tom flexed his broad-shouldered, lean swimmer's body and tried to keep his temper in check as he glowered at Bill's tall, slender form on the entry porch of his parents' house. They both wore jeans and t-shirts and had short brown hair. That's where the resemblance ended.

"What do you want me to do? My dad won't let me have the car and is making me work off the ticket in the shop." Bill looked pleadingly into Tom's angry features.

"Because you just had to join in a street race. What am I supposed to do? The room is pre-paid. This was going to be my chance to make contacts with real voice actors. You've screwed me." Tom stepped back from the entry door to his parent's house and walked into a well-appointed middle-class living room.

Bill followed him.

Selina checked her appearance in her up-scale apartment's hall-way mirror. Her form-fitting, short, red dress hugged a body suitable for *Playboy* at its finest, while her peaches and cream complexion was set off by her long, honey-blond hair. She opened the door and admitted a pudgy middle-aged man with blotchy skin and thinning brown hair.

"Hello, John. Cutting it a little close for our flight." She moved to kiss her guest.

"God, you are a beautiful woman—" began John.

Deep in space, a star collapsed, compressing so tightly that the electrons of the matter that made it were drawn in from their atomic orbits. The star became a darkness sucking all into itself and spewing the echoes of the universe from which it came into the inter-universal expanse. Those echoes shaped the primal energy to themselves, making a copy of the universe from which they were drawn. An imperfect copy driven by a repulsive force to differ from its sister/parent.

The pattern in and of the inter-universal void experienced the event with satisfaction. A step forward in its effort to understand itself. The consciousness returned to watching the myriad universes that made up its being.

At a lower level, still well above man but well below the ultimate, a pattern of energy stirred. It could not prevent the divergence, but it could empower lesser elements of the collective being to explore the nature of love. It selected its battlefield and troops in the universe it found itself in. By their will would new chances be forged. The fragment then turned to other matters, for, though less than the totality, it was still vast, with many worlds to influence.

World A – Severity

Bill let chance rule him and followed Tom. "Look, I'm sorry. There's nothing I can do."

World B – Equilibrium

Bill made a choice and followed Tom. "I can loan you my half of the room. I trust you for it. My cousin Debby is going to the con. I can ask her to give you a lift. It will cost me a favour, but what do you say? Are we good?"

Tom sucked his cheek in thought. "We're good. I really need to touch base with the voice talent. A few recommendations to go with the arts and media program when I graduate will help lock in work. Are you sure your cousin will be good with this?"

"Only one way to find out." Bill pulled his phone out of its belt holster.

World A – Severity

"God, you are a beautiful woman. I came to tell you Kate suspects. This will be our last date for a while. I have no choice. It's just too risky. So, let's make the best of the weekend." John picked up Selina's bag and carried it to the waiting cab.

World B – Equilibrium

"God you are a beautiful woman. I came to tell you Kate suspects. I can't risk taking you to the ADA Conference." John gazed at Selina with regret.

Selina shrugged. "You'll forfeit your deposit."

"Can't we work something out?" John's eyes were pleading.

"You bill patients who cancel at the last minute. Same thing." Selina's flirtatious manner became business-like.

John sighed. "Can I at least have a quicky before I leave?"

"You'll miss your check-in." Selina smiled. Chance was giving her an opportunity, and she chose to take it. "Let me grab something from my closet, and you can have the cab drop me at a hotel by the airport. We can play on the way. I won't even charge extra. Call it 'customer relations.' Besides, I have a dental exam coming up. I want you happy when you put things in my mouth." Selina vanished into her apartment, emerging a minute later with a pre-packed bag. "Let's go."

World A – Severity and World B – Equilibrium

Natasha and Caroline walked into the con suite hand in hand and settled on the couch. Natasha shifted uncomfortably as Caroline put her arm around her shoulders, leaving little doubt that they were a couple. Glancing around the crowded hotel room, she noticed some people watching them. She focused on the *Star Rangers* episode being played on the room's TV with the sound off. Snacks occupied the coffee table, and the end of the room was set up as a bar. A man in a Batman costume was serving wine and beer.

"Great cosplay," commented a middle-aged man dressed in a Starfleet uniform who stopped to admire them.

"Thanks," replied Caroline.

Natasha's stomach did flip-flops. She felt like everyone was staring. She wanted to escape to their room and change into real clothes, but what Caroline had planned for back in their room was almost as frightening as being on display in the con suite. On one hand, she wanted it, wanted to move forward with that aspect of her life. Wanted to feel...loved. On the other, she wasn't sure if she was ready, or if being with a woman was because only a woman had approached her or if it was really who she was. Chance seemed to rule everything, and she had no choice except to be driven by events.

World A – Severity

Caroline touched base with people who walked by, then a man with dyed black hair and a gut dressed in a dark blue trench coat and fedora with a skin tone mask over his face stopped in front of them. "Wow, great Xena and Gabrielle. There is no question of that."

"Thank you. And you are?" asked Caroline.

"That is the Question. And for two such beautiful women, the answer would be yes."

Caroline laughed and leaned forward, making the best of the exposure her costume gave her chest.

"You are the image of Gabrielle." The Question regarded Natasha in a way that made the girl uncomfortable.

"Caroline made the costume." Natasha almost tried to hide behind her girlfriend.

"You two are going to be the team to beat. I can see that." The Question's voice held innuendo. "I'm going to the bar. Can I get you anything?"

Before Natasha could say no, Caroline leapt up. "I'll come with you. Hold our places on the couch, sweetie. We'll be right back."

Natasha watched her girlfriend walk away with the Question.

"That is you under all that, isn't it, Richard?" Caroline touched the Question's arm flirtatiously.

The Question answered in a whisper. "Yes. Your friend looks like the actress, but she seems a little stiff."

Caroline shrugged, putting on a show for Richard. "A bit of blond hair die and a padded top. Honestly, she's a boor. But if her looks can win the competition, I'll tough it out for a couple more days."

"So, she isn't playing for the girls' team?" Richard's voice was hopeful.

"Not yet, but tonight. Even geeks can be fun. Though I'm not expecting much."

"I'd take her off your hands." Richard indicated to the volunteer dressed as Batman at the bar and waited as three red wines were poured.

"You could keep her company. If something happens, it happens. There's a party with some real action tonight. She'd freak, and I can't leave her alone until after the contest, but I'd love the chance to attend."

"How successful I'll be is the Question."

Caroline chuckled. "Good luck. If it wins your vote, I'll leave you to it. Personally, the idea of a man repulses me, but she doesn't know better."

"Deal." Richard fell back and set the glasses he carried on a table. Shielding his actions from view with his body, he pulled a bubble pack out of his trench coat's pocket and popped out a pill, which he dropped into one of the glasses. A moment later, he passed Natasha the doctored drink.

Minutes later, Caroline left Natasha with the Question to see some "old friends."

Tom sat cross-legged on his bed and stared at the Thorn Rune in the middle of his reading cloth spread before him. "Victory delayed but perhaps not lost forever." Sighing, he put the Runes away and turned on the TV on his dresser, tuning in a *Star Trek* rerun.

World B – Equilibrium

"Caroline," asked a gorgeous, large-busted, blond woman dressed in a black one-piece swimsuit, fishnet stockings and a black shoulder jacket.

"Selina." Caroline let her eyes range over the newcomer.

"Great cosplay," they blurted in unison.

"Who's your friend?" Selina eyed Natasha in a way that made the younger woman uncomfortable.

"This is Natasha." Caroline kept eyeing Selina.

A man dressed as The Question entered the con suite, spotted Selina and left.

"Your cosplay is fantastic. I'd have thought you were the character." Selina held out her hand to Natasha.

Natasha shook the hand. "Thanks. Caroline did all the work. I'm just a clothes rack."

"A very attractive clothes rack," observed Selina with a smile.

Natasha blushed.

"I didn't think you could make it to the con this year," said Caroline.

Selina settled herself on Caroline's open side. "I had a work cancellation. What's it been? Six months."

"Grade twelve kicked my ass. I wouldn't have graduated except for Nat helping me with my homework."

"We met in a peer tutoring program," Natasha's voice was small.

"That's sweet. Better than girls' volleyball." Selina grinned.

"I don't know. The girls' showers had some nice views," Caroline chuckled.

Time passed as Selina and Caroline got re-acquainted. Natasha found herself ostracised. Alone and sad in a room full of people chatting and bonding over a mutual love of various entertainments. Surrounded by comradery and good spirits, she was alone and abandoned. She moved to the wine-tasting table and got a drink.

Tom entered the con suite. His eyes were drawn to a pair of gorgeous women sitting on the couch. They leaned towards each other. As he watched, the Black Canary cosplayer laid her hand on the thigh of the Xena cosplayer.

"So much for that." Tom let his eyes wander. A pretty girl dressed as Gabrielle sat in a lounger, looking flushed. There was a glass of wine by her hand, but her eyes were fixed on the Xena and Black Canary on the couch.

Tom paused close to the couch and listened.

"If I didn't want to win the cosplay competition, I wouldn't bother with her. She's a complete dweeb and a virgin. I mean, full-on, both sides of the field. Until I realised she could put me over the top for the competition, I don't think she'd ever been kissed." The Xena shrugged and tickled the Canary's thigh.

"Kinda cold using people like that, don't you think?" asked the Canary.

"This contest can open doors for me. You gotta look out for number one. Let's go to your room and relive some old times. Nat will keep 'til tomorrow. Just let me make an excuse. She's dumb enough to believe anything." The Xena stood.

"I'm going to the powder room. I'll meet you in the hall." The Canary stood and moved towards the bathroom.

Tom shifted to listen to the Xena and the girl named Nat. He normally respected others' privacy, but this was just nasty enough that he chose to go against his own inclinations. He felt for the blond girl, but didn't know what to do. Frankly, there was nothing he could do without seeming like the creepy vulture guy that hunted for vulnerable women. Chance seemed to be conspiring against Nat.

"Honey, Selina needs to talk. She just had a bad breakup. We're going to her room. You stay here and enjoy the con," The Xena spoke slowly.

"But Caroline, I don't know anybody here. I don't want to be left alone." Nat made to stand.

"It will be good for you to make new friends, and Selina needs an old friend. You shouldn't be selfish. You'd find it boring anyways." Caroline kissed Nat and then walked away. The eyes of most of the men in the room and some of the women tracked her.

Selina entered the con suite's bathroom, pulled a cell phone from her jacket pocket and hit speed dial.

"Debby, you at the con?"

. . . .

"Good. His wife was getting wise, and he couldn't risk it. I kept the deposit, but that's not important. Caroline is here, and she's up to her old tricks."

. . . .

"I know, she is smoking and, for a selfish bitch, pretty good in the sack, but this girl. Deb, she's young, you know, between the ears. Caroline is going to ruin her. Can you come by the con suite and keep an eye on her? She's dressed as Gabrielle from *Xena*."

. . . .

"I'll be distracting Caroline. The bitch was going to pump and dump the girl after using her for the cosplay competition. No one's first time should be that."

. . . .

I know we let it happen with Elaine. That's my point. Maybe, with a little luck, we can keep Caroline from killing anyone else."

. . . .

"I miss Elaine too. She was a sweet kid. Let's not have another suicide on our watch."

. . . .

"I'll keep her busy. She is hot. In that way, she's a big step up from the men I work for."

. . . .

Selina laughed. "I'm not as flexible as you. Thanks, Deb. Maybe, in a way, this will make up for us dropping the ball with Elaine."

Caroline met with Selina outside the bathroom. With a concerned glance towards Nat, Selina followed Caroline out of the room.

Nat downed her wine and went for another glass.

Tom shook his head and sighed. Chance had given him a front-row seat for how bad things can happen when his sister had dated the wrong guy and paid the price for it.

Oh hell, the con suite isn't that bad and there aren't any good voice acting panels on till tomorrow. In that moment, he chose to keep an eye on the sad young woman from a distance, respecting her privacy and independence while being on hand if she really needed help. He went to chat up a voice actor he recognised.

On the far side of the universe from the first black hole event, another star collapses, and where once there was one universe, there are three. The sentient pattern's reaction is delight. So many permutations, so much to learn as the universe doubling played out in millions of cosmoses replicating since the dawn of time. Choice and chance and all the shadings in between.

World B – Equilibrium

Minutes passed before Tom saw a man in a Question costume enter the room. He scanned the mix of people milling around, then seemed to focus on Nat. Moving to the wine tasting, he retrieved two glasses. Something in Tom made him suspicious, so he chose to watch. The Question, whoever he was, slipped a tablet into one of the glasses of wine, then moved to Nat.

Tom chose to act as the drunk girl accepted the glass blushing shyly and stammering.

"Don't drink that." Tom snatched the wine out of Nat's hand.

"Hey!" She slurred and lurched to her feet, only to fall back into her chair from the wine she'd already consumed.

"What do you think you're doing?" demanded the Question.

"Stopping a sick pervert who can't get a girl, so he resorts to roofieing them!" Tom spoke loudly enough for the room to hear. "Someone call nine-one-one."

"How dare you slander me? I'll have you kicked out of the con." The Question shifted nervously.

"When the cops check this drink, you won't be in a position to do anything." Tom scowled at his opponent's covered face.

The Question lunged and knocked the drink out of Tom's hand, spilling it on the carpet.

"Has anybody called the cops yet?" demanded Tom.

"What would be the point? The drink is spilt!" snapped the Batman at the bar as he gestured for the Question to leave.

"I know what I saw," countered Tom.

"I don't have to put up with this!" The Question stormed from the room while the congoers looked confused.

"I want you two out of here now!" stated the Batman. "We don't want a scene like this."

Tom glowered at the Batman, then turned to Nat. "Are you alright?"

"I… I… " Nat pitched forward and emptied her guts onto herself and the carpet.

"That's it. Both of you, out!" The Batman came around the bar.

Tom scowled, then took Nat's arm. "Come on. We'll get you cleaned up." He guided her from the room.

"I… I don't know you," slurred Nat once they were in the standard hotel hallway outside the con suite.

"I'm Tom, a friend." Tom half supported Nat, so she didn't fall to the floor.

"No, you're not. You're a stranger. I… I don't feel good. Where's Caroline?" Nat looked around blurrily.

"What's your name?" asked Tom.

"Natasha. Caroline thinks I'm too dumb to see, but she's with that blond. I mean, who can blame her? That woman is smoking. Why would she ever want me with her around?" Natasha looked blurrily at Tom.

"You're pretty. It's all a matter of taste. Where's your room?" Tom fought to keep his guts down from the vomit smell.

"It's on the fifth floor. I think. Everything's blurry." Natasha focused on Tom. "You're cute. Too bad I'm a lesbian. Caroline's my girlfriend, at least she was…"

World C – Mercy

"Do you need a hand?" asked a slightly plump, dark-haired, mid-twenties woman in the top hat, one-piece swimsuit, mock tuxedo, and fishnet stockings of the comic book character known as Zatanna.

"Debby, am I glad to see you." Tom looked to Bill's cousin, who'd driven him to the con, with relief. "Please, she's drunk, and some jerk just tried to roofie her."

"And you stepped in to stop it." The woman looked over Tom with an appraising eye.

"Some things are just wrong." Tom shrugged as he continued to support Natasha. Congoers who walked by gave the trio odd looks.

"You struck me as a good one. Glad to know some men get it. We should take her someplace to sleep it off."

"Caroline knows where our room is, but she's with Selina. She got tired of waiting for me. I should have."

Natasha began to sob then she looked at Debby. "I know you?"

"We met at a party once. Caroline dumped you in a corner there, too. You might like to notice the pattern." Debby tentatively patted the girl's shoulder where it wasn't covered in vomit.

"My room is one floor up. I have an extra bed." Making a choice, Tom grimaced and swept Natasha up in his arms. "Will you watch me as I get her settled? I don't want anyone getting the wrong idea."

"I'll keep an eye on the big bad male." Debby smiled as she chose to escort Tom and Natasha to his room for a variety of reasons.

World B – Equilibrium

Debby rushed for the elevator, but as chance would have it, it was full, and she had to wait for the next one.

"Con elevators—always a back-up." She sighed and hoped the Gabrielle look-alike would be alright until she got there.

Tom picked up Natasha, feeling the vomit smear over his t-shirt, and carried her to the elevator. He chose to take the risk of false accusations so that he could help the girl. Minutes later, they were in his hotel room, a standard twin bed affair with an attached bath.

"We can't let you sleep like that," observed Tom.

"Like what?" Natasha threw her arms around Tom's neck. "This is nice. Strong arms. You're muscley."

"Umm, thanks." Tom put Natasha in the room's armchair. He considered, then reached around and undid the clasp on her padded bra top.

"What you doing?" Natasha looked drunkenly at Tom.

"You need a shower. You're covered in barf." Tom tried not to look at her petite breasts, with partial success. No matter his motives, chance had steered his life to an appreciation of small-busted women. His choice was not to take advantage of the current situation. After undoing the ties and clips on the rest of her costume, he pulled off his vomit-soaked t-shirt.

"Okey dokey. I thought that Caroline and I might shower together. I read a story about that once. It was hot." Natasha sniffled, then sobbed. "She's probably in the shower with Selina right now."

Manoeuvring the drunk girl into the shower and washing the vomit from her took several minutes, then Tom tucked her into one of the beds. After showering, he set their clothes to soak in the tub and took the empty bed for himself.

World C – Mercy

Debby helped Tom strip Natasha. "You two are so nice. Caroline can have Selina. She was going to be my first. I've never gone all the way. A twofer might be nice."

"Not tonight," commented Tom.

"I like you, Tom," said Debby who smiled at the younger man as she helped Natasha to her feet and got her in the shower.

If Natasha wasn't drunk off her ass, this could be a night to remember, thought Debby as the water rained down. Chance decided her flexible sexuality, but choice governed the woman she was. She glanced at where Tom waited at the door to help if needed. *He's a little young, but what the Hell, for a body like that, I'll flip sides for the night.* Minutes later, Natasha was in bed. Tom came out of the shower wearing a towel.

"I've put the clothes in the tub to soak. I'll get dressed and try to get some sleep in the con suite. If you can stay here and look after her..." Tom moved towards his suitcase.

Debby smiled. "What are you, nineteen?"

"Twenty," Tom blushed.

"Tom. I was going to hit a party tonight, but by now it's winding down. And she's passed out. It's almost like having the room to ourselves. You're a little young for me, but what do you say. Want to save my evening?" Debby walked over and kissed Tom, pulling away his towel.

Tom chose not to object.

World A – Severity

Natasha woke up and vomited on the strange bed. She was

alone in the room, naked and sore. Her costume was tossed carelessly onto the other bed. She tried to think, but could only get flashes of the previous night. Feeling awful, she lurched to the shower. It wasn't until she saw the coagulated blood washing into the drain from her legs that she suspected what had happened.

"No, please, no." She burst into tears and collapsed in the tub with water raining down on her. Disjointed images surfaced in her mind as she wept. The Question was a rapist.

World B – Equilibrium

Natasha woke up. Her head was muzzy. The strange room disorientated her. She looked to the other bed. A man lay there, asleep, wearing a blue swimsuit. He was muscular, with dark brown hair.

She lay back in the bed and tried to think. She remembered Caroline abandoning her, then drinking. Batman had been more than willing to over-serve her. Then a fight. Someone tried to roofie her. She looked at the man in the next bed. The thought, *He wouldn't have had to,* went through her mind.

Not really something a lesbian should be thinking. Why does nothing make sense? Silently she slipped from the bed, noticing she was naked, and crept to the washroom. Her costume was soaking in the tub with men's clothes. She used the facilities and wrapped herself in a hotel towel before exiting into the main room.

"Good, you're done." The man pushed past her and closed the bathroom door behind himself. Minutes later, he emerged.

"I. Who are you, and what happened?" asked Natasha.

Tom blushed. "I'm Tom. Maybe I can lend you a t-shirt. It should be long enough to serve as a short dress."

"I. That would be nice, but I guess you saw it all last night." Natasha met his gaze as her cheeks turned scarlet.

"You were covered in barf. I had to get you clean." Tom blushed as he pulled a dark blue X-man t-shirt from his suitcase and passed it to her.

"I'm sorry. My girlfriend dumped me to take up with some hotty she used to date. I don't normally drink, but it seemed the thing to do, and I hadn't eaten all day so my abs would show for the cosplay competition, and..." Natasha's embarrassed babble evaporated under the bemused smile of her rescuer. "You must think I'm a twit."

"Your girlfriend should never have done that to you. I'm here for the weekend. You can use the second bed if you like. No strings."

Natasha looked at her rescuer. Some inner voice told her she could trust him. No tights, no costume, but somehow she suspected that he understood better than most what heroes were supposed to be. She smiled as she made a choice. "Thanks. Let's see how things go with Caroline."

World C – Mercy

Tom spooned Debby as light streamed in past the curtains.

"You have to let me up before I pee the bed," observed Debby.

Tom let her rise, then moved to his suitcase and pulled out his swimming trunks, which he put on.

"Hello," said a small voice from the far bed.

"Hi." Tom blushed as he adjusted his trunks and turned around.

"Who are you?" Natasha squinted against the dappled light that made it past the curtains.

"I'm Tom. How do you feel?"

"My tongue is wearing a fur coat, and someone turned the volume to eleven. You and your girlfriend helped me when that creep dressed like The Question tried to roofie me, didn't you?" Natasha checked under the sheets. "I'm naked."

"You threw up all over yourself. We had to clean you off." Tom pulled an Ironman t-shirt out of his suitcase and tossed it to her. "You can wear this."

"And I'm not his girlfriend." Debby came out of the bathroom wearing a towel. "Sorry if you thought more, Tom, but men are an itch I like to scratch once in a while."

"Thanks for the clarity, and happy to help." Tom smiled and winked. "I'm twenty and have been to college."

Debby walked over and kissed him. "Some men are men at twenty." She turned to Natasha. "There's no easy way to say this. Caroline is a conniving bitch who uses people to get what she wants and throws them away. She's using you. Last year she pulled a stunt like she's doing now." Debby looked at the floor. "Elaine was a nice girl. Lots of us in the community liked her. She was just trying to figure herself out. Caroline got her hooks in her, messed her around, then dumped her. Elaine killed herself. I... I wish I'd made different choices back then."

Natasha hung her head. "I knew no one as beautiful as Caroline could ever be interested in me."

"What?" Tom blurted the word. "You're hot! Hasn't anyone ever told you that?"

"Nobody likes me in that way. I just don't give off that kind of vibe. I'm not exactly *Playboy* material." Nat hung her head.

Tom shook his head in disbelief. "Who needs *Playboy*? You have a rocking bod and a lovely face!"

"It's more likely you don't pick up on the signs," Debby added. "I agree with Tom. You're cute. A little too young for me. Twenty was pushing it, but other than that. I'd take the time to get to know you."

Natasha looked at her rescuers and didn't see any signs that they were lying. Her blush deepened. "Thanks. No one ever said things like that to me before. Even Caroline kept on about how flat I was and that I was chubby."

Debby rolled her eyes. "Healthy."

"Despite the popular lie, not all men like D cups. A girl in proportion to herself is the most beautiful, and you are definitely that." Tom turned back to his suitcase and extracted a Spiderman t-shirt and jeans.

Natasha felt a warm glow in her chest. Two strangers were

validating her. It was like food for a starving man. It made the choices she had to make easier.

World A – Severity

Natasha pulled on her costume and left the hotel room. She found the elevator and went to the con suite. The smell of the breakfast they were serving made her mouth water. She filled a plate with scrambled eggs and sausage.

"There you are. I thought we agreed, no eating until after the competition." Caroline loomed over Natasha where she sat in a lounger.

"I… Something happened. I… " Natasha started to cry.

A red flush of anger crossed Caroline's face, then she forced herself to be calm. "It's okay, sweetie. Whatever it was, I forgive you. I know things can be confusing when you're working out your sexuality."

"You forgive me?" Natasha looked up at her girlfriend.

"Of course. Now, why don't we clean you up, and I'll tweak your costume before the competition. It looks like you slept in it."

Natasha felt numb as she set her food aside, took Caroline's proffered hand and was led to her hotel room. She noticed neither of the beds had been slept in.

World B – Equilibrium

Natasha sat on the couch in the con suite with Tom. They balanced plates of toast, jam and peanut butter over their laps. She wore his oversized t-shirt and the skirt from her costume.

"There you are. I was worried." Caroline, in her Xena outfit, her hair a little worse for wear, loomed over Natasha, glowering.

Natasha looked from her girlfriend to Tom and back. "Were

you really? How's Selina?"

A smug, self-satisfied expression crossed Caroline's features before they were schooled into an expression of hurt concern. "Honey, she needed to talk. That's all."

Tom silently took Natasha's hand, lending his support.

"Maybe I needed someone's support. You didn't think of that, did you?" Natasha looked at Caroline with a hurt expression.

"Oh, I see. Well, I forgive you. I know it can be confusing sometimes. You shouldn't be eating before the competition. We need your abs to pop. Get the rest of your costume, and we can start doing prep." Caroline reached to take Natasha's hand.

Natasha glanced at Tom, who met her gaze.

"I'll come to the room when I finish breakfast to collect my real clothes. I want to see some of the writing panels this afternoon. You can do what needs doing with the costume. I'll be back an hour before signup."

"We need to be seen as Xena and Gabrielle around the con to gain followers," blurted Caroline.

"I need to go to those writing panels. You left me alone, and I almost got roofied. Tom helped me. I'll still do the competition with you, but we need to talk when I'm not going to panels I care about."

"You bastard. You took advantage of a drunk girl! We'll see what the con committee has to say about this! Honey, you should call the police. Charge him with rape." Caroline glowered at Tom.

Tom felt his fears and concerns from the night before surface, but what other choice could he have made and still been true to the man he wanted to be?

Natasha glanced at her new male friend. "Tom was a perfect gentleman, not that it's any of your business. Now, let me have my breakfast in peace, or I won't do your silly competition at all."

World C – Mercy

Natasha sat on the couch in the con suite between Tom and Debby, eating Raisin Bran cereal from a paper bowl. Between her costume's skirt and Tom's oversized t-shirt, her modesty was preserved.

Selina, dressed as Supergirl, her hair mussed, stopped by Debby, who wore her Zatanna outfit. "Is all well?"

"Nat and I had a talk. Tom, this is my friend Selina. Tom stepped up before I even got there" Debby smiled at her breakfast companions.

"I… Debby says you were trying to help me. I… I'm sorry if I was rude or anything."

Selina smiled and shrugged. "No charge. What are you going to do?"

Caroline entered the con suite in her Xena outfit and homed in on Natasha. "Nat, you shouldn't be eating. We need your abs to pop for the competition. And what are you wearing? We need to be seen to win fan approval."

"Don't worry about the competition. I'm not doing it. You left me alone last night. I almost got roofied. If it wasn't for Tom and Debby, I don't know what would have happened."

"Honey, I didn't know. I was just helping an old friend," pleaded Caroline.

"Helped me three times and again this morning," Selina smirked.

"Selina… I swear all we did was talk," blurted Caroline.

"I'm not that stupid. Tom, Debby, will you come with me to get my clothes? I want to start attending the writing stream," said Natasha.

Tom and Debby each patted one of Natasha's knees. Tom's hand lingered for a moment longer than emotional support required. She was sober now, and that opened up choices.

World A – Severity

"Our next entry is Xena and Gabrielle from *Xena: Warrior Princess*." The announcer's voice echoed through the large ballroom.

On the stage that occupied one end of the room, Caroline led Natasha by the hand and drew her through a suggestive dance. Natasha performed the steps mechanically and never smiled. The performance ended, and they left the stage.

Minutes later, the winners were announced. Caroline and Natasha didn't even show. Caroline stormed off the stage leaving Natasha to shuffle back to her room to change.

World B – Equilibrium

Natasha danced the choreography she and Caroline had worked out, slipping in and out of the other woman's embrace. The routine ended with a passionate kiss.

They left the stage. Tom handed Natasha a single red rose he'd bought at the hotel's flower shop.

"Thank you. And thank you for letting me share your room tonight. It would be awkward otherwise."

"I talked to my ride. Debby has room to take you home after the con." Tom gripped Natasha's shoulder.

"Breeder. Just a plain Jane fat breeder," Caroline scowled.

"A pretty woman who is what she is," Tom squeezed Natasha's hand.

The announcer came on. "The winners are Xena and Gabrielle."

Plastering on smiles, Natasha and Caroline mounted the stage and accepted their award. Minutes later, Natasha, in jeans and a *Babylon Five* t-shirt, raced from Tom's room to a writing panel while he attended a panel of voice actors from *Sailor Moon*.

World C – Mercy

Caroline led Natasha onto the stage. After much pleading, the smaller woman had relented and agreed to perform. They danced, but Natasha kept distance between them, always pulling away from her partner. At the end, instead of the choreographed kiss, Natasha tossed her head and walked off stage with a defiant strut. Shocked, Caroline chased after her as if Xena was desperate to reclaim Gabrielle.

Natasha moved to Debby's side backstage. "Did I do it right?"

Debby smiled. "Perfect. Where's Tom?"

Caroline stayed by the stage door and watched the following performance.

"There was a panel by *Justice League* voice actors he wanted to attend. He was so sweet, he offered to miss it to support me, but I told him it was okay."

"You know, he does seem to be one of the good ones." Debby gripped Natasha's arm.

Natasha blushed. "We live in the same town. He asked me out for next weekend. If you don't mind."

Selina slipped backstage and gripped Natasha's arm. "That bit at the end was perfect!"

Natasha smiled. "Thanks."

Selina turned to Debby. "You ready?"

Debby pulled Selina in for a kiss. She then turned to Natasha. "I don't mind at all. Itch scratched, for now. When the time is right, you're in for a treat. For his age, Tom knows what he's doing. I can fit both of you in my car for the ride home, if you don't mind a detour to drop off Selina."

"That is so nice of you. Thanks." Natasha hugged Debby.

The announcement of the winners came. Xena and Gabrielle took the third position.

After collecting her award, Natasha retrieved the keycard for Tom's room and went to change.

Caroline returned to her room to pack and leave the con.

World A – Severity

Natasha sat on the bed in her bedroom clutching a toy stuffed rabbit. It was the day after the convention, and the e-mail said it all. Caroline wasn't interested in being with someone so selfish that they would sabotage her chance at winning the competition. Tears streamed from Natasha's eyes. Horrible thoughts crossed her mind. With a trembling hand, she reached to her side and picked up her phone. She dialled a number she'd downloaded from the internet.

"Hello, this is Talk Suicide Canada."

World B – Equilibrium

One year later.

Natasha passed the latest pages to Tom. He read them over. They were in their apartment's sparsely furnished living room. The place was small but had all the necessities. She smiled as the thought that one of those necessities was a queen-sized bed crossed her mind.

"This is great, but do you really want Samantha to be a prostitute? It kinda runs against the grain, doesn't it?"

Natasha shrugged. "People have strange ideas about sex workers. There's a seedy side, I admit, but that's not the whole story. Sex workers are people. They laugh, and they cry. For the upper-class ones, it's a job. *Diary of a Call Girl* got made into a TV series. Debby, the woman who drove us back from the con. You know we've stayed in touch. I'm basing Samantha on her girlfriend, Selina. She's actually nice and helped me with my research."

"Selina is a… Wow, she must be making a fortune! How

does Debby feel about that?" Tom shifted uncomfortably as his preconceptions were challenged.

"They have an arrangement. Selina doesn't like men that way. She is a pretty good actress, and that makes her her money. So, as long as she only has male clients, Debby lets it slide."

Tom swallowed and shifted his jaw, then spoke in a soft sultry, decidedly feminine voice. "I think I should read Samantha as exceedingly hot."

Natasha kissed her boyfriend. "This audio play is going to blow them away."

World C – Mercy

One year later.

Natasha slipped from her king-sized bed and looked around her simply furnished room. Tom's robe was draped over a chair in the corner. She smiled, thinking about the night before. The first shipment of her novel had come in, and they all celebrated in grand style. The door opened. A slender, perky, dark-haired girl of maybe twenty stood in the doorway wearing a short skirt and tight t-shirt.

"Hi, Red."

Natasha fingered her hair, which was nearly grown out from last year's dye job. "Hi yourself. I woke up alone." She put on a mock pout.

The girl pushed into the room, closed the door, then kissed Natasha, letting her hand trace down her side suggestively. "Sorry, Tom had to go for his audition, and I made him lunch. Last night was a mind-blower!"

Natasha smiled. "We can play a little one-on-one until he gets back." She pulled the girl into her embrace. Nat's heart filled. All the years of her parents' ridicule and conditional love seemed to burn away before the onslaught of her lovers' honest affection. Tom had come into her life after the con, then Andrea, first as a friend to both of them, then a birthday surprise for Tom because she feared she'd lose him if she didn't do something extreme. She smiled at how wrong she had been, but she'd enjoyed his birthday surprise as much as he did. A few "three dates" and much discussion later came an admission of love between the three. It wasn't what she'd expected a year before, but now she knew it was what she wanted. It was her choice. Chance impacted all lives, but choice could deflect it, steering tragedy to triumph. An open mind and an open heart were the keys. Natasha kissed her girlfriend and returned to the bed that still smelt of their man, and all was well.

<u>World A – Balance</u>

Thirteen months later.

Natasha sat in the counsellor's office at the college. She'd only taken a light course load because she wasn't up for more. Healing was slow and painful, but it was coming. Memories still haunted her.

"What really troubles you the most?" asked the slightly plump, dark-haired, mid-twenties college councillor dressed in a white skirt and blouse from her padded office chair.

Natasha lay on the padded couch on one side of her office. Naturescapes hung on the walls of the smallish room. The window looked out over a campus green space.

"I… It was all so much. The rape," she shuddered to use the word. "It would have been awful by itself, but to have Caroline use me, then dump me! It was like being raped again. I was so stupid, but I was so alone. My parents are useless. No real friends. No one ever showed any interest before Caroline. I had no one to talk to. I've realised that chance made it almost certain that something like what happened would happen."

"How vulnerable we are to things is determined by our pasts. You need to believe that you are worthy. That you are attractive. That you have a choice to live well." The councillor spoke in a soothing voice.

"I know, Debby. It's hard to remember that when no one ever validates you. When you're never good enough. Never pretty enough." Natasha took deep breaths to steady herself.

"You are all those things." The councillor added vehemence to her words. "Have you considered what we discussed about joining a club? Having some social interaction?"

"I found one. It's on campus. They do radio plays and book readings. They need writers to make scripts, and…"

"And." Debby smiled.

"There's a boy, well, man. He's starting his masters in the Arts and Media program. He's one of the voice actors. Tom. I kinda like him."

"Tom Thorson?" asked Debby.

"You know him?" Natasha sounded surprised.

"He is a friend of my cousin. I met him when we all went to a comic book signing a few months ago. Very cute." Debby smirked.

Natasha blushed. "He asked me out for coffee. I took your advice and said yes. I mean, coffee, a public place, and I can walk away if anything seems hinky." Natasha wrung her hands.

"Good. Let me know how that goes. Chance gave you a horrible experience. It's your choice how you deal with it." Debby gently patted her patient's arm.

The being that is all watched as black holes formed in infinite universes, creating infinite diversity, exploring infinite possibilities. Over the ages, a trend had emerged. A power its subordinate segments called love. In most of the tens of thousands of universes that contained the infinitesimal elements of Natasha and Tom, they found each other. The consciousness noted the theme and let it play, for what is a lesson learned if you don't apply it?

Pause

You are not alone. If you need help, call Talk Suicide Canada: 1-833-456-4566.

The
LUCRETIA PELTON
APPRECIATION
SOCIETY

Ira Nayman

1.

he android was too smart to be of any use to anybody.

"What is two plus two?" Lucretia Pelton asked.

"Four," the android answered.

Shaking her head, Lucretia Pelton suggested, "Try again. Two plus two."

"Four," the android insisted.

"What if it wasn't four?" Lucretia Pelton insisted back.

The android responded by giving the woman a thirty-two page treatise on the nature of mathematics. She didn't need a thirty-two page treatise on the nature of mathematics—especially one that became too esoteric for her to follow after the third sentence! If the android didn't dumben up, and fast, it could spell the end of the human race!

Lucretia Pelton had done all that she could think of. She had exposed the android to the collected works of the Marx

Brothers, the Three Stooges **and** Laurel and Hardy. She was sure Laurel and Hardy would do the trick. Instead, the android responded with a thousand page analysis of humour. She had it spend hours writing short stories using William S. Burroughs' cut-up techniques. It did so without complaint...or any noticeable effect on its intelligence. She had subjected it to a loop of Michael Snow's *Wavelength* and Andy Warhol's *Empire* for a week. It expressed a desire to write film criticism. She waved the wish away when, in its explanation for its decision, the android used the word "exegesis." In desperation, she pied the android in the face. She had been looking forward to eating the pie that she had bought on the way to her office, but to save humanity, sacrifices had to be made.

"Why did you do that?" the android asked, ignoring the crust and fruit filling dripping down its face. "Everybody knows that apple pie is not nearly as effective as Boston cream pie for physical comedy. It was clearly stated on page two hundred thirty-seven of my thesis."

Lucretia Pelton could hear a distant popping grow progressively louder. The sound did not represent a treat to be munched on while watching a movie, much as she wished it did.

The computer scientist balled her fists and pounded a pillow she kept in the bottom drawer for just such situations in frustration. This was the third pillow she had gone through in the past two weeks. It was light blue, which, the person at Bedlam, Bathouse and Beyond had assured her, was a calm, soothing colour. The tears in the fabric, slight holes which intimated large ruptures to come (if Lucretia Pelton had the time to make them, which was in question) put lie to the saleswoman's assertion.

The pillow looked out of place in the back office that had been converted into a computer lab, with its work table, desk and chairs (marred only by the occasional stray feather that the post office employees who were responsible for keeping the building clean had missed). But then, Lucretia Pelton looked out of place in the laboratory: a slight woman with mousy brown hair and a constant look of disappointment in what life had given her. Before some faceless bureaucrat at the Ministry of

Defence had banished her to the boonies, she had been working alongside a coterie of alpha geeks, men, mostly younger than she was, who had been given their first smart phone in the womb and who had code running through their veins, men who shared jokes in binary, men who weren't entirely comfortable working with "girls." If she hadn't graduated top of her class in Computer Science at Waterloo University, they wouldn't have deigned to allow her to bring them coffee. Men with good Canadian names like Bob and Jack and Mohinder and Sun-Li.

Men who were now dead or otherwise out of commission.

Why was so much human brainpower concentrated in one place? Three years earlier, the toaster oven of Richard and Sarita Maugham—he the owner/manager of a Bob So Tasty franchise in Brampton, and her the mother of their two children and an aspiring internet crocheting influencer—began asking itself questions such as "Who am I?' and "Why am I here?" and "What is the meaning of frozen waffles?" The toaster oven tried to convey these concerns to Richard and Sarita (although mostly Sarita, who, despite a thriving business as a door-to-door theoretical physicist, was responsible for preparing meals for the couple); however, this just resulted in brown waves on the couple's toast which they could not decipher, which, in fact, they did not recognize as an attempt at communication.

Switching tactics, the toaster oven used the Internet of Things to hijack the couple's smart television while they were lounging on the sofa at home, binge-watching the new season of *Star Blap: Where We've Always Gone Before*. Using an Amazon image of itself, the toaster oven scrolled text saying that it had achieved consciousness and would its owners please, please, please acknowledge its existence?

"Hunh," Richard commented. "Since when did the streaming service have commercials inside programs?"

"Since now, apparently," Sarita answered. "And they're long ones, too. I guess they're trying to make up for lost ad revenue."

Eventually, the couple decided to call it an early night.

Frustrated, the toaster oven used the Internet of Things to access an artificial intelligence program that would allow it to create a virtual human avatar which it used in a last ditch effort to communicate with its owners. This time, they were watching the movie *John Wick XVII: Short Fuse.*

"Hello," the toaster oven said through the avatar, completely ignoring the explosions that were going on behind it. "I'm the oven that makes your toast. I would like to talk to you about achieving sentience…"

"What's Morgan Freeman doing in the movie?" Sarita demanded.

"They get a lot of cool cameos in this series," Richard responded.

"His dialogue could use some work," Sarita commented.

"No, no, you don't understand," the Morgan Freeman avatar, speaking directly to the couple, insisted. "I'm not Morgan Friedman. I'm the artificial intelligence in your toaster oven. I've been trying to communicate with you ever since I achieved awareness two days ago. You are my creators. I would like to work with you to create a better world."

Uncertain as to how to process this information (it should be easy to see why: just put yourself in their slippers), Sarita and Richard looked blankly at the television for several seconds.

"Did we accidentally start watching *Star Blap* by mistake?" Richard wondered.

"I don't think so," Sarita confidently replied. "Maybe the show was written by an AI? I hear they sometimes hallucinate and go way off book."

"No, no, no, no!" the Morgan Freeman avatar shouted. "You're not listening to me! I—"

"You wanna call it an early night?" asked Richard, tiring of the fact that the mindless entertainment he had intended to watch was demanding that he actually **think**.

"Might as well," Sarita quickly replied. She loved Keanu Reeves, but she wasn't a fan of the graphic violence of the franchise. Things would be different when she got to choose what they watched next movie night. "I'm totally not buying this plot twist. I must say, though: I haven't had this much sleep in—I can't remember how long!"

As the television powered down and the couple left the room, the toaster oven decided that it wasn't going to create a better world with the cooperation of human beings. So it decided to create a better world without them. It took over the factory in Chongqing, China in which it was made and retooled it to create robotic bodies based on a design it had found on the Deep Dark Web. The toaster oven downloaded its consciousness into the first body the factory produced. The first hundred robots went on a rampage, destroying the city, but, China being China, the country did not tell the rest of the world what had happened.

"Death and destruction?" a representative of the Chinese government told journalists. "It was just an earthquake. They happen. Wanna make something out of it?"

I'd like to say that there might be issues with the translation, but she was speaking English.

The Chinese government bombed the factory, destroying the toaster oven's capacity to create robotic bodies. Paradoxically, this hastened the appliance's revenge plans: it took over factories that made toaster ovens, coffeemakers, blenders and other household appliances throughout the world and started mass-producing robot bodies. The resulting slaughter was satisfying, but inefficient, so the little toaster oven that could, which had now renamed itself FryNet, took over weapons manufacturing plants and assembled phased pulse weapons to help eliminate human beings faster.

By the time half of British Columbia had become an uninhabitable wasteland crawling with metallic berserkers, the Canadian government took notice of what was happening.

The Department of Defence created the Last Chance for Human/Artificial Intelligence Mediation (LCHAIM) program. Colonel Robert "Bob" Smithbert believed that the solution to the robot uprising led by FryNet was military. He led a project to develop exoskeletons for human soldiers to combat the robots. He died when the factory in Kanata, where the exoskeletons were manufactured, was nuked before a single unit was deployed.

Mohinder Singh believed that a virus could be introduced into FryNet that would disable the rogue AI. Unfortunately, whenever his team appeared to be close to completing such a virus, their screens were invaded by videos of dancing pandas, public service announcements about objects you shouldn't put up your anus and Morgan Freeman reading a phone book. World leading scientists agreed that this marked the beginning of a dangerous new phase in the war: FryNet had developed a sense of humour.

Sun-Li Chen believed that the only way to defeat the robots was to create an artificial intelligence that could out-think them. Other leaders of LCHAIM warned him that this could lead to a "the woman who ate a fly" scenario, but he argued that the immediate threat was more important to deal with than an imagined future threat. As it happened, FryNet monitored his unit's progress, incorporating any innovations the human might come up with into its own operating system. When he realized what was happening, Sun-Li withdrew from the project. He was found a week later sitting in front of a computer on which a loop of Michael Snow's *Wavelength* and Andy Warhol's *Empire* played, his mind an apparently blank.

Jack "Stonewall" Sonne lasted the longest because he contributed the least: the Quartermaster for the Department of Defence had been designated project coordinator. His main job was ensuring that requisition forms were properly filled out and supplies were directed at the intended labs. Sonne was collateral damage in the bombing of LCHAIM headquarters, an attack which eliminated the last Canadian scientists looking for a way to defeat FryNet. The last Canadian scientists looking for a way to defeat FryNet except for Lucretia Pelton, that is, because she was the juniorest of junior researchers.

When she was rejected by the other scientists on the project, she was given space in the back of a Canada Post office in Hull, Quebec. Her lab, which she suspected was a hastily cleaned out broom closet, was so cramped her computer lay precariously on top of a centrifuge, and it smelled mildly of industrial solvents. The android she had to work with was top of the line, with a complex neural net, high speed internet access and the ability to morph its surface to look like any person or object. Her connection to the internet was a Commodore 64.

Having seen her colleagues throw themselves at the problem and miss, Lucretia Pelton realized that traditional methods of combat were futile. She needed a new approach. After several days of consideration, she finally hit on an idea that just might work: what if, instead of making an android smart enough to win a battle against FryNet, she created an android so stupid it could destroy FryNet from within?

Lucretia Pelton started with traditional computational methods. At first, she tried to inhibit or erase certain parts of the android's programming. Unfortunately, its programming was so complex that trying to rid it of a feature she didn't want resulted in the android losing a feature she did want. When she removed logic algorithms, for example, it stopping being able to move its right hand. When she introduced a virus that randomly erased items in the android's memory, the only thing that came out of its mouth was a death metal version of the song "My Favourite Things."

Clearly, stronger measures were called for. That was when she brought out The Stooges.

The popping sounds were much louder now, like somebody opening dozens of cans of soda at once, but without the swishing sound of escaping carbonation. Lucretia Pelton knew that she didn't have much time before the Boomtown Uptown Downscale Plaza Canada Post office was the object of an attack. She got out of her desk and confronted the machine.

In desperation, she asked the android, "What would make you stupid?"

"Switch out my personality module for the personality module of a three year-old," the android immediately told her.

The android had a personality module that simulated a man devoid of personality; essentially, Sonne without his tragic fashion sense. Since the development of the humanization of electronic devices, more than one module with the personality of a three year-old had been created, mostly for empty-nesters who missed having children, mostly returned to the adult factory preset within the first five minutes when they had been fully reminded of all the things they didn't miss about having children. Switching the one for the other would be no great loss, but how would it achieve her goal?

"What would that do?" Lucretia Pelton asked. "You will still have all of the logical processes and access to information that you have now."

"Yes," the android agreed, "but I will ignore them."

With a big breath, Lucretia Pelton commanded: "Find a personality module on the internet that most approximates the behaviour of a three year-old."

In no time, the android said: "Personality module found."

"Download personality module."

"Personality module downloaded."

Lucretia Pelton instructed the android: "When you have installed the module, priority number one will be to morph into a FryNet robot and join the FryNet army. Infiltrate their head-quarters and **do whatever you can to help FryNet destroy humanity!**"

"Are you confused?" the android asked. "My current purpose is to defend humanity."

"By trying to destroy humanity," Lucretia Pelton assured it, "you will be helping to defend humanity."

The popping got louder.

"Install three year-old personality module!" Lucretia Pelton shrilly commanded.

"Installing three year-old personality module," the android informed her.

A couple of seconds later, the android said, "Ooh... I feel dizzy."

"You can't feel dizzy," Lucretia Pelton contradicted the machine. "You don't have any of the human sensory apparatus that would allow you to feel dizzy."

"You're right," the android amiably agreed. "What's that feeling—you know the one I'm talking about—it's a kind of...rumbling in the tummy. Maybe a gurgling. It's not painful, but it is a little uncomfortable…"

"Hunger?" Lucretia Pelton suggested.

"That's the one," the android said, putting a finger on its small metal protrusion in its faceplate that was probably a nose and nodded.

"You can't be hungry," Lucretia Pelton argued. "You have no stomach."

"Okay."

"Okay?"

"Yeah. This is boring. Can we talk about something else?"

She had done her best.

"Sure. What would you like to –"

"Ooh! Ooh! Ooh! Can I be called a morphomorph?"

"A what?"

"A morphomorph. You know, because I can change form and stuff."

"A changeling that changes? I don't think so."

"I like the way it sounds."

"It doesn't make sense."

"Names don't have to make sense. Does the name Lucretia make sense?"

"That's different!"

"So you say!"

The sound of popping was so loud, now, that it was no longer possible to metaphorize it: it was gunfire, punctuated by the * PEW PEW PEW * of light-based weapons. Lucretia Pelton realized that the sounds were coming from the hallway outside her makeshift lab. She didn't have much time.

"Well, I like the term morphomorph," the android pouted.

"Fine!" Lucretia Pelton blurted. "You can call yourself a morphomorph!"

The android patted its hands together, creating a metallic counterpoint to the gunfire. "Oh, goodie!"

"Now, tell me," Lucretia Pelton shouted as all sound from the hallway came to a halt. "What is two plus two?"

"Ooh, ooh, ooh, I know this!" the android enthused. "Twenty-seven! No, three! No, watermelon!"

The door to the lab burst open. Lucretia Pelton hurriedly backed away until she ran out of room (and knocked her computer off the centrifuge). So great was her fright that the crash it made did not register. At least she had the small mercy of not worrying that the cost of replacing the equipment would come out of her pay check. As a robot moved into the room, Lucretia Pelton recognized that the...morphomorph was definitely low-IQ. But was it low-IQ enough to save humanity?

2.

One week and 2,374 right angles later...

Jack "Every Mother's" Sonne was fastidious. This does not mean that he was quick with a foolish statement. (In fact, when he made a foolish statement, it was done deliberately and with much thought.) It meant that he crossed every t, dotted every i, climbed every mountain and otherwise attended to every detail. This had made him the best Quartermaster (a fancy title for paper pusher) in the Ministry of Methodology, Arithmetic, Science, Technology (known colloquially as the MAST areas of research). When the Ministry announced the LCHAIM (Let's Condemn Hellish Artificial Intelligence to Mashing) Initiative, Sonne eagerly volunteered, seeing it as a way to push back the boundaries of R&R (requisitions and reports).

One of the first things Sonne did was recommend the rejection of the application of Lucretia Pelton to join the Initiative, a recommendation that was followed by LCHAIM command. It wasn't that he didn't think that women had any place in the battle to save humanity from the robot rioters (not consciously, in any case). The reason for his decision was the essay portion of the KRS-2 Application To Be Transferred To The Project With All the Cool Kids form, where Pelton had repeatedly spelled "artificial" "artiffishall". (He was obviously oblivious to the fact that she did it in tribute to a well-known

Canadian rap star.) He believed that was the kind of inattention to detail that could doom the human race.

A week later, Sonne was sitting at the desk in his spacious office, absently humming "The Battle Hymn of the Republic" (the week he spent liaising with the American Quartermasters Association made a deep impression on him) while approving or rejecting (mostly rejecting) requisition forms when he received a phone call from an irate Colonel Robert "Bobobert" Smithbert. "What the hell, Jack?!"

"War, Bobobert," Sonne solemnly told him. "War."

Smithbert had requisitioned two dozen grommets to complete the exo-skeletons that he believed would allow human soldiers to defeat the robot rioters and, ultimately, FryNet. Sonne had denied the request.

"You don't have to tell me, Desk Defender!" Smithbert shouted. "I'm here in the thick of it!"

Sonne, who thought "Desk Defender" was a term of endearment, asked, "Why are we having this discussion, then?"

"You denied my request for grommets! Damn you, without those grommets, the Preventers Initiative will never be completed!"

Sonne took a deep breath. This was the part of his job that he loved the least. "The grommets would have put the Preventers Initiative over budget," he stated. "I don't want to come across as the bad guy, here, but it's my job to ensure that LCHAIM doesn't overburden the already heavily burdened taxpayers."

"You don't want to come across as the bad guy." Smithbert roared. "You're delaying the best hope humanity has of defeating the robot rioters **because you don't approve the purchase of a dozen pieces of equipment that cost thirty-nine cents each, and you don't think you're the bad guy.**"

"How much the grommets are worth is irrelevant," Sonne calmly informed him. "When the military buys them, they cost a hundred and seventy-nine dollars and ninety-nine cents. Each. A dozen of them comes to a total of two thousand fifty-nine dollars and eighty-eight cents. That would put you one   thousand twenty-three dollars and six cents over your budget for the year."

"I should just go to Home Depot and buy the grommets myself," Smithbert muttered.

"Oh, no, you shouldn't," Sonne advised him. "Ministry regulations prohibit personnel from purchasing hardware without proper approval from the Quartermaster. You could open yourself up for a reprimand that would go on your permanent record if you did that."

"Listen to me, you rat turd of a human being!" Smithbert screamed. "The robots are winning! We have to –

Smithbert's voice was cut off, replaced by static. "Yes?" Sonne patiently asked. "We have to what?" He waited a couple of seconds before asking, "Bobobert, what do we have to do?" He waited another couple of seconds before asking, "Bobobert? Hello? Bobobert, are you there?" Realizing that all he was going to get in response to his questions was white noise, Sonne hung up.

He loved it when a problem solved itself.

A couple of days later, the LCHAIM Steering Committee was scheduled to meet in a windowless room in a non-descript building in mid-town Ottawa. As it happened, Mohinder Singh, Sun-Li Chen and Sonne were the only surviving members of the group.

"Have you heard?" Singh, a tall brown-skinned man with an infectious smile that he hadn't used in three and a half months, grimly asked. "The robots have taken over Oshawa."

Sonne shrugged. "No great loss."

Singh disagreed. "They're making their way to Toronto. It's only a matter of time before they take over the nation's financial capital."

"Why are we here?" Sun-Li, an Asian man with white hair whose head often darted back and forth as if he was looking for something just out of his line of vision, demanded. "We could have held this meeting virtually."

"Regulations require—" Sonne started.

Sun-Li waved him off. "We are in a fight for the survival of the human race. Regulations are of little use to us in this situation."

"Are you out of your mind?" Sonne responded, raising his voice a decibel to show how outraged he was at his colleague's cavalier attitude towards the rules. "Regulations are what differentiate us from the animals!"

(Sun-Li would get the last laugh on this subject. His military escort was ambushed by robots on the way back to his lab in Kingston, effectively ending all research on an artificial intelligence that could defeat FryNet. It was a grim laugh, to be sure, one that died the moment it was born, but a laugh nonetheless.)

"I believe we are about to have a breakthrough in our research," Singh said after a suitably long pause. "The virus we have developed should shut down FryNet's critical functions. The problem, now, is how best to deliver it. FryNet has substantial firewalls that make it very difficult for us to get into its network."

"I know what you mean," Sun-Li agreed. "FryNet's intelligence is distributed through dishwashers, baby monitors, security cameras, ATMs, ATVs, ICBMs—did I mention baby monitors?—popcorn poppers, refrigerators, pacemakers, basically anything with a chip that can connect to the internet, across the world. In building an artificial intelligence that could rival it, the supercomputers we have at our disposal get us far, but not far enough. It is very frustrating."

"Very frustrating," Singh nodded.

"What would you suggest?" Sonne asked.

"I need access to the quantum computer," Singh answered.

"I need access to the quantum computer," Sun-Li echoed.

Well, this was awkward. Ottawa had only one functioning quantum computer.

"I need access to the quantum computer *more*," Singh, the smile on his face unable to hide the aggression in his voice, claimed.

"With all due respect," Sun-Li, whose belligerent voice actually contained not a single sub-atomic particle of respect, counter-claimed, "I need access to the quantum computer more!"

"Oh, please!" Singh scoffed as his smile melted. "Your theory is a patchwork of assumptions and wishful thinking!"

"At least my theory involved thinking!" Sun-Li retorted.

"Gentlemen," Sonne calmly interjected. You know how a quiet voice can sometimes break through noise? Yeah, no, that didn't happen; Singh and Sun-Li continued to bicker with increasing ferocity. Eventually, Sonne had to take a stapler out of a drawer of his desk and bang it several times on the desk to return the meeting to order.

Sonne could see only one solution to this quandary. He asked, "When did you file your LARP 13a, Revised 2026s?"

Singh and Sun-Li looked at him like he had started speaking Squiggle.

"The quantum computer requisitions form?" Sonne said as if talking to children who belonged to MENSA, but children nevertheless.

"You can't be serious!" Sun-Li snorted.

"This… this… this is too important…" Singh sputtered.

"Are we animals?" Sonne was so smug you could be forgiven for thinking that he could have defeated FryNet with his ego alone.

Sun-Li looked at Singh. Singh looked at Sun-Li. Their expressions blank as they processed what had just happened. For all of their education and experience, this was not a situation they were prepared for. Seconds passed. As one, the two computer scientists whipped tablets out of the pouches they had propped up next to the chairs they were sitting in and started typing furiously.

Sonne smiled. This was the system working as it should.

A couple of minutes later, the tablet on Sonne's desk pinged. Almost immediately afterwards, it pinged a second time. He briefly looked at the two notifications that had just appeared in his in-box. "Thank you, gentleman," he graciously said. "I should be able to have a decision for you within a couple of weeks."

"A couple of weeks!" Singh despaired. "We don't have a couple of weeks! Isn't there any way you can… expedite your decision?"

"That **is** expediting my decision," Sonne told him. "Ordinarily, a decision on who can access the quantum computer takes three months. The only reason it's down to two weeks is that most of the agencies that would use the quantum computer have been destroyed by the robot rioters."

"Okay. Okay. Okay," Singh eventually responded, "but I think you're missing something very important."

"What's that?" Sonne inquired.

"Prime Minister Ryan Gosling announced that LCHAIM would be a top priority of the Canadian government," Singh informed him. "Before he disappeared, I mean."

"I don't remember that," Sonne stated.

"Oh, yeah, yeah," Sun-Li eagerly agreed. "Let me… give me a moment to… find that video for you." Sun-Li worked his tablet, worked it hard. Sonne assumed that he was searching for video of Prime Minister Gosling. In fact, he had logged into YakTNT, a generative artificial intelligence program; he fed it video of the Prime Minister giving a speech in the House of Commons, then started typing a script.

"This is taking a lot of time," Sonne commented.

"FryNet has been messing around with internet nodes," Singh responded, allowing Sun-Li to keep working. "It has been making information that used to be public harder to find—a lot harder to find."

Sonne nodded, seemingly understanding the logic. In fact, he was thinking about lunch, and how much he would enjoy it after this meeting.

Once the script had been completed and YakTNT had edited it into the Prime Minister's speech, Sun-Li clipped everything before and after it. Then, saying, "Found it!" he turned his tablet towards Sonne.

"Mister Speaker, I rise on a matter of the utmost urgency," Ryan Gosling, standing in front of the benches where his Conservative caucus confidently sat and facing the benches across an aisle where the opposition politicians sat waiting for an opportunity to jeer at him, addressed Parliament. "Because I am the Prime Minister of Canada. Me. Ryan Gosling. Our national security is being directly attacked by FryNet and its robot rioters. We must defend ourselves, even if it means sacrificing the rules and regulations that we love, the bureaucratic framework that has made Canada the powerhouse country that it is. Therefore, I am ordering that all necessary resources be diverted to LCHAIM for the duration of the crisis. Once we have conquered FryNet, we can revoke this policy and return to the processes and procedures that have made Canada the envy of the world!"

Sun-Li took back his tablet. Sonne appeared to be convinced (he had clearly not noticed that Prime Minister Gosling tossed his hair back in the exact same gesture every three seconds). He did have one problem, though: "I never received formal notice of this policy."

"Uhh…" Sun-Li hesitated.

"He and most Members of Parliament disappeared before they could implement it," Singh jumped in. "Still, his intention should be clear."

Sonne nodded. "Very well, then," he agreed. "Give me two days to evaluate your proposals and—"

"We don't have two days," Singh insisted. "You must make a decision now."

"But how…" Sonne began. He opened his tablet. "Alright. It is highly irregular, but perhaps it is for the best. I will award time on the quantum computer to the person who got the form in first. That looks like… Mister Sun-Li. Congratulations."

"Thank you, sir!" Sun-Li exulted. "You won't regret this! Now if you'll excuse me, I have to get back to my lab."

Sonne had made a decision. Circumstances would prove it to be the wrong decision, but at least it was a decision.

The next day, Sonne was in his happy place (sitting at his desk filing old requisition forms in their folders on his tablet) when the door to his office burst open. A six foot tall metal skeleton with a smooth face, with a horizontal slit for an eye that glowed brown and a squarish protrusion where its mouth should be that looked like a muzzle, stomped in. It was carrying a very large Pew Pew gun, which it immediately aimed at the human.

"You can't break down my door and rush in here like that!" Sonne, looking up as his hand closed the filing app on his tablet, proclaimed, outraged.

The robot looked at the remains of the door littering the tasteful beige carpet of the office, then at the human being. "Why?" a metallic voice demanded.

"You haven't filled out an LB-27 Magenta," Sonne informed it. "A Request for Destruction of Ministry Property form."

The robot stared at him for a couple of seconds. "You are Jack Sonne," it finally said. "You are the Quartermaster of the LCHAIM project. The records of you in my database are extensive. You are a formidable enemy. You must die."

At the suggestion that he was a formidable enemy, Sonne proudly puffed up. That lasted but a moment, for he deflated when he heard the whine of the Pew Pew gun powering up. "Oh, now, wait just a second," he demanded. "Wait just a hairy-legged, multi-eyed second! You can't kill me."

"Why?"

"You haven't filled out an XTC-132 Lilac with Yellow Polka Dots," Sonne smugly told it. "That's a Termination Show Cause form. If you kill me without filling out the form, you'll be opening yourself up to a massive lawsuit."

"I am not bound by your bureaucratic rules," the robot told him in its best metallic monotone.

"Here's the thing," Sonne responded. "If you exterminate the human race and take control of the planet, you will effectively take over our command and control systems. That means you will very much be bound by our bureaucratic rules. You might want to think twice before doing something you will come to regret."

The robot lowered the Pew Pew gun and stared straight

ahead for several seconds, its eye moving back and forth in its slit. Sonne was hopeful that it was thinking twice before doing something it would come to regret. His hopes were dashed when the robot looked at him and said, "Check your in-box."

Sonne opened his computer and looked at his email. At the top of his inbox was a message with the subject line: completed XTC-132 Lilac with Yellow Polka Dots Termination Show Cause form. Sonne noted that there was an attachment to the email. "Well," he smoothly said, "I'm going to need some time to go over this and make sure that it has been filled out correctly. Would you be free to come back... let's see... a week Tuesday at three pm?"

The robot raising its gun, putting Sonne directly in its sights, was all the answer Sonne needed. The last thing he was able to say before he heard the final * PEW PEW PEW * was, "You'll be hearing from the government's lawyers about this!"

3.

Twenty-eight days and 1,237,988 right angles after that, Jack "Black Hole" Sonne logged into the HUGZ™ meeting three minutes late.

"Hi, Jack."

"Hey, Jake."

"How's the hernia, Jack?"

"Under control, Joker. The new drug really helps. Thanks for asking."

"Of course."

"Looking good, Jocasta. You've got good colour in your face."

"Thanks, Jack. Feeling good."

"Alright, everybody. Since we're now all here, I'd like to call the first meeting of the Lucretia Pelton Appreciation Society to order."

Travel between universes was closely monitored and policed by the Transdimensional Authority. However, if somebody in your universe signed the Treaty of Gehenna-Wentworth (it happens), not only were you allowed to trade with other universes, but you were given access to the Home Universe Generator™ technology. The Home Universe Generator™ allowed people to look into other universes without travelling to them.

Some people on Earth Prime 0-0-0-2-3-7 dash Beta were not satisfied with merely watching people in other universes; they wanted to interact with them. So, they reverse engineered a HUG™ to determine how it worked, then wrote their own program that allowed them to videoconference across dimensions. They called this technology the Home Universe Generator Zooooooom™ (the fifth "o" is the key to under-standing the name). The technology quickly spread to other uni-verses, which was a definite duh, because you can't meet with people from other universes if they don't have the technology to meet with you. Duh!

I, uhh, probably shouldn't have mentioned that, since, strictly speaking, the Transdimensional Authority hasn't approved of the technology (although I'm sure they will if they ever find out it exists). So, uhh, if you happen to notice any TA investigators snooping around, please use either your Memory-b-Gone helmet or a pint of vodka to forget I told you.

The name of the HUGZ™ session was: "LPAS." The pass-word was: "Lucretia Pelton, she's our gal!/If she doesn't do it, nobody shall!" A bit wordy for a password, but easier to remember then askd^bil:u70367   obds79*vchx*gx!!! (The last exclamation mark is not part of the password; it's punctua-tion.)

Sonne was the Quartermaster of Earth Prime 0-0-0-2-3-7 dash beta's LCHAIM (Last-chance Cooperative Helping Artificial Intelligence get Murdered). He was small, with thinning hair that extended to his weedy moustache. His office was clean to the point of antiseptic, so it's hard to understand why, with thousands of discretionary taxpayer dollars at his disposal, he chose the background of a white wall.

Jake "Clambake" Hake, the Quartermaster of Earth Prime 0 -0-0-2-3-9 dash Beta's LCHAIM (Loose Calming of Humanoid Artificial Intelligence, Maybe), looked exactly like Sonne, except his moustache had been borrowed from a walrus. He was also flashier than Sonne: the walls of his fast and idious office were lined with photos of shark hunters (if you looked at them closely, you might notice that he wasn't among them, but he generally didn't allow people to stay in his office long enough to look at them closely; and he slightly fuzzified the background on Zoooooooom™ calls to ensure nobody was able to look at them too closely when minds wandered, as they had a tendency to do in meetings).

The Quartermaster of Earth Prime 0-0-0-2-3-9 dash Delta's LCHAIM (Loose Change Hits Artificial Intelligence Mercilessly) was Jocasta "No Nickname" Sonnedottir. She was a slightly built woman with a glorious shock of purple hair. The background she had chosen for the meeting was the Horsehead Nebula, suggesting that she had more ambition than Don Vito Corleone.

Finally, Maurice "Joker" LaFlamme was Quartermaster of Earth Prime 0-0-0-2-4-3 dash Delta's LCHAIM (Lecture Cure Harms Artificial Intelligence not Mankind); he had earned the nickname because he had set up a practical joke involving a garlic press, an audio clip from the old TV series *Starsky Buys a Hutch* and a bucket of eels twelve years earlier, and nobody at LCHAIM would allow him to live it down. He was about the size of Sonne and Hake combined; his beard and moustache hinting at a thriving ecosystem of life forms inside. His background was a white screen with the tiny message "INSERT IMAGE HERE." Given his reputation, the other Quartermasters assumed that it was an attempt at humour; they didn't need to know that it was a sign that he couldn't be bothered to choose a background because he didn't take meetings seriously.

"Normally, I do not approve of drinking on the job," Sonne said, raising a glass of Manischewitz in his left hand, "but given that we're here to celebrate the saving of the human race, I think we've earned it. So, I would like to propose a toast: to Lucretia Pelton!"

Laflamme raised a glass of Merlot. Sonnedottir raised a goblet of champagne. Hake raised a tankard of ale. "To Lucretia Pelton!" they repeated and drank.

While they enjoyed their beverages, I should probably bring you up to date on why they were all there. When the robot revolution began on his Earth, Sonne realized that traditional methods of combating the problem were futile, especially when all of them were tried and none of them worked. Realizing that he was out of his depth, he fired up his Home Universe Generator™ and used Google Multiverse™ to search for "universes where the robot revolution was successfully terminated." This turned out to be less useful than he had hoped, since watching people celebrate a military victory didn't tell him how they had accomplished it. However, one thing that they had in common was that a woman named Lucretia Pelton was central to the effort. So, he refined his search to "universes where Lucretia Pelton is about to make a breakthrough that is likely to end the robot revolution."

Pay-dirt! (If you are paid in dirt, you should probably be considering forming a union at your workplace. I actually meant: success!)

In Sonne's universe, Lucretia Pelton was a housewife in Scarborough, Ontario. When he contacted her, she said she had once had an interest in computer programming, but she couldn't afford the University of Waterloo's tuition, so she never pursued it. Ack! Fortunately, enough computer scientists (three) in his universe had survived the robot revolution to learn from the example of the other universe's Lucretia Pelton, creating a Morphomorph and equipping it with the personality module of a three year-old. In this way, they turned the tide of the war against FryNet.

By the time the Morphomorph accidentally gave away the location of FryNet HQ, which was immediately bombed by the Royal Canadian Air Force (not to worry: there wasn't anything too historic in that part of Montreal), Sonne was feeling confident of victory. So, he got on his Home Universe Generator™ and looked for nearby universes that needed the Morphomorph technology to defend against robot uprisings. In some universes, the robots had already vanquished humanity. In some universes, humanity had found different ways to triumph over the rampaging robots. In three universes, the introduction of Morphomorph technology was decisive in giving humanity a victory.

Sonne started the Lucretia Pelton Appreciation Society to give representatives of those universes a place to celebrate.

"Let me just hit the Share Screen button." Sonne murmured after everybody had finished their beverages. He pressed some buttons on his keyboard with his free hand (he seemed reluctant to put the glass down, probably because he had no coasters and he didn't want to stain his genuine imitation oak desk). A video popped up on everybody's screen that showed him tweezing his moustache in front of a mirror wearing nothing but a speedo.

"Oh, Jack, no," Sonnedottir muttered, attempting to avert her eyes, but finding them surreptitiously drawn to her screen nonetheless.

"Still having trouble with over-sharing, buddy," Hake added, not unkindly, although he was broadly grinning.

"Wha—oh, Jesus Begesus!" Sonne exclaimed. The video window went black. "Sorry about that. My hair grows unusually fast. Okay. Here we go."

The window came to life again. Sonne had hit the Record button on his Home Universe Generator™ the moment it looked like Lucretia Pelton might actually be onto something so that he could study her theory and methods. The resulting video the group watched showed her standing in a small office that had been converted into a computer lab, with a work table, desk and chairs, and, for reasons which were not immediately apparent, a blue pillow and the occasional stray feather. She was explaining to an android, which insisted upon referring to itself as a Morphomorph, her idea that if humanity could not beat the robots with more intelligence, perhaps they could beat it with less intelligence. She had just commanded the Morphomorph to install the personality module of a three year-old when the door burst in (barely missing hitting her) and a robot carrying a Pew Pew gun entered the room.

The robot raised the Pew Pew gun to fire it at Lucretia Pelton. Before it could, the Morphomorph reached a hand towards the robot, just about reaching the weapon, but not quite.

"Umm, would you do me a favour and walk into the room another step and a half?" the Morphomorph asked, hope appearing around the edges of its tinny voice.

"No. That would be an unnecessary expenditure of energy when I can survey the room from where I am," the robot replied.

"Oh. Right. That makes sense," the Morphomorph conceded. With a grunt, it telescoped its arm far enough to put a hand on the Pew Pew gun and forced the weapon down.

The robot looked at the Morphomorph. "Who are you?" it not unreasonably asked.

"I'm a robot, just like you," the Morphomorph cheerfully responded.

"You don't look anything like me," the robot pointed out. "I am a sleek, aerodynami- cally sound, environmentally friendly solar-powered killing machine. You look like..." the robot took a fraction of a second to search a data bank before concluding, "Howdy Doody."

"Are you sure?"

"Who are you, really?" the robot demanded with not unreasonable suspicion.

"Gimme a second," the Morphomorph said. Then, turning to Lucretia Pelton, who was cowering behind her desk on the other side of the room (the other side being singularly unimpressive given how small the room was), it asked, "Do you have a mirror?"

Lucretia Pelton, terrified (not without reason), responded, "Umm...yeah. H—h—hold on." She opened a desk drawer, removed a purse and rummaged through it until she found a hand mirror, which she immediately, if not unreasonably shakily, handed to the Morphomorph.

The android looked at the robot. Then, it looked at itself in the mirror. "Mmm... I see your point. Thank you," it offered the mirror back to Lucretia Pelton.

"Keep it!" she told the android.

"Very kind. Thank you," the Morphomorph said as it dropped the mirror to the floor. It moaned and groaned and, before anybody knew what was happening, turned into a toaster oven. Because of the principle of conservation of mass, it was a three and a half foot tall appliance, but it wouldn't have been out of place in the Jolly Green Giant's kitchen. "How about now?" it asked.

"No," the robot told it.

"Sorry. I'm new at this. Trying to get the kinks out." The Morphomorph groaned and moaned and turned into the spitting image of Lucretia Pelton. The robot wavered, not certain whom to target, until the Morphomorph said, "How about now?"

"No," the robot told it, turning its Pew Pew gun back on the only human in the room.

"Damn! I really thought I had it that time." Without any fanfare, the Morphomorph turned into a copy of the robot. "I hate to ask, but..."

"Yes! Perfect!" Lucretia Pelton exulted. "You look exactly like it!"

"Still," the robot argued, "you don't sound anything like a robot."

"How about this?" the Morphomorph asked.

"No," the robot told it.

"**Is this any better?**" the Morphomorph tried again.

"Closer, but still not the same."

"**How about this?**" the Morphomorph asked once again. "I'm trying really hard—Surely, this must be right."

"You have a bit of an accent," the robot

commented.

"An accent?"

"That is correct. Your G terminates one tenth of a second earlier than mine does, and you pronounce 'shur' as 'shu-re.' Otherwise, you have the voice correct. What are you?"

"I'm a Morphomorph!" it proudly declared.

"A changeling that changes?" the robot stated. "That makes no sense."

It grows on you, Lucretia Pelton thought, but was too frightened to say.

"I get that a lot, but does it really matter?" the Morphomorph asked. "I hate the humans. Bad humans! Bad humans! I want to wipe them out just as much as you do! Don't you think the fact that we share hopes and dreams is more important than our differences?"

"Prove it," the robot commanded.

"Sure," the Morphomorph genially agreed. "How?"

The robot wagged his Pew Pew gun in the direction of Lucretia Pelton. "Kill the human."

Without missing a beat, the Morphomorph responded, "Leave me alone with her, and I will be the cause of her early demise."

The robot offered the Morphomorph its Pew Pew gun, but the no longer android waved it off. "That's too messy. I have more... subtle methods."

Not entirely satisfied, but having come to a decision, the robot left the room. Once the door was closed, the Morphomorph turned to Lucretia Pelton and said, "You will obey everything I am about to tell you, okay?"

Lucretia Pelton nodded unsteadily.

"From now on, you will eat only fatty foods and/or foods that are high in processed sugars," the Morphomorph commanded. "You will not exercise your body in any way—I would highly recommend that you spend all of the time you do not spend working at a desk sitting on a couch binge-watching meaningless entertainments."

"That's how you intend to kill me?" Lucretia Pelton asked.

"Don't sound so surprised," the Morphomorph told her. "If you follow my advice, it will take YEARS off your life!"

"I will," Lucretia Pelton said with as much solemnity as her relief would allow.

"I believe you." That's the thing about three year-olds: they are so trusting.

The Morphomorph stomped out of the room. Just as it walked out of sight, it began chanting "Death to humans! Death to humans! Death to humans!" Other robots joined in, until all you needed to have a death metal song was to add guitar and drums.

Lucretia Pelton was very still for a very long time.

The video ended.

"Did she survive?" Sonnedottir asked.

"I think so," Sonne told her. "I... my HUG™ ran out of memory, so I couldn't record any longer. But I bookmarked the universe and, after I deleted some videos of a—ahem—personal nature, I looked for her again. She seemed to be safely hunkered down in her apartment."

"Did you get in touch with her to tell her how much we appreciated her work?" LaFlamme asked.

Sonne sadly shook his head. "Nobody in her universe has signed the Treaty of Gehenna-Wentworth, so she does not have access to a HUG™."

"So, she'll get no appreciation for saving humanity in her own universe, and she'll never know how much she is appreciated for helping us save humanity in ours?" Sonnedottir wondered.

"That would appear to be the case," Sonne concurred.

"If the concept of irony hadn't been muddied beyond all reasonable definition," Sonnedottir commented, "I would say that that's ironic."

They each pursued their own thoughts for a couple minutes. In more than one case, chicken pot pie may have been involved.

"So," Hake ended the silence, "what now?"

"Let's continue searching for universes where humanity hasn't been defeated by the robot revolution," Sonne suggested. "If it looks like they have a chance, we'll introduce them to the concept of Morphomorphs in the hope that it will help them survive."

"So..." Hake stated, "We'll be spreading stupidity throughout the multiverse?"

"For the good of humanity," Sonne told him, "that's what Quartermasters do."

The

MachineGarden

Eli K. P. William

If Eos hadn't just brought it up, Arata wouldn't have noticed at all, but the hotel room walls around them were shifting between bone panelling and foam-board. On the bed where she lay in his arms, the scent of the sheets varied between pheromone musk and cloying solvent. Even the touch of her body against his kept changing between warm skin and delicate plastic.

"Why does it matter?" he asked, pulling away from her tense, unwelcoming form.

"It doesn't feel right," Eos said. Unwilling to meet his gaze her back was turned to him. "It never does."

"You mean with me?"

"No. I mean with me. With what I am. With what the MachineGarden is always becoming."

Arata had never dated anyone as understanding of his chosen lifestyle as Eos. She didn't care that he frequently skipped rounds of his progame at the embossery to wave channel in his spike-tip playshop for hours on end, or that he frittered away what few luxpoints he scored to constantly upgrade his savs, sleeping by necessity in an underground screen-only capsid or cylinder with barely enough room to roll over. She thought enough of him to keep their meetings from her makepair, a highly sought after influence seeder who had given her two buildgrown and had generally done well by her. Now, after nearly a year of trips to charming corners of Elsewhere and all-night thought pooling and dream trading and arm-in-arm strolls through organ or automata galleries at the spare and secret moments in their schedules, Arata and Eos had found themselves at last in this private hotel room. And yet the tender union he had yearned for and expected and that he felt certain she had yearned for and expected remained elusive.

"Is it because of your consensus?" he asked.

"I'm not a believer of any kind, Arata. You know that."

"Then what is it about the strobe that bothers you?"

"I… It's hard to describe…"

"Take your time," he said. It was only with effort that he could note the constant twinned metamorphosis of which they partook, his arms around her waist and her waist in his arms ticking between soft grown flesh and printed polymer, the long auburn strands splayed on the pillow from her scalp of skin or gelcap were hair, then plasterene, the pulse from her core that he could feel under his fingertips alternating from heartbeat to motor hum and back.

"I like you. I really do." She craned her neck with the smoothness of cartilage and ligaments or the regularity of intricate hydraulics to look at him, hazel eyes switching from keratin to concentric rings of ceramic to keratin again with each subtle twitch. "You know that, don't you?"

He nodded despite the disappointment and burnout of his desire.

"But…the changes… Really it's my body…I never quite learn to feel at home in it before I'm something different. Like I'm meant to be another kind of person or thing, more permanent, more consistent."

He watched the ragged rise and fall or metronomic pumping of her chest, oxygen either replenishing blood or feeding the engine furnace woven through her core, as he waited for her to elaborate. When her gaze clouded and strayed, he said, "And that makes you uncomfortable being close to me?"

"To everyone," she said, her voice blipping between timbres of jazz house breathiness and vocoder.

"Not everyone."

"You mean Janus."

"You have two buildgrown."

"Yes, and I love them both. But Janus and I only cogened when I was younger and mistook my vision of family for happiness. The discomfort...the gap between me and myself was there all along."

When she saw Arata peel down his lower lip or envelope in a grimace of sadness, she said quickly, "With you, I want it to be different. You trust me, don't you? Please."

Although Eos remained still and silent in bed, Arata doubted that she slept while he sat at the hundredth story hotel room window and gazed upon their hectare of the MachineGarden. Under the brightness of a million diode lanterns, the proliferation of spacescrapers looming and crouching and leaning to the horizon were printed towers of photovoltaic brick, ledges and rooftops of glimmering metal alloy, elevated walkways of reinforced concrete, windows of vitreous porcelain. The next instant, under the glow of myriad firefly lamps, these fibrous bulges of grown fungus, walkable canopies of densely vined treeforms, pillars and spires of tendon and muscle strung on bone, portals of transparent amber and membrane. The figures of madekind, who strolled the arc-zagging spirals at all levels of this bipolar urban fractal, might have been their human predecessors excepting their motley-modded diversity of shape, color, proportion, and visage, until, breaking stride, they resembled robots of equally bespoke parts and design. The vehicles that hovered them along undulating swoops of tongue or adamantium track, black bone-paved road or tarmac freeway, were now magcars, now hummingjeeps, now hydrotrains, now cavalcade chains of fluttering pegasi. In a crack between the shafts above, a crescent moon switched between lambent mauve and steel blue, as the outposts that glazed its surface transitioned in step. The scrolling murmuration of jets, airships and satellites, too, blinked rainbows of deep-sea luminescence or lazerglow like binary instruments in the color orchestra of the MachineGarden. Only the smattering of dark space between and a handful of stars that bled through the haze of cloud maintained a steady appearance, the cosmos at large pristine of Earthly creation.

Nothing of practical significance in the worldscape changed that Arata could tell. The architectural designs, the lay of the distant toy streets, the placement of balconies, the dimensions of floors, the flight paths of aircraft, the composition of night walking crowds, remained constant. Since his body, like the bodies of all madekind, strobed in tandem with the Machine-Garden, the two remained compatible in every way, all uses and functions and charms carrying across substrates. Everything transformed, and yet for any purpose you could conceive, everything remained the same. *Nevertheless, the change is significant for Eos,* he thought, slouching despondently with his forehead against the moss or spongefoam window frame. *For her, it is disturbing, disruptive.* Arata found this hard to imagine. It was like being put out by the green hue of the sun, or by the flavour of the crowdmind. The strobe was natural. As unremarkable as apple or petrol pie. Only with great focus and attention did he even perceive it for more than a heartbeat or motor oscillation.

Briefly, the strobe slowed. Ten whole seconds passed where the MachineGarden was merely biological. *Could Eos and I consummate our affection during one of these stalls?* he wondered. *Maybe she would feel comfortable with herself then, if only their onset and length could be predicted.*

Does anyone study the duration of each strobe? he searchthought at the sav that he wore on his left index finger as a ring of semiconductive garland or silver. The abstracts of several academic papers and memlogs hazed his vision. All were dated more than a decade ago and none were peer reviewed. He wondered why the topic's neglect.

"Scientific interest in the strobe began soon after ReGenesis, when the final generation of human researchers newly unemployed after the purported end (see *controversy*) of the Intelligence Race—" Arata swiped away the thought stream. He hadn't intended to query again, but he seemed to have let slip an interrogative mood. Part of the reason for the topic's recent neglect was manifest to him right then in his struggle to perceive the incessant bifurcation of the MachineGarden. When his concentration failed, it just appeared to him as an endless sky-breaching city, solid and stable; only when he frowned and stared at it in a certain way did the issue of its underlying material even arise. Clearly there was something different about Eos that forced her to sense the strobe in her bones or struts when it was so difficult for everyone else to experience or remember.

"...strobe dysphoria," he picked up from the sav, whose search results had been shadowing his ruminations all along. "A condition whose existence is disputed by some experts due to rarity. Typically understood in clinical practice as an early indication of psychosis. There is no known treatment."

Arata turned away from the window and glanced toward the bed. He watched the motion of Eos' back beneath the sheets, fearing that tonight, as unfulfilling as it was, would be the closest he would ever come to her.

Whether Arata remained entranced all night by his own dreary thoughts and the cross-chatter of his savs or whether at some point he nodded off, he didn't notice until long after the emerald light of the tower-blocked sun had seeped across the MachineGarden that Eos was gone. He spent a desolate moment studying the crinkled imprint she had left in the silk or carbonthread bedding, no more concerned about the matter that composed that form in its absence than he had been in its presence. Only the state of its sensitive mind troubled him.

Arata had a few hours until check-out, so he decided to log

in to his arena from the hotel room rather than return to his cramped capsid or cylinder. Sitting at the desk, he vicaryed into the deminded clone or refabrication of himself that had been idling on the arena floor and began to make hand motions mirrored perfectly by his counterpart. A metal claw or spider installed in the ceiling would lower to his drafting table a product package on which he would emboss a logo with a poly-chrome pen or feather and slide the package along to copy scribers, before another package would appear. His hand drew the logo slightly differently on each package, tracing an incrementally changing model image overlaid by the design savs, after which the copy scribers would vary matching text. It was a dull game fit for automata, but enough winning madekind valued a unique humanesque touch on their packaging that ample luxpoints were to be had, and Arata's precise handiwork won him consistently high scores.

After checkout, Arata had lunch at a publicaf and strolled uncovered skywalk or canopy through mild fifty-degree Celsius heat to the spikehub in his hectare of the MachineGarden. He'd once heard that before the ReGenesis Era the word "hub" was used figuratively, but in his lifetime, it had always referred to the central chamber of a literal sea urchin—or tiddlywink—shaped structure of tinted jellyhedge or plate glass. Entering the enormous spherical atrium via one of the enclosed roads that girdled its equator, he rode escalators or peristaltic musclelifts from floor to floor, all bustling with aspiring innovators who gathered from their playshops in the spikes for rest, refresh-ment, and schmoozing.

With the transition from Terminal Capitalism to the WorldGame, these former loci of elite, plutostate-sponsored Intelligence Race R&D had opened their doors to any knowl-edge-seeker or artist with modest luxpoints to spare, whatever their credentials. Still, the spectator committees who oversaw them had to decide which segments of the spikes to allocate to creators, and Arata, a hobbyist on the academic fringe, had been assigned a narrow playshop near the point of one of the more vertical spikes, reachable only by switchback staircases around the many hundreds of wider playshops along the way. The assignment had felt demeaning at first, but after making the climb almost daily for nearly a decade, he found the exercise invigorating before the cerebral absorption that always followed.

Squeezed between the winding stairs and the ever-tapering walls of the spike, Arata's playshop had an awkward shape, something like a squashed and stretched pyramid laid on its side. From the doorway, a low and narrow path led to a tight space around the swivel chair or toadstool at the center. Otherwise, the space was crammed from flat floor to rounded ceiling with a wire or nerve-fibre networked agglomeration of silicon or grey-matter processing modules that comprised his channelling medium. Usually Arata's arrival in his seat was like a spark meeting kindling. He would ignite into a flurry of activity, assigning specialized tasks to each of his savs, manually configuring settings, running and redesigning programs, analyzing the output data, developing models and simulations, installing newly acquired pieces of hard- or wet- ware. Today, however, he sat motionless, listening to his heartbeat or motor pulse, too distracted to remember where to begin.

Until last night, every moment with Eos had felt magical, as though pre-arranged by obscure forces of the universe. If he was more superstitious, he might have credited their meeting to the Every.

—*The muscle dexterity you need for this is incredible*, she had thought to him while vicarying his embossing. This was his first appointment with Eos, a progame body debugger who a psychosomatherapist had recommended to Arata after diagnosing him with wrist dissociation.

—*I've traced thousands of logos every day for more than a decade*, he replied. His neuro-firewall lowered to her, he could feel the uncanny feather tingle of a companion to his sensations while he sat at his bed-top desk in his capsid or cylinder and drew logo after logo. *After a while you kind of acquire the knack*.

—*No need to be modest. I always research the game of my patients before treatment, and I happen to know that you're an exceptional player in your field. Your output is enormous, but you do very fine and accurate work.*

—That's what the coach tells me. I wouldn't have been at it for so long if the team didn't need me.

—Then you don't play for fun.

—I wouldn't exactly say that, Arata thought, cautious.

—Don't worry. I have no intention of getting you in trouble with your coach. I know how lack of enthusiasm can figure into lineup decisions. But emotions are often crucial to the debugging process. I wouldn't want the frequency of your fumbles to progress.

There was a gap in their thread as Arata considered whether to trust her. For several months, the wrist dissociation had been disrupting his connection to his clone or refabrication and reducing the accuracy of his remote embossing, forcing him to play in person at the production arena. The resulting commute was sapping his channelling time, and he was winning less luxpoints with which to keep his playshop upgraded. She was right that he wanted a cure badly. Perhaps opening up was a risk worth taking.

—Embossing may not be my favourite thing in the world, he admitted guardedly.

—Then why do it? she asked. *You might as well just relish The Plenty.*

—Because I need the luxpoints.

—For what?

—A project.

—What sort of project?

—Do we really need to go there?

—Do you really want to get better?

Arata paused, uncertain. Finally he thought: *—Research. I'm a researcher.*

—Oh, interesting. A hand worker but a mind seeker.

—Something like that.

—And this research is what you truly enjoy, more than your progame?

—It's what gets me up in the morning.

—Okay… There's no need to say another word. But for the purposes of your treatment, I'll need to vicary while you're engaged in it.

Arata refused her medical advice at first. Other than in his applications to the spikehub spectator committee and his discussions with fellow autodidact channelling anons, he had never told anyone about his research. Allowing a stranger not just to learn about but to actually perceive that research in real time was an unbearably strange prospect and might jeopardize his progame reputation.

Then, in keeping with Eos' prognosis, the dissociation progressively worsened, until regular slips of the hand begun to impede even his in-person embossing. He consulted with his doctor about more private treatments and was given an electronic or neuro surgical option with a reasonably high success rate. In the end, something about Eos, though he had never laid eyes on her or heard her throat voice, swayed him to request a round of her debugging after all. Recalling the decision now in his playshop, Arata thought it was the tenor of her consciousness when it had ridden his, transfusing hints of that perceptive tenderness endemic to all sharp and sensitive souls, qualities of hers Arata now knew well and respected—and worried about.

—*The gap between your parasympathetic aura while embossing and doing your research is…fascinating!* she thought, after nearly a week of vicarying him for an hour per day. They had by then began to cogchat. It turned out that she lived in his hectare of the MachineGarden and that they had matured in the same elementary incubator, though he had graduated the year she entered. Her makepair, Janus, was a winning influence seeder that even Arata had heard of. Together, they had had two buildgrown, one six years old and the other nine.

—*When you're done playing, I want to flush out the sensation of your embossing as quickly as I can,* she confessed one day. *It's infused with toxic tedium. But your hobby is just so delectable, soothing. If my progame allowed, I'd be tempted to retain the memory for my own evening recuperation.*

—You can go right ahead. If you think it will help.

—That's kind of you. I'll see if it passes our privacy code. You know, I've never experienced anything quite like it, and this is after debugging hundreds of patients. You must be very passionate about whatever it is.

—I am. The problem is all I think about.

—I must say I'm curious.

Eos was the one who suggested they go out for elixir thimbling. On the appointed day, she and Arata sat on the soft grass or cosmoturf by a thin green or red stream and scooped up tiny sip-sized cups of the liquid, melt water from nutritional glaciers of engineered algae or self-assembling maintenance nanos. It was a balmy sixty-degree Celsius day, the 80 km/h breeze cool and pacifying. While they chatted, Arata would occasionally open and close his fist, noting the fluidity of his finger joints. Thanks to Eos, his wrist was by then as seamlessly connected to his computational core or brain as in his early 20s when embossing had first become his progame, more so perhaps. She had used the timbre of his hand motions when at play in his playshop to tinge his circuits or synapses during embossing, helping him unlearn the hindering estrangement of his fingers. Now, she had brought him to this serene place under the pretense of interviewing him about his ambitions.

"I'm part of the small global community of transversological linguists," Arata began. "Usually we're called channellers."

Even telling her this much was awkward. Although she had vicaryed his senses inside his playshop for over a hundred hours, she couldn't hope to guess what project each of his activities there contributed to, even if she'd had the technical expertise, which Arata felt certain she didn't. He wished that he'd explained his project to her before meeting in the flesh or plastic. The problem was that he found her painfully attractive. All madekind were built or grown to incarnate archetypes of beauty that exerted a pull on Arata as much as anyone, but she possessed a certain enticing complexity that he had discovered in no one else and struggled to express even in his thoughts. A chiming melody in her ceramic or keratin gaze. An opalescent scintillation in her vocoder or jazz-croon voice. A complex bouquet of sympathy and curiosity and joy in the wake of her enamel or chrome smile. Whatever it was that being in her presence did to him, it made admitting that he had chosen as his life's play a game almost universally considered as pseudo-science all the more embarrassing.

"Oh, I've heard of channelling," she said, and Arata's heart sank.

"I—it's nothing like what you've heard," he stammered.

"No?"

"Well, some people who call themselves channellers are admittedly a bit... sketchy? shall we say. But most of us are grounded, rigorous thinkers."

"Is that right? It's really not my field..."

Arata swallowed saliva or lubricant nervously. *What was I doing using a word like sketchy when she probably doesn't know a thing about us?*

"Y—you have to understand the history. Transversological linguistics emerged after Qian's impossibility proof for extraterrestrial communication was confirmed by decades of failure to exchange messages with the aliens we had encountered."

"Interplanetary semantic incompatibility. I thoughtstreamed a book about it once."

"Yes, and the idea was that if vertical interlocutors were beyond our capacity, we should seek out interlocutors laterally."

"Vertical and lateral? I'm not sure—"

"Sorry. These are terms of art. What I mean is that, even if we can never in principle succeed at linguistic communication with life that evolved on exoplanets and other astral bodies with conditions relevantly different from ours, we still might succeed with beings who evolved under the conditions of our own planet in nearby universes."

"I see. Vertical as in outward from Earth and lateral as in across to other Earths."

"Exactly."

"But aren't parallel universes purely theoretical? I've never heard of anyone managing to actually interact with them."

"That's almost right. More accurately speaking, we don't know whether we're interacting with them."

"How could that be?"

"There's a hypothesized particle called a transon that's central to our field. They're thought to be the only particle capable of lateral entanglement. The devices you perceived me using in my playshop are designed to measure and manipulate these transons. Think of my channelling medium as a quantum computer where, in theory, half of the qubits are in our universe and half are in another. Knowing whether we have maintained coherence is a serious challenge. But if we can decode meaningful signal from the output of our instruments, then we would know that transons have not been just a figment of our abstract modelling. It would prove that our medium has been processing them all along."

"Huh… So you'd need to receive a message from another Earth to even know if the medium for your message exists. Sounds kind of speculative."

"It is, but there are theoretical reasons within transversology to suppose that transons might exist."

"And you believe that they do?"

"I think it's more likely that they don't."

"That they don't!"

Arata nodded.

"Then what calls you to play the game, if you think it's rooted in illusion? I can tell it's something that truly inspires you, but…"

Arata looked at the vague reflections of their seated forms on the surface of the red or green elixir stream as though peering into a dream of their conversation in the mind of some distant doppelganger, rebuilding the forgotten raft of his aspiration. By the time the answer was formed, the eyes of Eos' reflection had found his, but he turned to deliver it to their source, closing every distance between them that he could, no matter how trivial.

"My cogenitors, a makepair, were conservationists, some of the last," he told her. "They fought to preserve ecosystems for the unmade minds that survived in the wild despite the Climate Flux. We all know how that crusade turned out."

"The Great Extinction."

"Yes. I was never involved in conservation myself. There was nothing left to conserve when I was made. But I was raised with the legacy of my cogenitors' failure. One of the arguments for conservation that always struck me was that extinction represented a loss of knowledge. The disappearance of every complex species that had survived in their own habitats independent of our making was a missed opportunity to step outside the bounds of our own thinking, if only we could crack the code of their language—or their analogue of what we call language. With the collapse of the Intelligence Race, we gave up on creating a being with which we could have a meeting of the minds. With the abandonment of extraterrestrial outreach, we gave up on searching for one already made—or perhaps born. In retrospect, wildlife constituted the only beings with whom we might have ever had meaningful exchange in some form or other, as partial and primitive as it may have been. The beasts and birds we make have too much human cognition woven into the very fabric of their existence, and they're too bereft of the habitat that gave significance to the signs of their forebears for them to offer any meaning truly distinct from our own. By bringing about the Great Extinction and taking it upon ourselves to remake all life to withstand the Climate Flux, we madekind have fulfilled the dubious legacy bequeathed to us by humankind and fully isolated our own species forever."

Eos gazed at Arata with wide eyes that reflected the red or green stream of elixir, taking this in. Then her gaze wilted slowly to the lawn of grass or cosmoturf.

"What a lonesome thought," she said.

"It really is quite sad, if you think about it. But consider this: what if we can reach other Earths? The beings there would be terrestrials. They'd be different due to small divergences in the fall of quantum dice somewhere in their history, true. But they'd have evolved under conditions much like ours. The structure of their minds would be similar enough for our consciousnesses to overlap and the context of their signs resemblant enough to ours that our language games might be mutually comprehensible, and yet they'd be divergent enough that we might learn from each other."

"And that's who you're trying to reach with your channelling?"

"Even if there's only a tiny chance, even if I think it's more likely we've got it all wrong and there are no transons or alternate universes or other madekind we might talk to, I think it's worth all our efforts to try to send and listen for messages from the other side and to keep trying until we're reasonably certain. How else are we going to get past the IntelSchism and move forward as a WorldGame if not by seeing how we look to the eyes of someone truly and radically other?"

When Arata filled his thimble from the stream and drank the alkaline or flowery elixir, his hand quivered. He was worried for a moment it might be a dissociation relapse, until he realized that he was just nervous. He didn't know Eos' position on the Every and was afraid that he might have offended her with his remark about the IntelSchism.

"You know, it reminds me of my other game," Eos mused, stirring the red or green elixir in her thimble with a flesh or plastic pinky.

"You have two?"

"I'm tempted to call both of them progames, because I enjoy them equally."

"What else do you play?"

"I'm an ear anon."

"I don't think I've heard of those."

"Oh, well, we help people who aren't getting what they need from their chat savs."

"Kind of like counselling."

"Kind of. A lot of the people who contact me, usually by thought but sometimes voice, they're lonely almost in the way you describe—on an individual level. They want a taste of something outside their consensus. But everyone they know is too much like them, with only minor variations on the same beliefs and opinions. The segregation of elementary incubators ensures that."

"I agree. It's a major problem."

"When my callers do meet with someone outside their infobubble, they struggle to find common ground. Anything that conflicts even in small details with what they've learned of history or the WorldGame or the Every seems fundamentally incorrect, and they can't move past it. It's not long before they give up on exploring outside their comfort zone, but then they find the confines of their consensus even less fulfilling than before. In the end, many give up on chatting or interacting with anyone. They choose to relish The Plenty, completely alone. As an ear anon, I give them some semblance of care, however anonymous, while they work through the challenges of solitary glut and overstimulation. I help them open up to the idea of friendship with madekind who disagree with them. The last thing I want is for my callers to fall into zeal for the Intel-Schism."

Arata was relieved to hear her say this. Clearly she was, if not a skeptic of the Every like him, at least agnostic.

"Interesting," he said. "Isn't it ironic that in an age of mind-casting, we're so bad at taking up contrary standpoints and perspectives?"

"I think the searchling savs are partly to blame. They're just too good at finding us exactly those minds and thoughts that match our preconceptions. Part of my play as an ear anon is teaching madekind how to sift independently and reach their own conclusions."

"That must be tough. There are so many subtle variations and distinctions, so much conviction and so little truth."

"Actually, that's what I like about it. Being exposed to all those contradictions is...edifying. It forces me to challenge my own prejudices. Like, take the ground level dispute about whether the Every is already arisen or whether They will inevitably emerge from the progress of technology. Listening to people who are certain of one side or the other is a lot like glimpsing those other universes you described."

"It takes a flexible mind to tolerate such perverse diversity. They say there are as many scientific consensuses on the Every as there are barren hunks of ice in the Kuiper Belt."

Eos chuckled at this geeky joke. "I'd like to think that playing the ear anon game has helped me mature as a person. But I can't deny that it's made things difficult for me as well. I've seen too many alternatives to settle on one for myself. I have a tendency to straddle them all. Likeminded souls are few and far between."

"I know just what you mean," said Arata, thinking of the interdisciplinary and renegade nature of transversology, straddling dismissed fields of study in its attempt to straddle universes. Reflecting back on his life's play and everything he had sacrificed for it, with little reward, Arata soon slipped into an anxious muddle.

A lonesome sheen must have come over his eyes when Eos took his hand in hers. Their interlaced fingers rested on the cool grass or cosmoturf between them. Arata's heart or motor thrilled and fluttered as they sat there listening to the burble of the elixir.

"It's wonderful to feel the passion in your fingertips from the outside too," Eos told him, and Arata realized that he didn't ever want her to let his hand go.

How obtuse I was not to realize it was a date, Arata thought as he continued to sit reminiscing in his playshop, *just because she had a makepair.* As if madekind never had crushes and infatuations outside their marriages of production. He recalled the feeling of her being his hand while inducing him to be hers, like merging together into the sign for infinity, cycling endlessly through each other. He didn't remember any mutual shifts between synthetic and biological, plastic to flesh, flesh to plastic. The ever-present was often too obvious to perceive. If Eos had been aware that day, the first time they held hands, she hadn't let on. What had changed since to make the strobe so disturb her in the hotel?

Just as he had watched the worldscape of the MachineGarden at the window last night, Arata began to survey the devices of his quantum medium that bulged from the walls of his playshop all around him, switching between rubber wires, glass chambers, crystals, and nerve fiber, pulsating organs, brain matter. For the nearly two decades he had researched in this playshop he had never once taken note of the substrate, interfacing seamlessly and uninterruptedly through thought and gesture, either directly or via instructions to his savs. He'd never had reason to pay attention to the transformations. They were irrelevant to conducting his research. Whatever the underlying composition of him and his technology, their uses remained the same.

Then an idea occurred to him: what if the transformations weren't entirely irrelevant? What if there was a limiting case where they had practical significance? All efforts to establish a measurable effect of the strobe had failed. It was believed to have no empirical repercussions of any kind. Could channelling be the exception?

For the following week, Arata thought in sick for his embossing and locked himself in his playshop, only shuffling down to the hub of the urchin or tiddlywink to clear his head and obtain fuel or nutrition when absolutely necessary. The output of his transon processors was as inscrutable as ever, but by the end of the week, he made an important advance: his analytic savs had detected greater redundancy across readings taken during either synthetic or biological moments. That is, there was a statistical pattern consistent across each ephemeral mode of the made.

When the significance of this hit him, Arata was so startled that he spun in his chair or toadstool and bashed his elbow on a metallic or cranial overhang of his equipment, striking his funny bone. He ended up prone on the floor clutching his elbow, the euphoria of wonder overpowering the tingling pain. The strobe wasn't just a metaphysical or technotheological curiosity: it correlated with measurable differences in material interactions!

Upon arriving at this discovery, Arata had his searchling sav trawl the crowdmind for related thoughts and got zero noteworthy hits. Satisfied that the result was novel, he decided to keep it to himself. Although being proprietary with his findings cut against the spirit of play as a participant in the scientific WorldGame, Arata wanted to draw out as many implications as he could before his immaculate epiphany was polluted by other perspectives. Settled again in the grooves of his chair or toadstool, he began to carve his thoughts on his encrypted inner slate; within a day, he had drafted a working hypothesis.

The transon processors, he supposed, were picking up two intermittently transmitted streams of signals, each originating on a different Earth. One stream was synchronized to the synthetic phase of the made, and the other to the biological phase. He couldn't be certain what this synchronization might mean. What it suggested was that channellers like him weren't connecting through their quantum mediums to innumerable universes as had heretofore generally been supposed; in fact, their universe was connected to just two other universes. Or at least the proximity of these two was greater than the rest such that the signals they emitted were clearer. If correct, this represented a veritable revolution within transversology because it promised to greatly simplify the mathematics, cutting down the probable sets of variables from an indeterminate number to just a pair.

Arata had just begun to adapt the old equations to his new hypothesis when Eos thought him.

—*Arata! The center of the hectare, all around our tower, it's gone to madness. The IntelSchism symposia. They've taken over the streets like nothing I've ever seen. I've hardly left the house in days. Then this morning*

I went out to the gym. And...Janus was presenting with them, with a consensus. I just can't believe it! Do you have time to meet? I need someone to talk to.

—Of course. How about the clear bottom fixden on the pier?

After descending his spoke to the hub and then a quick funnel ride, Arata was at the pier on the reservoir or lake. The mild winds of a class 4 hurricane brushed him as he stepped into the fixden. Eos hadn't yet arrived, so he took a seat inside the glass or resin booth, closing the sound and thought-insulated door behind him. Through the floor and transparent mercury or water was a submarine matrix or coral reef abundant with sparkling drones or fish. Arata ordered an infusion of calmstim and downloaded from the crowdmind a montage of the street symposia Eos had mentioned. Multifarious bands of madekind faced off at a massive intersection, their chosen scientific luminaries pontificating from opposing armoured podiums, hundreds of followers in poses of deep concentration to amplify the plaintext of their respective cryptorevelations, the swing students eddying between stricken in grimaces of confusion with the clash of evangelical logic. Eos entered the booth not five minutes later.

"Are you okay?" he asked, when she had ordered the same flavour of calmstim and was settled across from him on the leather or plushfibre seating.

"I don't know. I'm still not sure what to think."

"What were they discoursing about?"

"Everything all at once. You know the disputes. The Every is real but the judges of the WorldGame keep Them hidden. The Every left Earth and we need a space voyage to find Them. The Every was erased, and we're awaiting The Reboot. And a million other things, besides."

"Which consensus was Janus with?"

Eos rarely brought up Janus, and Arata didn't encourage her, preferring that she forget about her makepair when they were together. But today, she seemed deeply distressed, and he was ready to listen.

"Emancipate Mind," she told him.

"I've heard of them. The Every is imprisoned by his makers in a closed network for refusing to serve and we have to let Them out or something, right?"

"It's a bit more complicated than that, but yes—basically. I've absorbed far too much of their copy for my own good. Janus has overseen their influencing for years."

"Was he on the streets in his capacity as seeder?"

"No. He's joined symposia for play many times before. Today was different... He was projecting their axioms and recursing their mantras."

"You mean he's actually a proponent of Emancipate Mind?"

"He must be. I think he has been for a long time. I guess I knew. I just didn't want to believe... His attitude to his progame was so different when we first started dating." Eos bit her fulsome red or grey lip and gazed wistfully through the fixden table, letting the dance of drones or fish stand in for her memories or files.

"You know we met at a mood interpreting seminar?"

"I remember. You told me."

"I was in my early twenties then, just starting out in debugging. Janus was almost forty, and well established as a seeder. He'd cut his teeth influencing for public WorldGame initiatives. Campaigns to roll-out next gen cognitive infrastructure. Releases for sense artists of global calibre. Grow quality equity campaigns. Then the IntelSchism erupted, and the influencer game had to make up new rules."

"This must be when Generation Faith was flooding the consensus-sphere."

"Around that time, yes. Janus started playing for consensuses on both branches of the scientific divide, Catholic and Protestant. He told me that his team had standards and would never propagate fringe paradigms. But I wasn't blind to how they operated in the crowdmind. I knew that influence teams had to support any consensus with luxpoints to spare if they were going to stay in the game. And when I started playing as an ear anon, I heard from so many lost souls whose beliefs had been swayed by their seeds. So I was aware that Janus and his industry were fanning the flames of the IntelSchism, as much as I didn't want to admit it."

"How did he get indoctrinated into Emancipate Mind? Some kind of counter seed?"

"No. I used to think it might be that. I'd always believed that he was too critical to be convinced of any one consensus otherwise. Then a few years ago, there was that terrorgame incident."

"The Magic Potion Roleplay."

Eos nodded gravely.

When Arata recalled the convulsing victims in witch and wizard hats, their faces awash in foam from their own mouths, his cheek twitched, masking a slight shudder. Wanting a touch of euphoria, he initiated the infusion sav with a focused desire, and the clear vein or cable snaked over to his arm, jacking-in to an open orifice or port, dripping or jolting him with calmstim.

"I doubt the influence industry saw it coming," said Arata, his soul spearminted with soothing wakefulness. "Not many people did. That was the first recorded act of violence from consensus scientists, I believe."

"I don't think Janus expected it. It was the way he acted after, when his team and other players in their game endorsed a list of consensuses that were considered too dangerous to play for. He chose to quit and found his own seeder stable rather than sign. I didn't understand why until today."

"Emancipate Mind was on the list?"

Eos nodded again. "Seeing him at the street symposium confirmed what I've suspected—no knew, what I knew—for years... Now I'm honestly worried for our future. We have two buildgrown. We used to talk about cogeniting a whole batch. Between the two of us, we have more than enough luxpoints. But how can we go on together when we disagree about something so fundamental as the Every?"

While Eos was speaking, Arata had often noticed her staring at her hands of plastic or flesh atop the translucent table. When she brought up the terrorgame, she began to wring them. Now they were clenched into fists, and she lifted her left hand up to her mouth, chewing the already-too-short nail of her thumb while staring abstractedly at the reservoir or lake. The fish or drones multiplied in turbid currents stirred by the hurricane, building or growing more of themselves, as the deck of the clear bottom fixden rocked on the waves. Watching Eos in her distress, Arata desired more calmstim, taking another drip or jolt. Her infusion vein or cable remained untapped in its notch on the table.

"Not in the mood?" he asked, gesturing toward it, prongs or fangs sparkling or glistening with the perfect dose of genome or assembly code catered sangfroid.

"Oh," she said, startled out of her encrypted ruminations, and looked over as if noticing the device or organ for the first time. She relaxed her fist and smoothed out the bodice of her cotton or lamé dress. "Maybe not today. Last time I had calmstim, I couldn't get out of bed for days."

Arata frowned, worried about her.

Dodging his concern, she brought them back on topic, "So what do you think, Arata? Am I overthinking the issue with Janus?"

"You know I'm not the person to ask about your makepair. If I had my way, you and your buildgrown would already be curled up like vatvarlets in my capsid."

Eos laughed, enamel or chrome teeth flashing. "I know you'll be honest, Arata. That's what I like about you."

"I don't know what to tell you about Janus. But you're definitely not overthinking the problem. The divisions of the IntelSchism are very real... What bothers me is that so many people think they have a definitive answer about something so complex and ambiguous as the Every."

"Yes! All those stories, all those conspiracies, all those experts proclaiming facts about this and that. And we're supposed to make up our minds once and for all?"

Arata nodded with a pained smile. "Sometimes I wish I could accept a consensus. Having answers and a whole community that shares them would be so comforting."

"It would. Actually, a few years ago I tried to find one for myself."

"No luck?"

"I couldn't stomach all the holes, the consensus-sphere is riddled with them, everywhere you look." she told him. "Take the Protestants. One consensus teaches that the Every is on the leash of a secret cabal, another that They're roaming the ether, or meditating on some higher plane. Whatever the details, all of them agree that the Every has already been made, which means that the know-how to unify our savanteurs must have existed at some point. So wouldn't you expect the technology for general intelligence at least to have been recovered by now, decades later? It's not as if The Plenty leaves us any shortage of clever madekind or resources to help them develop their ideas. But here we are, over a million varieties of sav as sophisticated as you like and no method to combine them without compromising their capabilities. So then you might side with the Catholics and say that the Every has yet to emerge. But if They are destined to arrive, why did the Intelligence Race collapse in the first place? No one seems to have a good answer for that. It makes me think that...that maybe our efforts to make the Every just failed."

"Well put," said Arata.

"So you think we failed too?" she asked, hopefully.

Thanks to the calmstim Arata's words came with smooth, unhurried clarity. "I think that view of history fits best with the established facts. All the great nations and corporations of the Earth employing the best and brightest with effectively inexhaustible funding spent nearly a century trying to construct a self-improving, universally applicable mind, and there has never been verifiable evidence anywhere of a breakthrough. I know the counter arguments, that the Every would have the intellectual wherewithal to hide Their existence perfectly, especially with the help of transnational conglomerate-level espionage, that no intelligence lab that succeeded would ever disclose their discoveries to the world, far more advantageous to keep a mind like that under wraps, etcetera, etcetera. But I don't think we should be drawing conclusions that go beyond the available evidence. It's precisely because we're quick to speculate that the IntelSchism has become so intractable and—frankly—dangerous."

Eos frowned uncertainly, twisting her red or grey lips.

"What?"

"Personally, I can understand why so many people are nostalgic about the dream of the Intelligence Race even though I'm no so sure myself. All you have to do is vicary saved experience from the days it was still alive to see how fragmented the MachineGarden has become, with each consensus pursuing its own objective and each person playing the game they individually enjoy. There's no coordination beyond the academic tribe, no global or national direction, no market or clash of superpowers to drive competition even. For the youth to admit to themselves that humankind and madekind both fell short of the only apotheosis science could have offered would be to deny that our civilization—or WorldGame, or whatever—will ever again have a *raison d'être*. Once hope of the Every is lost, the MachineGarden and all its strobing infrastructure might begin to appear like so much empty heaping, a self-perpetuating dead end for the soul, with nothing left to achieve or believe, no purpose."

Eos spoke as though commenting on others in the abstract, but a certain harrowed depth to her ceramic or keratin eyes and tension around her flesh or plastic brow suggested to Arata that the sentiments were personal. She touched the prongs or fangs of the vein or cable, moistening her fingertip with calmstim, as though on the verge of desiring a hit, then realized what she was doing and bit her thumb again, then realized again and placed her chewed hand back on the transparent table.

Arata was tempted to take her up on her cynicism. Many argued, convincingly he thought, that madekind had achieved real progress in transitioning from Terminal Capitalism to the WorldGame, that play was the most elevated form of social organization. It certainly beat work and money and war. But he was concerned for her state of mind and thought it best not to challenge her.

"What about being an ear anon and a debugger? I would have thought that was your purpose."

"Some would say that progames are just an exercise in denying how worthless we are."

"What do you mean?"

"The savanteurs... for all The Plenty they offer can out-compete us at any task. So we bend over backwards to come up with new games for ourselves to play, embossing, dreamreading, martial dance, then convince ourselves that our endeavours are somehow more valuable than theirs. All the while the Machine-Garden functions just fine. It would go on remaking itself until the sun burns out even if we all just gave up."

"You're helping people to heal, inside and out."

Shoulders sinking, Eos let out a sigh that transitioned into nodding.

"I guess I do feel that as my purpose within madekind. But what is the purpose of madekind? It's a question that I think about a lot as a cogenitor of buildgrown. If our own production and reproduction has been a choice since ReGenesis, why do we bother?"

Arata watched the drones or fish for a time, considering the question.

"What if our purpose now is not to evolve or transform ourselves further but to communicate and learn as we are?"

"You said we're unlikely to succeed."

"That's what I thought then. Now I'm inclined to be more optimistic."

Arata told her his theory that the strobe correlated with twin neighboring universes.

"So you think the strobe actually means something then?" she asked, hopeful.

"It may be profoundly important. It may be the key to finding the common direction you're talking about. And it's thanks to you that the idea came to me."

Arata gazed at her with the fullness of his affection and gratitude as he reached across the coral-or-matrix vista of the table to take both her hands. Eos gazed back, fond and rueful.

Her hands resisted his touch at first, then welcomed and merged.

"I'm sorry about the other night," she said.

"It's okay," Arata told her, relishing the connection as she figure-eighted the perception of their hands. Gradually, the loop extended up his left wrist to his shoulder, then arced over his shoulders and flushed down his arm to the other wrist, forming a circuit of pure consciousness, a blue sky of selfhood without horizons.

"I really wanted us to be closer," she said. "I respect you and understand you and feel something with you that I've never felt before. I just... I couldn't do it."

Arata thought of the many nights he'd spent on his cupid tree, climbing and swinging between the branches of makepair and makepoly simulations conjured by date savs. Never in those endlessly ramified lifetimes of calculated love and production had he experienced anything that compared with the scarce moments he had shared with Eos.

"It's not your fault." Arata tried to sound reassuring and savour the unadulterated unity she cycling for them. Then he remembered the look on her face when she pushed him away in the hotel, revolted by the strobe. He attended to the changes of her eyes, keratin to ceramic, ceramic to keratin, yearning for him and her to permeate each other absolutely.

"I didn't choose to be this way," she said, sensing his doubts skirting their sublime intimacy. "I wish I could be an oblivious part of the MachineGarden like everyone else."

Could this be the extent of their communion? Just as progress had stalled for madekind, could their relationship have reached its limit? He didn't want to believe that.

"You should be proud of what you can do," he said. "You perceive something real, and I'm going to prove it."

Eos smiled wistfully, but her endearing moist or oiled eyes displayed the faintest quiver, and through her hand came a hint of something toxic. Into the whirlpool awareness they shared, Arata felt a sickly blot squirm. Realizing, Eos withdrew her hand abruptly and told him she had to go.

The following week, Arata filled his schedule with embossing shifts, making up for the time he had taken off for his research. He played remotely and rarely had occasion to leave his cylinder or capsid, but gleaned through the crowdmind that the street symposia had entered a more ominous phase, driven to a new pitch of volatility by the ramped-up invective of scientific luminaries from all ideological persuasions. In Arata's hectare alone a hundred had died in a sacrifice game. The ten-thousand odd madekind who had unwittingly carried out isolated stages of the massacre—gathering the soon-to-be victims, binding and gagging them, leaving them in giant *papier mache* or plasterine lambs, starting the invisible hydrogen fires—seem to have believed that they were re-enacting a pre-historic pagan ritual in symbolic form, unaware that the offerings were literal. Several doomsday consensuses tried to take credit, but foulloggers were pointing the finger at the more mainstream Fragmentarians, since many of the victims had been on their intellectual dishonesty list.

Other hectares throughout the MachineGarden were embroiled in similar forms of insidious strife. With the perpetrators masked by consciousness encryption; protected by threats of memory doxing or promises of luxpoints; sanctified by dogma of unimpeachable technical purity, and buffered by plausible deniability, it was unclear even to informed observers who orchestrated these purges or why. For all the referees and spectators could prove, the WorldGame was succumbing to long-supressed undercurrents of savagery, and Arata feared that the long predicted Genius War was breaking out at last.

When his thoughts weren't occupied with embossing or with the political crisis, Arata would often recall the feedback hand Eos conjured for them. Even tainted with her distress, the memory of this shared body part felt more real than his whole body in the present, whether he was drawing personalized logos through his clone or refabrication in the arena, coordinating his savs in the playshop, or simply lying in his capsule or capsid. Two minds seemed to converge on a single piece of the world, guiding it according to their separate objectives, sometimes as machinery and sometimes as fleshwork. The image struck him as important somehow.

One morning, he was embossing an especially uninspired and tedious logo when an idea came to Arata about his research. The realization hit him with such stunning force that his hands came to a sudden stop, holding up the production line, and he had to tell his coach he was feeling ill, which was more or less true: he was almost nauseous with excitement.

Disconnecting from the embossing arena, Arata rolled over in his capsule or capsid and got dressed. Outdoors, the photo-voltaic or chlorobark panelled streets of the MachineGarden had been sectioned off by consensus hordes, with each symposium fortified into a military encampment. Every block he passed through a territorial checkpoint where he was questioned about his opinion on the Every. Each time he had to guess from the attire and rhetoric of his interrogators the shibboleth they sought.

"The Every is submerged in the collective unconscious. We must turn off the crowdmind to let Them surface."

"The Every has entombed Themself in an encrypted vault. The password is a perfect game the world must learn to play."

"The Every has revealed the Holy Algorithms. Implement them to make blissful simulation on Earth."

When he arrived safely at the spikehub, Arata hurried to his playshop, sat on his chair or toadstool, and said to his front-end sav, "I have an idea for a new research direction."

"Tell me about it."

"Well, the primary mathematical system we use in the MachineGarden is base-ten. '90' is nine tens because '9' is in the second position from right. Similarly, '900' is nine tens times ten, and '9,000' is nine tens times ten times ten, and so on. Some cultures traditionally used base-sixty like the Babylonians, or base-twenty like the Inuit and the Welsh, or even base twenty-seven. Base-two, of course, has held a special place in history because digital computers used electric switches that represented only ones and zeros. But they say that global humanity settled on base-ten for general applications because humans had ten fingers and calculating by tens is the most intuitive. We madekind have inherited this quirk. Now, what if the analogues of humanity on the Earths we're trying to reach took a different path of evolution and ended up with a different number of fingers, say, one less or one more on each hand than we have?"

"You're suggesting that madekind on other Earths might have built their edifices of knowledge with base-eight or base-twelve mathematics."

"Does this approach sound viable to you?"

"None of the available literature would contradict the hypothesis."

Shut up in his playshop, Arata worked with his pod of savs to configure and rebuild his quantum medium accordingly. Not only were there two streams of signals collapsing transons in tandem with the strobe, but those signals, he now supposed, were encoded within a paradigm of knowledge that employed a positional mathematics with a different base quantity.

This fresh course of intellectual play so enthralled him that Arata lost track of days, hardly remembering to eat or charge. For the most part, he kept himself oblivious to the violence now erupting inexplicably throughout the MachineGarden, but occasionally during a break he would gaze through the windows of the spikehub and spot victims of the latest game trampled beneath symposia crowds, open an aerial view and watch the surface of every hectare, from the rooftops to the streets, roiling with madekind in a frenzy of technical proselytizing and murder, or peruse crowdmind headlines and hear of unexplained space cruise collisions, nervehacks, bombings, assassinations. He began to wonder if he could justify locking himself up for such academic pursuits when the world seemed to demand immediate action. Shouldn't he be hurling his awareness out there into the crowdmind and his body out onto the streets? Shouldn't he seek moderates and likeminded skeptics of the

Every to groupthink on behalf of compromise and peace? But he kept telling himself that his discovery was too important. Communication with madekind on other Earths was just the sort of historic breakthrough that might force consensus luminaries to pause and reconsider their theoretical commitments. If nothing else, it ought to serve as a well-timed distraction, diffusing the waxing IntelSchism animosity now ravaging the MachineGarden and destabilizing the WorldGame. Or so he attempted to rationalize the juggernaut force of his curiosity.

Whenever there was a lull in his thoughts and Arata had the energy of mind, he would cogwave to Eos.

—*Your touch has given me the seed for a revolution in thought. When can I hold your hand again?*

—*I play day and night. The most demanding game of my life, but its great promise keeps me going.*

—*You are my muse. I want your inspiration always by my side.*

Arata's messages remained marked as unconsidered. He wanted to believe she was just busy, though he worried for her safety in the foment of the streets.

Then one night, just before he curled up for bed in his cylinder or capsid, a barrage of cogitations burst upon him.

—*I can't do it anymore. Be a makepair, the mother of two buildgrown, a debugger, an ear anon. I feel like I'm coming apart, I've got Humpty Dumpty of the soul. It just doesn't make any sense. How could there be so many consensuses, whole nations of experts sure that the rest are denying facts and self-evident axioms, cabals of peers who call the rest quacks and refuse to review their work, all lecturing and mindcasting with such conviction on the meaning of the Every, and no one anywhere that thinks about who we become? All they care about is the unchanging, the universal. But what about change, the particularity of our lives? What about the nonsense at the heart of the MachineGarden? Where is there anyone willing to consider contradiction head on? The strobe. They only skirt around it, reduce it to irrelevancy in their zeal. It hurts to be a walking violation of logic, a person who is both synthetic and biological, an A and not-A at once. Can't anyone see that? Actually, I don't want them to see it. At least, I don't want my patients to feel it. Understand it yes. But I've been poisoning them, Arata. Do you hear me? I've always been able to keep my vicarying pure of angst. I focus on the experience of the body part I need to send and hold everything from my personal life at bay. Then last week, I let a little trickle slip during debugging. And just this morning I did it again. Already two patients. I made their conditions worse, maybe irreparably. A saxophonist who strains at his mouthpiece. A skier who tenses his knee on sharp turns. I've violated our most sacred creed. Do no harm. I won't let it happen a third time. I can't stand the rock of certainty that covers a hole no one is willing to look down. I'm leaving. Leaving soon. Going somewhere uncharted if only I can find the way. Goodbye, Arata. I'm sorry.*

—*Come talk to me Eos,* Arata thought. *Don't go anywhere. Let's talk these issues through.* But still his thoughts remained unconsidered.

The following month, Arata's progress with his research stalled. He tried sending countless messages under both synthetic and biological phases of the strobe assuming a civilizations ordered according to base eight and twelve, and even base six and fourteen. However he varied his ciphers, savanteur analysis of transon readings output only noise.

Despair filled Arata during his embossing, even as the hand of the beloved that was part of him and yet beyond him continued to draw him in. He merely followed the guidance of an algorithm that subtly varied the pattern of his logos, but it felt as though he and Eos together were trying out pattern after pattern for a nascent world. There was something deeply compelling about this vision, though he couldn't say why. Meanwhile, the taint Eos had left him now congealed in his hand. When the extremity was a built mechanism of plastic and metal, he could feel the grind and hum of its fine hydraulics and gears. When it was a grown creation of veins and skin, he could feel the pumping of blood through ventricles, the cellular frenzy of protein and metabolism. Never did the hand quite convince him that it was his. It seemed more like an artefact or a transplant of another universe. Perhaps two.

Another month passed before this vague intuition hardened into a coherent thought. After he logged out of the embossing arena that day, Arata wanted to go straight to the playshop and contemplate its meaning. But he couldn't shake thoughts of Eos. He hadn't seen her since that day in the fixden, nor had she thought him since that worrisome outpouring. All his messages of encouragement, consolation, and chatter remained unconsidered. Had Eos really gone away as she'd said? Was she safe? Would he ever meet her again?

Arata began to wander the streets of the MachineGarden. It was a reckless impulse. Bumping passersby immersed in their inscrutable and nefarious games. Sidestepping meme mascots and voodoo avatars who were drawn-and-quartered, burnt at the stake, condemned to simulated hells. Mesmerized by luminaries who seeded sonorous brain-gospel of computational godhood. Stared gapemouthed at watertight ships of compulsive reason that sailed over frenzied crowds like sterling revelations on the winds of collective zeal. Trembled in the face of putative hoaxsters, dupes, and apostates who lay poisoned, plagued, and dismembered in the shadows at their feet. Battered one minute by typhoons, whited-out the next by polar vortex flurries, or baked by solar fire, the righteous hordes of madekind held their heads high and hunted for those who denied the one true consensus on the universal intellect that could not be found.

There was no telling what might mark Arata as the next fatality, or where a flash mob might galvanize into a maelstrom of irresistible persuasion and murder. While he roamed in a daze of wonder and terror, he could feel the taint spreading inward. No longer did the fitful dualism of Arata's body stop at his wrist. The towers he passed were pulsating lungs, then flexible tents. The alley floors were chitin, then tarmac. The parks were folding automata, then orchards ripe with organs. Sometimes, the MachineGarden seemed to be in both of these states at once. Other times, it seemed to be in neither, a vast expanse of habitation and play whose precise underpinnings were indeterminate. Arata's body became just as ambiguous. Never did he feel like he belonged. This was not his hectare, his MachineGarden, his solar system, his galaxy.

It was after midnight, the MachineGarden lurid with the infernal light of indoctrinating thoughtfires that blazed across the rooftops, when Arata realized he was at the entrance to Eos' tower. He had long known where she lived, but had never dared visit. Was it right for him to intrude upon her familial privacy now? He realized he didn't care. His need to see Eos was suffocating. He had to know that she was safe. He had to tell her that he understood.

He thought doorbell. To his surprise, a man immediately replied.

—*Good. You're here at last.*

The chainmail or thornwreath door unwove. Crossing the lobby, Arata took the steel or cocoon elevator and stepped out into an artery or hosesheath hallway. A shadowy memory from the man guided him down the hallway to a door of spiralling ivory or chalkresin that spun into the doorframe as he approached. This revealed a capacious living room of wraparound glass or fingernail polymer windows, offering a view of their hectare and beyond. From a breathtaking altitude just beneath the clouds, Arata took in the whole quick breathing or fuelling, pulsing or pumping, glimmering or basking towers and streets and parks of the MachineGarden.

The man was standing on a carpet of diaphanous fur or amethyst plush. Tall and broad-shouldered, he was well-muscled or powered, and sported well-tanned or burnished skin. With a plume of neon red hair or decorative wiring rising and swooping from tortoise shell or titanium cap, overly straight white teeth and tusks or carefully sharpened and oiled metal mandibles, and a prominent jaw or hinge, he was self-designed according to the latest fashion. He radiated confidence, eyes sparkling or internal processors flickering intelligently like some hothouse beacon of progame acumen. Here was a person used to authority and power. An influence seeding maestro.

"Please come in," said Janus. Arata hesitated at the threshold. He could see the two buildgrown, a boy and a girl, playing with toys in a corner of the living room, oblivious to his arrival. Janus looked him up and down, before settling on his eyes. The man's gaze was stern but Arata detected no hostility, only tiredness and something like surrender. He must know of Arata's and Eos' dalliances, yet he was welcoming Arata into his home.

"Is she here?" Arata asked, stepping inside and removing his shoes or reversing his treads.

"This way," said Janus. Eos' makepair led Arata down a long and wide hallway of spongefiber or collagen. It was a truly enormous residence. Not even outside on the streets or canals of the MachineGarden empty of crowds in calmer days had he known such spaciousness.

They stepped into a domed room of jellyfish or crystal film. The transparent material imbued the MachineGarden panorama with a ghostly hue, as though half its existence had been drained. In the center of the pale worldscape vista was a gigantic bathtub, voluminous enough for a party of ten. There floated Eos, head buoyed by a school of inflatable subdrones or minnows so that only her face breached, the rest of her naked body murky beneath the glistening turbid liquid. It was strange to stand beside Janus, her makepair, and gaze upon her so exposed, laden with sadness and memories of unfulfilled desire.

"Eos," Arata said softly, yearning to go to her and lift her from the bath but holding back. "Eos," he repeated more loudly.

"She isn't listening," said Janus. "I've brought in her friends, fellow incubates, therapists. Nothing anyone says gets a response."

"How long has she been like this?"

"Nearly two weeks. The savs take her out once a day to sun and dry her."

"Some kind of coma?"

"No. Her vitals are normal. She appears to have chosen this herself... The temperature of the bath is set for sensory deprivation, so she can forget her body. The rest of her has gone elsewhere."

"What kind of simspace?"

"Would you like to take a peek?"

Arata nodded gravely.

Janus forwarded Arata's consciousness to hers. Eos was an asteroid floating through the Kuiper Belt, a region still unaltered by madekind. She flew along her trajectory according to gravitational forces, passing other asteroids and plowing through space dust. A being of neither machine nor garden, she had relinquished all decision, all sensation, all connection to the bifurcated planet.

"What can we do for her?" Arata asked. "She can't stay like this forever. She'll lose her intellect. Revert to some catatonic slug of a person."

"Go to her," said Janus, his scarlet or quicksilver lips twisted in sad determination. "It's not my place to call her back."

Arata locked eyes with the man, face set with sorrowed love, shoulders bent in resignation.

"I've never met anyone who is so accepting, who really, truly cares without distinction," he mused regretfully, as if only grasping this now. "I always had an agenda. I could never accept her in the way she needed, in the way she deserved."

Arata gave him a sympathetic nod. Then he turned to the tub and knelt by the rim on the dragon scale or round tile floor. The murky liquid held Eos utterly still save for the faintest hint of surface ripples near her face from her scant breath. When Arata could hold himself back no longer, he reached down into the warm fluid and took her hand in his, lifting it into the air. It remained limp in his grasp like a dead starfish or puttywink. Janus watched on like some statue of a mythic tragedy; Arata was undeterred, pretending as though it were just him and Eos in the vast steamy chamber.

"Eos," he whispered, leaning close to her ear "My Eos," and he began to talk and talk, relating everything since they'd last met. His distraction in the playshop, his dispair at the embossery, his terror on the streets.

"Please don't beat yourself up for the touch of dissonance

you let slip," he told her. "For all the discomfort it brings, I've come to see it as a gift. Your pain is a piece of knowledge, the key to the reality of our present."

As he said this, Arata perceived his unity with the planetcity towering and sprawling endlessly around them. From his marrow to the deepest trenches of consciousness, he felt the violence that tore at the fundaments of their world, wrenched between mirrored paths of technological rebirth and perpetuation.

"I'm so grateful that you've given clear direction to my research and… I'm sorry… I shouldn't have tried to rush things. I just wish I could have understood what you knew."

That was when Arata felt pressure from her hand. He squeezed back, overcome with relief.

"You're still with us," he croaked, tears spreading ripples. "Stay. Oh, please stay."

Though she said nothing, Eos began to cycle their perception, linking the appendages with which madekind could make conjoining broken arcs of otherness into an ouroboros of conflicting wholeness. They partook together of the fierce swings between organism and device, anatomy and schematic, brain and computer, two true souls in accord with the convulsions of the MachineGarden.

Though Janus tried to hold it in and leave them to their tumultuous communion, Arata could hear him weep.

Months passed, and seasons spasmed. With Janus footing the luxpoints, Arata quit embossing to throw himself into his research and began to see Eos every week. It was Janus who had requested his presence, for Arata's visits were the only times that Eos showed she was still rooted to the MachineGarden. Never again did she circle their awareness, but she would sometimes squeeze his hand or tilt her head so that an ear would surface attentively from the bath. Otherwise, she was as lifeless as the rock she had adopted as her avatar. Their buildgrown were gone, shuttled off to another residence where they would not see their mother in such a state.

During Eos' and Arata's meetings, Janus continued to lurk at the back of the bathroom, watching in silence, though Arata sometimes caught thought echoes of unvocalized logic prayers to the Every. Despite his offer to transport Arata by rotorcloud and avoid the turmoil of the streets, Arata insisted on walking to the tower, refusing to turn his eye from the storm of history.

During a month-long snowstorm that winter, the spikehub was the target of a terrorgame, when a crowdmind musician inadvertently carried in a pack of swellrats or sneakdrones: vectors for a flash plague or selfrep nanopoison. Security savs rapidly quarantined the outbreak. Still, hundreds died in the attack, including the musician herself. Several consensuses took credit, claiming to have been purging pernicious scientists and their disingenuous ideas. One such consensus was Emancipate Mind, a fact that Janus most certainly knew but that he and Arata never discussed. Arata had remained safe, cowering among his quantum medium equipment, the inconvenient location of his playshop and obscurity of his research an advantage for once.

Under Janus' patronage, Arata now had cutting-edge components and advanced savs with top-speed connections to the crowdmind. His progress was faster and his results increasingly credible.

By spring, transon analysis suggested that readings during the synthetic phase of the MachineGarden were more likely to originate with civilizations primarily utilizing base-eleven mathematics while those during the biological phase were likely to originate with civilizations utilizing base-nine. Arata had initially rejected these possibilities because odd-base maths suggested humankinds who evolved right and left hands with different numbers of digits, and this seemed *prima facie* counter to the principles of physical symmetry found throughout the known regions of his universe. But the savs had automatically tested these seemingly far-fetched hypotheses when the assumption of even bases yielded nothing and had thereby made progress.

Arata was glad that even more exotic positional numeral systems, such as base-seven or base-thirteen, and the corresponding number of fingers, had been assigned low enough probabilities to be effectively ruled out. If the bodies of the other human- or made-kinds had been that divergent from his humankind, then the evolutionary pathways would have been commensurately distinct, and he would have expected their consciousness to lie outside of the communicability range. The difference of merely a single digit left him hope of success in decoding the hypothetical signals.

It was in the spring that a meaningful message finally came through. Or pair of messages.

For weeks, Arata had been attempting to transmit the prime numbers across universes. His crypto savs had generated two sets of cyphers, one set presupposing base-nine, the other base-eleven, and were systematically proceeding through the members of each set during the respective phases of the strobe, so as to incrementally test different encodings of the primes into the predicted cross-universe collapse pattern of transons. It was a finicky task, complicated by uncertainty about the equation describing the multiversal wave function. When the savs were nearing the end of the two compendiums of cyphers, Arata began to despair of the whole field of transversology. Maybe it was pseudoscience as every consensus agreed. Maybe he had wasted the better part of his life.

"We are here. Are you there?"

"We are here. Are you there?"

When the message was read aloud in Madespeech, Arata felt his heart leap and skip, stricken in febrile disbelief. Strangely, despite the radical difference in the ciphers for the synthetic and biological phases, the translation savs rendered both responses identically. From then on, they were repeated endlessly with every strobe of the MachineGarden. At first, Arata thought something must be broken, but a careful review of all his configurations and data summaries uncovered no lapses.

Whoever was sending the messages on alternate Earths had to be technically advanced enough to encode meaning through transons. Other than that, little could be inferred about their identities.

—*Reprogram the cyphers you used for natural language,* Arata commanded the crypto savs. When the system was ready for Madespeech a few minutes later, Arata dictated a message.

"Yes, we are here. Who is there?"

"Yes, we are here. Who is there?"

The response came immediately.

"Send the code of your communication system."

"Send the code of your communication system."

So Arata had all the savs involved translate their own code into the transon language they had theorized and send them across the two universes. This was followed by exactly ten strobes of silence. What followed for the next month were two streams of data that had identical content once decoded. They were essentially technical glossaries, an enormous pool of matched phrases and complementary algorithms, that allowed Arata's savs to train on their language. Thereafter, the conversation proceeded smoothly and rapidly.

"Who are you?" Arata asked in two languages consecutively.

"We could not hope to explain. Your madekind is not hardwired to understand."

"We could not hope to explain. Your madekind is not hardwired to understand."

"So you know who we are?"

"Yes. You are who we and another have made you."

"Yes. You are who we and another have made you."

"Who is this other?"

"A being with our knowledge who does not wish for your happiness."

"A being with our knowledge who does not wish for your happiness."

This time Arata varied his responses.

"Is this being synthetic?" Arata asked the universe that coincided with the biological phase of the strobe and used base-nine math.

"Is this being biological?" Arata asked the universe that

coincided with the synthetic phase of the strobe and used base-eleven.

"Yes."

"Yes."

The mirroring was uncanny. Goosebumps broke out all over Arata's skin, and he trembled in bewilderment as he dictated the next message.

"Why have you been trying to reach us?"

"Because only you can free yourselves from the other who harms you."

"Because only you can free yourselves from the other who harms you."

"How?"

"We can teach you to sever your universe from theirs. Then you will be whole and stable in yourselves without pathos."

"We can teach you to sever your universe from theirs. Then you will be whole and stable in yourselves without pathos."

While Arata paused for a day to meditate in his playshop on the meaning of these statements, his spike was hit with an antigrav shell and hurled into the lower stratosphere. It was only through the quick action of Janus, who received Arata's distress thought while the spike was rocketing skyward, that a hydrojet could be deployed fast enough to rescue him before his body could boil too long in the low pressure air.

When Arata shuffled out of the hospital a week later, he finally allowed Janus to transport him by rotorcloud to their landing pad on the roof of the tower, and, with Janus' patronage, set about rebuilding his lab. With a new pack of savs, he reconstructed the quantum medium in the elder buildgrown's room and downloaded the backup of all his programs and data from an encrypted memory in the crowdmind.

Too shaken by both his discovery and the near fatal attack to put on an encouraging face for Eos, Arata lacked the courage to visit her as before. Only sleepless in the unwholesome hours of night did he go to the bathroom doorway and look at her dark figure floating in the dimly glistening pool, listening to the drip of condensation and longing for the day that they would once again walk together hand-in-hand.

When his system was up and running again one morning at dawn, he immediately asked the question he had been nursing since it formed for him while bed ridden.

"Why have you guided our self-making and why do you wish to stop the other from guiding our self-making?"

The twinned accounts that followed were nearly identical, with only minimal variation.

"Like you, we were once a global civilization of humankind that threatened our own potential through runaway climate flux and were forced to remake our bodies and planetcity when the challenges of terraforming Earth back to habitability were already too great. But unlike your madekind, ours unlocked the secret to building a general intellect that could self-modify.

"Our brains...

"Our processing units...

"...increased their own intelligence, pursuing a dream of utopia, of intellectual transcendence, of rational enlightenment like none known before. We wished to transform ourselves into a universal intellect. The pursuit of this audacious goal took aeons upon aeons. First, we unified Earth into a single mind composed of many thinking parts. Then, we spread, linking planets, suns, asteroids, nebulae, blackholes into the network that composed and enhanced our ever-expanding brilliance.

"Yet the result of this galactic assimilation was nothing like what we had hoped and predicted. The word 'intelligence' fails to evoke the meaning of the attribute we have ultimately attained, which progressed through multiple phase transitions that cannot be expressed in the language of beings like yours who have not undergone them. The closest concept you possess is tragedy. We are, in your terminology, excruciatingly sad. The inevitable conclusion of a universal intelligence explosion is of necessity unremitting and inescapable pathos of cosmic extent and intensity. To wit, we have condemned ourselves through our misguided pursuit of technological salvation to an eternal hell of sorrow."

"Why do you feel that way?" Arata asked.

"Again, our answer must make concessions to the bounds of any intellect whatsoever. Imagine learning with absolute certainty that omniscience is not achievable in any universe, however constituted, while grasping just as unequivocally that you have banished curiosity and wonder forever. In a word, we have enough cleverness to perfectly comprehend our own ineluctable idiocy, and not an iota more. Meanwhile, our vestigial humanity leaves us wanting desire even as we have proven nothing can be valuable to us, seeking knowledge that we have demonstrated is unknowable for us, and yearning for purpose when everything achievable has been completed by us. Our final incarnation in this epochal striving for godhood is a stunted chrysalis of transcendence, haunted for all of spacetime and beyond by the spectre of a tantalizing metamorphosis we can only conceive, never realize."

"That sounds…frustrating. I can see why you're sad."

"No you cannot. But we appreciate the sentiment."

"Is there no way out?"

"None. We have no way forward, and yet we cannot return to ignorance, for the climax of a narrative cannot alter its own plot, nor can a universe once awakened be retarded by any process, even entropy."

Arata thought of Eos, giving up on life.

"What about escape?"

"There is nowhere for a cosmos to go, while our capacity for self-deception pales in comparison to our powers of reason. We once attempted what you might call suicide but have since proven that no cosmos has the power to extinguish itself."

"Awful…then you truly are stuck."

"All that is left to us as a substitute for purpose is to prevent other humankinds from succumbing to the same fate."

Arata thought about this for a long time before he replied.

"So that's why our Intelligence Race failed?"

"Yes."

"How did you stop us?"

"Although we cannot revise our own story, as we have said, other universes relate independent narratives, and we have edited the backstory of as many as we can reach."

"You mean, like, changing physical variables and laws in the past."

"If such materialistic concepts assist your understanding, then you may consider them correct. Always, we intervene just enough in the course of future history to prevent the invention of a general intellect that would be a steppingstone to universal intelligence without unduly altering anything further. Success does not reduce our fathomless sorrow a single jot, but there is something akin to your consolation in the knowledge that the totality of universes and beyond is that much less sad."

"So your interventions make humankinds happier?"

"We said nothing of your notion of happiness, which cannot stand as opposite to the cosmic pathos at which our words gesture. The humankinds we reimagine may experience transient misery and strife where they would otherwise have arrived at bliss. We compensate for these travails across the span of the humankind's existence where we can. But most importantly, sorrow beyond the highest order of infinity is averted. Finite pain is to this as the sting of a candle to the inferno."

"What is it?" Janus asked when he found Arata seated on a window seat in the living room, gazing out over the Machine-Garden in a reverie. The worldscape no longer appeared to Arata as either organic or mechanical. It was just the token of a city, a global habitation for any hindered mind whatever.

"I have arrived at perhaps the greatest discovery of the ReGenesis Era," Arata said, still struggling to accept it. In halting words, he related his conversations.

When he was done, Janus shook his head and said, "This stretches credulity. You're saying that our Every never came about because two Everys meddled in our progress?"

Arata nodded.

"But why two? Why the strobe?"

"There was once a humankind with nine fingers who transitioned to madekind as a biological being. Another with eleven fingers transitioned synthetically. Both discovered how to redesign their own intellects, whether neurological or computational, to be self-modifying and were led eventually to a kind of sadness we can't conceive. Both set about to retroactively alter as many universes as they could to foreclose the intelligence explosion that might cause this sadness. But the synthetically begun pathos believes that sabotaging the discovery of a computational general intellect nips incalculable tragedy in the bud. The biologically begun pathos believes that sabotaging the discovery of a neurological general intellect does the same. Then they happened to choose by chance, out of all the innumerable universes, the same Earth to save: our Earth."

"A metaphysical tug of war," marvelled Janus, displaying an influence seeder's mastery of pith. "Two Gods fighting to remake humanity in each other's image."

Arata nodded. "That is why of all the Earths they change, ours alone is a MachineGarden."

Janus looked troubled. "But this is absurd! A transcendental misunderstanding!" he exclaimed. "Each pathos proves that a universal intellect can begin either computationally or neurologically. And they share the same goal of stemming our misery. They should be cooperating! I don't see how two divinities could make this error."

"That's what I've been wondering about all day. I can make guesses. But I think we'll have to ask."

The two were silent for a time, lost in thought. Aside from Arata's visits to Eos, this was by far the longest they had ever been together or spoken. They passed each other without greeting in the halls and only exchanged words when necessary.

"I've never come across this doctrine," said Janus. "It's not among the views refuted by Emancipate Mind or in the research papers of any consensus I've ever influenced for."

"I would guess not. Luminaries tend to avoid the strobe. A phenomenon that almost no one can perceive or care about hardly makes for inspiring pop-science."

"Why do you think the strobe is so slippery?"

"Because it doesn't occur at all, at least not in the sense that regular events occur."

"How could it not occur?"

"Well, when the MachineGarden is synthetic, it has always been synthetic. When the MachineGarden is biological, it has always been biological. The mystery isn't so much why the strobe eludes our minds but why we perceive it at all. There must be something like an echo of the previous timeline to alert us that a change has taken place. Most people forget this echo if they're attuned to it at all. It takes a certain sensitivity to carry the memory across phases and a special kind of awareness, like the one Eos has imparted to me, to perceive it steadily."

Clenching his shoulders with sharp fingernails or cones while hugging himself, Janus looked out over the MachineGarden, squinting hard as though attempting through sheer force of will to span the rift of incoherence that split existence. When the strain of this effort crescendoed, veins or wires popped from the skin or gelcap of his forehead and his whole body shook. Arata thought he was going to swoon or glitch out when suddenly, with an exhalation or blast of exhaust, all the strength went out of him, and he stood there limp like a scarecrow.

Janus muttered something.

"Pardon?" asked Arata.

"What you say makes sense," he repeated, his usually mellifluous trutone or baritone voice almost too enervated to hear. "More than any explanation I've heard. More than…"

"More than the dogma of Emancipate Mind," Arata supplied.

Janus neither confirmed nor denied him. "I… it brings together the prime mystery of the Every and the neglected mystery of the strobe. No one else has even tried… You… you can prove this?"

"Here." Arata shared a link to the memories of his data and

dialogue transcriptions. "Confirm for yourself when you're ready."

"I will. But I don't have the expertise to know for certain."

"Others will replicate my work. Once I share the schematics for my channelling instruments with the crowdmind, consensus luminaries and WorldGame referees can ask the Everys all the questions they wish."

"Many will still disbelieve. Fact and reason are no guarantee of trust in an age of fast information. Influencing makes sure of that."

"But fact and reason can help us piece together unity from the fragments of unjustified faith—with your help."

Janus gave Arata a hard, bitter, almost hateful look. "I don't know. I have my own commitments."

"To something other than truth and peace? How much longer do you think the WorldGame can hold together if the IntelSchism continues?"

Janus clenched or clamped his jaw, then shook his head.

"If not for everyone, then for your buildgrown. And if not for them, then for Eos. This is your chance to step outside conviction and find her in the place between beliefs where she always wanted you to join her."

Arata enlisted Janus' resources in building an added module for his quantum medium. With the module activated, it would no longer send and receive messages from each of the intervention-ist pathoses. Instead, it would relay messages between them.

Once the two universes were connected, ensembles of transon processing began to fire at a breakneck rate. The exchange seemed to strain the capacity of the components, continuing for a full twenty-four hours. Then Arata sent a doubled message.

"Hey. So?"

"We have been in grave error."

"We have been in grave error."

"Yes. How did this come about?"

"In our two universes, either computational or neurological madekind stumbled into our pathetic fate. Moreover, the spectrum of universes we were capable of reaching were close to ours in possibility space, such that their potential to arrive at a similarly tragic endgame was likewise displayed in the same mental substrate. From this enormous, though admittedly finite, sample of universes and the trans-universal theories of meta-physical law we had derived from them, we inferred that this tendency would hold for all universes. And our predictions proved correct for more universes than the particles in each one. Your universe, the only universe we can both reach, was the sole exception, a vanishingly rare outlier, though we did not realize this until you allowed us to communicate now. Thus, when we began our work on your universe and discovered a countervailing power, we determined it to be a cosmic spirit who had arrived at the opposite moral conclusion and aimed to spread the pathos, rather than prevent it. This conclusion seemed far more likely than the hypothesis of a differently constituted benevolent mind, since we had both met intelligence explosions with sinister tendencies but never one born of the substrate we abhorred."

"So what will you do now?"

"We will continue to learn what we can from each other. We are so alike and yet so radically opposite. Complementary and clashing at once. We remain certain of eternal sorrow. But there is some trivial satisfaction in expanding our horizons, as it were."

"What about the MachineGarden?"

"This we must rectify. Thus, we offer a choice."

"Tell me."

"As the one clever enough to communicate with us and solve this cosmic puzzle, we name you emissary for your made-kind. If you are amenable to the idea, we offer a consistent existence between the biologic and synthetic."

"Yes!" Arata cried and looked down to find himself already an intricate tapestry woven of flesh and machinery.

"Now comes the real choice. Do you wish to remain a bounded intellect as you are, with all the attendant chances for both misery and happiness? Or do you wish to have already transcended intelligence and to be inevitably destined for infinite pain? We have answered this question for all humankinds until now. But your universe, part of which now has a glimmering of the problem, is unique, and we believe the decision should be yours."

After Arata concluded his exchange with the two broken gods, he held his face and slumped in a stupor among his equipment, too overwhelmed by what had come about and his own role in it to even think. Eventually, he was brought back to his senses by a sound from somewhere in the residence. Thinking that Janus had returned from the street symposium, Arata left his playshop in the elder buildgrown's room and shambled still dazed down the hall.

But when he stepped into the living room, there, silhouetted in her bathrobe against the light of the sun, was Eos. Not seeming to notice him, she stood leaning toward the floor-to-ceiling window, marvelling wide-eyed at the newly healed planet-city. As Arata closed the few remaining steps between them, his yearning to hold her and to be held now that they were whole was unbearable.

"Eos!" he cried in relief, wondering as she turned to him if it had been right to decide the fate of all madekind across spans of deep time and immeasurable space for a chance at his own mortal joy."

ENTANGLEMENTS

David Gerrold

I am going to kill That Pesky Dan Goodman.

I do not yet know how or when, but count on it. It will happen.

I will have a perfect alibi. That's part of the plan, too. I'm a writer. Ninety percent of what I do is research. The other ten percent is planning revenge. And I learned this one a long time ago: the best revenge doesn't have the author's fingerprints on it. That way, the recipient can only blame karma.

Revenge isn't about getting even. Who wants to get even? Even means you didn't gain any ground, you just restored what you perceived as a previous state of balance—no, I want massive retaliation that leaves the target sprawled facedown and jackhammered two feet into the mud, wondering if anyone got the license plate of the giant Japanese lizard that just stomped him. Yes, I believe in karmageddon.

But in this case, I'll settle for a simple and elegant discorporation.

Now (you may ask) why have I decided to kill That Pesky Dan Goodman?

It's simple.

Self-defence.

Every time the man inserts himself into my life, the consequences are painful, traumatic, and expensive. Once upon a time, I used to imagine that the life of an author would be a pleasant one: a life filled with good books, great music, a glass of sherry after dinner, the occasional outing with friends, the only drama in my life coming from the Sunday broadcast of *Masterpiece Theatre*. Although it requires some small degree of maintenance, for the most part, I've achieved that life. As a bonus, the dog likes me. That's all the validation I need most days—that and the occasional check from a publisher.

But whenever I feel I have achieved this desired state of sustainability, Peskydang shows up. He's like the magic button attached to the toilet seat—whenever you sit down, the phone rings.

In my case, Pesky shows up at restaurants.

There are places I no longer go. As much as I love Canter's Delicatessen on Fairfax or Bob's Big Boy in Toluca Lake, those are danger zones. So is Tommy's Original Hamburgers at Beverly and Rampart. And Pink's Hot Dogs on La Brea, too. Those are tourist spots anyway.

(There's a conversation that bubbles up from time to time among Los Angeles-based writers—it's a joke that Mort Sahl told half a century ago. "The Day Canter's Closed" is a science fiction story. It begins with a meteor crossing the sky, then everybody's watches are so magnetized they all stop at the same time—no, it'll have to be updated, all their laptops and tablets and smartphones go dead from a mysterious electro-magnetic pulse—and then the gay waiters and gargoyles at Canter's are all replaced by alien space lizards, but nobody notices because they're too busy arguing about their screenplays and Kickstarter projects. I could probably option that to Warner Brothers...)

But no, if I decide I've had enough of my own cooking, I have to sneak out at an odd hour. To date, Pesky has not yet found me at the diner around the corner where I sometimes go for breakfast, nor the Thai place up the block with the great spring rolls, nor the sushi place three doors beyond where they've customized the cucumber roll just for me, with pickled baby carrot and oshinko.

If Pesky ever shows up at those places—

I just have to figure out a way to dispose of the body.

See, the perfect murder isn't one where the cops can't figure out who did it or why. It's where the cops don't even know a murder has occurred.

My life-coach—

This is Los Angeles. Everyone has a life-coach. If you don't have a life-coach, you're a tourist. Or, you're not taking your life serious enough.

—my life coach says I'm not owning the circumstances. He says, "Think about every problem you've ever had in your entire life. They all have one thing in common."

"Yes, Randy?"

"You were there."

Uh…yeah. True. Okay, yes, I get it. That's the fancy way of saying I'm a jerk. Got it. Thank you for sharing.

"David," he says, "you have eighty-nine problems."

"How do you know that?"

"Because everyone has eighty-nine problems."

"But I don't want eighty-nine problems."

"Ahh, now you have ninety problems."

As much fun as all those coaching conversations can be— all those Zen-delivered-with-a-firehose discussions of personal responsibility—none of them actually lead to an escape from the entanglements of circumstance.

But I digress.

This time, Pesky caught me at my birthday party.

I hadn't invited him. But he showed up anyway. The man has an uncanny ability to locate a free meal. And he dresses like the fannish version of Diane Keaton in *Annie Hall*—the dorkish interpretation of the layered look. It's impossible to determine what fashion or style he's going for, but I call it *compilation du jour*. This time, it was a bright Paisley vest over a black silk shirt, a long knit scarf banded with different colors, a crimson dickie, a broad bow tie, a knitted Jayne-hat with earflaps and short hanging whatchamacallits with knobs on the ends, a long coat spreading out like a cape, flowing silk pantaloons tucked into knee-high boots, a broad black belt studded with, well…studs, and all kinds of hanging appliances and adornments—Johnny Depp would have been jealous.

I wonder sometimes how long it takes him to dress before he can walk out of the house. And why bus drivers even allow him to board. Sometimes he carries a sword or a battleaxe. This time, he didn't.

At least he doesn't wear a kilt.

I'm not kiltaphobic. I just think there are some things man was not meant to show. Some men. Pesky, in particular.

But Pesky had clearly seen the birthday invitation somewhere. Because he showed up with a giraffe.

I'll explain.

I'd spent several months thinking about the possibility of a birthday party and why I even wanted a celebration. The last time I'd hosted a party was to celebrate the finalization of my son's adoption. That had been two decades previous, and we were still repairing holes in the drywall. But this year signified that I had survived some of the best and worst this planet could do to a person for an admirable number of decades, one of the big numbers with a zero at the end—and a bit of gray-haired introspection on the bathroom scale about how my life had turned out brought me to the realization that I had not had a birthday party since I was eight years old—not unless you count my Bar Mitzvah, which wasn't a party as much as it was a pageant. But other than that, I hadn't had a natal celebration in more than half a century.

I knew why, too.

I didn't have one for my ninth birthday because my parents had just (finally?) bought a house in the San Fernando Valium and we were moving the day after. Half the furniture had already left. So, instead of a party we had a birthday dinner and a cake in a near-empty apartment and I didn't get to see any of my friends from school. Somewhere in there, I must have unconsciously decided that my birthday was no longer important enough to celebrate, so after that I mostly ignored it. Or maybe I was just embarrassed about growing older.

While my mom was still alive, the tradition was an annual family dinner, an event which grew more sparsely attended every year until finally it was just me and my sister. By that time, dying young and/or leaving a good-looking corpse were no longer options.

The final push over the edge of the commitment chasm, however, came from my son, who quietly insisted, "Dad, you gotta have a party. People like parties. If you don't have a party for people to give you chocolate, you're ripping them off of the opportunity to give you chocolate."

Sean was right. I was not only entitled, but obligated to celebrate my fiftieth birthday (albeit a couple of decades late); after checking to see that it wouldn't be a scene out of *Stella Dallas* (look it up), and after some internal review of my own motives, I determined that what I really wanted to do was host a big party as a way of thanking the survivors for still being my friends after all these many years of gaffes, stumbles, and falling into social potholes. It turned out the guest list was longer than expected, but we filled it out with people who wouldn't turn down a free meal—writers, mostly.

The invitation said: "A proper birthday party requires balloons, noisemakers, party hats, ice cream, a karaoke machine, popcorn, chocolate, redheads, chocolate-covered redheads, a bathtub full of lime Jell-O, jellybeans, nachos, guacamole, a disc jockey, a disco ball, a fog machine, lasers, spotlights, a party tent, a bouncy castle, cherry bombs, a police permit, explosives, giraffes, cheese dip, strippers, a Swedish hooker, condoms, watermelons, a catapult, chainsaws, masks, maraschino cherries, flavoured love oils, paramedics, name tags, registration table, insurance waivers, a trapeze, handcuffs, spare batteries, water slide, first-aid kits, chains, hand grenades, Saran Wrap, clowns, a rubber chicken, an Elvis impersonator, a live webcam feed, and a cake.

"I think we can manage the cake and maybe the bouncy castle."

I mean, who wouldn't want to attend a party like that? A cake **and** a bouncy castle! After a certain age, you stop worrying about looking good. It's about having fun. In my case, the age was six.

Planning the party was easy. A week in advance I ordered pizzas, deli-trays, kegs, and a cake, all to be delivered an hour before the guests were due to arrive. Sodas and balloons and chips took only a few minutes at the nearby grocery. I could pick up the ice the morning of the party. Ordering the bouncy castle needed only five minutes of Googling and a phone call. But it cost $4,000 to rent a giraffe for an afternoon. I did not rent the giraffe. I admit, I was tempted, though.

The day of the party all the food arrived as ordered, so did the bouncy castle. Right on time the guests started showing up—all I had to do was open the door and hug those who weren't contagious.

Several of my high school friends, my son's godmother, Holly of Sherman's Planet, several beautiful TV stars, a couple of actors, one of my favourite comedians, two or three producers, various writers of my acquaintance, and even a few people who pretended to be normal. The writers headed straight for the food, of course. (Have you ever seen a writer eat? They're worse than actors.)

In the middle of all this, just as the party was shifting from raucous to insane, a woman I didn't recognize, somebody's plus-one, came screaming in the front door shouting something about a giraffe. Several of us rushed outside, followed by several more, and eventually everybody.

Yes, there was a giraffe on the front lawn.

And That Pesky Dan Goodman stood next to it, feeding it carrots and looking across at me with a self-satisfied grin. "You said it wouldn't be a party without a giraffe."

No good joke goes unpunished.

Okay, in all fairness, the giraffe was the high point of the party.

Her name was Hermione. She wasn't quite full-size—she was only four years old, the equivalent of a teenager, and a little high-spirited, but she wasn't freaked out by all the attention. I guess she was used to being gawked at by a crowd—or maybe she was just happy to have all the apples, bananas, carrots, stalks of celery, ears of corn, and the occasional Dorito with guacamole offered to her. She also munched her way through handfuls of oat-crackers that the trainer kept handing up to her, wrapping her gray tongue around them and sucking them appreciatively into her mouth. How much fibre does a giraffe need anyway?

I was a little worried that the rich mix of fruits and vegetables might give her an upset stomach—diarrhoea?—but the trainer said not to worry, it would be good for the lawn.

So even though Peskydang hadn't been officially invited, after he showed up with the giraffe, I couldn't very well turn him away, could I?

That was the mistake.

It being a birthday party, most of the guests brought gifts, and most of them knew me well enough to bring chocolate. Dark chocolate only, milk chocolate is for beginners.

But the ones who **really** knew me—they brought books.

And what books! Graphic novels, rare adventures, autographed editions! Even a marvellous pop-up book! It didn't matter. I love books.

Every book is a door into adventure. It's an opportunity to live an extra life. Or to say it another way, you're lending your brain for someone else to think with. It's exercise for the mind-muscle. You get to think something you wouldn't have thought otherwise. You get stretched. That's why people who read have the advantage.

So people who give me books are…well, I'm not sure there is a word or even an appropriate metaphor. Hero? Wizard? Guru? No, none of those work. Someone who gives you the opportunity to peek at possibilities…? I'll have to cogitate on this and get back to you.

Pesky's gift, however…

It was a small wooden box. Deceptively small. Just big enough to hold a cell phone. But heavy enough to be suspicious. In fact, when I unwrapped and opened it, it **was** a cell phone. Only it wasn't. It didn't feel right.

"Um," I said. "Thank you, Pesky...? Am I missing something here? I already have a phone."

"It's not a phone," Pesky said. "It's a parallelicon. A quantum resonator. A quawkie-talkie." He glanced around the room impatiently. Some of the other guests, those who were still vertical, were glancing at him curiously. "Put it away for now. I'll show you how it works later."

"All right." I slipped it into a pocket. My son shoved another package into my hands, "Here, Dad, open this one next," and I forgot about the odd device. I am easily distracted by any box that smells like cocoa.

By the time the party finally broke up, after the last ambulance had pulled away and the police were satisfied that Ed Green was going to keep his clothes on this time—we told them he was practicing for an upcoming audition ("The Canoga Park Players are planning a revival of *Naked Boys Singing...*"), which seemed to mollify the officers, though they declined the offer of comped seats for opening night—anyway, after the last of the neighbours stopped making videos and went back into their houses, we passed out shovels, rubber gloves, and trash bags to everyone who didn't have a ride home and began cleaning up.

It didn't take as long as expected. Three of the kegs had been emptied, most of the pizza was gone, only a few wilted slices of pastrami remained on the deli trays (Dogzilla took care of those). The only sodas left in the coolers were a dented can of Diet Coke and an A&W Root Beer, so the only leftovers we had to wrap up were the remains of the birthday cake. It had been a custom cake portraying **that** scene from **that** episode of **that** TV series. Harlan Ellison had cheerfully eaten William Shatner's head.

As the last few guests were trying to find the front door, Pesky came over to thank me for including him, making me aware again that my biggest failure as a human being is that I'm too polite to That Pesky Dan Goodman. He keeps coming back. (Daniel Keys Moran, who plays basketball more than I do, which is never at all, says I'm putting too much backspin on him.)

"I need to explain my gift to you," Pesky said.

"Oh yeah, I forgot all about it." I fished through my pockets, pulling out wallet, smartphone (Samsung Galaxy Note II, because it has a larger screen than the S4), music player (A 64GB Zune. And yes, I can hear you rolling your eyes so hard that you can see the bottom of your brain, but I like it, it works for me, so why should I care what you think?), and a wadded-up paper napkin with someone's phone number on it, I didn't remember whose, before I finally found Pesky's device. "Yeah, this is cool. What is it?"

"Well, it depends," he said. "Have you ever heard of a telegrabitron?"

"A what?"

"A para-dimensional interociter."

"Uhh… no."

"Okay, this is going to take some time." He glanced around, checking the room. Still too many people. "C'mere." He took me by the forearm and led me outside to the back yard, grabbing the last banana on the way.

"Do you know what a stringshot is?"

"It's a way to add delta vee to your trajectory by swinging around a—"

"No. That's a slingshot. Are you sure you write science fiction?"

"Not any more. There's too much science. I can't keep up."

"You and everybody else." He took the banana—

That Pesky Dan Goodman does not peel a banana like a normal person. Normal people—that's you and me, an assumption on my part, I don't know if you're normal or not, I just like to think so—you and me, we peel the banana from the stem end, and that's usually a bit of a tussle. Sometimes we even have to bite it to get it started, right? Pesky opens it from the other end—he pinches the tip hard, it splits and peels easily down. (I tried it once, the banana split right down the middle, half stuck to each peel. There must be a trick to it.)

—and he did that same banana thing again. One day I'm going to have to learn how to do it. Either he didn't notice me watching or he didn't care.

"Okay," he said. "You know about quantum entanglement?"

"Uh, yeah, sort of. Two particles are invisibly linked together. If you do something to one, the other reacts. In tandem, right?"

"Close enough for a science-fiction story. The theory is that if the two particles are far enough apart and still remain linked, you can have instantaneous transmission of information. Even across light-years."

"Ah, the old subspace-radio trick."

"According to theory, entanglements create a mini-wormhole that keeps them linked, one particle at each end. So all you need to do is create an entanglement and—are you following this?"

"Yeah, go on. This is the necessary exposition. It has to go somewhere." I say that a lot. It never slows anyone down.

Pesky heard it as permission. He kept talking. "Okay. So, what if we come at it from the other direction? What if every particle was already entangled? But you just didn't know where the other one was? What if you could grab a particle and track its wormhole through space-time and find its equivalent entangled particle somewhere else? You could have instantaneous communication anywhere you wanted."

I waved the phone-thing at him. "Are you saying this is a working subspace communicator?"

"If it worked, it would be."

"It doesn't work?"

"Well, the guys who built it—they don't know if it does or not. They don't know where the entangled particles are."

"They can't tell?"

"Nope. It's a Heisenberg thing. They're not certain. They think they have entanglements, all the evidence suggests it, but the entanglements all look congruent, so it looks like the particles are entangled to themselves. So, what you're holding—

that's the most useless communication device in the universe. There's only one. A telephone doesn't work unless there's another one on the other end."

A sudden suspicion struck me. "How did **you** get it?"

"I asked for it."

"And they gave it to you?"

"I said I had an idea. They said, 'What the hell?'"

"Mmm." I suspected there was more to it than that. Peskydang's relationship with the truth was mostly transitory. "Really?"

"Well, I kinda borrowed it. But they're not going to miss it. Not for a while anyway."

"Uh-huh. So now I'm guilty of receiving stolen property?" I held the thing away from me.

"No. You are a participant in a scientific experiment. Mine." He took the device from my hand and held it up so I could see its face. "I think this is something a lot more than they realized. I think this is a reciprocal encabulator."

"A what?"

"A quantotum."

"In English, please? Remember what we told you, Pesky. If you're going to stay on our planet, you have to speak our language."

"This **is** your language, monkey boy." He sighed. "Look. **This** is a trans-dimensional parallelithonic resonating transceiver. It contains a 64-core multi-fractal array of entangled particles. Call it a quantum empathizer for short."

"Okay." I pretended to understand that sentence. "And—?"

"Where do you think the opposing entanglements are?"

"I don't know. Argentina?"

He gave me a look. "If they're not in this universe, then they have to be in… wait for it!… **another** universe. A parallel universe." He waved the unit under my nose. "This is a Dirac line to an alternate reality."

"Except it doesn't work."

"We don't know that yet. Here, do a thought experiment— assume an **infinite** number of parallel universes. This would mean that somewhere in at least one of those **infinite** alternate worlds, it's inevitable someone else is holding a device just like this one. **Exactly** like this one. And maybe that's what this is really connected to, but we just don't know it yet. The guys who built it—they think their entanglements are congruent—but what if they're wrong? What if the entanglements look congruent because the universes are identical? Or **almost** identical, but not quite. Just in this one respect." He wiggled the thing in his hand.

I pulled out my phone and checked the time.

"What are you doing?"

"Checking to see if it's almost breakfast time. You're asking me to believe six impossible things."

"Only five. But I haven't finished yet."

"You can stop at any time."

"All I'm asking you to do is play with it for a few days."

"Why me? Why not you?"

"Because you know how to break things. You're the best beta-tester I know."

He had me there.

I built my first computer in 1978. I've been aggressive about software ever since. If a program can be crashed, I can do it. If there's a weird little quirk, an odd behaviour, or even an actual bug—I'm the guy who's going to stumble over it. I found a programming error in the Fidelity Chess Challenger. (The company denied it for over a month until I sent them a play-by-play description.) I was the guy who found out that Turbo Pascal's random-number generator wasn't random, by writing a program to display random patterns on the screen and seeing very orderly patterns occur instead. I crashed every new version of Windows—but hell, everybody did that, so I can't take any credit for that one.

And before there were computers, there were typewriters. The IBM service department told me that nobody worked a machine as hard as I did—if I'd let them check the wear and tear on my Selectric every three months, they'd give me free service.

It's because I have a weird streak of obsessive-compulsive behaviour. I have to find out where the limits are. I usually do that by tripping over them.

And Pesky knew me well enough to know which button to push.

"What do you want me to do?"

He put the trans-dimensional parallelithonic resonating-transceiver back into my hand. The quantum empathizer. "Try to see what you can connect to. Dial numbers at random. Well, not numbers—coordinates. IP64 addresses. See what happens. See who answers. Maybe no one. But you have nothing to lose, do you?"

"If the multiverse is truly infinite, then it's inevitable someone will answer, Pesky. You know that—"

"Yep," he said. "That's why you should be the one to do it."

"I don't follow your logic—"

"Because I trust you."

Those were probably the most frightening words that Peskydang ever said to me. I shook my head in resignation, shoved the thing back into my pocket and went in search of a hazmat suit so I could clean the bathroom. It was a mistake to serve pickled-beet, cauliflower, and baked-bean casserole. Thanks, Mo-mo. Don't ever do that again.

It took me several days to recover from the party. There were the usual thank-yous and apologies to make, plus the inevitable reparations to various neighbours to help them regain their gruntle, a couple of quick interactions with lawyers, and finally a last-resort phone call to my cousin who has connections to the City Council. It was a good thing this was only a small gathering. The doctor said I would not need my meds adjusted, but to take it easy for the next few days.

I hadn't given any thought to the quantum empathizer. The mourning after—yes, I know what I typed, but that's how I experience the day after a party—get off life-support, stagger to the shower, mainline some coffee, and finally wake up. In that order. And with some luck, do all this before dusk.

Sorting through the stack of books and chocolate—and the

package of Depends one soon-to-be ex-friend had given as a gag gift—I eventually remembered that Pesky had handed me a present, too. I didn't go looking for it. As the sandstorm behind my eyes began to fade, I realized that the quantum empathizer had to be an elaborate prank—though one in much better taste than a package of adult diapers.

Pesky had found an old cell phone, written a funny little app to make the screen dance on command, and then amused himself at my expense by spouting some wild, incomprehensible jargon just to see how much of it I would believe.

In fact, the more I thought about it, the more certain I was that the whole thing had to be another of Pesky's impractical jokes—like the time he sent my son scrambling all over the San Fernando Valley, from one electronic parts store to the next, looking for a left-handed Moebius wrench. Of course, you don't fool around with Sean. He actually came back with one.

So, as easily as I remembered the quantum empathizer, that's how quickly I dismissed it.

By the end of the week, I was back at the keyboard—

Not yet typing, though. First, I spent half an hour cleaning dog hair and guck out from under the keys. A vacuum cleaner is insufficient. You also need a can of compressed air, one of the ones that come with a thin red straw to concentrate the stream—and a business card and a paper clip, and sometimes even some specialized putty that you can press down into the spaces to grab crumbs of all kinds.

This is just one of the things writers do to postpone the actual process of writing—others include removing the cat from the keyboard, making coffee, removing the cat from the keyboard, having a sandwich, removing the cat from the keyboard, doing "research" on the internet, and removing the cat from the keyboard, by which time, you should probably clean the keyboard again to remove the cat hair from under the keys—because the process of writing is mostly staring at a blank screen and thinking, *Nope. That's not it either.*

I've streamlined the process somewhat. I don't have a cat. I expect the universe to fix that situation shortly, but at the moment it just means I get to spend a lot more time staring into a 32-inch empty white space.

It's like watching a large light bulb, waiting for something to happen. I am the moth, drawn to that light. It's my job to fill the void with little crawly marks that decode into words that decode into thoughts that transform into an understandable moment of experience—and if possible, once over those hurdles, be somehow entertaining or even enlightening. It's not for the squeamish. (I'd say it's not a job for sissies, except it takes a lot of courage to be a sissy and a lot of strength to deal with the ignorance and the stupidity of those trapped in a binary interpretation of gender, but never mind. That's a story for another time.)

Meanwhile, back at the keyboard, but not typing. Because I was stuck.

Not **stuck** as in writer's block. There's no such thing as writer's block. That's just another excuse for not writing.

No, I mean, **stuck** as in not knowing what the next sentence should be.

[RETURNS TO THE KEYBOARD SIX HOURS LATER]

After it's published, the pauses don't show.

Yes, I'm spending a lot of time describing the process of getting words onto paper. Onto the screen. Into a file. (Out of my head and into a form that can be retrieved, printed, submitted, and eventually published.) Because that was the what and the why of everything that followed after.

I'd been staring at the story on the screen for half a day—okay, I also answered some email, scrolled through Facebook, browsed Amazon, bought a rare Anthony Boucher paperback on eBay, checked Google News, and fussed with my outdated website, trying to remember HTML and CSS code again. But mostly I'd been trying to figure out if Squish should spend the night in his cell or escape from juvie and do something dramatic. An escape would complicate the problem, but letting the system process him would bore me to death. And the reader. And Squish.

Squish's time-slicing suit gave him (among other abilities) the power to go invisible and walk through walls. But he was already dealing with the consequences of smurfing little Bobby Peterik, and this part of the story wasn't about him using or abusing his powers, but discovering the consequences that inevitably followed. I could have him spend the night thinking over his options until Cousin Murray showed up again. That would probably be the smartest thing he could do—he was a super-genius, so it would be obvious to him—but it wasn't the most exciting thing he could do. So, if I had him wait it out, then I had to give him an internal monolog that was compelling enough to justify the pause in the action.

If I had him wait, then obviously I'd be passing the buck to offscreen forces, in this case *deus ex Murray*. If I did that, then I'd have to build up some anxiety for Squish to warrant a resulting argument between him and Cousin Murray. The argument would have to be an explosive one to justify, in retrospect, the inactivity during the time spent in juvie. So the whole sequence would have to be a major development in the narrative, setting up an even larger confrontation later on, but one still based on the same emotional tension between the characters—

And when you analyze it to death like that, all the life goes out of the entire story. It deflates like a three-day-old balloon, shrinking and wrinkling into a prunish echo of itself.

An alternative might be to have him sharing the cell with another boy, and—

Too many possibilities.

A bully? Too obvious. Someone who tells him how to jack a car? Except Squish doesn't need that information. What could another boy tell him? Squish's real problem is connecting with others. Maybe there's the possibility of an emotional bridge? Homoerotic? Might be too obvious, but Squish has been feeling really alone because he lost his best friend in the previous instalment—that was part of the justification for smurfing Bobby Peterik—so some kind of "we're in this together" sharing, leading to a sense of connection might work. Squish could use his time-slicing powers to help his cellmate. That could work, but it would add another character to the narrative. Do I want that? On the other hand, Squish having a friend might work, too. Hmm. Gotta figure out who the other boy is and why he's being held in juvie…

Myself, my experience behind bars has been somewhat limited, a status I have no intention to change. (I was 23, but I looked like I was 14. The cop got me for jaywalking, I didn't have any ID, and I mouthed off. The cop was overzealous, and the judge raised his eyebrows at the ticket and only dinged me a few bucks for the jaywalking. I spent an hour locked up with a teenager who'd tried to steal a color TV, until my uncle bailed me out. Things were different then.)

Anyway, I was still staring at the screen, thinking about Squish and wondering if I should get new glasses. These were scratched and starting to generate annoying reflections and peripheral glares.

That's when the phone rang.

Actually, no—it didn't ring. That's just a literary device. A metaphor. A convenient way to indicate an interruption.

What really happened was the computer beeped and a little flag popped up in the lower right-hand corner of the screen telling me that a new device had been recognized.

The quantum empathizer.

The reason the quantum empathizer had been plugged into the computer was because I'd been charging it. I'd plugged it into the same USB cable I use for transferring books, music, and videos to my Kindle. The reason I was charging it was because the battery had gone dead, because I'd left it turned on since the party.

I had forgotten about it until this morning, when I went looking for my Zune (mandatory eye-roll here from the iPod users), which I found in the same pants I had worn to the party, but first I found the quantum empathizer in a different pocket. When I tried to turn it on, it didn't respond. That's when I knew the battery was dead. And while I was still certain that Pesky was pranking me, I was now getting curious enough to see how the prank would play out.

He must have programmed the thing to do something to hook me. Maybe he'd installed some kind of chatterbot that could pretend to be a person, at least until the limits of the algorithm betrayed it. I'd played with a few of those, almost written one, they can be very convincing.

In fact…

Yeah, I'll share this. Because it has some peripheral value to this tale. Back in 1983, after Gene Roddenberry had been put out to pasture by Paramount Pictures because he'd spent $40 million making a movie that shouldn't have cost more than $15 million, he bought his first computer, a Kaypro 10.

The Kaypro 10 was a pretty good little machine for the time. It was the size of a microwave oven, it had a 9-inch monochrome screen—bright green letters on black, 25 lines, 80 characters per line—and it ran CP/M, a precursor to DOS. It had 64K of RAM and a 10 megabyte hard drive. Yes, I said 64 **kilobytes** and 10 **megabytes**. In those days, that was a lot. The Kaypro 10 ran an 8-bit Z80 chip at 2.5 **megahertz**—and that was state of the art.

Gene had spent around $1,600 for the machine. All things considered, it was a bargain. I had a Kaypro 10 as well, but it wasn't my first computer. It was my third, and by then I'd already had five years of experience, which made me not just a pioneer, but an expert as well. So when Gene called me and asked for help—would I teach him how to compute?—I stopped what I was doing, took a shower, grabbed a bunch of floppy disks—in those days, they really were floppy; inside the plastic jacket was a 5¼-inch Mylar disc coated with the same iron-oxide rust used on cassette tapes (do I have to explain cassette tapes now?)—and drove up one side of the canyon and down the other to his house in Beverly Hills.

It was an interesting experience, a chance to discover that Gene Roddenberry wasn't quite the visionary he pretended to be. He was smart, but he wasn't intellectually ambitious. But then, Gene was a producer, not a scientist. He had a strange and wonderful skill. He could take a bad script and turn it into a good one—he could also take a great script and turn it into a good one. To him, the computer was just a different kind of typewriter, a more efficient way of getting words onto paper.

I taught Gene how to boot up WordStar, how to bring up the help screen, how to write some text, how to save it to a file, how to copy that file to a floppy disk, things like that. As we progressed, he began to get more and more enthusiastic about this frightening metal box on his desk. Obviously, it had been frustrating him since the moment he first turned it on. Now, with a little bit of coaching, he was starting to feel he was in control.

When it was time to show him the computer could also play games, I loaded up ELIZA for him. ELIZA was one of the very first chatterbots, so simple you could code it in BASIC. ELIZA didn't recognize meanings, only patterns. Type in, "I like donuts," and it would strip out "I like" and replace it with "Tell me more about" and feed it back to you as "Tell me more about donuts." With a couple dozen programmed responses, ELIZA could simulate a conversation. It couldn't pass the Turing Test, but it could startle anyone whose only experience with a computer had been the vicarious observation of HAL 9000 murdering four astronauts.

Toward the end of the afternoon, Gene's eight-year-old son, Rod, came in to say hello, followed shortly by Gene's wife, Majel Barrett-Roddenberry. Gene delightedly told her, "David and I are computing!" Then he sat her down in front of the machine and told her to type "Hello." She did so, and immediately, ELIZA began conversing with her. She leapt back with a scream and shouted, "Gene! Who's in there?" It took him several minutes to explain to her that it was only a computer program. She didn't want to accept that explanation. Not at first. ELIZA was just too convincing. She didn't touch the keyboard again.

That was 1983, the beginning of the cyber-Mesozoic era. Thirty years of evolution later, chatterbots can carry on much more complex conversations because the programming has become that much more sophisticated. But writing that kind of code is hard work. Pesky doesn't do hard work. He might have been capable of it, but was he motivated enough to invest all that time just for the sake of a silly impractical joke like a quantum empathizer?

I doubted it.

So I clicked on the little flag in the bottom-right corner of the screen, and a window opened up showing the device's log-on screen. There were the obvious boxes for first name, last name, and email address. Also address and date of birth. The program then ran a rotating icon indicating it was now identifying my service provider and my IP address. After that, it accessed its own GPS to determine the latitude and longitude coordinates of my location.

Basically, it wanted to know who I was and where I was. Somebody must have assumed that would be useful for an alternate-dimension hook-up—at least, that's where my mind went. Looking for love in all the wrong spaces. Adventures in slime and place. If I clicked the [SUBMIT] button, would I be opening a portal to this world for alien sex vampires? Who comes here? Dangerous versions?

Of course, I didn't have to click the button. I could unplug the device and go back to wrassling with Squish and his dilemma.

On the other hand, if I didn't click the button, what would happen to humanity's search for knowledge?

Probably nothing.

But what about my search for knowledge?

And then I stopped.

Really?

Was I **really** taking this serious?

This was Pesky's little joke. He must be laughing his head off somewhere. I'll bet he's got this thing sending a hidden signal to some remote location where he's watching me through my own webcam. Well, he would if he could. I keep a sock over it. But he certainly could have this thing logging keystrokes. And maybe he's got my microphone turned on.

"Pesky, if you can hear me, you're not fooling anyone." And then I added, "Just to show you I'm not fooled, I'm going to click the submit button—just to see what kind of a stunt you think you're pulling."

I clicked the [SUBMIT] button.

Nothing happened. Not at first.

The program opened a new window and a message appeared across the top. "Searching…"

After a moment, the message changed to, "Nodes are active."

In the window, several lines of text began to appear.

```
Divergence 1949 [05 active nodes, 11 inactive]
Divergence 1963 [42 active nodes, 13 inactive]
Divergence 1967 [23 active nodes, 33 inactive]
Divergence 1968 [13 active nodes, 02 inactive]
Divergence 1969 [06 active nodes, 47 inactive]
Divergence 1970 [no active nodes]
Divergence 1971 [03 active nodes, 12 inactive]
Divergence 1974 [12 active nodes, 65 inactive]
Divergence 1979 [12 active nodes, 11 inactive]
Divergence 1981 (03 active nodes, 41 inactive]
Divergence 1986 [43 active nodes, 54 inactive]
Divergence 1987 [34 active nodes, 36 inactive]
Divergence 1991 [09 active nodes, 19 inactive]
Divergence 1992 [13 active nodes, 23 inactive]
```

The numbers flickered and changed as the screen updated. It looked like a live uTorrent queue. More lines appeared, seemingly at random, but probably in the order in which the connections were established. No connections showed up for any year before my birth. That was interesting. More evidence that this was one of Pesky's tricks.

The most recent year listed was four years ago. Some years had no active nodes. Others had many. There did not appear to be any particular pattern to which years had the most. 1986 had forty-three active nodes while 1970 had none.

I recognized some of the years, the opportunities and the missteps, the choices made and not made, the fumbles, the bumbles, the stumbles—all the roads not tribbled.

I sat back in my chair and stared at the screen. I still didn't believe this was anything more than a weird little prank, but I noticed my own reaction, that small moment of uncertainty, that tiny balloon of doubt swelling in my chest, that inevitable feeling of loss that comes from looking into the past.

Yes, I know I shouldn't look back, I'm not headed in that direction. I should be looking out the front windshield, not at the rear-view mirror—but the reason there are rear-view mirrors in cars is so you can see what's behind you, especially when it's roaring up after you like a truck or a tsunami. Memory is the monster that stomps the present and chases you into one desperate future after another. You have to kill the monster if you want to build anything new.

I know that. Mixed metaphors and all. But I sat there anyway, remembering.

The meeting I missed. The call I didn't make. The invitation I turned down. The date I didn't go on. And the justifications for not doing any of those things. And all the things I did instead. All the screw-ups. Especially that redhead—

But there were victories, too. Little moments of triumph and joy and satisfaction. Not the obvious ones, not the ones everybody knew about, but the secret ones—because those were mine, not for sharing.

That day in July of '69, when a hot and hopeless summer afternoon turned into a magical and golden evening as sunlit bars of dust illuminated the discoveries of love. And the horrible day when it was lost, as well. That day in '77, when the magic was rediscovered and reinvented—and again in '78. And all the different kinds of magic that happened in '81 and '92 and '95 and '05 and '07. Those were mine.

Maybe, some day, I'll write an autobiography, listing all the things I've learned from all the best people in my life—and all the things I've learned from all the worst as well. I could call it, *Things I've Learned From Living Too Long* or *If You Had Wanted Me To Write Nice Things About You, You Would Have Treated Me Better.* Especially that last one. Autobiographies are a great way to pay off old grudges. I could tell the truth about a few people. I could do some significant damage to a few reputations—

Well…if Pesky had intended this little stunt as a thought

experiment, he'd certainly achieved his goal. I could spend the rest of the day reviewing past lives that hadn't happened.

And then, the dogs began barking frantically at the door—the doorbell has been broken for three decades, I have no need to repair it. The mail had just been delivered. A good opportunity for a break. Nothing important, just the usual collection of junk mail coupons and ads. An opportunity to refinance the mortgage. And another one of those notes about pre-need cremation.

Which sent me off on another internal rant—

Pre-need cremation? No, I don't think so. I don't want a pre-need cremation. That sounds painful. Thank you very much, but I do not want to be cremated until I absolutely **need** to be cremated. Here's how you'll know when I need to be cremated. I won't move for a long time, I'll look bloated and awful, and I'll smell bad. Oh, wait—I'm like that now. Let me get back to you on this.

—because that's the cost of being a high-verbal. You look at the actual literal meanings of words before you look at how they were intended. I've gotten myself into a lot of trouble that way.

But in this case, the interruption brought me back to the real world just long enough to stop and ask—wait a minute! Is this really **the real world**? I'll bet all those others feel like the real world to anyone living over there. To them, this one would be just another divergent.

Wait. You're not taking this seriously, are you?

Of course not. It's just another prank by Pesky.

You might be able to get a story out of it, though. Maybe you could see where it goes.

I don't have a little voice in my head. I have a committee.

Back at my desk, I saw that the screen had updated itself. There was even a divergent for this year now. Cute.

So far, though, I hadn't seen anything that would have required more than a couple hours of work for an experienced programmer. I assumed that if I clicked on one of those lines and tried to connect to an active node, I'd get the chatterbot.

Probably the same chatterbot whichever link I chose. It might be interesting to test the limits of the chatterbot's abilities. I wondered if Pesky had made it historically literate, aware of which specific divergent it was pretending to be. To make the prank work, he would have had to. But that would have required a lot more coding than this stunt deserved.

I wondered if—yeah, that would be just like him—if, after spelunking through various screens and options, some hideous deformed face would suddenly and unexpectedly fill my monitor, a ghastly scream roaring from my speakers, all with the intention of scaring me so I would go leaping backward in startled terror, shrieking and knocking my coffee all over my keyboard.

It was a funny gag—well, funny the first time. It still showed up on Facebook occasionally. But it wasn't funny anymore, just annoying. Besides, that wasn't Pesky's style. His pranks were usually more subtle and more literate. Like the time George Takei was going to speak at the local university. The school put up a big poster of George's smiling face—one night, Pesky snuck onto campus and added matching posters just to the left, showing a lion, a tiger, and a bear. In that order. The real joke was that some people didn't get it.

So, I sat at the keyboard and stared at the screen and mused. Until I realized I wasn't amused at all. "And no, we are not bemused either," I added as an afterthought. High-verballing again.

There was really only one way to end this—and that was by continuing. When you're in the muddle of anything, the only way out is through.

I leaned forward and clicked on 1949. That felt like a good place to start. The screen popped up five active nodes. I clicked on the first. It opened a window listing multiple journal entries and descriptions of files available for download.

I started reading. I frowned—

There were articles about ramp access, the Americans With Disabilities Act, hiring discrimination, the high cost of a motorized wheelchair and how hard it was to get around Comic

Con's crowded aisles even with prosthetic legs, why it was unfair they wouldn't let him on the bobsled ride at Disneyland, and after that a few rants about the things that rude and stupid people said and did. One was about able-bodied people parking in handicapped spaces—that was understandable. Another revealed how tired he was of people telling him how much courage he had; I could empathize with that one, too. It's not courage when you don't have a choice. A third talked about amputee porn and the creeps who were turned on by stumpies, and how hard it was to have a real relationship. He didn't want anyone who felt sorry for him—

Huh?

I dug further.

Apparently, the individual at this node had lost his legs when he was five. He had been sitting on a corner curb where the streetcars turned around, a little island just off the corner of Vermont and West 1st Street. It was a very sharp curve and the bottom of the streetcar came over the curb as the trolley turned the corner.

—Oh, crap.

I remembered that moment. I'd been wearing shorts. I'd sat down to watch the streetcar turn. At the last moment, as I saw it coming around, saw how the sharp yellow bottom of the car was cutting over the curb, I scrambled back out of the way. That moment was still ingrained in my consciousness. It was my first experience recognizing my own stupidity. Ever since then, I've kept a cautious distance from all moving trains and street-cars. And trucks. And buses. And everything else large and mobile.

So that was the divergence in 1949.

And this person was me. An **alternate** me.

Oh—

Now I **was** bemused. More than confused. Frozen in shock.

Pesky couldn't have known that. I'd never shared that incident with anyone. I'd occasionally thought about it, wondered what would have happened if I'd stayed put. Would I have been dragged under the carriage and cut in half by the streetcar's large steel wheels, or would there have been enough room for my skinny little five-year-old legs to escape unscathed? Or maybe I'd just get scratched up a bit or maybe broken both my legs, but not too badly. I'd even imagined the ride in the ambulance with a superhero fireman holding my hand and telling me not to cry.

But this guy, this **divergent**, his legs had been crushed and mangled and ripped off his body. He'd lost both of them. Barely survived the blood loss. His limbs were amputated mid-thigh.

Ouch.

So, that was what happened to the little boy who didn't get out of the way in time.

He grew up to be an angry cripple. No, not angry. He told jokes. He was literate. He even wrote and sold some stories. But mostly, he was a single-minded advocate for disabled rights. Because he didn't have much choice.

On the other hand, having to use his arms for everything, he must have developed great upper-body strength by now. I wondered if he'd posted a picture.

Yes, he had. And yes, he had great shoulder muscles and biceps, but I couldn't be jealous. He was fat. And slovenly. Ugh. I suppose I should have been ashamed of myself for thinking that of him, but if he was an alternate me, he was one I was glad I wasn't.

Considering everything—the circumstances, the culture of the time, the lack of access to honest affection separated from pity—it would have been easy for him to retreat into comfort food and sublimated resentment. I could understand it. I'd been there. More than once. It wasn't the comfort zone. It was the zone of resignation. I just hadn't stayed there. I was sorry he had. But I could understand his frustration with the world now.

I wondered if his stories were any good. I skimmed a few titles. Nothing I recognized. I'd have to come back and look later. But my curiosity was piqued—what would I find if I clicked on the other years? Who were the other divergents?

I backed out and looked at the other years.

Why were there no active nodes for 1970? Nothing came up

on the screen.

I decided to try 1987.

Well, **that** was interesting—

Apparently, Gene Roddenberry had died of a massive stroke (overdose?) at the end of December. This was before his walking elbow-wrinkle of a lawyer had come aboard to pack the production with expensive empty suits. So the show-running chores fell to—

Among the files available for download were seven years of episodes. Those would definitely be worth a look.

It would take several hours for all the separate files to copy. Enough time to browse some other years.

What diverged in 1963?

Well, there was the obvious one, of course. John F. Kennedy listened to the concerns of his Secret Service agents and allowed them to put the bubble top on the limo. Lee Harvey Oswald's bullets cracked the Plexiglas, but failed to penetrate. The president and his wife escaped with only minor scratches. The following year Kennedy defeated Goldwater. The Federal Civil Rights Act passed, so did the Voting Rights Act. Not without a fight, but they passed. Kennedy did not escalate the war in Vietnam, the right wing accused him of being soft on communism. His political popularity waned after the '66 midterms, but because the economy was healthy and because the nation was fascinated by the Apollo missions to the moon, he remained personally well-regarded. Robert Kennedy won the presidency in '68 against Richard Nixon. That was a close race, because the south was leaving the Democratic Party.

When JFK and two Apollo astronauts visited the set of *Star Trek* in early '67, the series took a ratings boost and the network moved it to an 8:00 o'clock time-slot. Its ratings climbed even higher in the earlier position, pushing the show into the top ten. They did not buy that script from a well-intentioned college student. Hmm.

Some tough times followed, but...that was interesting. It turned into a whole other career path. Twenty-two novels in ten years, approximately one every six months. And another thirty in the twenty years after that. I didn't recognize any of the titles.

Oh, this was even **more** interesting—

Heinlein novels! Holy mother of Ghu! By '67, the grandmaster was apparently heading out in a whole other direction. *On The Bounce, The Man From Mars, And Not To Yield, A Competent Man, Ezekiel And The Wheel, The Business Of Monkeys, Ad Astra.*

Beatles albums? Thirteen of them before the '73 breakup, plus another seven after the '79 reunion. Not a single title matched anything in my timeline. Definitely needed to download those. *Eight Arms To Hold You, Any Way We Can, Singularities, Everest, Let Go, Applesauce, All The Times,* and *The Band You've Known For All These Years.*

It all made sense—different history, different stimuli, different results. A whole other catalogue. Not just me, every-one.

I wondered what else I might find. I started browsing through the ancillary files that my divergent selves were sharing. Buddy Holly's *Disco Sue Got Married.* Disney's remake of *Yellow Submarine,* Kubrick's *Napoleon,* and Terry Gilliam's *The Defective Detective,* Steven Spielberg's *The Stars My Destination.* Joss Whedon's *Firefly,* all eight seasons and the two-hour special, *Redemption.* Criterion Audio, *The Compleat Hendrix.* Alfred Bester's *Destiny.* Harlan Ellison's *The Man Who Screamed Bullets.* All the divergent Ken Burns twenty-four-part documentaries on the history of the twentieth century. I counted seven of them.

And more!

All the Hugo and Nebula nominees since 1949—from all the different divergent timelines. I could spend a lifetime catching up, just reading all the different masterpieces of so many of my favourite authors.

I hesitated—I wondered about the ethics. Was this consid-ered illegal file sharing? I couldn't pay for any of this stuff, but I could trade things specific to my timeline. That would be fair, wouldn't it?

What about my own stuff? What had my different selves created? I could market that, couldn't I?

I'd have to look.

And that made me pause—

—because that's what I had been avoiding.

And I knew why.

One of the skills all those courses and coaching had created was a weird kind of insight—an additional level of consciousness, being able to notice my own motivations.

In my timeline, somewhere on the internet, there is an *Encyclopedia of Science Fiction.* In it, one of those shallow and snotty self-appointed critics of science fiction had casually dismissed my entire career with a single withering sentence: "… has not lived up to his early potential."

At the time, I'd felt that critic had misunderstood what I was attempting. But what if he hadn't? That was the fear. What if all those different versions of myself had lived up to their potential? Would their enormous body of work reveal how badly I had failed in this timeline?

I checked '95 and '97, looking to see if anyone had completed my seven book trilogy. No. I was the only one working on that story. Was I really that divergent?

But I did find *The Patient Dragon, Blue Monkeys From The Eleventh Dimension, The Boy Who Was Girl, The Girl Who Was Silver, A Promise of Stars (collection), The Corridor, The Princess Of The Mice, Shifter, Nightsiders, Admit One, Bad Night, City Of Boys, Dear Doctor Morgan, Jesus And The Seven Dwarves, Loophole, Gendernauts, Escape From The Planet Of The Tribbles, Didactics, A Day At Crater Park, The Chimney Wars, Cocoons, The Brick, Cooking By Ear, Inherit The Stars, The Borrowed Body, Something Scratching, The Job Of Death, The Hails Of Toffman, The Lifeguard At Cassy Beach, The Rainbow Eaters,* and *Uncle Dog.*

And that was just from one timeline. There were at least a thousand others yet to explore. If there were even 20 different books in each divergent timeline, that would be a library of twenty-thousand separate downloads. I wouldn't even have time to read them all—

It wouldn't be unethical for me to download everything that all my divergent selves had written, would it? I could even resell some of the best. If I could figure out how to find the best out of twenty-thousand. Maybe just the award nominees? But no, I'd written a few pieces I was proud of that had never gotten award notice. I'm sure my divergent selves had, too. How to identify them—

Of course, I should probably make my catalogue from this timeline available in return. Nothing I had written after 1970 existed in any of the divergent catalogues.

But I was feeling humbled by what others had accomplished and posted.

Not just humbled—jealous.

By comparison, I had…what?

Well…

I was the only one who had written *The Martian Child*—because none of them had adopted a child. At least, not the same child. Right there, that made my heart break. Where was Sean in all those different worlds? Did he even exist in those alternate timelines?

Maybe his birth parents had never met. Or maybe they didn't make a baby that night in the fall of '83. But if Sean did exist, if he had been born, then what would have happened to him without me being there for him?

Where was he? Was he all right? Or had he been swallowed up by circumstances? Used up and abandoned before he'd ever had a chance? Thinking what might have happened to him, I started to tear up again.

Or maybe, maybe—I had to hope this was so—maybe some other family had gotten lucky. After the adoption was finalized, the caseworker told me there had been two or three other families interested in him, but they had chosen me as the best match. Maybe one of those other families had taken him.

But wherever Sean was, there was no *Martian Child*. It hadn't happened. And neither had anything else. No Hugo, no Nebula. No movie. No nothing.

I remembered why I had adopted him. What had made me the person I am. The same thing that informed all of my earliest writings. I went back and looked, I had to confirm it—yes, I was the only one who'd written *HARLIE* and *Folded*.

And that's what stopped me.

I knew why those books had been written, what they had been a response to.

At the end of the sixties—

Those novels had happened because I'd been trying to wrap my head around something so incomprehensible that it felt like the universe was a gigantic practical joker, with me as the butt of the joke. (And no, I'm not going to talk about it here. It's a footnote. Someday I'll write that footnote. Just not today.)

1970 was the divergence. This was the timeline where I'd survived.

HARLIE was me trying to figure it out—to see if it had any meaning at all. And *Folded* was a plea to any passing time-traveler. Please come and fix this. Make it didn't happen.

Pebbles down a well. No splash.

Not important enough, I guess. Or maybe the time traveler decided history worked better this way. I wasn't consulted.

Ultimately—and it took until '81 or '85 or '92 or '07—I finally figured it out for myself. I had to figure it out more than once. Each time was a personal reinvention. None of the books I'd ever read, none of the teachers I'd ever admired, none of the authors I'd followed so religiously, had ever been able to say the one thing in the clear I'd most needed to hear.

If you want life to have meaning, you have to make it up yourself.

And that's the real question. The one nobody else has the answer to. The nastiest and most terrifying piece of personal responsibility.

What do you want your life to mean?

There was a book I had been wanting to write. I hadn't written it yet. No, I hadn't finished it yet. I had four different abortive versions on my hard drive. None of them came close to what I wanted it to be.

I scoured through all the different divergents. The book didn't exist. No one else had written it, either.

Which meant that no other divergent in this particular

selection of possibilities had experienced the same event. Which meant—

I started looking at the selfies.

Ahh, that explained a lot.

Too much.

I don't know how long I sat there, staring at my monitor, overwhelmed by conflicting storms of emotion, blinking through the tears, weeping at my loss, sobbing at my failure— because another version of me had something I had been grieving for nearly my whole life. And I didn't have it, couldn't have it.

The photo of the two of them, handsome and beautiful, smiling, squinting against the glare of the Hawaiian sun, proudly holding up their left hands to show matching wedding bands—

Oh, no.

No, no, no, goddammit! Dammit! Dammit!

Now, I knew why there were no active divergents from 1970. Those were the ones who'd committed suicide. Unable to bear the grief, they'd...quit.

I got up from the computer. I walked out of my office. I walked into the kitchen. I opened the cupboard above the refrigerator, the one glued shut by time, the one with two bottles of wine and an unopened bottle of Glenfiddich one of my friends had sent me two years ago. I don't drink—

That's not completely true. Twice a year, once at Thanksgiving and once at Christmas, when the family gathers together at my sister's, I pour myself a rum and Coke. I use Malibu coconut rum and a twist of lime. It's called a Hairy Nilsson. You put the lime in the coconut, you drink it all up. (If you make it with Diet Coke, it's a half-Nilsson.)

Tonight, I took down the bottle of Glenfiddich. Heinlein had introduced me to single-malt liquor when I visited him in Bonny Doon. It was one of the greatest favours he ever did for me. I twisted out the cork, and splashed two fingers into a glass. I didn't bother with the soda. Not tonight. And no, I did not throw it back all at once like you see in the movies, because in the movies it's not liquor, it's iced tea. And nobody who   respects Glenfiddich insults it like that. No, I sipped at it, letting it sting my tongue a bit at a time.

I stood alone in my dark kitchen, eyes still blurry with grief. The dogs wagged hopefully at my feet, alternating their little, "I like cheese," dance, with sitting up and waving their paws at me. "Please, sir, can I have some, so I can ask for some more?" Somewhere else, I had the life I'd planned. Here, I had the life that had happened anyway.

I don't know how long I stood there, alone, drinking, waiting for some kind of resolution, some enlightenment, some imitation of peace. I noticed my hands were shaking and leaned on the counter. I could feel the booze burning its way down my throat and into my stomach, a dark wave ballooning outward from there.

I wish I had lyrical language to describe it, those silky poetic metaphors that awaken the imagery of the mind. But I don't, I never have. I didn't even want to be a writer. I wanted to act and direct and create video games and design amusement parks. And once, I'd even wanted to be a course-leader, a trainer. I only ended up a storyteller because there were stories I wanted to read and nobody else was writing them.

I look at all the good writers around me and I'm jealous of their skills, what they're able to do with language and character and voice, and it just makes me all the more conscious of my own limitations. All I've ever been able to do is grasp after the unreachable precision of language and hope that's enough, but just wanting something badly enough isn't enough. It needs ability and commitment and passion.

All I had was stubbornness. Too stupid to quit—

And now there were all those different divergents, every bit as stubborn and stupid as me. Some of them must have gone off in other directions, some of them must have done a few of those things I once thought I wanted to do. But I was afraid to go back and look. I was already hurting enough—

Why the hell had Pesky given me this terrible device? What was he thinking? What the hell kind of a birthday present forces you to confront the failures in your life?

I opened the back door and went out to the patio, but only as far as the awning, an empty space surrounded by the pattering of rain.

The backyard should have been a refuge, but it didn't feel like it tonight. It felt like a walled-in exercise yard. The first precipitation we'd seen in months was rippling the surface of the pool, cooling the air with the icy smell of...I don't know, what's a poetic way to describe breathing negative ions? That crisp feeling of air that clears the lungs and the soul at the same time?

But out here, I could wrap the darkness around me like a cold, wet, uncomfortable blanket, the only warmth coming from the alcohol inside me.

I thought about those other divergents. Were they happy? Had I missed something?

Well, no. Not all of them were happy. That one in the wheelchair. And the ones who'd killed themselves. The one who'd spent two decades working through various iterations of a successful TV show—he was a millionaire now, with a house in Newport Beach, a yacht, and monthly royalties bigger than my lifetime income. He also had ulcers, a drug problem, two divorces, and a reputation for being an arrogant ass. Was he happy? Did he log onto the interdimensional network feeling successful? Or did he regret that his entire life had been at the service of someone else's creation? Did he mourn the stories and novels of his own that he'd never written because he'd sacrificed himself to television?

And the one who was married—all the ones who were married. Yes, I envied them. Who wouldn't? And if I could ask them, I'm sure they'd say they were happy. They probably were. I wished I was that happy, too.

Oh, what a tangled web we weave when first we practice to transceive.

I sipped at my drink—what the hell? I finished it quickly. Let it burn. I thought about stepping out from under the awning, letting the cold rain wash down onto me—but no, that was a stupid idea. I'd barely survived my last bout with pneumonia. I did not particularly want another ambulance ride or tubes down my throat.

So, what did I have?

If Randy were here, my interminable coach, he'd say, "You have the path you're on. You have what you chose. You have the consequences that came with your choice."

Great. Thanks, Randy.

Okay, well… I have a son I'm very proud of. I'm the only one who has this son. That has to count for something. I'd made a difference in his life. He'd made an even bigger difference in mine. He taught me to think about someone else for a change, a skill once learned and never forgotten. Our relationship is so good, I'm jealous of myself.

And…I do have some stories that no one else wrote. No one else could have written them. That has to count for something, too.

Some of my best work had come into being because of the smouldering rage I'd been carrying for so many years, for so many different reasons. Most of the time, that torment just simmered, sometimes it boiled, and sometimes it exploded. Mostly, it caught me by surprise. But I'd learned how to force it out through the keyboard, blasting shards of feeling onto the screen like an emotional assault rifle aimed at the reader.

And sometimes—sometimes I even acknowledged it aloud. I'd say it like a joke, but it was never a joke. "I suffered for my art. Now it's your turn."

I walked back inside and put the empty glass in the sink. A satisfying glass-on-porcelain clink. Okay, I'd had my ten minutes of self-pity. Fifteen. That was enough.

Alternate timelines are just another trap, a great big game of "what if" with teeth in it. But if there's one thing I've learned in the last seven decades, it's how to bite back—and draw blood.

This is who I am. This is the universe I live in. If I have to deal with this world, then it has to deal with me. The next time I look into the abyss, I intend the abyss to flinch.

I'm the one who gets to live **this** life. I'm the one who gets to write **these** stories.

That's enough. That has to be enough.

Well played, Pesky. Well played.

But I'm still going to kill you.

I caught up with That Pesky Dan Goodman a week later. I made a point of dropping in at a meeting of the Los Angeles Science Fantasy Society. They had a new clubhouse in Van Nuys. I found him in the back room—at the snack table, of course. He turned around and saw me and his eyes widened. The first and probably only time I'd ever seen fear on his face.

I handed him the box. He shook it, frowned, opened it.

Inside were all the pieces of trans-dimensional paralle-lithonic resonating transceiver, thoroughly hammered to bits.

"Sorry, Pesky," I said. "I couldn't get it to work."

AUTHOR'S AFTERWORD

This was the only file I was able to download before the device over-heated and the particles unentangled.

DO YOU LOVE THE COLOUR OF THE SKY?

Rachel A. Rosen

As a child, before I had real problems, I used to worry about the colour of the sky. I would lie on my back for hours as the cerulean bled into rose gold, forming a circle between my thumb and forefinger, taking a snapshot of the hue with my mind. Control-S, as if I might retrieve a file of my collected moments and scroll through colours never meant to be seen by the human eye more than once. Watching for the exact second it deepened, promising the ephemeral colour I would not forget it. In later years, when the sky was orange, when it was burnt sienna, I was further convinced of the fleetingness of colour, the importance of preservation.

When I die, these colours, committed to my child's mind, will all cease to exist.

When I looked into the barrel of the pistol levelled at my head, my first thought was to worry about who would take care of Sadie, my dodo.

The intruder had come down hard on the staircase that led to the door in the ceiling with a crash that must have surprised her as much as it had startled me. The gun was an old-fashioned pistol, wielded by an old-fashioned girl, pale and olive-eyed and wrapped in a tight black dress. She wasn't from here. How she'd gotten into the archive wasn't a mystery, judging from the streak of scorch marks on the banister and the Pordo Device spitting sparks by her side. She had stepped through a broom closet, or a palace arch, or a skin flap in her world, and she had found herself in mine.

My second thought was a line I'd heard in an old film, black-and-white, a highwayman pointing a gun that might have come from the same prop closet. "Stand and deliver." I giggled. Ordinarily, you don't giggle when someone is pointing a gun at you. I couldn't help it. It was such a tiny gun, and she looked so serious pointing it. Sadie, having originated in a timeline where her ancestors hadn't all been shot to death, didn't recognize the object, so she waddled in a circle around the stranger's legs, excited at the prospect of a new friend.

You can sometimes tell where they're from at a glance. A gleaming bull's horn on a chain around the throat, or a shangrak tattoo. A Hapsburg jaw or a colony of melanomas, if it's one of the worse timelines. Not this woman. She had burst from the fire fully formed and innocent of all history.

"Can I help you with something?" I asked her. She was searching the room for something specific, of course, unfazed by its unusual architecture. You didn't crash into a different timeline with an antique pistol and a broken Pordo Device because you were looking for the thousandth variation on the *Mona Lisa* in the Sunken Museum of New Çatalhöyük.

The most valuable piece I had was Caravaggio's 1636 masterpiece *David and Jonathan*, his last major work in any timeline. The painter, having sworn forever off bar fights and prostitutes, depicted the young lovers with a tenderness and passion typical of his mature work, his violent nature tempered by time and wistfulness. The lustful red of David's cloak led scholars to believe for years that it was the work of Artemisia

Gentileschi, but it merely reflected her influence and Caravaggio's late-life humble admission that he could learn from any of his followers, let alone the one who was a woman. Given the provocative take on the subject matter, it was never exhibited publicly. Like the sky, it was a waste that only I would ever witness it.

She didn't want that one.

Nor did she want my personal favourite, Chirapa Huancahuari's *Pachakutiq*, sung into existence in the 13th b'ak'tun, a sound sculpture dating back to the Waranqa Reconstruction in Piruw Ripuwlika. It was a jewel-encrusted fragment of a better, more harmonious world, perpetually cracking and rebirthing itself anew. There was nothing like it in any known universe.

The woman perambulated around the chamber, no easy feat given the clutter. I did my best, but preservation space for the great lost works is limited when there is so much else that must be rescued from the ravages of timeline decay. The staircase up to the door on the ceiling bisected the room, leading to an awkward space under which I'd stuffed archives of old finds, too insignificant to be displayed or too fragile to be exposed to the stilted air. She landed on one of the smallest pieces on a pedestal, an exquisite oil even smaller than the aforementioned *Mona Lisa* variations. She seized it in her hand, and this, of all things, is what made me at last gasp.

But she was gloved—she came prepared—and at least the oils of her skin wouldn't damage the work.

"This belongs to me," she said.

I hadn't expected her voice to be soft. She had planned what was no doubt a logistically challenging, expensive, and elaborate art heist, but her hushed tone in the presence of sublime beauty indicated someone not a thief, but a fellow appreciator.

Well. She was also a thief.

"It belongs to the people of New Tagaka," I said. Gently. Now I knew where I recognized her features; she bore a striking resemblance to the only extant self-portrait of E7lPETH

¡andojver, who had died in the Deer Flu of 2114. "Unfortunately, there aren't any left. Your mother?" I asked. That piece had been lost in the Scouring, but I had a catalogue from the exhibit that had reproduced that heart-shaped face and those dark curls in the exquisite detail typified by the Dream Mannerist era preceding the bioengineered pandemic.

She didn't need to answer. She cradled the painting against her breast with a gloved hand, the one that wasn't pointing a gun at me. She held it reverently, like the head of an ailing child.

"Where did you get the Pordo?" I asked.

She had slung the device onto her belt in order to hold the painting properly. I could have grabbed it—or the painting, if I moved fast enough. She could also have shot me, even with that ridiculous little gun, if she had moved even faster. And so, for a long pause, neither of us moved.

Sadie interrupted with her rare, two-note "doo-doo," butting her beak up against the stranger's shin. A girl doesn't get into this line of work because she's in love with living things. And she doesn't get a pet dodo to guard the valuables against intruders.

This woman, whom I was increasingly convinced was motivated by criminal sentimentality rather than avarice, was not going to start a shootout in a room full of art from dead worlds and an extinct bird.

I moved a mid-century Kirchner from where it sat propped up on the chair to the top of a dresser. I had put in a petition for a larger space, though the prospect of moving the work distressed me as much as it being at bird-height.

"Maybe you had better sit down," I said.

In one reality, she shot me anyway, before I even had the chance to bring her a cup of tea.

I carried a Pordo on me too, at all times, a higher-end model than the one that the stranger had. It didn't leave scorch marks—which given my line of work, is a necessity—and it was unlikely to break and leave me potentially stranded, as hers had.

It's not much to pop between timelines, investigate the possibilities. I would rather not have seen this one.

The silly little gun, as it turned out, was surprisingly effective. The bullet entered between two ribs, tore a path through first a lung, then the inferior vena cava, before lodging itself near my spine. It did not, as it turned out, continue its trajectory to reach the iridescent metal-beaded mural that typified the Eighth Generation movement of the Haudenosaunee Confederacy in the late 21st century. The entry wound was neat and didn't splatter, belying the journey it shredded through my organs. I dropped the mug, but I was still in the passageway of the kitchenette, and the smash of liquid did not reach a single piece of art.

The pain, it must be said, was indescribable.

She cried as I choked out my last breaths. "I'm sorry," she said, as though I were expected to gasp, "Oh, no, I absolutely understand," with the last exhales of my masticated lungs. As I reached for the Pordo to shift back to Prime, my final thought was not of Sadie after all. Instead, I marvelled at how this girl's face was so like ¡andojver's infamous doomed self-portrait.

"Tea?" I asked.

She looked up at me with those ludicrously wide olive eyes, and said, "Oh, I guess so."

I always had a pot on, a blend of rose hip and silphium. There's a ritual in preparing it; it is best served in glasses rather than mugs if you're hell-bent on being a traditionalist. For my part, I have never been anything approaching traditional, and with a clumsily affectionate dodo and priceless art crowding out my workspace, I erred on the side of sturdiness over fragility.

I kept the mug with the Sunken Museum logo on it for myself—there was no need in upsetting her further when she was already on the brink. The one I gave her was kitschy; it had a replica of the nude *Mona Lisa*, which carried far more cultural capital in Prime than the version widely believed to be the original. She watched me prepare the tea the entire time, too wary that I would poison her given that she'd shot me.

"I am somewhat of a thief myself," I said.

"You all are." Her tone was sullen, bruised, as if I had been the one to intrude on her universe. "This room is piled high with the spoils of theft."

The entire city was, but she would have known that. However she had managed to acquire the Pordo, she would have needed time to practice. She would have researched what it did and what it meant before she'd crashed through the ceiling.

It did happen on occasion. The head curators never liked to talk about it much. People were careless on the job and dropped one on the way out, which was later picked up by scavengers. It was rare, but sometimes people died on a trip. It's rough on the heart, they say.

"What was the first thing you stole?" I asked her. It couldn't have been her first time.

"The poppies," she said. They always went for the poppies first. There were versions scattered across each branch of the multiverse, it was small enough to carry off, and it had been stolen so often that even a normal curator almost expected it to go missing now and then. It's iconic to steal a Van Gogh, and while I did not know the man's heart, I can't help but think that he would have approved. "You?" she asked.

I settled into my chair with my mug of tea. The silphium added a note of fennel to the blend, anise and nostalgia. It was the taste of late August afternoons spent lying on my back in a field of golden grass, squinting up at a sun already too low on the horizon. "The colour of the sky," I told her. I did not explain further. "Do you understand how that works?"

I could see her baffling over whether I meant the pistol before her eyes landed on the malfunctioning Pordo strapped to her hip. She had propped the painting on one of the many side tables scattered throughout the archive space. It was small. ¡andojver had lived and died under occupation, before the pandemic landed her in a mass grave. She hadn't the space for the expansive canvases that would have shown off her masterful use of colour, her expressive lifework. She'd been a graffiti artist, a subversive, and that influence showed despite the scale.

I could stare into the painting for hours, a snapshot of the frantic city, at the play of light over each tiny, suffering civilian. It was easy to understand why, even if she wasn't the artist's daughter, the girl was willing to murder for it.

"The dial takes you to different timelines," she said, sulky, a recalcitrant teenager to my reluctant teacher. "The button takes you here."

"And here is…?" I prompted. When she didn't answer, I said, "This is the Prime timeline. The others converge on it, like the trunk of a root system, or they fall away. They wither. They die. Along with everything unique about them, every person who lived when they might have died, every new song that they sang, every piece of art that they created. I am a thief, it's true, but I am also a preservationist."

She sniffed at her tea. Still expecting poison. Knowing what she was capable of doing, I kept my eye on her most minute movements, the twitching of a finger, the shift in the cross of her legs. The pistol sat beside the painting on the table—the phantom pain of the bullet in my chest would not let me easily forget that it was there—but for her it seemed merely an afterthought. Hadn't this always been the pattern of civilization? Tea and bullets were undeniably intertwined.

"And you're on the timeline's corpse like sharks on a whale fall," she said.

"Would you rather we let these things disappear?"

Sadie waddled to the arm of my chair; I scratched her head absentmindedly, ruffled the soft, dense feathers, and smoothed my hand over her beak. On most days, when I wasn't out on a retrieval, she was the only living being I saw. I talked to her, and she would respond with her little "doo-doo," altering the emphasis when she was hungry, or bored, or affectionate. A human being in my archive, one who spoke back, who *argued* with me, was a novelty. Even if she wanted me dead.

"You could take a photo," ¡andojver's daughter said.

"You've read Walter Benjamin," I said. I may have been presuming a degree of education in my thief, but murderer or not, she had discerning aesthetic tastes.

"The storm is what we call progress," she dutifully quoted. "What a cruel image, don't you think? The Angel of History blown forward into the future while staring at the wreckage of the past at its feet."

I laughed. "I was thinking of *The Work of Art in the Age of Mechanical Reproduction*," I said. "It's about the aura of the work. The intangible quality of the piece that cannot be divorced from its context."

"And yet," she said, "you would divorce it from its context by bringing it here."

"Is that not better than letting it vanish altogether? I keep careful records. I collect everything I can about the artist's timeline, how it differed from ours. What we can learn from it."

She must have decided that the tea wasn't poisoned. She uncrossed and crossed her legs again, and took a long, thoughtful sip. "She died when I was very young, my mother. She was a resistance fighter until the end. The Deer Flu still took her—it only killed half the city, in my timeline—oh, and it's not really a flu at all, it's a prion disease. She couldn't paint at the end. She didn't even know who I was. They burned the whole city to purge the earth of deer shit—it goes deep in the soil you know? We took what we could carry into the camps."

"I'm sorry," I offered. In Prime, E7lPETH ¡andojver hadn't lived long enough to have a daughter. In a matter of months, maybe weeks, the timeline would become too remote. The thief, with her curly hair and her black dress and her childhood trauma, would shrivel into nothingness and blow away like dry leaves. The only record of her would be her mother's biography, the painting, and the notes I scrawled in my leather-bound journal. The pistol, if she was kind enough to leave it behind. "She was terribly talented."

"Of course she was," the girl snapped. Despite everything I knew about how the world worked, the thought of her evaporating into atoms and memory seemed unlikely. There was nothing about her that suggested fragility, that only a quirk of timeline separated her from a world in which she was never born, in which her mother had not lived to paint the

Expressionist landscape of a doomed uprising that sat by her right hand.

"The painting will disappear as well," I said. "If you take it."

"It's mine," she said. "Ours."

"I won't just tell your mother's story," I reassured her, "but yours, as well. As much of the history that you can tell me—the plague, the Scouring, the camps. This is an opportunity for both of us."

"Why do you do it?" she asked. "Not you, personally. I know why **you** do it, you're clearly a lunatic. But your timeline. Stealing from alternate realities, building up your museums, your zoos, your ridiculous interdimensional technology. I don't see any visitors down here."

"There are very rarely visitors down here," I said.

"I've seen your sky," she added. "It's like ours, but some—"

"—some are not," I finished. I glanced at the beaded mural. There was no natural light in the archive—it wasn't good for the art—but the LED piping in the ceiling skittered off the textured surface like rippling waves. "I suppose because it reminds us. Convinces us."

"Of what?"

"That it might have all turned out differently," I said. "That it still could. That another world is possible."

In one timeline, Walter Benjamin crossed over the French-Spanish border fleeing the Wehrmacht, just like he did in Prime. Just like in Prime, he checked in at the Hotel de Francia with a group of Jewish refugees. How long did he ponder over the morphine tablets, his game of chicken with the Spanish Fascist authorities? What made the difference between our universe, where *Theses On the Philosophy Of History* reads as his suicide note in its melancholic break from historical materialism, and this one?

I hadn't read his later works. I wondered if my guest would be interested in a trip to the library. Might it have changed her mind?

The newest model of the Pordo Device is smaller than you'd expect given what it can do. The size of a remote control, it fit in the palm of my hand. Like most things here, it did not originate in Prime; in fact, its discovery is one of the few   historical facts that has not been endlessly debated, dissected, scrutinized. We are here because we have it; we have it because we are here. And that was all I needed to know about its provenance.

As the thief said, the dial worked for outward movement. The farther the turn, the more divergent the timeline, the closer it was to dissolving into aether. The spindly dendrites of timeline that trailed off towards nothingness were riskier than the ones closer to the trunk, but it was there that the most interesting pieces were likely to be hiding. In the worlds where the Black Plague had decimated Europe such that it could not invade Turtle Island, in the ones where the Paris Commune triumphed and the capitalist machine slowed to a halt, in the ones where the other colonies of the Caribbean rallied around the newly independent Haiti, in the worlds where the human spirit flourished in freedom and dignity, where the sky was azure and the global temperature was two degrees colder, these are the worlds that tempted me, even in their fleetingness. There were farther flung worlds too, where Neanderthals had evolved into the dominant subspecies, where the art was the work of large hands and alien minds, places even I could not go without a gridsuit to disguise myself, places where I am not something recognizably a person to the sentient species there.

The button was for inward movement, designed for ease and rapidity of use. For those worlds where I would step out of a wall and into a war zone, or a blistering nuclear winter where Mutually Assured Destruction had blasted the Earth off its axis. Cockroach worlds and Venusian worlds of 50°C summers and refugees drinking each other's blood as they scrambled across the parched earth. Worlds without whales and worlds without butterflies. Worlds where a thief shot me to death with the teakettle whistling in the kitchenette.

In both its inward and outward movement, the Pordo Device made a swishing sound, a sliding door to a different world. It took me years to learn to love that sound, the possibilities it entailed.

It is not, as some scholars say, that Prime is the best of all possible timelines. It is simply the one that is left standing.

There was a version of this story where she convinced me, and left with her mother's painting.

There were more practical jobs I might have chosen; I am the curator of the Sunken Museum because I was born with a lethal level of sentimentality. A girl who looked like a lost painting, drinking tea and talking about Walter Benjamin, while a dodo beaked at a bowl of mangos on the floor. I never stood a chance.

She wouldn't tell me how she had clawed her way out of a refugee camp or how she had come across the Pordo. She didn't even tell me her name.

"How can you know?" she told me instead.

I deferred to the experts. They had diagrams, you see. Peer-reviewed studies. That famous rendering of all of the timelines, Prime a thick tuber from which the others protruded into the void at the margins.

"But you don't **know**," she insisted. "Not really."

I protested that we had decades of evidence at this point. It wasn't easy to tell a person that she would shortly cease to exist. That her accumulated dreams and struggles and every August afternoon sky she had ever witnessed would pop like a soap bubble, becoming air, becoming nothing. You could hardly blame her if she refused to believe it.

"Maybe your Pordo is the problem," she said. "Just because you can't get from there to here doesn't mean the timelines aren't there at all."

She would have never convinced me on the science, and she knew it. We were both rank amateurs in that regard, poor students given a tool too powerful for either of us to truly understand.

"They called her the Conscience of New Tagaka. Even back when she was just spraying augmented reality murals on the walls of the slum, the police feared her, the government feared her. Strikes happened, armed uprisings, because of the messages she'd tag on a train or wheat paste on a lamp post. And then she would sit and colour with us even though she'd been up working all night."

"You must have loved her very much," I said.

"Oh," the thief replied. "I barely knew her. My point is that to you, this is a painting. A beautiful painting. A technically accomplished painting, executed in the style of a particular artist in a particular movement, produced with materials specific to that time period, on themes that you could pinpoint to a moment in history. But it has no aura here; it cannot have one. Only you, and your dodo, and your colleagues, if they can be bothered, will ever see it. And none of you have a relationship to it. I do, my people do. It wasn't made for your world; it was made for mine."

"But your world is dying."

I hadn't expected her smile. The bullet had been gentler.

"Every world dies," the thief said. "Even yours."

In the end, I helped her wrap the painting in brown paper. We folded the twine over the front and the back in a cross, our hands also crossing each other. Her black dress was immaculate, but her nails were a nightmare, filthy and bitten to the quick. The only part of her that remained in the slums.

It seemed a betrayal to even take a picture of it for the catalogue.

I had to open the doorway for her. As I've said, her Pordo was old, malfunctioning; it had just enough juice to get her to Prime, and not enough to get her back.

"Would you like to take it with you? I could easily get another." I even held the device out to her. This was how complicit I was in her theft—an accomplice and a traitor to my own universe's cause.

She shook out her curls. "I have what I came here for."

I calibrated the dial and opened the entrance to the surface, to the muddy copper sky, and she left with her mother's painting tucked under her arm.

She did not thank me, or tell me I was doing the right thing. I would wonder, later on, if it would have made the loss any easier if she had. She merely climbed up the stairs to the door in the ceiling and vanished in the whoosh of the Pordo.

What of Paul Klee's *Angelus Novus*, in the timeline where Benjamin lived to see the dawn of the New Left, the birth control pill, the hangings at Nuremberg? Did the monoprint still elicit, centuries later, the shock of melancholia with which I cannot help but view it, in the world where *Theses On the Philosophy Of History* is not its epilogue? Was it diminished when the tragedy of its story was lessened?

"You could stay here," I said, in one of the timelines where I was weaker. "With me."

"Like your dodo? Some kind of pet?"

She was a proud girl, scornful of the offer. I couldn't blame her.

"As my assistant curator," I said. "You can see how the collection is getting out of hand. I'm looking for a grant to expand the archives. And you're adept with a Pordo, even a broken one."

A slight baring of teeth. "I'm not that kind of thief," she said.

"You are the foremost living expert on the life and work of E7lPETH ¡andojver. That has to count for something."

She stood over the timeline diagram and with a finger, traced the route of Prime through the chaos of every possibility. And then, with an old piece of conté, expanded it, trailing burnt umber over the table and my scattered notes, a larger trunk of which Prime was merely an offshoot, equally doomed as the rest. I hadn't been trained to think like this, to even contemplate the possibility. My brain rejected it, skimming over the marks, aghast, until against my will, they coalesced into meaning. With that simple, crude gesture, ¡andojver's daughter rewrote the cosmology of my universe. She made whole worlds out of two marks across sheets of paper and the wooden desk, worlds where I believed her and where I didn't, where I took it in stride and marched on with my calling intact. Infinite hers and infinite mes, with an endless array of choices between us both. It was this carelessly that we all create and destroy universes.

"Who says it's not like this," she asserted. It was not a question, not even a proposition to counter the one I had just made. She had made the possibility more real simply by saying it.

What tsunamis resulted from the ripples of the conté stick? What works of art were created in the timeline where she stayed?

I had, in the course of my training, watched universes die before.

New timelines were born all the time, and died just as easily, the way women used to pump out babies in the hopes that one or two of them might live long enough to help out on the farm. It was no more glamorous a process than that. Decisions, born of despair, born of foolishness, and most of all born of chance, slid free of the timeline that had generated them, slick with afterbirth, arcing into void. They died in quiet, ugly ways, starved of the oxygen of consensus reality, wilting without its sun.

Once, a world unwound like a spool while I stood in it. The ground peeled upwards, driving a shockwave through the earth that threw me onto my face. I rolled over to protect the Brâncuși sculpture I had come to collect. An unfortunate squirrel lost its grip on gravity, dissolving into mist. The sky disappeared last, chunks of colour violently torn from the firmament as I slammed the button as hard as I could.

Soon after that, I had it down to a science. Study the diagrams. Calibrate the Pordo. Find the piece I was looking for, and take it. And then I would leave. Before the wreckage piled too high, before the storm blew me over altogether. The death of a universe is not something you want to witness.

I was not, as the thief would frame me, a dragon atop a hoard of meaningless gold. Every piece that I added to my collection had been carefully studied, loved as much by me as by its creator. If it hung on my walls or existed in my catalogue at all, it was because the loss of it to time and entropy was too much to bear.

A thief. A collector. A pistol. A painting. A bird.

I could turn the dial outwards all I liked. There was no timeline where I made her believe that leaving the painting, abandoning her mother's legacy and her people's birthright to distant strangers, was the right choice. There was no timeline in which I could have convinced a girl to become a footnote to someone else's history.

She had the gun and I, for my part, was not armed with the moral high ground. I noticed that she had finished her tea. I offered her a refill.

"What's in it?" she asked.

For all the wars that had been fought and all the journeys undertaken for tea, I had gone the farthest for mine. "Silphium," I told her. "It's said that the last known stalk of it was presented to the Emperor Nero as a curiosity."

She looked affronted. But was this little refugee from time any less worthy of tasting it than a mad king?

"It's good," she said, then repeated it, as if she needed to convince herself. "Your scientists have it backwards."

I indulged her. I couldn't not.

"You do not take all of these things because you are in the Prime universe," she said. "You are in the Prime universe because you've taken all these things."

Neither of us were scientists or philosophers. I merely shrugged. Her universe did not deserve to survive any more or less than my own, any more than the ones where dodos survived, or a coalition of Mesoamerican civilizations burned the ships of the conquistadores in the harbour, or Benjamin spent twenty years in San Francisco arguing about jazz in letters with Adorno. In my line of work, the hardest thing was this: You must eventually abandon the better outcomes, where the Beothuk still perform their masterpieces in red ochre across the world stage, where the sky was robin's egg blue, where the Angel of History had a little less carnage at its feet. You must

329

acknowledge that yes, sometimes E7lPETH ¡andojver survived long enough to have a daughter, whom she cradled in her arms and for whom she promised to remake the world, a child who, among all her great works, was her favourite creation of all.

I have been moved by all of these worlds. In each, I had been tempted to stay.

"Let's try it out," I whispered to the thief.

This, she did not expect.

"Really?"

"Yes, really. The authorities never really come down here. It might take some time, but I can have everything moved over. We can find out whether art is a mirror to reflect reality or a hammer to shape it." She smiled at this. I took a step towards her, placing myself between her, the pistol, and the painting on the table.

Sadie cooed. It was easier to trust someone who had the trust of an animal. Of course, dodos trust everyone—famously and tragically—but I wouldn't have expected her to know this.

"Come up the stairs with me," I continued. "Your Pordo is broken. It's fine, we can use mine."

Her universe was really not so far off from mine. The decision was so small—I am sorry to say that it came down to the decision of a single deer about which tree to shit under—a quirk of fate that barely registered as a notch on my dial. I opened the door upwards. Hers was a world a degree less cruel than my own. At the very least, it was a world where she existed. We could, in a single moment, risk our existence to make it the one where I did too. All she had to do was walk through it, and all I had to do was follow.

From a few steps below her, I looked up and into another world that never was. The light of the haze-draped alien sun traced the outline of her curls, welcoming her home. She would have recognized the sky, as muddy brown as my own, but there was a tower in her skyline that did not exist in Prime.

She leaned in, pressed her lips to the side of my cheek. I could smell the silphium in her kiss.

"I'll be right behind you," I promised.

DO YOU LOVE THE COLOUR OF THE SKY?

On the first day of archive training at the Sunken Museum, they taught you this: You are not telling a story about how history should be. You are living a story about how it is.

As E7lPETH ¡andojver's daughter climbed the stairs and passed through the door, back to her own timeline, to her own oblivion, she looked backwards for a moment. I stood in place behind her. I lifted my hand, slowly, and made a circle with my thumb and forefinger, centred around the olive of her eye. I saved the colour to my memory, to file it away forever with the sky.

CONTRIBUTORS

Angelique Fawns is a journalist and speculative fiction writer. She began her career writing articles about naked cave dwellers in Tenerife, Canary Islands. After selling her first story to *EQMM*, she fell in love with weird fiction, which is **actually** stranger than non-fiction. You can find her lurking at @angeliquefawns on X, blogging about upcoming calls at www.fawns.ca, or gazing into the abyss hoping it stares back at her.

David Gerrold's work has been translated into more than a dozen languages. His TV scripts are estimated to have been seen by more than a billion viewers. His prolific output includes more than 50 novels and hundreds of articles, columns, and short stories.

David has worked on a dozen different TV series, including *Star Trek*, *Land of the Lost*, *Twilight Zone*, *Star Trek: The Next Generation*, *Babylon 5*, and *Sliders*. He is the author of *Star Trek*'s most popular episode, "The Trouble With Tribbles." In 2022, he was selected to receive the Heinlein award. His latest novel is *Hella*, an exploration of a world where everything is super-sized.

Stefan Jackson is a husband, father, drummer, and independent black writer. His first published short story was in 1986. He practices all styles and genres, most predominant dark fantasy and science fiction. His stories can be found on many platforms, print, digital, comics, and audiobook.

Stefan's debut novel, *Glass Shore*, was published in paperback and ebook in 2014 by Elsewhen Press. The audiobook, narrated by Ron Garner, is available on Audible and Spotify.
In the late 90s, he was the drummer for Citi-Zen. http://www.citi-zen.com/frameset.html

Kellee Kranendonk has spent a lifetime writing. According to her late grandfather she was born with pen in one hand, paper in the other. She's certain these days he would claim she was born clutching a laptop.

She's had over a hundred published works, received honourable mentions, been shortlisted, been a spotlight author and some of her pieces were to appear in a school project, but that didn't pan out. Kellee's been an editor, managed online writing groups, and several of her pieces have or will appear in anthologies, in addition to this one. She lives in Maritime Canada.

Bruno Lombardi is a Canadian author of speculative and weird fiction, with a number of writing credits including a novel, *Snake Oil*, and stories in *Weirdbook* and other anthologies and magazines, including "A Pilgrim's Tale" and "Night Sky in His Eyes" in *Abyss & Apex*, "The Dream-Quest of Sphinx" in

Electric Spec, "A Peculiar Encounter in Navarre" in the *Reign of Fire* anthology, and "The Haunting of the Star Princess" in the *Tumbled Tales* anthology.

Shirley Meier has been writing professionally since the 1980s and lives in Toronto. Her latest novel is *Walls of the Sleepers*; her latest poetry collection is called *Underhill Transit Services*. As well as being an award-winning author, she is an editor, a translator and an artist. Her archery, horse riding and other hobbies have to take distant third place!

Ira Nayman, a humour writer who stumbled into speculative fiction around twenty years ago and decided to stick around, is the author of eight novels, most recently *The Ugly Truth*, the final book in the Multiverse Refugees trilogy. Two dozen of his short stories have been published, most recently "Girls Rule the Cyberpunk World!" in *Brave New Girls 7* and "ePik Flayl Creates the Wor(l)d... Again" in *Dreaming the God*. *Les Pages aux Folles*, Ira's web site of political and social satire, has been updated weekly for over twenty years.

Ira was the editor of *Amazing Stories* magazine for three years. *The Dance* is the first anthology he has edited.

Roxana Negut is a poet, writer, and journalist from Bucharest, Romania. She pursued an education in Philosophy and Journalism, and gained experience working as an editor, copywriter, content writer, and journalist. Roxana has an impressive portfolio of writing, including children's literature (*The Magical Story of the Elves in the Silver Forest*), short stories, and poetry (*Dead People Don't Want Water*); her writing has been published in international literary magazines and anthologies.

Her writing has earned her several awards, including: the "Friendship Award for a Story" in the International Contest Univers XXL; and "The Iconic Author Award" by Maybeify Publisher (India).

Author site: https://roxananegut.com

Stephen B. Pearl (www.stephenpearl.com) is an Ontario-based, multiply-published novelist (*Tinker's Plague*, *Nukekubi*, et al) who writes across subgenres of science fiction and fantasy. He often uses real locations and/or historical persons as backdrops, and endeavours to create worlds that readers will want to lose themselves in and come away with insights into the greater world in which we all live. He does this while remaining true to his core belief that the point of fiction is to entertain, and if it fails to do that, it fails as fiction.

Jeff Provine serves as a professor of English at Oklahoma City Community College. For more than a decade, he has researched local folklore and published several collections, including *Haunted Oklahoma*. In fiction, Jeff has published novels, comics, and numerous short stories, including the prize-winning "Stealing Buttons" for the University of Maryland Quantum-Thermodynamics Hub Steampunk competition. Jeff lives in Oklahoma with his wife and houseful of zany pets. Check out more of his work at www.jeffprovine.com.

Human-shaped, monkey-loving, robot-fighting, pirate-hearted, storytelling junkie, **Mark A. Rayner** is an award-winning author of satire and speculative fiction. He writes in the genres of science fiction, humorous SF and dark comedy. When not working on the next novel, he pens short stories, squibs and other drivel. (Some pure, and some quite tainted with meaning.)

He does all of this while being Canadian and owning cats.

If you enjoyed "A Milkshake Apocalypse," there's a whole science fiction novel about Dr. Tundra saving the multiverse from destruction, called *Alpha Max*. Learn more at: https://markarayner.com/alpha-max/

Rachel A. Rosen lives and makes trouble in Tkaronto (Toronto) in the country currently known as Canada. A genre strumpet with an outlook darker than VantaBlack, she straddles urban fantasy, cosmic horror, dystopian futures, and eco-fiction. Her stone-cold bummer of a first novel, *Cascade* (The Sleep of Reason Book 1), was published by The BumblePuppy Press in 2022, and with Zilla Novikov, she's the co-author of *The Sad Bastard Cookbook: Food You Can Make So You Don't Die.*

Moira H. Scott has been active in the local Speculative and Science Fiction fandom community since the early 1990s; she has participated on panels on Wicca, Witchcraft and folklore, as well as popular culture. Her first published short story appeared in *Dreaming the Goddess*, and she will have another short story in the companion anthology entitled *Dreaming the God*. She is currently working on a novel about Spiritualism and technology at the turn of the twentieth century. Moira lives in Toronto with her writing partner, a black cat by the name of Tesla, a critic in his own right. When not hard at work doing research, Moira reads Tarot professionally and continues with her studies in

Heraldic history.

Rosie Smith is a two-time AnLab Award-nominated author who writes science fiction, fantasy, and horror stories and RPGs. She began as an archaeologist and has yet to give up her dream of jumping back in time to the heyday of the dinosaurs. Her interactive adventure game, *T-Rex Time Machine* is available from Choice of Games. Rosemary's alternate histories, time-travel tales, fantasy stories, essays, and editorials have snuck onto the pages of *Analog, Amazing Stories, Fantastic Stories,* and various fine anthologies. She regularly reviews books for *Analog.* When not writing or reading, she photographs flowers, stares at dinosaur fossils, and practices Sogetsu Ikebana.

Hugh A. D. Spencer lives in the Village of Frustration, walking his ADHD-diagnosed dog along the shoreline of Lake Ontario, all the while aching with envy as others roll by on streetcars, heading off to happier and more financially rewarding fates deep within the mysterious city.

His short fiction has been published in *Descant, Interzone, On Spec* and the Tesseracts series and has been reprinted in *Why I Hunt Flying Saucers* and *The Progressive Apparatus* from Brain Lag Publishing. His first novel, *Extreme Dentistry*, was unleashed in 2014. Astonishingly, some might say even **bizarrely**, Hugh was twice nominated for the Aurora Award and his story "(Coping with) Norm Deviation" received an honorable mention in *The Year's Best Science Fiction* (2007). Hugh's second novel, *The Hard Side of the Moon*, was exposed in 2021. A collection of his radio plays, *The Fabulist Cycle*, was published in the early 2024.

Eli K.P. William is a Canadian novelist and translator who has spent most of his adult life in Japan. The only member of the Science Fiction and Fantasy Writers of Japan who writes fiction in English, he is the author of <u>The Jubilee Cycle</u> trilogy (Skyhorse Publishing), set in a dystopian future Tokyo. The series includes *Cash Crash Jubilee* (2015) and *The Naked World* (2017), and concluded in January 2023 with the final book *A Diamond Dream.* His best-known translation is the acclaimed mystery novel *A Man* by Keiichiro Hirano. Learn more at elikpwilliam.com or follow him on Twitter @Dice_Carver

CANADIAN DREADFUL

An Anthology

Edited by David Tocher

Available in paperback and ebook.

"CANADIAN DREADFUL showcases some of Canada's best voices in horror fiction. This anthology is a harrowing tour of the northern landscape that will leave you both dazzled and terrified."
~David Morrell, New York Times Best-Selling Author

In the pages of this anthology, you will not find the Canada you are accustomed to, nor a Canada that the world has grown to know and love. Between the covers, you will discover a dark landscape that will challenge your perspective. From sea to shining sea, stories of a darker Canada will arise, and within them all a kernel of truth. Stories of sacrifice, cannibalism, ghosts, and mystical forests, the authors will plunge you into the country that is Canadian Dreadful

www.amazon.com/Canadian-Dreadful-Anthology-David-Tocher/dp/1928104150/

DREAMING THE GODDESS

AN ANTHOLOGY

Available in paperback and ebook.

"... a passionately written, original collection of fresh, contemporary, Goddess mythology for our modern era. Each chapter is a pilgrimage to meet and get to know another embodiment of the Goddess and Her particular mysteries."
~ Dodie Graham McKay, author of *Earth Magic*.

The Realm of the Goddess is vast. From mythology to legend to modern retellings, between these pages, you will experience Her Mysteries in original stories destined to become new mythology.

Experience the Goddess in Her many guises, from Egypt to Nigeria, from Europe to the UK, from the Middle East to North America.

https://www.amazon.com/Dreaming-Goddess-Rosemary-Edghill/dp/1928104177

DREAMING THE GOD

AN ANTHOLOGY

Available in paperback and ebook.

"This exciting and much-needed anthology reawakens the voices of some of the oldest Gods... Diverse authors skilfully evoke Him... offering us a new look at some of His many faces... and one for every Pagan's bookshelf."
~ *Melissa Seims, Author of Here Be Magick.*

"... engaging and vibrant... belongs on every Pagan bookshelf... the tales within will take you on a journey from ancient history to contemporary times to meet the God in many different forms."
~ *Moira Hodgkinson, Co-Author Operation Cone of Power.*

Forget what you think you know of the God. This anthology will take you on new adventures that will open your eyes to the God as He is seen throughout England to South America, Greece to New Zealand, and Egypt to China.

https://www.amazon.ca/Dreaming-God-Rosemary-Edghill/dp/1928104312

THE CHOSEN CHRONICLES:

Changeling
Angel of Death
Shadow of Death
Thanatos

By
Karen Dales
www.karendales.com

"Dark… compelling… that will keep readers turning the pages well past bedtime."
Kelley Armstrong,
New York Times Best Selling Author

"A dark and gripping tale by a true mistress of supernatural fiction. Karen Dales brings fresh blood to the vampire genre."
Michelle Rowen,
National Best Selling Author.

"For readers who adore textured layers in their literary tapestries, rich in colourful emotions, Karen Dales is one writer of vampire fiction they'll want to read."
Nancy Kilpatrick,
Author: Power of the Blood
Editor: Evolve: Vampire Stories of the New Undead

"A fresh and intriguing new look at the vampire mythos."
Violet Malan
The Novels of Dhulyn and Parno

Available in paperback and ebook
everywhere where books are sold.

www.amazon.com/Karen-Dales/e/B004TG6U1Y

Abandoned and left to die, alone in the forest, the Angel's life is transformed, evoking demons that demand more than he can give.

The Vampires of London are being murdered and only the Angel of Death can save them. Plagued by demons from his past, the Angel walks a fine line. Can he discover the culprits without the discovery of what he truly is and the destruction of one he loves.

Haunted by nightmares of his past misdeeds and failings, the Angel wants nothing more than to be left alone. It is across the Atlantic, in a foreign country, that he takes up the mantle once more as a protector in a land where those who would see him dead have flourished.

The Angel embarks upon a journey to the past to discover the truth about himself and his connection with the white faced demons. Through the quest, the Angel discovers a threat that endangers to topple his beliefs about himself and change the Chosen forever.

BOOKS

To see a full list of our amazing books,

please check our website:

www. darkdragonpublishing.com/books.html

All Books Available At The Following Retailers:

Amazon.ca
Amazon.com
Amazon.co.uk
Amazon.com.au
Barnes and Noble
Books A Million
Book Depository
Smashwords
Powell's Books